Glittering parties, scandalous liaisons,
passionate encounters…

Regency

High-Society
Affairs

They're the talk of the Ton!

The Wagering Widow
by Diane Gaston

An
b

Regency

High Society Affairs

Regency

HIGH-SOCIETY
AFFAIRS

Diane Gaston &
Georgina Devon

M&B™ and M&B™ with the Rose Device
are trademarks of the publisher.
Harlequin Mills & Boon Limited, Eton House,
18-24 Paradise Road, Richmond, Surrey TW9 1SR

First published in Great Britain in 2004

REGENCY HIGH-SOCIETY AFFAIRS
© Harlequin Books S.A. 2010

The publisher acknowledges the copyright holders of the
individual works as follows:

The Wagering Widow © Diane Perkins 2004
An Unconventional Widow © Alison J. Hentges 2004

ISBN: 978 0 263 86881 4

052-0210

Printed and bound in Spain
by Litografia Rosés S.A., Barcelona

The Wagering Widow

by

Diane Gaston

As a psychiatric social worker, **Diane Gaston** spent years helping others create real-life happy endings. Now Diane crafts fictional ones, writing the kind of historical romance she's always loved to read. The youngest of three daughters of a US Army Colonel, Diane moved frequently during her childhood, even living for a year in Japan. It continues to amaze her that her own son and daughter grew up in one house in Northern Virginia. Diane still lives in that house, with her husband and three very ordinary house-cats. You can find out about Diane's books and more at her website: www.dianegaston.com

Don't miss the next in Diane Gaston's shocking Regency series, *A Reputable Rake*, available in Regency High-Society Affairs next month.

Chapter One

Guy Keating straightened his spine and glanced about the blacksmith shop that he'd wager had never seen a forge. The voice of the anvil priest rang throughout the room. 'Repeat after me…I, Guy Keating, take thee, Emily Duprey, to be my wedded wife…'

Barely able to make his mouth work, he finally responded, 'I, Guy Keating…' His words sounded like a funeral dirge.

What the devil was he doing in this place, speaking these words? The final vow nearly caught in his throat.

'…'til death do us part.'

The priest, who Guy would hazard was neither priest nor blacksmith, turned to the young woman dressed in a plain brown travelling garment, standing on the other side of the never-used anvil. 'Repeat after me,' the anvil priest said. 'I, Emily Duprey…'

The young woman answered in a soft, but clear tone, 'I, Emily Duprey…'

Guy tried to give her a smile, this woman whose appearance was as unremarkable as her personality. She was neither short nor tall, thin nor stout. Her hair, worn with curls framing her face, was in the popular fashion, though its colour was the same bland brown as her dress. He could never quite recall the colour of her eyes, but whatever they were, her eyes did not enliven her always-composed face.

She gazed at him, almost a question in her expression, but not quite that animated. He ought to be flogged for bringing her nearly four hundred miles, to court scandal for them both at Gretna Green. Oh, he might tell himself she was better off wed to him than having her fortune gambled away by her wastrel father or plundered by one of the rakes who had lately been courting her. Guy had a much better use for her money. Did that not make him less reprehensible than those gentlemen ready to exploit her for their own gain? Certainly less reprehensible than her father, Baron Duprey, who was as addicted to the roll of dice as Guy's own father had been.

She continued the vows in modulated tones. 'I take these folks to witness that I declare and acknowledge Guy Keating to be my guideman.'

Guideman, indeed. Pretender, perhaps. Deceiver?

Rogue.

The anvil priest, who looked more like a prosperous merchant, come to think of it, took both their hands and clasped them together. 'Weel, the deed is done. Y're husband and wife.' The man laughed, jiggling his considerable girth. 'Kiss the bride, mon.'

Guy jerked up his chin. He'd forgotten about this part of the ritual. He had kissed her once, upon proposing, because it seemed what he ought to have done, but he'd not thought of kissing her since.

She coloured and glanced shyly at him through her lashes. He leaned down and placed his lips on hers.

God help him if her lips did not seem expectant, as though she anticipated more than this sham of a marriage could deliver. She deserved more, after all.

'Now shall we go on to the inn, then?' The anvil priest raised his brows. The inn was another of his enterprises, no doubt.

Guy swallowed. He had not forgotten they were required to consummate the marriage. Would she be as hopeful on that score as with the kiss? First they would have a leisurely supper and then… He offered her his arm. 'Shall we go, my dear?' What he meant to say was *I'm sorry*.

He escorted her around the puddles left in the street from the afternoon's rains. What sunlight there had been that day waned in the sky, slipping as low as his confidence. He'd once thought this the wisest course, but now he felt like the veriest blackguard.

A wide puddle of water blocked the entrance to the inn, not a problem for his boots, but deep enough to dampen the hem of her skirt. He scooped her up and carried her over the threshold. Her face remained subdued, but she trustingly settled in his arms, feeling to him almost as a wife ought.

He made a vow more genuine than the ones he'd repeated after the anvil priest. He vowed to be a good husband to her. He vowed she would never know the truth of why he'd married her.

Their meal was a stilted affair, the two of them confined together in a private parlour. He tried his best to be as solicitous as a new husband ought.

'Would you like some fish, my dear?' he asked.

'Do you care for another piece of tart?'

'Shall I pour you another glass of wine?'

She responded with similar politeness and managed to dredge up conversation, mainly about the food.

'This tart is delicious, do you not think?…The pastry flakes wonderfully…The raspberries are sweet, are they not?'

And he responded as he ought. 'Very delicious…very sweet.' In truth, he could not taste the food at all, and he'd availed himself of the innkeeper's whisky far more than was prudent. Surely all their future meals together would not be so excruciatingly dull.

After they finished the last course, no other choice remained but to climb the stairs to the bedchamber the anvil priest/innkeeper had promised them.

Guy's boots beat like a drum against the worn wood of the staircase, matching the loud tattoo of his heart. He'd bedded his share of women. Any man in regimentals was bound to, after all, but those simple exchanges were honest ones. How could he bed Miss Duprey—his wife, he meant—when he'd kept the truth from her? He'd feared she would not marry him if he had been totally honest about needing her fortune, though many a *ton* marriage took place for that very reason.

The innkeeper led them down a hallway to the bedchamber where a cheerful fire flickered in the hearth. The oak floor was covered with a figured rug, and a large bed, its linens turned down, dominated the room. A bottle of wine and two glasses sat on the small table next to it, and a branch of candles further illuminated the charming scene.

Miss Duprey—his wife—wandered over to the window and stood peeking through the gap in the curtains. She still held her hat and gloves as if not certain of staying.

'I weel leave y', good sir.' The innkeeper gave Guy a broad wink and grinned wide enough to expose the gap between his teeth that had not been visible during the brief wedding ceremony.

The thud of the closing door broke the silence, while Guy's disordered emotions continued to rage inside him. Miss Duprey—his wife, dammit! he *must* recall—turned at the sound.

Her eyes were wide, but her countenance composed. She clutched at her hat, crushing its ribbons.

He tried to smile. 'Do you care for some wine, my dear?'

'Thank you,' she said.

He poured two glasses, wishing it were the good Scottish whisky instead. She glanced around and finally found a bureau upon which to place her hat and gloves. With hands clasped like a schoolgirl, she walked over to the bedside table. He handed her a glass and took one himself, almost raising it to his lips before he caught himself. He ought to make a toast.

His mind raced to think of something, hoping he did not appear as witless as he felt. Her expression conveyed no hint that she guessed his thoughts.

'To our future…' he managed, clinking his glass with hers.

'Yes,' she replied in a whisper.

Their wine consumed, he stared awkwardly. She made no move. He supposed it was his responsibility to decide how to go on.

'Do you desire me to call a maid to assist you?' he asked. 'I could step downstairs to allow you some privacy.' And consume how many whiskys while she readied herself for her wedding night?

She shook her head.

A wave of panic rushed through him, the latest of many on this day. Would he be able to perform his husbandly duty? How ironic. If he could not perform, he would provide her the means to have the marriage annulled. One could almost laugh at the thought.

She was a well-enough appearing female. There was nothing to object to in her. So why could he not dredge up some modicum of desire?

Guilt prevented him, of course. Lying to her, telling her that her father had refused permission when, in truth, he'd never approached the man. Guy had tricked her into this flight to Gretna Green, leading her to believe there was no other way for them to wed.

He tried to conceal his emotions. 'We do not have to…to consummate our vows this night, if you do not wish to,' he said. 'There is no one to know but ourselves.'

The hint of concern flitted through her eyes. 'The bed sheets?'

Ah, the bed sheets. Some chambermaid or another would be changing the linens and might notice the lack of evidence. Would that create any difficulty? He failed to see why any of these people would care. They'd been well paid. What's more, she could easily be a widow or something. He shrugged. He'd come too far to take a risk now.

'I could contrive something.' Blood was a ready commodity, as any soldier knew. He might pierce his arm above his sleeve, bleed on the sheets and no one would be the wiser.

'I am willing to proceed,' she replied.

How was she able to keep her tone so temperate? She might as well be conversing with afternoon callers, but he, on the other hand, felt his voice might crack and fail him at any moment.

Her expression remained equally as mild as her fingers reached for the buttons of her spencer. He watched her free each button and pull off the garment. Placing it neatly on a chest at the end of the bed, she reached behind her back and struggled with her laces. He closed the distance between them.

Feeling as if he were perched on the ceiling observing himself, he undid her laces and slipped the dress off her shoulders. She remained as still as a statue as it slid to the floor. His fingers trembled when he set about removing her corset, but he soon had her free of that garment as well.

She turned to face him dressed only in her shift.

Perhaps if she conveyed some emotion, he might be more easy in this moment, but she was as colourless as she ever had been. He held his breath, watching her take the pins out of her hair and wondering how the devil he was going to be able to perform.

She ought to have a husband who greeted this moment with joy instead of obligation. She ought to run from him now and deny there had ever been a wedding. Bribe the avaricious anvil priest to destroy the marks in the register and hire the fastest post chaise back to Bath.

Such spirit, he would not blame—he might even admire it—but her compliance made him feel like a cad.

Taking a deep breath, he sat down on the bed to remove his boots.

Emily stood by, watching her husband as she smoothed her hair neatly behind her shoulders. She could not recall ever seeing a man remove his boots, even her father and brother, but certainly they would not have done so with the same masculine grace as Guy Keating.

Her heart fluttered at this intimate sight of him. He was by no means the tallest of gentlemen, only perhaps five or six inches above her own height, but there was such an air of compact energy about him that he seemed to take up more space.

That first glimpse of him came back to mind, in the Pump Room, her eyes drawn to him almost of their own accord. He had been leaning down to speak to two elderly ladies whom she now knew were his mother's aunts, an expression of acute tenderness on his face. That look alone had disarmed her. When he'd picked up one lady's shawl and wrapped it lovingly around her shoulders, Emily had thought she would weep for the sweetness of the sight.

Later that week at the Assembly he had walked up to her at her brother's side, having begged an introduction. *To her.*

Emily still marvelled at it. She watched him now pulling at his other boot, his dark hair curling around his head, his blue eyes shadowed by dark lashes any woman would covet. Why this good man had sought her out for attention, she still could not countenance. Nor could she explain why he had offered for her, when for three London Seasons no other man had fixed his interest on her.

She'd feared he must be mad or playing some cruel trick, but her brother assured her Guy Keating was top o' the trees, come into a handsome property, as game as he could go.

She'd also asked her brother why such a man would be interested in her, for it seemed so mystifying that he should be, when no other man had been.

Robert had said, 'Wager you ten to one his mama and those old crones of hers gave him a wigging for not setting up his nursery. His brother never did, y'know. Never fell in parson's mousetrap, never got an heir. One or two by-blows, but that is of no consequence. Shot himself, y'know. Lost at hazard. Lucky for Keating. Inherited the title.'

She had not asked her brother to speculate further, but, once begun, Robert tended to chatter on in his affected way of speaking. He added that the new Viscount had still been wearing black during the last Season. Robert suspected Keating, with his elderly charges in tow, had come to Bath to find a wife.

Still, there had been other eligible young ladies in Bath; why had Keating fixed his interest upon her?

It had been every bit as mysterious when Keating told her that her father refused his suit. Keating was so perfectly respectable. He was a viscount, after all.

Perhaps her father had been exacting revenge, because she had ruined his deranged scheme to trap the wealthy brother of a marquess into marrying her. She suspected her father had also set the town's unpleasant rakes upon her as well, showing her what sort of men were left to her, since she'd refused his plans. What other explanation could there be for the false flatterers to suddenly court her and pay her their absurd compliments? Such men preferred women with some looks or fortune, so it could have been nothing else but a trick.

Keating had been her only respectable suitor.

She must have been mad to agree to this Scottish elopement with him! But, what if she had not dared to sneak off? She might never have had another chance to marry a decent man.

So now she stood next to an unmade bed, dressed only in her shift, watching him remove his coat, waistcoat and shirt.

She hoped she was not gaping like the silliest of maids. She had tried so diligently to be correct. She wanted nothing more than to do everything correctly, though she had only the vaguest of notions of what was to come.

He stood, his chest bare, and it was all she could do not to stare at the wide expanse of skin. Each muscle looked as if it had been sculpted by some Greek master long ago. Her heart raced again as it had done when he'd removed her corset, touching her with only the thin fabric of her shift between her skin and his fingertips.

Was she to do something at this moment? She was conscious of a desire to place her hands on that wide chest, to feel the muscles for herself, but she dared not appear too forward. He looked away at that moment, and she took the opportunity to glance at his trousers, bold enough to eagerly anticipate what a man really looked like.

He glanced back at her, a half-smile on his face. He reached his hand to caress her cheek, and a surprising bolt of sensation shot to her female parts. Her face grew hot, and she was suddenly very impatient for this matter to progress.

'Shall we...shall we lie on the bed?' he asked, his voice low and raspy.

She nodded, too fearful of appearing incorrect to ask why he did not ask her to remove her shift nor he remove his trousers.

She climbed on to the bed, its linens cool through the thin muslin of her shift. He settled next to her and her heart raced again. He covered them both with the blanket and, after a pause in which she had no idea what to do, he removed the remainder of his clothing. Somewhat relieved she would not yet have to gaze upon a man's anatomy, she took that as her cue to remove her stockings and her shift, for the first time in her life naked in bed.

He stiffened for a moment when she tossed those undergarments to the floor. 'I forgot to extinguish the candles,' he said, hurriedly slipping out of bed.

She trembled as she watched his bare form walk across the room. He looked quite like a Roman statue she'd glimpsed once at a wealthy London townhouse.

The light from the fireplace did not prove bright enough to show more than a shadow of the front of him when he returned. He crawled back under the covers and faced her in the darkness, his handsome features only dimly visible.

Would he be able to see how full of anxiety she was at this moment? She dared not appear too forward, as carnal as her sister had undoubtedly been, but it would certainly displease him if she shrank away.

He took a deep breath and reached for her, pulling her towards him so that her bare skin touched his. She felt the parts of him she had not been able to discern press against her own intimate parts. He was softer than she would have imagined. His hands stroked her back, creating an unexpected thrill of pleasure matched only by the sensation of her breasts against his chest.

His hands continued to explore her in what seemed to her a resolute way, but, then, she'd had no experience with which to compare. His body broke away from hers while his hands stroked her breasts. The sensations he created were almost frightening. Were these the emotions that had caused her sister's downfall?

'I have no wish to…to hurt you,' he murmured haltingly.

'I am certain you will not,' she replied.

She knew that the first time was painful, but that was all she knew. It was difficult to imagine pain when her whole body had never felt so suddenly alive.

'I must try to ease it for you,' he said with a strong tone of duty.

His hand slid from her breast to her abdomen, her belly, to between her legs. She gasped, momentarily clamping her legs together. She quickly forced herself to relax.

He fingered that secret place of hers. Was it wicked for him to do so? She certainly had been taught by nurse-maids and governesses that she must not touch it unless absolutely necessary. The sensations created were almost unbearably intense. Not painful, really, but not at all comfortable.

His fingers became slippery, and she worried for a moment that her courses had started. She could not bear that particular humiliation. It seemed not to deter him.

Without warning his fingers entered her and she could not help gasping in surprise.

'I must,' he said.

She had no idea such actions were possible. Surely it was not as wicked as it felt! Her husband was not a wicked man, was he? To her surprise, her hips seemed to convulse without her willing them. She tried to remain as still as possible for fear moving might offend him. Maidens were supposed to hesitate at this moment, were they not?

His fingers created a strange, almost pleasureful pressure inside her. It made it quite difficult to think. Suddenly he pulled them out.

'I will enter you,' he said, sounding very solemn.

He gently urged her on her back and rose above her, the entire length of his body above hers held up by the strength of his arms. Slowly his muscles eased and he lowered himself, his legs between hers.

The part of him that had been so soft was now mysteriously hard and so much larger than it had been. Surely it was too large for her. He pushed against her and slowly, gently, the tip entered. It was difficult for her not to rise to meet his stroke.

He lunged and pain shot through her. She could not help but cry out. He immediately ceased.

'It is all right,' she managed, not wishing him to think herself truly injured.

The pain, in fact, could not compare with the other sensations, burning ones, insistent ones, ones that seemed to beg him to continue. It was a great relief when he did so, pushing in and out of her, faster and faster.

He suddenly gave a deep guttural cry and tensed. As he collapsed on top of her, her body still pulsated with such an intensity she thought she might shatter. Unbidden, tears sprang to her eyes.

He eased himself off her, and she felt like her body had been strewn into broken shards. That part of her where he'd entered hurt, but the rest of her ached. She wanted to rage at him, but was unsure why. He had done what men were supposed to do, had he not? Was she supposed to feel the way she did, wanting him to repeat the act, but wanting more to never feel such carnality again?

Her eyes had long adjusted to the dim light, and she gazed at his face, the arch of his dark brows, the way his lower lip was thicker than his upper. It was a handsome face, but the face of a stranger.

His brows knit together, and his blue eyes looked piercingly at her. 'I am sorry,' he said.

One tear rolled down her cheek.

Chapter Two

Each rut and furrow in the long road back to Bath jarred Emily's already aching heart. She managed to feign composure, although she imagined jagged pieces of her heart dropping like bread crumbs all the way back to Scotland.

Her husband, with amiable formality, made polite conversation. Asking after her comfort. Desiring to assist her. Apologising for the tediousness of the journey. She thought she would go mad with it.

Such a journey together in a snug carriage might have become a treasured interlude, a bridal trip as pleasant as a Parisian sojourn or a Venetian gondola ride. Instead, gloom permeated the atmosphere, and Keating's solicitude did nothing to banish it.

The carriage dipped in what must have been a very deep rut.

'Are you all right, my dear?' Keating asked. 'I dare say the roads are in a fair way to impassable.'

'I am not harmed in the least, sir,' she replied. Not harmed by the road, perhaps. With her husband, it was more difficult to say.

His words were all that was proper, but he seemed as distant as Buenos Aires or even the Sandwich Isles. Places reached in dreams. She might as well be alone. She had been alone the past two nights when her husband thoughtfully arranged separate rooms. 'For your comfort,' he'd said.

Her comfort, indeed. It simply gave him an excuse to avoid repeating the act that consummated their marriage.

Men were supposed to desire that act. She must have done something wrong, however, something so objectionable he could not bear to bed her again.

Between the bumps in the road, she tried to devise some manner of discovering what she'd done to displease him. She could not think of the correct words to form the question and thus remained silent on the subject. It put her to the blush to even contemplate speaking to him about what they had done. And what if speaking of it would be considered too forward? What if performing the act with her had been distasteful to him? How could she bear it?

Eventually the golden buildings of Bath came into view, shimmering in the sunlight of the crisp autumn day. They passed the King's Circus, proceeding up Brock Street. Her insides twisted into knots as their carriage pulled up to a building on Thomas Street where Keating leased a set of rooms.

'We have arrived,' he said in a tone she thought nothing less than ominous.

He spoke a few words to the coachman and picked up their travelling bags, carrying them into the building himself. They walked silently down a hallway where Keating set down their baggage and rapped on a door. An ancient man, thin as a stick and dressed in a nearly threadbare coat, stuck his head out.

'My lord.' The man spoke as if Keating had merely

spent a morning at the Pump Room instead of several days' absence. He gave a dignified bow and batted not an eyelash at Emily, half-obscured behind the Viscount.

'Bleasby.' Keating's one-word greeting managed to convey genuine fondness, even amusement at the butler's ability to remain composed. He stepped aside and brought Emily forward. 'I have brought my…my wife, Bleasby. Lady Keating.' Her husband presented her without actually having to look at her. 'Bleasby is our trusted butler, my dear.'

Bleasby maintained the hauteur of a high man in the servants' quarters in light of what must have been a very big surprise. He barely flickered an eyelid.

'Delighted to meet you, Bleasby,' Emily said.

The old man executed an arthritic bow. 'Very good, my lady.'

Bleasby reached for the baggage, but Keating had already retrieved it. 'No. No. Do not attempt moving these.' He placed them inside the doorway. 'I will attend to them directly. Is my mother in?'

'In the parlour with the ladies,' Bleasby answered.

'Ah,' he said with a cryptic nod. He turned to Emily. 'My dear, I suspect it would be better for me to seek a private audience with my mother and aunts. I hope you do not mind.'

What she did mind was being called 'my dear,' as if he could not trouble himself to recall her name.

'I am sure you are right,' she said.

Would his mother despise her for agreeing to the impropriety of an elopement? Would she think Emily had put him up to the mischief? She could not recall ever seeing the now Dowager Lady Keating. The aunts had not looked formidable, however, at least from a distance.

'I shall be but a moment.' He took two long-legged

strides before pressing his fingers to his temple and turning back. 'Bleasby, convey Lady Keating to…to the library and see to some refreshment.'

Bleasby limped, staggering a little with each step. Emily found herself wishing to give him her arm to lean upon, but the library was just around a corner. The small room had shelves, but no books to speak of and no fire in the grate. Managing to retain his dignity in spite of his infirmities, Bleasby limped out, closing the door behind him.

Emily stood in the centre of the room. She'd not even removed her hat and gloves. She could barely form a coherent thought. Her throat tightened and tears sprang to her eyes, blurring her vision.

No, she scolded herself. She would not become a watering pot like her sister Jessame, who wept over the slightest difficulty. Jessame had shed buckets at her wedding, a modest affair in St George's Church at the end of her first Season. Jessame's husband had been perfectly respectable, though a good dozen years her senior. If their father had ever thought to milk that gentleman's fortune, he'd been sadly mistaken. Jessame's Viscount had whisked her away from the family with creditable success. Emily had had barely more than a letter or two from her sister since.

She dug into her reticule for her handkerchief and dabbed at her eyes with its corner. If only she could be more like her other sister, Madeleine, who'd been daring enough to land on her feet after being banished from the household and passed off to everyone as dead. Madeleine had lived in sin with a man, borne a child out of wedlock, and still managed to marry well.

But what did it gain Emily to think of Madeleine marrying Devlin Steele? She'd once had the fantasy he would marry her, but discovering her sister alive and sharing his house had put an end to that. In truth, her parents' reprehensible behaviour had killed that illusion.

They had let her believe Madeleine dead for three years, when, in fact, they'd simply given her to Lord Farley, a man twice her age and a scoundrel.

How could Emily remain under her parents' roof after learning that evil? How could she resist the escape Lord Keating offered when he pressed his suit?

Her husband entered the room, looking a little grim. His interview must not have gone well.

'Come,' he said.

She followed him, but paused before they entered the parlour. 'Shall I remove my coat and hat?'

He had the grace to appear abashed. 'By all means.'

To her surprise, he assisted her. His hands only lightly brushed her shoulder when he helped her off with her spencer, but an echo of his touch lingered as he escorted her in to the parlour.

The parlour was another small room, but rendered cheerful by a flickering fire and personal items placed about the room. A chair held a piece of mending in progress. A copy of *La Belle Assemblée* lay open on a table.

Less cheerful, three ladies stood awaiting her entrance as if expecting a dragon to appear.

Keating brought her to them, first to a regal-looking woman with dark hair shot through with silver and the same startling blue eyes as her son.

'Mother, may I present to you my wife, the former Emily Duprey.'

Emily found not a hint of friendliness in those eyes. 'Ma'am,' she said softly. 'I am pleased to meet you.'

Lady Keating did not speak, but accepted the hand Emily extended to her.

Keating continued to the elderly ladies standing next to his mother. One, as if made of only bone and skin, leaned heavily on a cane. The other appeared sturdier, but was hump-shouldered and bent over.

'Let me present my mother's aunts,' Keating said. 'Lady Pipham and Miss Nuthall.'

Miss Nuthall glared at her, but Lady Pipham regarded her with a shy smile.

Emily extended her hand to each of them, shaking gently, a little in fear of breaking them. 'I am honoured.'

The arthritic butler at that moment entered, carrying a tea tray, the cups rattling like window panes in a storm. Emily held her breath as he made his precarious way, sure the pot, cups and small plate of ginger cakes would topple on to the floor. Keating took it from his hands and placed it upon the table. The butler bowed himself out of the room.

'Shall we sit,' said the Dowager Lady Keating. She dipped gracefully on to a satin-covered armchair. The elderly ladies found chairs for themselves, but sat with more effort.

Lady Keating added with a note of sarcasm, 'I suspect you need refreshment after your *long* journey.'

'You are very kind,' said Emily.

To her relief, Keating sat next to her on a sofa. She did not know if his support was genuine, but she welcomed it. The news of their marriage had obviously not been met with happy wishes.

Lady Keating poured. 'You understand this news of your…elopement comes as a great shock to us. Guy was not reared to perpetrate such folly. Indeed, he gave us no idea of this plan.'

'I am sorry it distresses you,' Emily said. 'It was not our intention to do so.'

'It is not quite the thing, you know,' added Miss Nuthall. 'A Gretna Green wedding is not quite the thing. It is not done in our family.'

Lady Pipham murmured, 'There was cousin Letitia...'

'Never mind *her*,' said Miss Nuthall repressively.

Keating rubbed his brow. Emily wished he would speak, because she did not know quite what to say. None of her exact attention to behaviour in polite society quite covered this situation. Lady Keating handed her the cup of tea and she sipped, relieved at having something else to do.

'Our housekeeper is preparing a room,' Lady Keating said. 'The chamber adjoining Guy's. It shall be ready directly.'

Had Lord Keating—Guy—given instructions to put her in a separate room? It was the way of married people in society, she knew. She was uncertain if she were pleased or disappointed that he'd not insisted she share his room.

'I hope this will not inconvenience you,' she said politely.

'My daughter will have no room.' Lady Keating folded her hands in her lap, but her fingers pressed into the skin.

'Oh!' exclaimed Emily. 'I am sorry—'

'No need,' said Keating quickly. 'Cecily is at school and has no need of a room here.' He paused. 'As you well know, Mother.'

Emily had not even known Keating had a sister. She opened her mouth to remark again upon this, but stopped herself. It would not improve matters to admit she knew so little about her husband. She took another sip of tea.

'Dear Cessy,' murmured Lady Pipham.

'Tell me, Miss Duprey—' began Lady Keating.

Her son interrupted her. 'She is my wife, Mother.'

'Oh, yes.' She smiled, but mirthlessly.

'Perhaps you could call me Emily, if that would be more comfortable for you.' Emily truly sympathised with Lady Keating. It must be difficult to give up one's title and status without warning, and to a stranger as well.

'Emily.' The Dowager pronounced her name with asperity. 'Do your parents know of this...this escapade of yours?'

Emily felt her face flush. 'No, ma'am.'

'I am a little acquainted with your mother,' said Lady Keating with disapproval. 'And my husband spoke of your father on occasion.'

Oh, dear. The discreditable Baron and Baroness Duprey were obviously not a desirable connection, but Emily was well aware of that fact. Her parents were a blight upon herself as well.

Keating stood. 'I will check on your room.'

Half an hour later Guy settled his wife into the bedchamber prepared for her. He could barely speak, he was so ashamed of his mother's shockingly poor manners. Even Aunt Dorrie had been disagreeable. He knew the news of his elopement would upset them, but he'd no idea they would behave so abominably. He marched back to the parlour.

His mother looked up from reading her magazine. 'Is your *wife* quite comfortable in Cessy's room?'

'My...wife is due any room I wish to rent for her,' he snapped.

'Then perhaps she will take over all these rooms, and we shall be on the street.' His mother's voice caught on a strangled sob. 'How could you do this, Guy? Marry into such a family and court such scandal? The Dupreys are not good *ton* at all. He's a gamester, you know, and she is said to drink.'

'The daughter had pretty manners, though,' murmured Lady Pipham.

Guy walked over to his frail great-aunt and placed a kiss on the cap covering her thinning white hair. 'Thank you, Aunt Pip.'

He stood next to Aunt Pip's chair, regarding Aunt Dorrie and his mother. These three ladies had always doted upon him and his sister Cessy. His mother had never made any secret of her hope for a fantastic match for him, teasing him to offer for young ladies whose papas would never have given him the time of day. The sad state of the family finances could easily be guessed by anyone who had encountered the perennially unlucky and now deceased Lord Keating and his elder son.

Emily Duprey had been a godsend, though he doubted God would approve of his methods of snaring her any more than his mother and great-aunts would. Or he himself.

'Emily is a respectable girl, Mother,' Guy said. 'No scandal attaches to her, and I'll wager you will not complain when her money pays your bills.'

'Money? Hmmph!' His mother glared at him. 'The family is headed for River Tick.'

'The family may be done up, but Emily has an inheritance,' he continued. 'If anything, our marriage prevents her father from throwing away her fortune on his gaming.'

Aunt Dorrie stared at him with a horrified expression. 'Can you mean you eloped with that girl for her money? It is the outside of enough.'

The dignified, but impoverished and impractical Miss Nuthall was indeed correct to a fault about his motive for marrying Emily Duprey. By God, the ladies knew their finances were in a sad way, even if they did not know the true extent of their difficulties. Why would they fault him for marrying his way out of it? Was this not preferable to his father and brother's empty promises of fortune at some faro bank?

His grip tightened on the arm of Aunt Pip's chair. 'My reasons for marrying Emily Duprey are none of your concern, and I will thank you to accord her every courtesy in this house.'

Aunt Pip bent her head. Aunt Dorrie and his mother glared at him.

'We have no choice, do we?' his mother whispered.

'No,' he agreed. 'You do not. I must also tell you that I took the liberty of asking Kirby to attend to Emily.'

His mother straightened in her chair. 'You gave my maid to that girl?'

Guy gritted his teeth before speaking. 'I borrowed her. And you would have done better by offering my wife her services yourself. You have been sadly remiss in hospitality, Mother.'

His mother did not even have the grace to look ashamed.

Guy forced himself to take a breath and to regain some composure lest he say more to his mother than was prudent. He knew she had always been unrealistic in her aspirations for her children. He could forgive her wishing he'd made a better match.

Still, she ought to have been kinder to Emily. There was no excuse for her rudeness. Her open disapproval made the whole business worse.

If his mother insisted upon keeping her head in the clouds as she had done during her marriage and the succession of her eldest son, it was none of Guy's problem. Rupert had been as big a wastrel as their father, but their mother thought the sun rose and set upon his sallow complexion and bloodshot eyes. To be fair, she could never think ill of any of her children, nor begrudge them any of their heart's desires. Why, she'd insisted upon sending Cessy to that dashed expensive school. Until his marriage, Guy had been racking his brains as to how to pay the fees.

Emily walked back in to the parlour, where there remained a tense silence. Guy's stomach clenched as it always did when he saw her. Would his guilt over marrying her ever dissipate?

She addressed his mother. 'Lady Keating, thank you so much for the services of your maid. She was most helpful.'

His mother barely looked up. 'You are welcome, I am sure.'

Emily turned to Guy. 'I wonder if I might speak to you a moment, sir?' She looked as if the tension in this household had indeed taken a toll.

'Of course,' he said, conscious that her discomfort ultimately lay at his door.

He stepped out into the hall with her. 'What is it, my dear?'

She winced a little. 'I…I think I should call upon my parents. It is not yet the dinner hour, and I might still find them at home. I feel it my duty to inform them of…of my marriage.'

He nodded. 'I will go with you.' Another unpleasantness to endure this day. Might as well get it done with.

She looked faintly surprised. 'Do you wish to come with me?'

He tried to smile at her. 'It would be shabby indeed if I allowed you to go alone.'

A ghost of a smile flitted across her face. 'I thank you. I need only don my coat and hat.'

She fled back to her room and Guy found his own coat and beaver hat.

Minutes later they were on the street. Her parents' rooms were close by, but in a more fashionable building. As they walked in the fine autumn afternoon, Guy could think of nothing to say to her, except to warn her of cracks in the pavement or bid her take care as they crossed the street.

When they reached the door of the house, Emily hesitated. He squeezed her arm, and she gave him a grateful look.

Guy sounded the knocker and a footman opened the door. From a doorway, a stately butler appeared.

'Miss Duprey,' the butler said in a monotone.

'Sutton,' she returned. 'Are my parents in?'

'Indeed,' intoned Sutton with barely a glance towards Guy. 'Your mother is in the back parlour.'

'Would you ask my father to join us there?'

Sutton flicked his fingers at the footman, who had been more open in his curiosity. The footman bowed and rushed off as the butler disappeared into another room.

Emily took a deep breath. 'Well,' she said. She cleared her throat and led him to the back parlour.

She knocked on the door before entering. Lady Duprey reclined upon a sofa. She looked up and adjusted the fine shawl that had slipped from her shoulders. 'Oh, Emily, it is you. I thought perhaps I had a caller.' She noticed Guy and sat up, patting her curls, still untouched by grey. She remained a very handsome woman, though she must be well near her fiftieth year.

'I see we do have a caller.' Lady Duprey's eyes kindled with interest as she extended her hand to Guy.

'Mama, may I present to you Viscount Keating,' Emily said.

Guy took the lady's hand, returning her limpid grasp and smelling sherry on the lady's breath. 'I am pleased to meet you, Lady Duprey.' What kind of mother was this, that she greeted a stranger with more interest than a daughter who had been absent for several days?

'Mama, I have been away, you know.'

Lady Duprey's gaze reluctantly wandered from Guy to her daughter. 'Yes…' She appeared lost in thought for a spell. 'Did you leave us a note? I cannot recall what it said.'

'I did,' Emily answered, as if this were the most normal conversation in the world. 'I told you I would be away for a while. Now I am back.'

Lady Duprey appeared to lose interest in this conversation. She turned her attention back to Guy. 'Won't you sit down, Lord Keating?' She patted the space next to her.

The door opened and Lord Duprey rushed in. 'What the deuce is so important, I ask you, that I must be interrupted? I have better things to occupy my time.' He saw Guy. 'Oh, Keating. What the devil are you doing here?'

'Papa…' Emily spoke in a wavering voice.

By God, perhaps this marriage had been right after all, Guy thought. Anything would be better than living with these unnatural parents who had not even heeded that their daughter had been gone almost a fortnight.

Guy interrupted Emily. 'Lord Duprey, Lady Duprey, we have come to announce our marriage. Your daughter and I were wed not more than five days ago.'

'What?' exclaimed Lady Duprey.

Lord Duprey gave a bark of a laugh.

'Yes, Mama, I am married,' Emily said. 'To…to Lord Keating. We will place an announcement in the papers in due time. I came to tell you of this and to arrange for my possessions to be sent to Thomas Street.'

'Well, we must drink to this, mustn't we?' said Lady Duprey eagerly. 'Pull the bell and desire Sutton to bring something fitting.'

Emily meekly did her bidding, but Guy fumed that his wife was made to arrange her own family celebration.

A bottle of French champagne was produced and poured. After the butler left the room, Lord Duprey lifted his glass. 'Here's to another daughter launched without me spending a groat. I must say, I thought this one too plain to catch a man without exerting myself. My luck has been running capital well lately.'

Emily turned bright red, and it was only with effort Guy managed not to plant his new father-in-law a facer. Baron Duprey tossed down the contents of his glass, while his wife poured herself another.

'I must be off,' Duprey said. 'Pressing engagement, you know.'

Guy stepped into his path to the door. 'One moment, sir. When may I call upon you to discuss business?'

Lord Duprey laughed. 'Business, you say? What the devil. You may call tomorrow, if you have a mind to. Not too early.'

Guy watched in stunned silence as Baron Duprey rushed out of the room without having said one word of a personal nature to his daughter.

Emily was certain her cheeks must be beet red. She was so mortified at her parents' behaviour, she could not bear to look up from the Aubusson carpet for fear of what expression she might see on Keating's face. What must he think of them? It was humiliating.

'If you will excuse me,' she said to her mother and Keating, who still gaped at the doorway through which her father had fled. 'I believe I shall attend to the removal of my things.'

She hurried to the room she'd occupied while her parents were in Bath, it seeming as foreign to her as the room in Thomas Street. Neither felt like home.

Once, perhaps, Malvern had felt like home, with its sunlit bedchambers and cheerful nursery. The family estate had seen many carefree childhood days, but even its walls seemed tainted now.

Besides, Malvern was rented for the time being and given that she could not expect her father to cease his gaming, it would probably remain rented, the revenue used to keep her family afloat.

She stood in the middle of the room, not sure what to do first.

'Excuse me, miss.' Lady Duprey's maid hovered at her door, her young niece with her. 'Is it true, miss?' Shelty asked. 'Is it true you are married to that gentleman?'

News travelled very fast among servants.

'Yes, it is true, Shelty.' Emily replied. 'He is Lord Keating. And I am afraid I must beg your assistance in packing up my possessions.'

'Hester, do whatever Miss Duprey—oh, I mean, her ladyship requests.' The older woman pushed her niece into the room. The girl, about sixteen years of age, had come to Bath from Chelsea where her father, a cobbler, owned a small shop and had been blessed with five daughters. Two of the others had gone into service. Hester was the last to be placed.

'My lady, would you be needing a maid in your gentleman's house?' Shelty looked at her hopefully. 'I would be beholden if you would take Hester here. It has become a mite difficult for her here.'

'Difficult?'

Shelty looked abashed. 'Well, you know, she is a pretty thing, and I'm afraid your father has taken notice of her.'

How much worse could her family get? Emily closed her eyes, remembering her sister Madeleine. Much worse.

'Of course she can come.' Emily smiled at the girl. 'Can we find a portmanteau to pack up some clothes for a day or two? And a trunk for the rest?'

Emily opened the drawer of her bureau and unrolled one of her spare corsets. Out fell a cloth purse. She breathed a sigh of relief. She'd no doubt her father had searched her room for her grandmother's pearls and emerald ring, but her guess had been right that he would not disturb her undergarments. She put the purse into the portmanteau. She rooted around in the drawer until she found the envelope containing the money she'd hidden from him.

Half an hour later she returned to the parlour. When she told Keating she would be bringing her maid with her, he'd looked rather grim, but perhaps that was due to being forced into her mother's company for such a spell.

When they made to leave, Lady Duprey extended her hand to Keating again. 'Do come to call any time, dear boy,' she purred. 'Welcome to the family.'

Keating mumbled something Emily could not make out. He turned to her. 'I'll give the butler the direction to deliver your trunk.'

After he'd left the room, Emily planted a dutiful kiss upon her mother's cheek. 'Goodbye, Mama,' she said, but her mother had poured herself the last of the champagne and had returned to perusing the magazine on the table beside her.

The young maid stood waiting with a portmanteau,

looking much more eager to embrace her new life than Emily felt.

'I am forever beholden to you, my lady,' the girl said in a shy voice. 'I will do anything you wish, I promise.'

Emily gave her a reassuring smile. 'Thank you for your willingness to change houses, Hester. I am in need of a maid.'

She glanced around the place. At least there was nothing to regret in leaving behind this old, so very empty part of her life.

As she and Keating strolled down the pavement towards Thomas Street, the maid trailing them, he threaded her arm through his.

Emily thought she might weep for the kindness of the gesture.

Chapter Three

Nothing imaginable could have put Guy so much in charity with his wife than this visit to her parents had done. Why, he could almost conceive himself a champion for whisking her away from that bleak atmosphere. The behaviour of his mother and great-aunts paled in comparison to Baron and Baroness Duprey, and surely, his mother, Aunt Pip and Aunt Dorrie would warm up to Emily in time. There was nothing to dislike in her.

Guy's heart actually felt buoyant. He managed to exert enough diplomacy to make their dinner go on comfortably. Aunt Pip, bless her heart, even ventured to ask Emily a few polite questions. And Emily, as ever, behaved in a perfectly proper fashion, saying nothing incorrect. He could not precisely remember anything she'd said, but he was certain of its faultlessness.

It had been an exhausting day, and Emily could not be blamed for retiring to her room early. His mother and aunts shortly thereafter bid their goodnights.

Guy remained in the parlour, pouring his third glass of brandy by the light of the fireplace. He'd extinguished the candles out of a habit of economy. Soon such miserly ways would be unnecessary, however.

He experienced only a twinge of guilt for being glad
Emily's fortune was nearly in his hands. He would pay
her back every penny, he vowed he would, once the estate
became profitable again. In the meantime, she would
never again suffer the slights of attention he'd witnessed
at her parents' house. He might have no affection for her,
but he would care for her, as was his duty.

Guy drained his glass of its contents and rose to his
feet. His wife might be asleep by now, warm between her
blankets, smelling as only a woman could.

Perhaps he ought to contemplate performing his husbandly duty. He'd not attempted a repeat of that first
night, knowing he'd hurt her.

Come to think of it, though, she'd not complained.
She'd not acted as if the marriage act was abhorrent to
her. Perhaps he could be very gentle with her.

All concerns about his ability to perform on his marriage night had disappeared after he'd forced himself to
go through the motions. Ultimately he'd experienced all
the pleasure a man could expect. Perhaps he had been too
long absent from a woman's bed, but that was not it. He'd
remained celibate for longer periods. Perhaps it had been
his wife's rather sweet response to him, so frightened, yet
compliant, even willing.

Still, it seemed devilish shabby of him to enjoy himself
with a woman he'd tricked into marriage in order to plunder her fortune. Reprehensible.

Such thoughts had prevented him from approaching her
again in those uncomfortable inns. Tonight, however, he
felt a decided tenderness towards her. He had rescued her
from that dismal family. That had been good of him, and
he owed it to her to give her what all women coveted. A
child.

He lit one small candle from the dwindling fire and,

keeping a hand on the wall to steady himself, walked down the hallway to his bedchamber. Once inside, he placed the candle on a side table and pulled off his boots. He untied his neckcloth and flung it aside. Shrugging out of his coat and waistcoat, he stared at the door connecting his room with his wife's.

It was his duty, he repeated to himself, though the stirrings of arousal suggested baser motivations. With a light knock of warning, he opened the door. The bed linens rustled and she sat up, a blur of white muslin in the dim light of his little candle shining through the doorway.

'My lord?' she said. The sound of her voice, husky from sleep, and the thought of her dressed only in a nightdress further stirred his senses.

How did a husband ask his wife if he might bed her? He smiled reassuringly, though she could not possibly see the expression on his face. 'Do you wish my company?'

She remained still, like a ghost about to dissolve into the air. 'If it pleases you,' she finally said.

The blood already coursed through his veins. 'It pleases me.'

She drew back the covers and slid over, making room for him. His loins ached as he made his way to the bed. Removing his shirt and breeches, he climbed in beside her. Her hair was bound in a braid and he longed to release it, but dared not, lest it offend her sensibilities. He pulled her towards him, savouring the feel of her feminine curves from beneath her nightdress, but wanting, needing to feel more. He drew the thin nightdress over her head and dropped it to the floor.

His hands explored her breasts, gently at first. She gasped, but did not move away. Encouraged, he stroked with more intensity until her nipples peaked under his fingers. His breath quickened.

The candle in his room guttered and went out. Darkness wrapped around them like a blanket, heightening the sensation of her skin beneath his touch. Her scent, lavender and something indefinable, filled his nostrils, and the cadence of her breathing sounded in his ears.

Desire shot through him. He wanted her pliant beneath him. He wanted to take her quick and rough and ease the aching need inside him.

But he resisted, determined to make the experience pleasant for her as well. She'd been so tight when he'd entered her that first time, but warm and wet and firm around him. He wanted this again. Needed it, but he would take care not to hurt her.

He let his hand slide down her abdomen. She arched beneath his touch, the change in position slight, but enough to encourage him. He moved his hand between her legs. She was already sweetly slick, and he'd be damned if he'd wait too much longer.

But she deserved some pleasure from this experience as well as he. He gently stroked between her legs. She made a tiny noise, and her breath came faster, the sound intensifying his arousal.

He could wait no longer. He mounted her, and her legs spread open almost as if to welcome him. He forced himself to enter her slowly, carefully, but no sooner had he done so than all control fled. A primitive rhythm overtook him, and he moved to it, feeling her hips rise to meet him at the perfect beat. Faster. Harder.

He felt a flutter from her body, like sweet tiny fingers squeezing him from inside her. He could bear no more. His release erupted in a spasm of pleasure even more intense than he'd hoped.

He collapsed on top of her, all energy spent, all muscles relaxed into liquid. Conscious suddenly of how heavy he must be, he slid off of her, but held her in his arms, as soft as if he cuddled a kitten.

All would work out well, he was certain. He would not regret this marriage. He could almost feel hopeful about it. They faced each other, so close her breath cooled his passion-heated face. He stroked her cheek and rested his fingers beneath her chin, closing the distance between them, tasting her lips and pulling her flush against him. She sighed and relaxed in his arms.

Yes, their marriage would be a good one, he was certain.

With that final thought, he plunged deeply into sleep.

Emily woke to the sound of rain rattling against the window pane. The light from the window barely illuminated the room and it had taken her a few seconds to realise dawn had come.

She rolled over to survey the man still sleeping next to her, his hair so dark against the white linens, his face relaxed and boyish. The bedcovers were tangled between his legs and all of his glorious body was exposed to her view. She felt wicked looking at it, but was unable to help herself. He was a truly beautiful man, all lean muscle, shoulders broad enough to carry her burdens.

She felt near to bursting with joy. Who would have thought marriage could bring such pleasure? It had been all she could do to remain still and quiet during his love-making. Her body had seemed to move without her saying so, and she almost cried out when that explosion of delight erupted inside her. She'd almost behaved like a wanton woman.

Smiling, she dared to touch one lock of his hair.

His eyes opened, their intense blue startling her. He

stared blankly at her, then comprehension seemed to come to him, and one corner of his mouth turned up.

'Good morning,' he said.

'Good morning,' she replied. What more was there to say? Surely ladies did not thank their husbands for making love to them. Or did they?

He reached out and touched her cheek. For a moment she thought he might make love to her again, and her heart skittered in anticipation, but instead he rose and groped for his breeches, slipping them on with his back to her.

He picked up her nightdress and handed it to her. 'Your maid may knock at any moment.'

A maid could be sent away, though, could she not? Emily dared not suggest this, however. She did not wish to risk disrupting the magic of the previous night. She sat up in the bed and donned her nightdress.

As he put his muscular arms through the sleeves of his shirt, she asked, 'Is there anything you wish me to do today?'

He looked at her. 'I can think of nothing. I will ask my mother to acquaint you with the workings of this household, though there is not much to learn on that score. I hope to provide better for you soon.'

His mother would derive little enjoyment out of that task, she was certain, but it would please him if she could find some way to ease the tensions her presence brought to the household. She wanted so very much to please him.

'Perhaps there is some service I might do for your mother,' she said.

'That is too good of you.' He again touched her cheek, his expression softening. 'My mother will soon learn to appreciate you, I promise. She was merely taken by surprise.'

The feel of his fingers on her face nearly drove out all

rational thought. 'I do understand. I will endeavour to put her mind at ease.'

He leaned down and kissed her, and she thought her spirit might soar through the heavens in pure ecstasy. She could barely keep from plunging her fingers into his hair and opening her mouth to taste more of him.

He broke off. 'I will call upon your father today.'

She could not imagine why he would wish to do so.

He regarded her with a serious expression. 'Emily, I promise to do right by you. The sooner I get control of your fortune, the better. I would not have your father plunder it.'

'My fortune?'

His face stiffened. 'The money your aunt left you.'

'My aunt?' She wrinkled her brow. 'But that is hardly a fortune, Guy. I have it here in the drawer.'

She hurried to the bureau and removed the leather envelope, handing it to him. He opened it and pulled out the five ten-pound banknotes.

He gave her a questioning look, bordering on alarm. 'What is this?'

Emily felt a rock forming in her stomach. 'It is my inheritance.'

Guy fingered the banknotes, staring at them as if they were some mysterious Chinese currency. Fifty pounds? No, this could not be the sum of her inheritance. She must be mistaken. There had to be more, there had to be.

His fingers trembled and he crushed them, the paper crackling. 'This is all of it?' His neck was so tense he could barely talk.

Her brows knit in confusion. 'Yes, all. I would not withhold it from you.'

Only fifty pounds? Guy's insides twisted into coils. Panic threatened to cut off his breath.

'You may keep the money, of course,' she added, her eyes wary.

He smoothed the notes and put them back in the envelope. He handed it to her, took it back again, and finally thrust it at her. 'Keep it,' he snapped. 'I must get dressed.'

What he needed more than anything right now was to get away from her before he lost total control of his temper. She must be mistaken. There must be more money, or what would become of them all?

Leaving her incredulous, standing with the envelope in her hands, he spun on his heel and rushed into his bedchamber, slamming the door behind him.

Guy's caped topcoat and beaver hat were soaked from the rain, as he paced outside the building where the Dupreys lived. He'd spent much of the morning walking the streets of Bath, heedless of the weather. The sense of foreboding was strong, as strong as before a battle when one went through the motions of eating and sleeping, knowing the next day life might be snatched away.

It was finally past noon, though the clouds obscured any confirmation of sun high in the sky. Holding his breath, he sounded the knocker.

The butler opened the door, took his coat and hat, and ushered him into the same parlour where he'd been the day before. He cooled his heels there a good half an hour before Baron Duprey sauntered in. The man chuckled, interrupting Guy's anxious pacing in front of the fireplace.

'Well, Keating, I always took you for a man of sense. Knew your father, who hadn't a groat of the stuff, but word's been you're cut from different cloth.'

Guy could only stare at him.

The Baron went on. 'Can't imagine what maggot got

in your brain to marry that daughter of mine. Thought I'd never be rid of her.'

Guy took a step towards him. 'Do not speak of my wife in that manner.'

Duprey laughed. 'Next you will persuade me you have a *regard* for her.'

Guy's right hand closed into a fist. He'd relish the opportunity to vent his disordered emotions on this poor excuse for a man.

Still chuckling, Duprey sat on one of the chairs and fingered the sleeve of his coat. 'Now what business must you conduct with me? What is so important you disturb my peace at this early hour?'

A porcelain clock on the mantel chimed one o'clock.

'My wife's assets are no longer yours to control,' Guy said bluntly. 'I came to arrange their transfer to me.'

The Baron pressed folded hands against his chin and gave Guy a blank stare. 'Assets?'

'Do not humbug me, sir,' Guy persisted. 'You have been bantering it all about town that you have control of your daughter's fortune. I demand you turn it over to me. If we need a solicitor to draw up papers, I shall arrange it.'

A smile slowly creased Duprey's face. 'Ah, the clouds clear.' He chuckled again. 'This is a famous one.'

'Pray include me in your jest, sir,' Guy fumed.

The older man's eyes brimmed with a malevolent mirth. 'Quite an inventive story, do you not agree? It kept my creditors at bay, I assure you. How fortunate I no longer require the ruse, since you make further use of the tale impossible. Won a big sum off young Jasperson, fool that he is.'

Guy's heart beat erratically. 'Explain yourself, if you please.'

'I did explain myself,' said the Baron pleasantly. 'I concocted that story about Emily's inheritance in order to extend my credit. I was in Dun territory, my lad. What else would you have me do?'

Guy felt blood drain from his face.

'The tale contained but a speck of truth,' Duprey went on. 'All the best tales do, you know. The girl did inherit. About one hundred pounds. I managed to get my fingers on half of it before she snatched it away. Never could find the rest and I looked for it, indeed I did. Everyone knew Lady Upford cocked up her toes, so could I help it if they believed she'd dropped a huge sum instead of that damned pittance? Left the bulk of it to some scientific society, for which I shall never forgive her.'

A pittance, not a fortune? Nothing but a ruse? Like a simpleton, Guy had fallen for Duprey's story. It did not console him one bit that a myriad of other fools had done the same.

'And don't be looking for a dowry,' said Duprey, waving his finger at Guy. 'That went last Season after she wrecked my plans to marry her off to Heronvale's brother. What a honey pot that would have been.' The man sighed. 'I despaired of being rid of her, I tell you. Who could have guessed a fool like you would marry a dull piece like her? Ha!'

Guy marched over to the man's chair and grabbed him by the lapels of his coat. 'Do not ever speak of my wife in that manner.' He lifted Duprey from his seat and thrust him down again, heading for the door.

'Do not tell me yours was a love match,' the Baron called after him.

Guy heard the man's laughter all the way out of the building and down to the street.

What the devil was he to do? No fortune. No damned

fortune. No money at all. Just one more charge upon his finances.

Damn his idiocy. He'd bought the tale of a fortune, lapping it up as the milk of his salvation. Not only had Duprey boasted of it, others had passed it on. There had been no rumour of it being false. Ordinarily he would have waited for some verification, but Cyprian Sloane, that notorious fortune hunter, had begun to turn his charm on Emily, and Guy had feared he'd be cut out if he did not seize his opportunity now.

He'd gambled on the rumours being true. Did his folly know no bounds? He'd gambled. And lost.

Guy strode back to Thomas Street and entered the house still in a towering rage. He shoved his coat and hat into Bleasby's frail hands and headed to the library, slamming the door behind him.

What the devil was he to do now?

He searched the cabinet in the room for a bottle, finding some old port. He poured himself a glass and downed it in one gulp. He poured another glass.

From the corner of his eye he saw a movement and swung around.

There his wife sat, in a chair by the window, a book in her hand. He had the insane thought that she must have been desperate to read whatever was in this room. Three books about farming methods he'd rescued from rot at Annerley. One dusty volume of sermons that had been left on the shelf when they'd leased the place.

Her eyes widened. Indeed, he must look like a wild man. He felt like a man who had lost his senses.

'What is amiss?' she asked, her voice coming out hoarse and nearly inaudible.

He laughed and downed another full glass of port. He

poured a third. 'What is amiss? I have been to see your father. That is what is amiss.'

Two spots of red appeared on her cheeks. 'What did he say to upset you?'

'He said that you are penniless.'

Her brows knit.

He had no patience for her confusion. 'Do not tell me you were not aware he was passing you off as an heiress.'

She paled. 'I was not aware of it.'

He gulped down more port. 'Well, neither was I.'

She stood. 'My father said I was an heiress?'

'He led the world to believe you were. A big inheritance from your aunt, Lady Upford.'

'It was not a big inheritance,' she said.

He laughed again and finished the port. 'Yes. Now I know.'

She stared at him, her bland face showing only a glimmer of confusion. Did it make it better or worse that she'd not known of her father's tale about her? Perhaps it would have been some meagre comfort to think she'd deceived him as much as he'd deceived her.

Her distress convinced him. She was innocent. The villains in this sordid mess were her damnable knave of a father—and her husband. God help him, he resented her anyway, hated that blank expression on her face, despised the fact that he was saddled with her for life. If not for her, he could search for a genuine heiress. Marry his way out of this fix.

How would he now rebuild Annerley? How would he return its fields to planting, its tenants to prosperity instead of wasting away for lack of food and decent shelter? How would he provide for his mother? Would his elderly aunts end their days in a poorhouse, cold and hungry? What harm would befall his little sister, so blissfully unaware of their troubles? How would he pay for her school? Find her a husband? The list was endless.

Waterloo had seemed like a walk in the park compared to the devastation he'd discovered when he returned home. Annerley House was a crumbling ruin. His brother had put a bullet through his own head, leaving a bloody mess and a mountain of debts. It had taken Guy months to sort through the disorder of the family finances. His father's man of business had long abandoned the family as a lost cause, and his brother had continued in his father's footsteps, raiding the capital and leaving nothing more than entailed property. Crumbling, rotting, fallow entailed property.

Emily's fortune was supposed to settle the debts and turn Annerley around. The land would be prosperous again. All he needed was time.

Now what would he do? What would he *do*? She'd let him down, and now he had one more person to worry about. Two, if he considered her maid. He supposed the maid was also his responsibility. By God, he'd pensioned off his father's valet and done without, but now he had an extra maid to support.

He glared at his wife, his penniless wife, aware of the injustice of his anger, but who else was there to vent his temper upon?

Her expression changed, her eyes widening and her mouth dropping open, then closing into a thin, grim line. Her eyes narrowed, and her voice came out low and filled with suppressed emotion. 'You married me to gain a fortune.'

Guy's level of anxiety was so high he snapped back at her. 'Of course I did. I needed the funds.'

She continued, her fingers clutching the book, her body

trembling. 'And what of your story of asking my father's permission to court me and he refusing?'

He was feeling perverse enough to tell the truth. Hang his vow to protect her from it. 'I never asked your father. I wish to God I had.'

'You lied to me?' Her voice shook.

He met her eyes. 'Yes.'

Then she did something he would never have anticipated. She threw the book at him, the action such a shock he barely had time to raise his arm to deflect it.

'That is for lying to me!' Her eyes flashed, and her face flushed with passion. Inexplicably, he felt a flash of carnal desire as unexpected as the book flying across the room.

'Why did you need this fortune of mine?' she cried. He'd not known her voice could have such volume, nor as much emotion.

'I haven't a feather to fly with, my dear,' he said.

'Do not call me that!'

He blinked. Her words struck him with nearly the same violence as the missile she'd thrown.

She paced back and forth in front of him, her arms folded across her chest. 'Where did you meet my father?' she demanded. 'Where did you hear these tales of my fortune?'

He'd once seen a mechanical doll, one that moved after a key was turned in its back. She was like such a doll coming to life, suddenly filled with genuine animation. He almost forgot to answer her question. 'At a card game.'

She twisted around as if to look for something else to throw at him.

'I cannot believe it!' she cried with a voice low and harsh and echoing his own rage. 'You are like him.'

'Like who?' he couldn't help but ask.

'Like *him*.' Her eyes shot daggers at him. 'You are a liar and a gamester, and I cannot believe I have married a man like my father. I thought I had escaped him!'

Her words stung as sharply as if she'd slapped him in the face. He stooped down and picked up the book, *Modern Concepts in Agriculture, 1732,* hardly modern, but a book he thought might be useful should he ever again have crops to plant.

Words leapt to the tip of his tongue. He would tell her he was nothing like her father. He'd done it all to save his family and estate and all the people who depended upon him.

What was the use? He had lied to her. Manipulated her. Tried to take her money from her. He was too painfully like her father.

She brushed past him with a swish of skirts, leaving the room like a Fury of ancient Greek mythology. It felt like she sucked the air from the room as she left.

Guy sank into a chair and put his head in his hands. He could not spare a thought about what he had done to her. He needed to think his way out of this morass.

What else could he do to save them? He had to try to reverse his ill luck in some manner.

Nothing came immediately to mind. If one could no longer marry for money, where was one to win a fortune?

The answer reluctantly dawned, but he could only feel like a condemned man awakening to the day of execution.

He would become a gamester, haunting gentlemen's clubs and gaming hells for the next big game. Just as she accused him, he would wager all their futures on a turn of the cards, exactly like his father and brother before him.

Exactly like her father as well.

Chapter Four

A week later, Emily walked into the Upper Assembly room on the arm of her husband, her first public appearance as his wife. She would have gladly forsaken the opportunity, but his mother pined for entertainment, and he had relented. Emily could hardly refuse her husband's request she accompany them.

Only two tiers of seating had been set up on the sides of the large room, and perhaps a hundred guests filled it. Not a bad showing for early October, but not even approaching the numbers at the height of the Bath Season. She glanced nervously around.

Her mother sat on the opposite side of the room next to the ageing Lord Cranton, whom Emily knew to be her latest flirtation. She leaned over the gentleman, giving him an ample view of her generous bosom. He laughed and whispered something in her ear. Emily touched her cheek, hot with embarrassment. Even more mortifying, her mother-in-law and husband were also gazing in Lady Duprey's direction. Her mother-in-law gave a disapproving huff.

Emily supposed she would have to greet her mother for propriety's sake. She dearly hoped her mother would be civil and return her greeting. Much depended upon how many glasses of wine her mother had consumed at dinner. On the other hand, if her father was present this evening, she hoped to avoid him altogether. He was bound to be in the card room, where her husband would certainly be headed.

Like a true gamester, her husband had been out every night since their arrival in Bath, coming home with the first glow of dawn. She knew because she was often still tossing and turning when he came in and could hear him moving about. Sometimes his step was light. A winning night, no doubt. Sometimes he moved like his feet were bound with irons. A losing streak. Only when the sounds from his room ceased could she sleep.

A dozen or so people looked towards the new Lord and Lady Keating, the ladies whispering behind their fans. Emily knew her marriage to Guy had been announced in the papers, because she'd read it there, but she and her husband had seen little of each other. They had conversed less, although he seemed inclined to put up a good front in the presence of his mother and the aunts.

'You have made us the latest *on dit*, Guy,' Lady Keating said in a petulant voice. 'I confess, I thought it might be worse. I don't suppose anyone will cut us, not that it would be of any consequence. Half of them are from the navy or the army, for goodness' sake. I declare, Bath has been overrun by military men.'

'You forget I was once a military man. Retired soldiers have to live somewhere,' Guy said.

She sniffed. 'Well, they are fair to ruining Bath. In any event, we ought to be at Annerley this time of year.'

'You know we cannot be at Annerley,' he said.

Emily wondered at the reason they could not go to the family property for the winter months. Was it rented like

Malvern? She would not be surprised, but she would not ask. She had decided to converse as little as possible with the man she married. Otherwise, she feared losing her temper again.

'Let me find you some seats,' he said.

Emily noted that he spoke more to his mother than he did to her, so perhaps he felt the same as she. He was angry with her for having no money, even though her father had been the real villain in this perfidy. Not Emily. She had not deceived Guy Keating. He had deceived her.

Was there ever a man who could be trusted? Even Lord Devlin had deceived her, making her think he would offer for her when he was living with her sister and in love with her. At least he'd done right by Madeleine. Their marriage had been announced months ago.

She sighed. She'd never truly believed Devlin meant to marry her anyway. But she'd thought Guy Keating to be different. Why? Simply because he'd shown such kindness to his great-aunts? It seemed an absurd notion now, to believe that one glimpse of his kindness meant he'd be kind to her.

Guy seated them near friends of his mother's and very properly introduced her as his wife. Emily endured the ladies' appraising looks, knowing they were dying to ask why this attractive man had married the very plain Emily Duprey, daughter of the shocking Baron and Baroness. Never mind. As was her custom, she would behave so properly no one would have a thing to say about her.

She chatted politely to Lady Keating's friends, and within moments, her husband excused himself, promising to return in time for tea. Emily supposed he'd been eager to escape to his cards. He'd certainly not felt compelled to ask her to dance, though eight couples were at this moment forming the first set.

Her mother-in-law, having her friends to converse with, required nothing of her, so Emily occupied herself by watching the dancers perform their figures. The ladies' dresses swirled prettily, like flower petals in a breeze. She found her toes itching to tap time to the music. She kept still, however, and tried to appear perfectly content.

Her mother glanced her way and gave her a half-hearted wave. Emily acknowledged the greeting with a nod of her head. She quickly continued to scan the room, lest she see her mother beckon her to walk over. Her eyes lit on an impeccably dressed gentleman, tall and elegant.

Mr Cyprian Sloane.

He caught her looking in his direction, and she could almost feel his steel grey eyes travelling over her in that manner that always made her think he knew what she looked like without her clothes. His full lips stretched into a knowing smile.

Oh, dear. He probably thought she'd been staring at him, but she never stared at gentlemen.

Not that Sloane was a gentleman precisely. By birth, perhaps, but he had the most shocking reputation as a rakehell. Ladies, from much younger than his thirty-odd years to much older, were said to throw themselves at him every bit as much as Caroline Lamb had at Lord Byron.

To Emily's total dismay, Mr Sloane excused himself from the people he was with and crossed the room. He could not be coming to speak to her. He could not.

He walked directly to her. 'Good evening, ladies.'

His white-toothed smile encompassed the whole group and brought their chatter to a sudden halt. Emily saw more than one set of raised eyebrows when he turned exclusively to her.

'I understand I must wish you happy, Emily…Lady Keating.' He spoke her Christian name as if she'd given him permission. She most assuredly had not. He extended his hand. What could she do but raise her own hand to him? He lifted it to his lips.

Her cheeks burned. 'Thank you.'

He held her hand a moment too long and she was forced to pull it from his grasp. He continued to discomfit her with the intensity of his gaze.

'If your…husband has not otherwise engaged you, I wonder if I might have the pleasure of the next dance.' His smooth voice paused significantly on the word *husband*.

Emily wished he would simply go away, but she could think of no excuse to refuse his request. Besides, she longed to dance. 'Very well.'

He bowed and walked away, leaving her to endure the knowing looks of her mother-in-law's cronies. The attention of Bath's most notorious womaniser did her reputation no good at all.

Emily could never quite comprehend why Sloane had bothered to pay his addresses to someone as plain as she, but, in the weeks before her elopement, he'd begun to notice her. She'd been so relieved when Guy began courting her. She'd fancied Guy had plucked her from the salivating jaws of a veritable wolf.

That was nonsense, of course. She knew that now. Guy had been far more dangerous. She'd fallen for Viscount Keating—no, for his kindness. She'd fallen for his kindness. But he'd turned out every bit as false as Cyprian Sloane.

Her gaze lifted to the crystal chandelier above the dancers, and she pretended to blink from the brightness of the flickering candles. Suddenly all was as clear as those twinkling crystals. Sloane must have heard her father's tale about her being an heiress. That was why he'd given her the scant attention he had.

But she was married now. Why attend to her still?

When the musicians tuned up for the next set, Sloane appeared at her side and threaded her arm through his to lead her to the dance floor. Emily could hear the murmurings of her mother-in-law's friends wafting behind her.

Sloane faced her in the set, his intense grey eyes riveted on her face. 'Well, Emily, my dear, you have desolated me entirely.'

My dear. What maggot entered these men's brains to assume she'd believe herself *dear* to them?

'I do not understand you, sir.'

They needed to complete the figure before he could speak to her again.

One corner of his well-defined mouth turned up. 'You have eloped with Keating and quite broke my heart.'

The steps parted them and they had to thread through the other couples before coming close again.

Emily narrowed her eyes. 'Do not speak nonsense to me.'

His brows shot up in surprise, but he retained the amusement in his countenance.

For the remainder of the set Emily endured more pretty words, more falsities. She pretended she did not hear them, but instead let herself keep step to the music. At the end of the dance, he bowed and she curtsied. He escorted her back to her seat.

To her astonishment, Guy stood there, a grim expression on his face.

'I return your lovely bride to you,' Sloane said to him with a wicked smirk.

Guy merely inclined his head, but when the man sauntered away, he gave her a stern look. She'd clearly dis-
pleased him by dancing with Sloane, but where had he
been when the music started?

'You are finished with cards so soon?' she asked in a
casual tone, determined to get her barb in first.

He did not appear to notice. 'It is time for tea,' he said,
turning from her to his mother. 'Shall I escort you both
to the tea room?'

As a good husband ought, he fetched tea for her and
sat next to her at a table shared by his mother and two of
her friends.

As the older women engrossed themselves in their own
gossip with words such as *that man* and *shocking* audible,
Emily was left in Guy's company.

He gave her a sombre look. 'I do not wish to criticise
you, my dear—' those words again '—but Cyprian Sloane
is not precisely the sort of company to keep.'

'Indeed?' she responded, having difficulty maintaining
her precise standard of composure. 'And, pray tell, how
am I to fend him off without creating a scene and calling
even more attention to myself?'

A flash of surprise lit his eyes. 'I concede your point.'

She took a satisfying sip of tea, disguising it as an ordinary one.

The look he gave her next seemed almost…caring.
'I…I would not wish your reputation to suffer. Sloane's
partiality cannot bring any good.'

He reached over and for a moment she thought he
might touch her, but he did not.

'I shall not behave with impropriety, I promise you.'
She kept her voice low. 'But I cannot prevent him from
seeking me out and I cannot stop those who wish to comment on it.' Her insides were churning, but she was not

sure if it were because he sat so close that she could feel his breath on her face, or because he dared comment on her behaviour. After all, he had rushed off to wager sums at whist, leaving her to fend for herself.

'True.' His ready agreement unnerved her more than if he'd given her a good scold.

It was his turn to sip his tea and for her to wonder what thoughts ran through his head. It was inconceivable he took Sloane's attentions seriously. She had never been the sort sought after by rakes. Or any other type of gentleman, for that matter.

He turned to his mother. 'Mother, would you enjoy some cards this evening, or do you prefer to watch the dancing?'

'I had hoped to play cards, I must confess,' Lady Keating replied. 'Are there other ladies in the card room?'

'Several ladies,' he said. He leaned towards Emily. 'Perhaps if you came in the card room with me, Mr Sloane would not disturb you further.'

In spite of herself, her heart fluttered.

'You can partner my mother,' he added.

Ah, he did not desire her company after all. Emily lifted her cup to her lips again. After a fortifying sip, she said, 'If your mother wishes it, I should be happy to partner her.'

Very shortly after, Emily found herself seated across from her mother-in-law at a whist table shared by an elderly gentleman and his wife, who were acquainted with the Keatings. Unfortunately, she was positioned so that her husband was in her view, seated in a corner with other black-coated men who hunched over their cards with grave, resolute expressions on their faces.

She'd seen an identical expression on her father's face.

He was in the room this very moment. She'd seen him when she entered, but, to her relief, he was too engrossed in his play to notice her.

Emily picked up the cards to deal. As soon as the deck was in her hands, habit took over. The cards rippled rhythmically as she shuffled. She could almost deal the cards without looking. Such were skills honed in a household obsessed by card-playing. She, her sisters and brother had been weaned on whist and piquet and quadrille. When her father could find no one else to play cards, he sought out his children. It was the only time he sought them out. In those days Emily would play whist until night left her yawning and rubbing her eyes, if it meant having her father's regard. Like a good father's daughter, she'd prided herself on playing better than her sisters and brother. If she'd thought it would win her father's respect, she'd been mistaken. When she won against him, he became furious.

The dealing done, Emily picked up her hand and spread the cards in a fan. A shiver ran up her spine. She felt the spades, diamonds, clubs and hearts call to her, as if beckoning her back into her father's influence.

Lady Keating and the other couple appeared not to notice. They seemed rather to find great enjoyment from the game. Lady Keating turned out to be merely competent as a player, and their opponents not as skilled. Emily held herself back from getting pulled totally into the game. Instead, she let her gaze drift to where her husband sat. He was an effective distraction.

She marvelled at the sheer symmetry of his face, the fineness of his chiselled features, the softness of his lips. She could swear the blue of his eyes glowed like sapphires in the room's candlelight. He concentrated on his cards, sitting very still in his chair, while the other men shifted at times, even occasionally rising to their feet when taking a trick.

So her husband was as cool a player at cards as he was at marriage. She shrugged. She did not care, did she?

She allowed herself to be lured back into the card game.

Cyprian Sloane leaned lazily against the door-frame of the card room, an amused expression on his face. So Keating had persuaded the so very plain and all-too-correct Emily Duprey to elope to Gretna Green? How daring.

He gave a mirthless laugh. With parents like the Baron and Baroness Duprey, a daughter might do anything to get away, even a woman as lacking in spirit as Miss Duprey.

When several gentlemen, including Keating, had turned their attention to Emily Duprey, Sloane had joined the competition. Now he could not help feel that Keating had won and he had lost.

Too bad he hadn't thought of asking her to run away with him. Not that he'd have contemplated taking her to Scotland like Keating did. Rather out of character for Keating to be so on the ball. Sloane had misjudged him.

He glanced at Keating, deep into his cards. That was a surprise as well, but he ought to have known. Bad blood always won out. Keating looked to be cut from the same cloth as his father and brother after all and would probably complete the family's journey to the River Tick.

An idea struck Sloane. Maybe Keating had believed Duprey's hum of a story about his daughter inheriting a fortune. Poor fellow, if he had. Would serve him right for winning the girl.

Sloane gave an imperceptible shrug. Virgins were more trouble than they were worth anyway. Besides, taking a maid's virginity was below even his low standards of conduct.

There were plenty of other women in the world. His eyes swept the card room. None of them, unfortunately, were in Bath.

He cast one more regretful look towards the new Lady Keating, turned around, and left.

Chapter Five

Guy sat at the desk in the library, rubbing his cold hands. He'd not bothered to light a fire, though it seemed a small, useless economy against the enormity of their debts. In a moment he'd be throwing a shawl over his shoulders like Aunt Pip.

He counted his money a third time. Last night's winnings had been modest, but then he'd been off his game shockingly. His wife had been the distraction, no doubt. True, she'd made no demands upon him during their visit to the Assembly Rooms, but he was not accustomed to having his attention divided. Dancing attendance upon a wife took much away from concentration on the cards.

He rubbed his face and stood.

Let him not fool himself. He'd scarcely given his wife a moment of his time at the Assembly. He was looking for excuses to explain the hands he'd lost, the money he'd pushed over to the winners.

The Bath crowd would certainly talk more of his card playing and lack of solicitude towards his new wife than gossip about her dancing with that rakehell, Cyprian Sloane. The man's presence vexed him, however, and he was not sure why. Perhaps because Sloane courted trouble. Other people's.

Guy ought not to be so concerned. His wife was too respectable to interest Sloane for more than a moment. Still, Guy disliked him paying any attention to her. What was the fellow about? Originally Sloane might have been after her fortune—her purported fortune—but that possibility vanished when Guy married her.

Perhaps he ought to commend himself for being the one to trick her into marriage. If Sloane had done the deed and discovered her penniless, what would his response have been?

Guy paced over to the window.

Could Sloane treat her much worse that he himself had done? He had neglected her at their first public outing. She did not deserve such treatment. None of the trouble he was in had been her fault.

Even so, he could not help resenting her. This anger did him no credit at all, but, devil take it, marrying her had made his financial situation worse. He could not even bed her now, could not risk repeating that one moment of pleasure with her, not as long as their future was so bleak. He did not dare produce an heir into this life of penury. What sort of irresponsible act would that be?

He placed his forehead against the cool pane of glass, but it did nothing to lessen the emotions boiling inside him like a cauldron of some noxious brew.

His resentment went deeper than her lack of fortune. His meagre glimmers of hope aside, he could only resent her complete lack of spontaneity, of life.

He ran a hand raggedly through his hair. He almost wished she would rail at him again. Throw another book at him. Damn him to the devil. At least there would be some excitement between them.

Any chance of making this a true marriage had disappeared when he told her he'd lied to her. He doubted she could forgive him for what he'd done to her by marrying her, for what life would be like for her if he could not reclaim their fortune.

Shivering with the chill, Guy gazed into the street.

More rain.

No relief to be gained by a brisk walk in this weather, he thought. Even the Royal Crescent would look dismal.

Like his future.

From beyond the library door he heard his great-aunts' shrill voices and other sounds of the household stirring. Poor dears. He supposed they were becoming a bit hard of hearing. He ought to join them for breakfast. He had some responsibility to keep up everyone's spirits.

And to smooth the tensions his wife's presence caused. Aunt Pip seemed inclined to be friendly to her, but Aunt Pip was no match for his mother and Aunt Dorrie. They seemed determined to continue to make Emily's life even more miserable than he had done.

Walking back to his desk, he plopped himself in the chair and placed his winnings back in the leather pouch. At least he'd come by enough blunt to buy some winter supplies for the tenants of Annerley and to pay for Cecily's fancy school. Along with the pouch, he placed the politely worded letter from the headmistress back in the drawer.

Still, these winnings were only meagre patches in a dam that was bound to burst. Postponing the inevitable, unless he could raise more blunt. There was no doubt he needed to find games played for higher stakes.

He must go to London. In London betting ran deep and huge sums were won and lost every day. In London he might win enough money at one seating to set them up for life.

In London, of course, plenty of skilled gamesters would be equally willing to take his last ha'penny. Still, what else could he do? Quietly let Annerley go to rot and its people with it?

Guy slammed the desk drawer and turned the key in the lock. His heart pounded in anxiety, for what he was about to propose to his mother and her aunts—and his wife. London could mean salvation or it could hasten the end. What a choice.

He entered the dining room, where Aunt Pip and Aunt Dorrie sat at the table, sipping their chocolate.

'Good morning,' he said, trying to put some cheer into his voice. He gave each of them a quick kiss on the cheek. 'I hope you ladies slept well.'

'That bed is an abomination,' grumbled Aunt Dorrie. 'It's a wonder I get any sleep at all.'

'Oh, I'm sure you get some, Dorrie, dear,' Aunt Pip said in her soft voice. 'I do hear your snoring from my chamber.'

'I do not…' began Dorrie in a huff.

Guy laughed. 'Well, I am certain you both look well rested, at least—' He cut himself short.

He'd not noticed Emily at the sideboard, filling a plate. 'Good morning, my dear,' he said stiffly.

She placed the plate down in front of Aunt Dorrie, giving him the barest glance. 'Good morning.' She turned to Aunt Pip. 'Lady Pipham, what shall I place upon your plate?'

Aunt Pip gave her a little smile. 'Oh, an egg, I suppose. And toast… No, a biscuit and ham.'

Guy walked over to his wife at the sideboard, reaching for his own plate. 'Bleasby usually serves them.'

She did not look up from her task. 'He woke with a dreadful cold this morning. I sent him back to bed.'

'And he went?' Guy said with surprise. 'It is not at all like him to shirk his duties.'

'I ordered him.'

She took the plate to Aunt Pip and waited at the table until he'd made his selections and sat down.

'Would you like some tea?' she asked, reaching for the pot.

He nodded. 'Thank you.'

Her demeanour remained perfectly composed. How did she accomplish that? he wondered. He feared all his worry would show on his face unless he battled constantly to conceal it. Another drain on his nerves.

She poured his tea and without a further word returned to the sideboard to place two pieces of toast on her plate. She sat down on a chair opposite his aunts and delicately spread raspberry jam on each slice.

'That is not much breakfast,' he said.

She darted a glance at him. 'It is what I like.'

He did not know what else to say to her. He watched her lift the piece of toast to her mouth and take a tiny bite. No relishing gulp of food for the self-contained new Lady Keating. A drop of jam clung to her bottom lip and her pink tongue darted out to lick it off. He remembered how her tongue had felt against his own, how she had tasted. He had to look away.

Aunt Pip and Aunt Dorrie intently chewed their food, offering no help in filling what seemed to Guy to be an oppressive silence. It was his responsibility to make the conversation, but what of? He could not speak his thoughts about tongues and tastings. He would not divulge that he meant them to go to London without his mother present. He cast about in his mind for something to say.

'I suppose I should check on Bleasby,' he finally came up with, though he ought to have thought of saying so when she'd mentioned Bleasby's illness.

'That would be good of you,' was all she responded.

His mother's entrance saved him from having to invent something else to say. He stood.

'What a dreary day.' His mother swept into the room. 'I declare I shall have nothing at all to do.'

'The rain makes my joints ache,' Aunt Dorrie said.

'It will not last, I'm sure,' assured Aunt Pip.

'Good morning, Guy,' his mother said, lifting her cheek, which he dutifully kissed.

Her complaints about the weather continued as she fixed her plate and sat down. He noted she'd neither spoken to nor even glanced at her daughter-in-law. Damn her. It made him ashamed.

'Mother, did you enjoy your cards last night?' Perhaps reminding her of Emily's willingness to partner her would help.

'Oh, indeed. I won some money.'

'How much?' His voice came out a little too eager. He hoped the ladies did not notice.

'A guinea and five shillings.'

Not precisely a fortune. 'Your share of the pot, or Emily's, as well?'

Emily stood to pour his mother a cup of chocolate. His mother did not look up at her. 'She gave the winnings to me.'

Emily sat down again and took a bite of her toast.

Guy stared at her. 'That was a generous deed, Emily.' His mother most assuredly did not deserve it.

She glanced up, looking surprised. 'It was a trifle,' she said.

Guy took another sip of tea lest he vent his temper on

his mother. She deserved a scold, but it was best done privately. As soon as he could get her alone he would speak with her about her treatment of his wife. Again.

But since they were all present and a change of subject would have its advantages, Guy decided to seize the moment.

He cleared his throat. 'I thought we might spend some time in London. Perhaps stay through the winter.'

His mother clapped her hands in glee. 'London! How delightful!'

'London air is bad for my lungs,' said Aunt Dorrie.

'Whatever you think is best, Guy,' Aunt Pip said.

His wife glanced up at him, but said nothing.

'Would it suit you, my dear?' he pressed.

She paused before answering in her bland way, 'I'm sure it will be very pleasant.'

He supposed he ought to be grateful that she was so accommodating, but, dash it all, he'd liked it better when she'd thrown the book at him.

'Won't be pleasant,' grumbled Aunt Dorrie. 'I'm sure to get an inflammation of the lungs.'

His mother rose to her feet and danced over to him, giving him a big hug. 'Oh, it will be a delight. Thank you, Guy. There will be some other important people in town as well, I'm sure. Some entertainment, at last.'

Another matter to speak with his mother about. It would not do for her to spend his money as fast as he could win it. He'd have to speak with her about economising. Again.

He glanced at his wife, who quickly averted her eyes. It would ease his conscience if he thought her as delighted as his mother to travel to London. It would ease his conscience if he knew anything he did pleased her.

He stabbed his slice of ham with his fork and let his mother's exuberant chatter wash over him.

* * *

Emily washed down the last crust of her toast with a sip of tea.

London.

Did she not have a considerate husband, asking her if a decision he'd already made suited her? Not that she had any illusion that a husband gave a wife any say in matters. Her father's luck or lack of it had always dictated where they would go and what they would do. Her mother went along, managing to find her own enjoyment. Perhaps that was what Emily would do as well, find her own enjoyment, though she could not imagine herself seeking out the sort of entertainment her mother craved.

She'd spent years ensuring that her behaviour did not entice the sort of men who danced attendance upon her mother, men like Cyprian Sloane.

She swallowed another mouthful of tea. She was certain Sloane's attention to her the previous night has been some sort of jest. Perhaps some other gentleman had put him up to it. 'Bet you a quid you won't get her to dance with you.' She could imagine it.

At least Sloane had sought out her company, whatever the reason. It was more than her husband had done. But she would not think of her husband. She would think of London.

Was she pleased to return to London? It could hardly be worse than Bath, and perhaps their London accommodations would give her less reason to be in her mother-in-law's way. Or her husband's way, for that matter.

Her maid would like the change, Emily was sure, as it placed her so near her parents. For Emily, the distance away from her mother and father was an advantage.

She wondered if her brother would still be in London. After his brief visit to Bath, he'd said he was returning there. Robert had never been very pleasant company for

Emily, loving cards as much as their father did even if he lacked the wit to be as conniving. Still, she would not mind seeing him.

She felt her eyes sting with tears and quickly poured herself another cup of tea. She must be lonely indeed if she pined for her brother's company.

'I thought we might leave in a week, if that would suit you.'

It took her a moment to realise her husband had spoken to her. 'If Bleasby feels well enough to travel by then.'

Her husband murmured, 'Yes, of course. I had quite forgotten.'

Did he think she'd chastised him? Good. His servants were his responsibility, after all.

'What about Bleasby?' her mother-in-law asked, still chewing her food.

Emily let the others answer. Her mother-in-law would like it so much better to listen to them explain, even though it had been she who had noticed Bleasby's cough and ordered him to rest.

Peering through her lashes at her husband, she pressed her lips together. What was the real reason he wished to go to London? Was he fleeing creditors? That had always been her father's reason for a change of location. Perhaps she ought to again offer him her vast inheritance of fifty pounds.

No, she said firmly to herself. As long as he did not require her to turn over the money, she would use it to help herself.

But help herself do what?

She sighed inwardly. Life had seemed so uncompli-cated when she'd simply gone along with whatever her parents decided. She'd always known her father liked his cards excessively and that her mother was a frivolous creature, but she'd always thought she could trust them to see her well married.

All that changed when she discovered her sister Madeleine was alive.

She'd been a fool to trust her parents with her future, and she'd be no less a fool to trust Guy Keating. He was as willing to deceive her as her mother and father had been.

The only person she could depend upon was herself. She alone must determine her future.

Looking as if she were merely lifting her cup to her lips, Emily secretly gave herself a hearty toast to her new resolve.

A few days later Emily called upon her mother. She'd not bothered to mention her intention to do so to her husband, and she knew the ladies of the household would have little interest in her whereabouts. Indeed, she herself had little interest in making the call, but it seemed the dutiful thing to do. Though her parents had not noticed her absence when she'd eloped, it still behooved her to let them know she was bound for London.

The day was brisk and still damp from the nearly constant rain. Rain may have prevented some activities, but it had not stopped her husband from leaving the apartments every night. Did he truly go out only to play cards? Or perhaps did he also meet a mistress? She shivered at the thought. What a humiliation that would be for a new wife, but he certainly had ceased taking care of his manly needs in his wife's bed.

Telling herself she did not care what her husband did, Emily walked up to her parents' door and sounded the knocker.

In a moment, the footman answered. 'G'd afternoon, Miss Emily,' he said.

She did not bother to correct him. 'Good afternoon, Samuel.' She pulled off her hat and gloves, and he assisted her with her pelisse. 'Is my mother at home?'

'Indeed she is. She's in the parlour.' He placed her items on the hall chair.

It was the fashionable hour for afternoon calls, but she hoped to find her mother alone. 'Does she have other visitors?'

He frowned. 'A gentleman, Mr Sutton said, miss, but he did not give me the gentleman's name.'

Just her luck. She was probably interrupting one of her mother's assignations. Perhaps with Lord Cranton. She had no wish to walk in on them. 'Perhaps you should announce me.'

He bowed and went to the task, returning in a moment. 'Lady Duprey says you may come up directly.'

She thanked him and proceeded up the stairs, trying to be optimistic. If her mother had company, perhaps her visit would be a short one. As she neared the parlour she heard a man's voice and her mother's trilling laughter.

As she stepped inside the room, her mother twisted around on the Grecian sofa. The gentleman stood.

Cyprian Sloane.

'Emily, my sweet,' her mother gushed, extending her hand. 'Look who has come to call.'

With the briefest of hesitation Emily walked over to her mother and clasped her outstretched hand. 'Hello, Mama.' She nodded. 'Mr Sloane.'

He bowed, his lips stretching into his most charming smile. 'Lady Keating.'

Emily sat primly in a chair, facing her mother.

Her mother giggled. 'Yes, can you countenance it, Cyprian? I am old enough to have a married daughter! It is too bad.' She fussed with the lace on her dress. 'Of course, I was married very young.'

Yes, Emily thought, her mother would most probably pretend to be a good ten years younger than her age, and neglect to inform the gentleman that she had an older married daughter as well, and a son nearing age thirty. As well as another daughter, younger than Emily.

'Indeed you must have been, ma'am,' he said agreeably. He turned to Emily and gave her that kind of appraising look that made her so uncomfortable.

'I hope you are well, Mama,' Emily said, trying to ignore him.

'Oh, famously well, darling.' She gave Sloane a flirtatious flutter of her eyelashes, before turning back to her daughter. 'Emily, be a dear and have Sutton bring our guest some refreshment. I believe your father has some very nice sherry put away.'

She crossed the room to the bell cord and a moment later met Sutton in the doorway to give her mother's instructions.

'I must not stay so long, my lady,' Sloane said, his glance sliding to Emily as she returned to her chair. 'My errand was with your husband, after all, and I would not intrude upon your visit with your daughter.'

Her mother flung out her hand as if to stop any attempt to flee. 'Oh, nonsense. You must have a glass of sherry with us. I insist upon it.' She made room for him to sit next to her on the sofa.

He laughed. 'I never could resist the entreaty of a beautiful lady.' He sat down.

Emily gave an inward groan.

After Sutton delivered and poured the sherry, Emily asserted herself to break into the bantering between her mother and Sloane. 'Mother, we are bound for London in two days' time. I came to inform you.'

'London!' her mother exclaimed. 'Oh, I envy you. How naughty of you to leave me when I am in such need of diversion.'

As if her mother had given her daughter's presence in Bath a moment's thought. Since Emily's marriage, her mother had not once called upon her.

'I believe my husband's affairs require it.' One way of describing a flight from creditors.

'Oh, that is right,' chirped her mother, acting as if she'd forgotten all about her daughter's marriage. 'Where is that handsome husband of yours?'

Sloane's eyebrows rose in anticipation of her answer.

'He has much to do to get ready.' Another half-truth, though her husband had been very busy cramming in as much card playing and who-knew-what-else as he could.

'Bath will be much duller without your presence, Lady Keating,' Sloane said, his voice silky.

Her mother tapped his thigh with her fingers. 'Oh, we shall contrive to stir up some excitement, will we not?'

He laughed, carefully placing her hand back upon her own person. 'Lady Duprey, you must not say such things. Your daughter will get the wrong notion of my visit.'

Emily's lips thinned.

Sloane inclined his head towards her. 'See, she looks at me very disapprovingly.'

Was he mocking her? Emily could not tell. In any event, he made her difficult interview with her mother much worse.

'I must not stay, Mama.' She stood and placed her nearly full glass on the table next to her mother's empty one. 'There are many preparations to be made.'

Emily had assumed the task of arranging the household's transfer to London. It kept her busy and relieved her mother-in-law of a tedious chore, though she expected no thanks from that quarter.

'Wait,' her mother said, again flinging out a hand. 'You may perform a task for me.'

She sat again. 'Certainly, Mama. What is it?' Likely something troublesome, and something she would rather not do.

'Take a trunk back to London for me.' Her mother used a tone of voice as if talking to a servant. For some odd reason, it irritated Emily that Sloane witnessed it.

'A trunk?'

'Yes.' Her mother nodded. 'A trunk of old dresses. I do not know why Shelty packed them. They are hopelessly out of fashion. All from last year.'

Emily stole a look at Sloane. He caught her, and a smile slid across his face.

She quickly looked back to her mother. 'Perhaps Shelty expected you to give them to her.' It was the custom, after all. A way for Shelty to make a little money on the side by selling them.

'She has no need of them, I assure you,' her mother shot back. 'Besides, they might be altered. Who knows what fashions will be the rage next year?'

Emily had a fair idea of how many boxes and trunks the Keatings needed to transport to London. 'I am not sure if—'

'You must take them,' her mother wailed. 'I am tripping over that trunk every time I take a step. I threatened to make Kirby store it in her own room.'

Emily sighed. She knew better than to oppose whatever her mother wanted. There would be no peace if she did not acquiesce.

'Very well,' she said in sinking tones. 'Have Sutton send it over not later than the day after tomorrow.'

'Will you tell him before you leave?' her mother pleaded.

She sighed again. 'Certainly.' Rising from her chair, she said, 'I really must leave.'

'Oh, if you must.' Smiling, her mother gave a sideways glance to Sloane, who also rose.

'And, dear lady, I must depart as well.' He took her hand and blew a kiss over it. 'I have left my card for Lord Duprey.' He turned to Emily, an amused expression in his eyes. 'May I escort you home, Lady Keating?'

'It…it is not necessary, I assure you, sir,' she stammered.

He smiled like a cat who'd got into the cream. 'It would be my pleasure.'

The walk back to Thomas Street seemed inordinately long to Emily, though Sloane behaved like a gentleman and spoke to her in the most proper of ways. They finally reached her door.

'Well, thank you, sir,' she said with nothing more than politeness.

'As I anticipated—' he grinned '—it was my pleasure.'

She opened the door and entered, feeling like she'd narrowly escaped getting tangled in a snare. Before she closed the door, he said, 'My regards to your husband.'

She hurried inside.

Sloane paused a moment before proceeding on his way. He smiled to himself. The new Lady Keating. It was amusing to rattle her, to see what cracks he could make in that armour of perfect primness.

Well, it was of no consequence. Now that she was off to London he must give up that mild amusement. How grim. Bath society had been thin enough that she had once been an attraction.

As he strolled down towards Union Street, he wondered if Baron Duprey would make good his gambling debt, the sole reason Sloane had made this call. He suspected not. Shocking when a gentleman shirked a debt of honour. If one wanted to sink low in society's eyes it was much more enjoyable to be known as a rakehell. That sort of dishonour earned a man some respect.

Chapter Six

When Emily stepped into the hall of the Keating London townhouse, she was unprepared for such a fashionable residence. Tucked into the corner of Essex Court, it was a few doors from the grand Spencer House, tiny in comparison, but perfectly large enough to accommodate them all in some style.

The journey had been tedious. Poor Miss Nuthall had complained of every bump and jolt, which Lady Pipham immediately countered as trifling. Lady Keating had much to remark upon about the countryside, about who might be in London and what entertainments they might find there. Her remarks were not directed to her daughter-in-law, however. Emily spent most of the trip looking out of the window. She'd found herself wishing she were outside the carriage, riding on horseback, like her husband, though she was merely a passable horsewoman.

The housekeeper and a footman rushed to greet them all, receiving a barrage of instructions from the elder Lady Keating while assisting in the removal of hats, gloves and outer garments. Guy had remained in the street, watching for the coach carrying the baggage, the ladies' maids, and a still sniffling and coughing Bleasby.

Emily examined the surroundings. The hall was bright with white flagstone floors and marble staircase, pale grey walls, plaster mouldings with gilt trim. A white marble statue of some Greek god gave the entrance its focal point.

A beautiful entranceway, like the interior of a small Greek temple, but perhaps a bit old fashioned. It wanted colour, she thought.

Lady Keating gave the footman, whom she called Rogers, three different instructions at once, and the man bowed and hurried out of the door to do one of them. The housekeeper became disengaged from her ladyship for the moment, and Emily took the opportunity to introduce herself.

'Good afternoon,' she said to the somewhat flustered woman. 'I am Lady Keating, Lord Keating's wife.'

The woman clapped her hands to her cheeks. 'Goodness,' she said, belatedly remembering to curtsy. 'We did hear his young lordship had married. I am Mrs Wilson. I did not realise who you were, ma'am. I beg pardon.'

What had the housekeeper expected? A more beautiful lady? Or had she merely thought the new Lady Keating would be introduced by the Dowager? That, of course, had not happened.

Emily extended her hand. 'I am very pleased to meet you, Mrs Wilson.'

Mrs Wilson clasped it briefly and curtsied again. 'Do you have any instructions, ma'am? I had planned for dinner at seven, because her ladyship always likes it that way. I hope it is to your liking. Do you wish to approve the menu first?'

Emily was lady of the house. She had quite forgotten. Apparently her mother-in-law had forgotten, too, since that lady was busy directing everything and everybody, though merely adding to the confusion.

She smiled at the housekeeper. 'I'm sure whatever Lady Keating likes will be quite acceptable to me. She is so used to making the decisions, is she not?'

Mrs Wilson looked relieved. 'Yes, my lady. She's been mistress of the house a long time, but I cannot say she likes making the decisions.'

Guy strode in. 'The baggage has arrived.' He saw the housekeeper, who curtsied once again. 'Good day, Mrs Wilson. Would you be so good as to supervise?'

Bleasby was ushered in on the arms of the maids, protesting all the while he did not need their help and should not enter the front door, but he was clearly in no position to direct the bags, boxes, trunks and portmanteaux. Guy firmly insisted he retire for the rest of the day, also directing Mrs Wilson to have Bleasby served hot broth and whatever else he might request.

The Dowager Lady Keating and the aunts climbed the staircase to the first floor, Lady Keating tossing instructions to Mrs Wilson to bring some refreshment.

'Yes, ma'am,' the housekeeper called back. She turned to Emily with a panicked look.

Emily took her aside. 'Ask the footman—Rogers, is that his name?—to take care of the baggage, then have the cook prepare Lady Keating's refreshment. It will take Mr Bleasby a bit to settle in. You may discover his needs later.'

Mrs Wilson smiled gratefully and started to rush away. She stopped, turning back to Emily. 'The bedrooms are prepared as Mr Guy...I mean Lord Keating's letter instructed. Do you require anything else, my lady?'

She had required nothing at all to this point. 'No, indeed. I am well satisfied.'

'Thank you, ma'am.' Mrs Wilson curtsied and hurried away.

The hall suddenly quieted. Emily stood at its centre, none too certain where to go.

Her husband spoke from behind her. 'Thank you, my dear.'

He startled her and she forgot to be annoyed at his typical salutation. 'For what, sir?'

The corner of his mouth turned up in a half-smile. 'For bringing some order to the chaos.'

She tried to think of what she had done. Nothing of consequence.

They were alone and they stood for a moment without speaking.

He finally said, 'Would you care to retire to the drawing room? Or do you wish to refresh yourself in your bed-chamber?'

She knew where neither of those rooms could be found. 'Wherever you wish.'

He stepped towards her. 'My apologies for the commotion. It was hardly a fit introduction to your home.'

Her home? It did not feel as if she would ever belong here. 'There is no need to apologise.'

He made no effort to look at her, but said, 'Perhaps tomorrow you can properly meet the servants.'

It seemed to her as if he were merely being polite, saying words he was expected to say.

'I hope you had a pleasant journey,' he added.

She clamped down a desire to tell him exactly how unpleasant it was. 'Very pleasant,' she said instead.

His eyes still slightly averted, he offered his arm. With a hesitation she accepted it. He escorted her up the stairs. 'Do you join my mother in the drawing room, then?'

Emily did not think she could endure a moment more of her mother-in-law's company. Not after that intermi-nable coach ride.

'Do you mind very much if I refresh myself in my bedchamber first?'

'Not at all, my dear,' he said. 'I will show you where it is.'

She forced a smile. Of course it made no difference to him what she did. 'Thank you.'

He left her very quickly at the bedchamber door, before she could ask where to find the drawing room. This was not some sprawling country house, she thought. She doubted she would have to wander too far.

Hester, her maid, was already in the room, busy unpacking her trunk. The girl looked up, face flushed with excitement. 'Good afternoon, my lady,' she said. 'I cannot believe I am back in London.'

At least someone besides her mother-in-law was happy about the change in locations. 'I expect you will be eager for a visit to Chelsea to see your mama.'

'Oh, yes, ma'am.' The girl grinned.

'Then we shall have to contrive a day off for you as soon as possible.'

Hester's eyes grew larger. 'Oh, thank you, ma'am. My aunt—Miss Kirby, I mean—said I was not to ask you and I wasn't meaning to. Not at all.'

Emily gave her a reassuring smile. 'Indeed, you did not ask me. I offered.'

Hester grinned. 'You are so kind.' She darted around the trunk to put clothes in the tall mahogany chest of drawers against the wall. Another pleasant room, Emily noticed. Except the carpet was worn of its nap in places, and the curtains looked frayed.

The footman appeared in the doorway with a trunk hoisted on his shoulder. 'Where shall I put this, my lady?'

It was her mother's trunk.

She looked about the room. 'Perhaps we can tuck it in the corner out of the way.'

'There's a small dressing room over here where it might fit.' Hester skipped over to a door and opened it.

On the other side was not a dressing room, but another bedchamber. No lamp burned there, but a large trunk and portmanteau stood in the centre of the room. Her husband's, undoubtedly. No one was tending to his unpacking.

She'd not had time to consider, but should he not have a valet? Bleasby helped him on occasion in Bath, and she'd not thought to question it, except to fear the family expected too much of the elderly servant. Here in London, however, it seemed odd indeed for a gentleman to be without a valet.

The footman noisily shifted the trunk.

'Gracious,' said Hester. 'It is the other door.' She danced around to a door on the opposite wall that indeed opened to reveal a small dressing room.

'That will be an excellent place for the trunk,' Emily agreed. The footman placed it in the little room.

Hester quickly pushed it to the best corner of the dressing room. Emily envied her maid's energy and enthusiasm. She was glad to have rescued the girl from her father's household. Indeed, now she could not fathom how to cope without sweet Hester. The maid was so grateful to her, it was almost like having someone on one's side.

Indeed, it was difficult at times to keep the energetic maid busy.

Emily glanced into her husband's room. 'Hester, I suspect Bleasby would have unpacked Lord Keating's belongings had he been well. Would you mind doing so? It should not be too difficult.'

'Yes, my lady. I would be happy to do so.' Hester

grinned again and said with a sigh, 'His lordship is a very nice gentleman.'

At least his lordship did not grope young maids or try to get them into bed as her father did. That was one thing to her husband's credit.

'Yes,' she replied. 'He is a nice gentleman.'

Emily sat at the mirrored dressing table and fussed with her hair, tucking away tendrils that had come loose during the journey. She'd wait until the dinner hour to change her dress, though a change of clothing was a tempting excuse to delay her appearance in the drawing room, but soon she rose and made her way to the first floor. Her husband was ascending the stairs at the same time.

'Ah, there you are, my dear. Shall we go in together?' he said.

My dear, again. She almost lost patience. 'I had thought you already there.'

'I decided to see how Bleasby goes on.' He waited for her.

How kind of him. Sometimes she hated being reminded of his kindnesses. It made her feel like weeping. 'How does he fare?'

He offered his arm, another kind gesture. 'He is quite fagged, but no more than that, I think.'

It felt almost companionable.

They turned to the first room on that floor and he opened the door, stepping aside to let her pass.

Her mother-in-law rose at their entrance, but looked beyond her daughter-in-law. 'Guy, dearest, where have you been? You have not yet told me how your journey was.' She presented her cheek for him to kiss and gave him no chance to respond. 'Ours was uneventful.'

'I'm a mass of bruises, I'm sure,' said Miss Nuthall. 'That hired vehicle was not well sprung at all.'

'I thought it most comfortable,' murmured Lady Pipham.

Guy left Emily's side to greet his aunts. 'I am sorry it gave you pain.'

'It did not give *me* pain,' Lady Pipham said.

Miss Nuthall tossed her sister a scathing glance. 'I cannot see how anyone could tolerate being jostled about like mail-coach baggage. Why could we not ride in one of the Keating carriages?'

Guy darted a quick look at Emily. 'They are at Annerley, Aunt Dorrie.'

Emily watched her husband more closely. Why look guilty about carriages? The coaches were very likely to be let to the tenants. Why not just say so?

He tucked his aunt's shawl more snugly around her, and fondly patted her back. Another kind gesture.

He looked back at her again and this time she quickly averted her eyes. 'Did you have a difficult ride as well, my dear?'

She wanted to blurt out, 'My name is Emily!' but she would not. Neither would she complain of his mother's poor manners towards her. If he cared, there was plenty of opportunity for him to witness it.

She made herself assume a pleasant expression. 'I had not noticed any undue discomfort, but, of course, I am perhaps less delicate than your aunt.'

Lady Pipham nodded vigorously, and the hint of an approving look crossed Miss Nuthall's face. Her mother-in-law took no notice at all.

Her husband placed a chair near the fire and invited her to sit. He turned to Lady Keating. 'Mother, I'm sure Emily would appreciate you introducing her to the servants. There is much for her to learn of the household.'

His mother pursed her lips. 'Guy, I declare, I am too exhausted to contemplate such a task.'

'Tomorrow will do,' he responded in a tight voice.

'I would be most grateful for anything you might teach me, Lady Keating,' Emily said. 'But I do not wish to trouble you.'

No matter Lady Keating's behaviour towards her, she vowed no one would accuse her of being an improper daughter-in-law.

Lady Keating, however, turned her back.

'Mother!' her husband cried sharply. 'My wife was speaking to you.'

The sharp tone of his voice took Emily by surprise.

The Dowager turned back and spoke in a clipped fashion. 'I will show you the house tomorrow and introduce you to the servants.'

'Thank you,' Emily said.

Lady Keating began talking of other things, matters which did not concern Emily, who took some time to recover her equilibrium. She glanced around the room, warmed by a small fire in the carved marble fireplace. More colourful than the hall had been, its walls were pale green trimmed with rectangular white moulding. The furniture was also in the classical style, sofas and chairs in the same pale green as the walls.

There was a very subtle air of neglect in the house, Emily thought, though the scent of beeswax suggested someone had recently dusted and polished. Perhaps the house had been unused for a time. She could not recall any of the Keatings present in town during her last two Seasons, but it was more than that. This décor belonged to her grandmother's time. It was as if no one had cared enough to tend to it since the last century had passed.

In Malvern, where she'd grown up, her mother always

kept up with the latest styles, no matter how big the expense or the debt. But that was a mere illusion of caring for a house.

Emily gazed at her husband, mother-in-law and his aunts. They formed a circle where they sat, a circle that kept her on the outside.

The footman arrived, bringing the refreshments, and Emily busied herself pouring for the others.

After the ladies retired to their rooms to await the dinner hour, Guy remained in the parlour alone. He searched a cabinet, pleased that Mrs Wilson had been thorough enough to stock it with port, the bottle still smelling of the wine cellar from which it had been unearthed. He poured himself a glass and plopped down in a chair by the fire. He would give his mother a few moments, but then he would have more words with her.

The gulf between himself and his wife was difficult enough, but her presence was a reality none of them could—or should—ignore, as easy as it seemed. His mother must be made to understand that her disregard of her daughter-in-law was not to be tolerated.

He downed the contents of his glass. His guilt at trapping Emily into marrying him was not eased by her perfect manners, her quiet way of doing whatever was required. With a few kind words, she'd already made a conquest of Mrs Wilson. And goodness knows what would have happened to Bleasby if she had not noticed his illness. He felt certain his mother would rush to report any sharp words from Emily, but none existed. Each day brought new evidence of what a fine woman he had married, how much more she deserved than a man who must make his fortune with cards and neglect her in the process.

Guy stood. The very reserve he admired in her dealings

with his mother rankled him at the same time. It left him at sea as to how to make amends to her, how to go about begging her forgiveness.

A few minutes later he knocked at the door to his mother's room, announcing himself. She bade him enter.

She lay upon her bed in a dressing gown and cap, but sat up as he walked to her side. 'I had not recalled what a small room this was. Kirby was barely able to find places for my clothing.'

He glanced around. It was more snug than she was used to, but perfectly adequate. 'What would you have me do about it, Mother?' he asked in a flat voice.

She waved her hand dramatically. 'Oh, there is nothing to be done.' She flung herself back on the pillows and gestured for him to sit in a nearby chair. 'She has quite taken over.'

He chose to remain standing. 'Now you know that is unfair. I made the decision. She, by the way, has asked for nothing.' He gave her a direct look. 'Emily is the new Viscountess Keating, and she is due all the advantages to the title.'

His mother closed her eyes, as if that would prevent her from hearing what he had to say.

He came closer and took her hand in his. She opened her eyes again. 'Mother, Emily is an agreeable creature. I urge you to treat her with more consideration.'

She sighed, clasping his hand tightly. 'I do apologise, Guy. But I simply do not like her.'

He pulled away from her fingers. 'And why is that? What is there to dislike in her?'

Her brows knit and she pursed her lips. He waited for her response. It did not come.

He leaned down and kissed her on the head. 'See, there is nothing to dislike in her. Do try, Mother. Introduce her to the servants tomorrow. Be gracious. Take her with you when you make morning calls, when you wish to go to entertainments Aunt Dorrie and Aunt Pip will not attend. She will be useful to you in that way, will she not?'

His mother met his entreating gaze. She gave a grim smile and patted his hand. 'I will try to be civil.'

He kissed her again, on the cheek this time. 'There's my girl,' he said. 'I'll leave you to rest now.'

But dinner was no more comfortable than it had been in Bath. As soon as he was able, Guy excused himself and left the house, intent on a visit to White's in search of a good card game and to get wind of where the most money was to be won.

Chapter Seven

All too soon days in London became routine. Emily smoothly assumed the management of the household. Her mother-in-law did not fancy the tedium of such mundane tasks as approving menus, overseeing expenditures and dealing with servant problems. The Dowager much preferred spending her time in more social pursuits, to which Emily was often expected to accompany her. Their visits were always very cordial, but such afternoons and evenings did nothing to raise Emily's spirits.

In one low moment, Emily had written to her brother at his rooms in the Albany, to inform him she was in town and to beg him to call on her. She had not heard from him. It was nonsensical to believe that Robert, of all people, could banish the blue-devils that so often plagued her, but she still longed for his companionship.

She did not seek companionship from her husband. He absented himself each evening, presumably to pursue his love affair with diamonds, spades, hearts and clubs. On the rare occasions he escorted his mother and wife to evening parties, he always left promptly after delivering them home, disappearing into the night like a stone thrown into an inky pond. Emily typically woke when he returned in the wee hours of morning, still listening carefully to the sound of his footsteps to tell her if he had won or lost. It became increasingly difficult to tell.

She dared not think what other nightly pursuits he might engage in, but it stood to reason he frequented the same gaming hells her father knew, places where one's fortune rose and fell upon the roll of dice or the turning of a card, and where there would be female company offering celebration for the wins and consolation for the losses.

The loudest sounds Emily heard from her husband's room were the clink of coins when dawn barely peeked into the windows. When her father had returned from his late-night gaming, he, like as not, would stumble in, mumbling to himself or yelling for a footman to assist him on the stairs. At least her husband avoided getting so foxed he could not walk. His footsteps were always steady.

Any day now Emily expected to see sure signs of a losing streak. Creditors should appear at the door. Her husband's even temper would then crackle like Vauxhall fireworks, and he would take to hiding in his rooms. How familiar that would be. Soon they would dash off to a country house party, or, perhaps, back to Bath. Anywhere the payment of gambling debts might be avoided.

There were no such signs, however. No creditors hounding them. No outbursts of temper. In fact, her husband was always painstakingly agreeable. Nor were there signs of great winnings. No lavish spending, no extravagant entertaining, no gifts purchased that shortly thereafter must be returned.

It was all so difficult to understand.

This night was to be one of the exceptional evenings when her husband would escort his mother and herself to a *musicale* and card party. Lady Keating was quite as mad for card playing as her son, and it well suited her to have her daughter-in-law as her whist partner. With Emily as her partner, she seldom lost.

Her mother-in-law had chattered all the week about the new gown she was to wear that evening. Emily had accompanied her when she'd ordered the dress from the mantua maker. She had been unable to convince Lady Keating to economise.

Emily did not know the exact nature of their present finances. Her husband always approved whatever household expense she brought to his attention, but she had a horror of the debt that would certainly come. She refused to spend any of her husband's money on herself, preferring to mend her old dresses rather than purchase new ones. It turned out Hester had a talent with the needle and an ability to slightly alter a garment so it appeared a bit less like one from two Seasons ago.

When it was time to depart for the *musicale*, Emily descended the staircase wearing a pale lavender gown she'd worn often, but with new lace trim. She carried her black cloak over her arm.

Guy waited in the hall, rocking on his heels, looking splendid in his snow-white knee breeches and dark black coat. She wished he were not so handsome. She wished he would not take her breath away at times like this.

As always, the smile he gave her seemed tinged with regret. 'Ah, you are ready, I see.'

At least he had not called her *my dear*.

'Yes.' She half-wished she had fished for a compliment. Even false flattery might feel more pleasing than none at all.

His mother arrived at the top of the stair, and both

Emily and her husband were saved the awkwardness of having nothing to say to each other.

Lady Keating put on her gloves as she descended. 'Guy, I hope you have a carriage ready. We are late.'

'It is waiting,' he replied.

He assisted his mother into her cloak. Bleasby, who had been standing aside, stepped forward to assist Emily.

'Thank you, Bleasby,' she said.

He bowed in his dignified, if arthritic way. Though apparently recovered from his recent illness, he'd slowed down considerably. He ought to be pensioned off, set up in a nice snug cottage on the family estate, perhaps.

'Shall we go, my dear,' her husband said, waiting by the door.

Bleasby limped over to open it, and Emily hurried to follow her husband and mother-in-law out to the waiting carriage.

They rode the short distance to the townhouse on Hanover Square, and were announced into a room where the chairs were lined in rows. The musicians were set up at the front of the room: a piano, viola, cello and two violins. Lady Keating exuded good spirits, greeting her friends, remarking on the lovely arrangements of flowers throughout the room. Emily stood quietly at her husband's side. The musicians began to tune their instruments, and Lady Keating rushed to find seats. Guy followed his mother through the line of chairs. Emily trailed behind him.

Soon strains of Haydn and Mozart filled the air. Emily closed her eyes and let the beautiful music wash over her. She almost felt as if she were floating on the melodies played by the strings, rising and falling with the notes, like a feather tossed on the wind.

The programme concluded with one of her favourites, *'Quasi una fantasia,'* a Beethoven sonata, once scandalous, now so fashionable its sheet music could be found in all the best parlours. The piano sound began peacefully, threading itself into and around her heart. It continued, growing, surging, like a storm about to erupt, a storm of emotion, pure and raw. She gave herself over to it, let it whip at her like a gale, until she felt the emotion clutch at her, taking her breath away.

When the ending came, she sat stunned, unable to move. Those around her rustled to get out of their seats.

'Are you feeling unwell, my dear?' her husband asked, placing his hand on her arm.

She glanced at him in some surprise, having forgotten even his presence during the turmoil of the music. 'No, I...I was merely listening.'

He let his hand remain for a moment, staring at her.

'I am quite well,' she said, embarrassed that her reaction to the music might show.

'Come, Guy,' her mother-in-law broke in. 'The card party is about to begin.'

There were several rooms set up with card tables. They wandered through them, looking for a place to sit. Being one of the last to make their way out of the music room, most guests had already chosen partners.

'See, we are late,' Lady Keating fussed. 'We shall not find anywhere to sit.'

A silver-haired gentleman approached her. 'Good evening, Verna, dear. What a pleasure.'

Lady Keating burst into smiles. 'Sir Reginald! I have not seen you in an age!' The gentleman took her hand and lavishly kissed it. She giggled like a girl, and turned to her son. 'Guy, do you recall Sir Reginald? He was one of your father's particular friends. My son, sir!'

'Ah, yes, Keating.' Sir Reginald shook Guy's hand. 'Spitting image of your father, I declare.'

Too much like the father, Emily thought, recalling her brother's assertion that the deceased Lord Keating had been every bit as bad a gambler as their father.

Guy presented Emily to Sir Reginald, and she shook his hand graciously.

'Come, let us make a foursome!' the gentleman said, ushering them to an empty table in the corner. 'Verna, be my partner, will you? A pleasure. A pleasure.'

Lady Keating pulled back. 'I want my daughter-in-law to be my partner,' she said, avoiding the use of Emily's name as did her son.

'No, no,' Sir Reginald cried. 'Not done. Not done at all. We cannot have two gentleman playing against two ladies.'

'But I like to be her partner,' Lady Keating persisted. 'We always win.'

Sir Reginald dramatically clutched at his heart. 'You wound me.'

Lady Keating giggled again.

'If you wish,' the gentleman continued, 'you may partner your son, and I will hook up with his lady. I assure you any son of old Justus will be a formidable opponent of mine.'

Lady Keating wrinkled her brow, considering this.

'I will be happy to partner you, Mother,' Guy said.

She acquiesced and they settled down to play.

Only a few hands showed Emily that Sir Reginald was a skilled player, and her husband as well, but then she'd expected him to be. She and Sir Reginald easily won the first game. Guy and his mother took the second, but only due to Honours points. Lady Keating, the weakest at the table, seemed also to be the sole person who cared about the outcome.

Until the third game. Guy had intensified his attention

to the cards, as any true gamester would do. Winning was always an object. Emily understood this perfectly. The gamester in her rose to the challenge.

'By jove, you are quite a player,' Sir Reginald declared to her as the last round of the third game was played. They'd won again, but it had been very close. 'I swear you would give any gentleman of my acquaintance a run for his money.'

Emily glanced at her husband, who was gathering up the cards. Perhaps if she played cards at those places he went at night, she would beat him as she'd done her father. If Sir Reginald were correct, she might even win the kind of fortune for which her husband married her. What she wouldn't give to win enough to tell them all to go to the devil.

Guy dealt the next hand and Emily stared at her cards. Her heart beat faster. If she could easily win at these *tonnish* card parties, why not with serious gamesters? Did not her father always say fortunes could be won at cards? But she would not give her winnings to her husband to gamble away. She would keep them for herself.

Could independence be purchased if the fortune won was large enough? Such a feat would require even more secrets than her husband kept from her, she'd wager.

Emily nearly trembled with the boldness of the plan forming itself in her head. Trying very hard to hide her growing excitement, she carefully restrained her card play to allow her mother-in-law the final win.

Supper was announced and they all retired to another room. Guy solicitously filled her plate, but she ate with very little appetite.

Her husband made the effort to converse with her. 'Do you enjoy whist, my dear?'

What ought she to say? That she thought it might be her salvation? 'Well enough,' she said.

He soon abandoned engaging her in conversation, getting drawn in to his mother and Sir Reginald's talk of old times.

After they'd finished their repast and wandered into the parlour, now free of card tables, Emily glanced across the room and saw a young man standing stiff in his form-fitting evening attire.

Her brother. So he was in town, the wretch. He had not bothered to answer her letter. Without a word to her husband, whose ear was bent to listen to Sir Reginald, she hurried across the room.

Her brother, seeing her approach, glanced to each side as if seeking an escape.

'Robert,' Emily said, almost out of breath. 'I am so glad to see you. Why did you not respond to my letter? I asked you to call on me.'

He flinched. 'Very busy, Emily. Meant to call. Really.'

Her brother much resembled her in colouring, but he presented a flashy appearance, fancying himself among the dandy set. This evening his collar points nearly touched his ears and his neckcloth was a labyrinth of intricate knotting.

She grabbed his arm, and he gave a quiet shriek at having his coatsleeve wrinkled. She led him aside, to a more private spot. 'Robert, I would very much like for you to call upon me. I insist upon it.'

He tried to pull away, but she gripped the fabric of his coat in her fingers. 'Have a care. My coat, Emily.'

She merely glared at him and squeezed more tightly.

'Let go,' he pleaded. 'Won't run. Promise.'

In addition to dress, Robert also affected what he considered a dandyish way to speak. In phrases. The habit annoyed Emily to distraction.

She released him, but stood in his way, blocking any sudden impulse he might have to run.

He eyed her sheepishly, patting his carefully curled hair and fingering his neckcloth. 'Must wish you happy, I suppose. Married Keating. Good fellow.'

'You ought to have warned me about him being a gamester,' she whispered.

His eyes widened. 'But he ain't a gamester. I mean… never was.'

'You've gammoned me, but no need to discuss that now,' she said.

He released a relieved breath, as if he'd escaped some dire catastrophe, like her pulling the chain of his watch and ripping his fob pocket.

'But you must call upon me, Robert. Tomorrow, if you can.'

'Tomorrow?' His voice rose uncertainly. 'Might be busy.'

'Tomorrow,' she insisted. 'Promise me.'

He shuffled his feet. 'Don't get in a pet. Will do it.'

Only then did she step back. 'Thank you.' She turned to leave him, but hesitated. When she swung back to him, he flinched again. 'You promise?' was all she said.

'Yes. Yes,' he grumbled.

Emily crossed the room to where her husband and mother-in-law stood. Two other ladies, friends of Lady Keating, had joined them with Sir Reginald. They had probably not even noticed her absence.

Guy spent the next morning in the library puzzling out how much of his winnings to reserve for debts, how much for daily expenses, how much to risk at the tables that evening. It was a daily balancing act that seemed more like constructing a house of cards than safeguarding the future. One careless step and the whole would tumble down around him.

As he'd hoped, he managed to gain ground by coming to London. He'd barely ventured from White's, where play was deep the year round, but still kept his ears open for more lucrative settings. He'd not always won. There were some nights his losses were deep, but slowly he'd gained enough reserves to play for higher stakes. He should do so soon.

He glanced at the figures he'd written on the paper in front of him. Not bad, but the icy, insinuating fear of losing everything was constant. So was the intoxication of winning. He'd felt that same intoxication even at the tame card party with his mother and Emily.

Emily was a good player, as Sir Reginald had said. For that one hand Guy had been locked in combat with her to win—the game of cards, that is. He'd enjoyed sharing that excitement with her, though, typically, he could not tell if she cared to win or not. She had the perfect face for cards, giving nothing away.

He gave a grunt of frustration.

He placed a packet of his winnings in his pocket and returned the rest to the desk drawer to lock away. He was off to the bank and to the post, to send another sum back to Annerley.

He walked past the front drawing room. Emily was seated by the window, peeking through the curtains.

His wife.

She looked pretty with the sun illuminating her features and shooting gold through her brown hair. Had he ever told her she was pretty?

She'd looked pretty the previous evening in the

lavender dress she'd worn several times before. She'd done something new with it. He did not know what. He ought to have told her she looked well in it, but his mother arrived in what was obviously an expensive new dress. Emily should have had a new dress to wear. He ought to have given her money for a dress.

He might tell her now, how pretty she looked by the window, her face aglow. Maybe she would smile. He longed to see her smile as she had the morning after they'd made love, before all went wrong between them.

She glanced to the doorway. For a moment, her expression was almost animated, but had he imagined that? When she saw him, the veil dropped over her eyes.

He forgot his intended compliment in his disappointment. He tried to smile. 'Good morning, my dear. Or is it afternoon by now?'

'A bit after,' she said, her voice without expression.

He paused, but then decided to enter the room. She clearly was not eager for his company. 'My mother and aunts are not with you?' he asked, then kicked himself. This was nothing like what he'd intended to say.

With perfect equanimity she responded, 'They prefer the small sitting room. There are fewer draughts, Miss Nuthall says.'

He smiled again, more genuinely. 'Yes, she would say that, wouldn't she?' He picked up a chair and moved it close to where she sat. 'You are not cold by the window, my dear?'

She continued to look at him, but without apparent emotion. She finally spoke. 'I am perfectly comfortable.'

'Ah,' he said.

More silence, as usual between them. He hated the silence.

'You are well, I hope,' he tried again.

'Yes,' she said.

The silence returned.

His head always flooded with all manner of things he ought to say to her, beginning with, 'I'm sorry.' Her composed expression stopped him. He was a bundle of emotions with her, but she seemed to have no emotion at all. He halfway wished, as before, she would rail at him, throw more books at him, torment him with what he had done to her. It was what he deserved. It was what he would like. He said nothing.

She glanced back to the window, fingering the fringe on the curtains. 'My brother is supposed to call. I am watching for him.'

'Indeed?' At least she'd spoken to him. She rarely added to a conversation. 'How nice for you.'

He'd met Emily's brother a time or two. A frivolous young man. A poor card player. When Guy decided to marry Emily, he'd reasoned Robert Duprey would be no threat to the scheme. He was not the sort of brother to chase after a carriage headed to Gretna Green.

She fixed her gaze out of the window again, and the silence returned.

'Emily?' He spoke her name so softly he was not sure he'd even done so.

She turned to him, slowly, it seemed. 'Yes?'

He faltered. 'I…I hope all is well with you here. That is…I hope you are enjoying London.'

Good God, he might be addressing a guest in his house instead of his wife. Why was it so difficult for him to talk to her?

'I assure you,' she said, her voice composed, 'all is well.'

Guy met her nondescript eyes, which did not waver. If eyes were supposed to be windows to the soul, hers were shuttered, curtains drawn. He doubted he would be able to open them to the light. With an inward sigh, he stood, his body suddenly heavy with fatigue. 'Enjoy your visit with your brother,' he said and walked out the door.

Emily remained at the drawing-room window, her husband's brief visit putting a pall on her excitement. He'd seemed so sad. A part of her had yearned to comfort him, but not for gambling losses, for that surely must be what troubled him. What else would bother him? Marrying a woman and regretting it?

Her mother-in-law appeared at the door. 'Do you accompany me? I have several calls to make.'

'I fear I cannot, ma'am,' she responded. 'I must stay here.'

Lady Keating gave her a sour look and left in a swish of skirts, never asking one question about Emily's plans.

Emily waited, trying to pass time by catching up on some mending for Miss Nuthall. She glanced at the clock on the mantel. Nearly four o'clock. Robert would not come. She needed him so, and he would fail her.

She'd been mad to think Robert could be trusted to help her. He was as consumed by his own interests as were all men. Why did she think she could bully Robert into helping her as she'd always done when they were children? He was a man now. A very foolish man, but a man none the less.

With a sigh of resignation, she stitched the rent in Miss Nuthall's lace cap. An approaching carriage sounded in the street below, and she nearly decided not to bother to look.

Her brother drew up in a stylish curricle. He had come! She fairly flew from the room. By the time Bleasby had admitted him into the hall, she had already fetched her bonnet, gloves and warmest pelisse.

Her brother barely lifted the hat from his head when she descended the stairs. 'Robert, take me for a turn in the park.'

'The park?' His hat remained in mid-air. 'Dash it, Emily. Cold out there.'

'Nonsense,' she replied, donning her pelisse with Bleasby's assistance. 'It will be refreshing.'

She pulled him out the door, assuring Bleasby she would be home in plenty of time for dinner.

Grumbling the whole while, Robert flicked the ribbons and the horses pulled away from the house. Emily's chest was a-flutter with excitement, as if this were truly the moment of her escape.

They reached the end of the block, and she saw her husband turning the corner on foot. She hurriedly looked away, pretending not to see him. She did not wish to think of him.

'Dash it, Emily. Why do we have to drive in the park?' her brother complained, using a rare complete sentence. 'It's cold.'

'I wished to speak with you in private,' she said, tucking a rug around her feet.

'Me?' He gaped at her, neglecting to attend the horses.

A hackney driver shouted, and he barely had enough time to pull on the ribbons and avoid a collision.

'Don't talk now,' he grumbled. 'Driving. Not a Four-in-Hand fellow, y'know.'

After a couple more close calls, they turned into Hyde Park where the pace was more sedate and the paths nearly empty.

'What the devil, Emily?' he said, which she took for permission to speak.

'I want you to take me to a gaming hell.' No sense in mincing words, not with her brother.

He nearly dropped the reins. 'G-g-gaming hell?'

She nodded vigorously.

'Hoaxing me,' he said.

'No, indeed. I am very serious.' Her heart beat rapidly. To speak her plans out loud made them seem very real. 'I need money, and the only way I can get it is to play cards.'

'Bamming me,' he said. 'Can ask Keating for money.'

She drew in a breath. 'No, I cannot. Besides he gambles away the money, but never mind that. I'll explain, but you must promise to tell no one.'

'Very well,' he said in a resigned voice. 'Won't like it one bit, though.'

She began by telling him of the rumour their father had spread around Bath and how Guy had believed it and married her, expecting a fortune. Best to start there instead of telling him their sister Madeleine was alive, no thanks to their parents. Madeleine had never made her existence public, so Emily felt she could not. Neither did Emily remind her brother again that he'd been the one to assure her Guy Keating was not a gamester like the previous Lord Keatings. What a Banbury tale that had been. Fussing at him now would serve no purpose. She desired his help.

'So I wish to win enough money to live alone,' she concluded.

'Jove, Emily,' Robert exclaimed. 'He ain't beating you?'

She waved her hand dismissively. 'No, he does not beat me. He's perfectly civil. It is just—'

'Nothing to it, then,' he said.

'There is something to it. He…he does not wish to be

married to me, you see. It is unbearable.' Her voice cracked.

Robert cleared his throat. 'Dash it, don't bawl like Jessame. Won't abide it.'

She drew in another deep breath. 'I want to have money enough to set up my own household. Nothing fancy. A cottage somewhere.'

'Can't do it,' he said firmly. 'Married now.'

'Oh, I know. Anything I won would be his, by rights, but I plan to run away where he'd never find me.' She expected her husband would not even trouble himself to look for her.

She'd been round and round about this in her head. It was her duty to give him an heir, true, but he'd not approached her bed since that first night in Bath, when he'd thought she would bring him a fortune. She must conclude he had no wish to bed her now, heir or not. For all she knew he might have another woman to fulfil those manly needs.

But she could not bear to think of that.

'Won't fadge,' Robert said.

'It will so,' she countered. 'I have fifty pounds from our aunt's inheritance. I can stake that money on cards. I want you to take me to a place where ladies can gamble. Where I can win huge sums.'

He neglected the horses, but the beasts trudged ahead anyway. 'Botheration, Emily. Don't play the cards much any more. Lost a bundle. Stay away from those places.'

'Take me to one just one time, so I might be introduced. You don't have to play. After that, I will go on my own.'

'Can't go on your own, Emily,' he said. 'Ain't proper. Bound to see you. Tell your husband. Talk all about town.'

'I have no intention of going as myself,' Emily said. 'I will go in disguise.'

Robert dropped the ribbons and nearly lost his seat retrieving them.

Chapter Eight

Guy finished dressing for dinner, assuring Bleasby, whose assistance was often more taxing than doing without, that he had no further need of the butler's services and would indeed follow him downstairs directly. Bleasby finally ceased fussing over his master's coat and his neckcloth and left the room. Guy followed a pace or two behind.

A quick footstep sounded on the stairs, and Guy heard Emily's voice. 'Good evening, Bleasby,' she said brightly. 'I told you I would return in time for dinner.'

'Indeed, ma'am,' Bleasby answered.

She turned the corner at the top of the stairs, hurrying to her room, her face aglow with colour, a smile on her lips. The smile stopped Guy in his tracks.

'Oh,' she said, seeing him. Her smile fled.

He tried to disguise the plummeting of his spirits. 'I see you enjoyed your visit with your brother.'

Her cheeks turned a darker pink, the effect unintentional but most becoming. 'We…we took a ride in the park.'

Guy felt a stab of envy, which ought to have been some relief from the guilt he felt about her, but it wasn't. Her face had come alive for a fleeting second. Until she spied him.

What did he expect? Her brother had given her enjoyment. Her husband gave her nothing.

'The air did you good.' Guy's voice emerged stiff.

'Yes,' she said.

The familiar silence returned.

'I must hurry to dress for dinner,' she said.

'Of course.' He stepped past her, but turned before heading to the stairs. 'Emily?'

She paused at her doorway. 'Yes?'

'I am glad you enjoyed yourself.'

She stared at him, unspeaking, then entered her room.

That night Emily again could not sleep, her mind flooded with schemes. She'd extracted a promise from her brother to introduce her to a private gaming club where ladies could play. He would take her there a week to this day, an evening when no other obligations would impede her.

She'd dosed off finally, only to wake when she heard her husband open his bedchamber door. Wide awake again, she could not help but listen to him moving about the room, more restless this evening than other times. He'd probably lost.

His footsteps came towards the door connecting their rooms, and her heart nearly stopped. She held her breath. Surely he would not come in her room. To what purpose?

Memories of the two nights he'd spent with her came flooding back. How he'd gently undressed her on their marriage night. How his hands had felt on her skin that night in Bath. The thrill of him entering her. The sensations that erupted.

His footsteps retreated and soon all was quiet in his

room. She bit her lip to keep it from trembling. She'd promised herself never to think of the nights she'd spent with him. *Never.* He'd thought her wealthy then. He did not want her now.

How like a gamester, when holding aces and kings all full of bonhomie, but if the hand contained twos and threes, suddenly consumed by self-pity.

She would show him she was more than a widow hand, the hand dealt but left on the table for no one to play. She would be in the game at last and she would win.

The widow hand would win.

After breakfast she called Hester to her room. If her scheme was to work, she needed to call in the young maid's debt to her. Hoping her credit with Hester was high enough to ensure the girl's assistance and discretion, she described her plan.

Hester listened with widening eyes. 'But, my lady,' Hester interrupted her. 'Why ever would you want to do this? Won't it make his lordship angry if he discovers what you are doing?'

'He must not discover it, of course,' Emily said, trying to think of a reason the maid would accept. 'He...he needs money, you see.' True enough. 'And I wish to help him.'

'Aye.' Hester nodded. 'I've heard the others speak of his lordship needing money.'

Emily was a bit taken aback by Hester's statement, but she supposed the servants knew very well of her husband's gambling. 'Yes, and I wish to help him. I am skilled at cards, but he has refused to let me play at the places where good money may be won.'

'Lady Keating thinks you are a very good player,' agreed Hester.

Lady Keating had made that known? What a surprise.

'So I am. I know I will be successful, but Lord Keating must never know what I am doing. No one must know. I need a disguise, and that is where I beg your assistance.'

'Mine? I know nothing of gambling.'

'No, I need you to craft me a disguise,' Emily said. 'You are good with a needle.'

The girl beamed at the compliment. 'I thank you, ma'am, but you said you must be ready in a week. I cannot make you a disguise in a week. I do not know how to make a disguise.'

Emily opened the door to the small dressing room. She opened her mother's trunk. 'You shall do very well. We will alter my mother's dresses, and craft a mask and hat to obscure my face. I have it all worked out in my head.'

Her mother's clothes were nothing like what Emily wore. They pulled out rich silks in a rainbow of vibrant colours, gold, red, green, blue—not a muted tone among them.

Hester fingered the fine material, 'Oooh. They are beautiful!'

Emily pulled up a small chair and draped several dresses across her lap. The fabrics were lovely, but she could never wear so many frills. Her mother loved frills.

'Do you think you can work with these?' she asked the maid, still exclaiming over each new discovery in the trunk.

'Oh, my lady,' Hester responded dreamily, 'I don't know about making a disguise, but I can make these dresses into the prettiest in all London.'

A week later, Emily stood in front of the full-length mirror in her room. Her mother-in-law had retired in a miff when learning Emily would not be home to play

cards with her and the aunts. Lady Pip and Miss Nuthall
had said their goodnights shortly after. Her husband had
gone out hours before. There was no one to concern themselves about her preparations.

She and Hester had selected an emerald green dress
from her mother's trunk. Hester had removed much of the
lace and ribbon on the bodice and narrowed the skirt. The
result was a plain but elegant drape of satin, though the
neckline was daringly low. With the extra material, the
girl had created a hat, an elegant cap of satin and silk that
included netting to pull over her face.

The mask, however, was Hester's real masterpiece. A
buff-coloured silk, almost flesh in tone, it seemed
moulded to the top half of Emily's face, leaving holes for
her eyes. Hester had so cunningly crafted the mask it was
barely noticeable, but managed all the same to obscure
her identity.

In the trunk Emily had discovered a box of face pow-
ders and tints that her mother had either discarded or forgotten. Emily used them to rouge her cheeks and tint her
lips and eyelashes, though she did so with a much lighter
touch than her mother would have done.

She had also found an envelope of paste jewellery,
more likely misplaced in the trunk. She chose an emerald-
like pendant, surrounded by false diamonds.

Emily stared transfixed at her image in the mirror. She
saw a stranger, an exotic, mysterious woman, nothing like
herself. Surely no one would know who she really was,
if she did not.

'You may call me Lady Widow,' she practised, using
her mother's voice and holding her head up proudly as
her top-lofty aunt had always done. It came more naturally
to her than she would have supposed. 'Is there any gentleman kind enough to partner me in a game of whist?'

Yes, she sounded nothing like herself.

There was a soft knock on her door. Hester jumped to answer it, opening the door a mere crack. Rogers, the footman, had come to announce Mr Duprey's arrival.

Emily's heart leapt into her throat. She carefully removed the cap and mask and reached for her black cloak.

'Good luck, my lady,' Hester said, helping her into the garment.

'Oh, Hester,' Emily exclaimed, 'I shall need luck.'

She carefully tucked the hat and mask in an inside pocket, and impulsively gave the girl a quick hug.

Hester skipped over to open the bedchamber door. Emily hesitated. It was not too late to abandon this wild scheme. She could send her brother away—he would be delighted, she was sure—and continue her days as the new Lady Keating, wife to Guy Keating, in name only.

She set her jaw firmly, squeezed her hands into fists and strode purposefully through the doorway and down the stairs to where Robert waited, twirling his hat in his hand and bobbing from foot to foot.

Bleasby stood nearby, looking as if he might topple over from fatigue.

'I'm ready, Robert,' she said unnecessarily.

He responded with a look of gloom.

As Bleasby opened the door for them to depart, Emily whispered, 'Go to bed, Bleasby. That is an order. You will not be needed this night. Have Rogers attend the door.'

A grateful but guilty look passed his face. 'As you wish, my lady.'

Robert assisted Emily into a waiting hackney coach. Like another lucky card drawn off the top of the pack, Hester had a brother who drove a hackney coach and who, for a hefty fee, agreed to transport Emily on her nightly jaunts. Her brother's worries about her welfare were thus appeased, for the burly young man had also agreed to look out for her.

The cards had fallen so neatly into place, Emily had to believe in the rightness of her course of action. It was not a mistake to take her future into her own hands. Card hands, that was.

The hackney made its way down St James's Street. Emily thrust a pocket mirror at her brother and aimed it to where she could see to don her mask and turban.

'Zounds, Emily,' Robert said when she'd completed her disguise. 'Don't look like yourself.'

She flashed him a smile. 'Exactly so. And I am not Emily, you must remember. I am Lady Widow.'

'Ghastly name,' he said. 'Makes no sense.'

The name made sense to her, however.

They pulled up to a sedate-looking house on Bennett Street and Emily was relieved it looked like a respectable residence. Robert helped her out of the coach and escorted her to the door opened by a giant of a man dressed in livery. Robert nodded familiarly to the man, and they were admitted without question.

Inside, the house was ablaze with light, and the murmur of voices could be heard from rooms above stairs. They passed by a gentleman who greeted Robert by name and who ogled Emily with open curiosity. Robert quickly led her into the large gaming parlour. Its walls were bright yellow with carved white moulding, so bright she almost had to blink, as if in strong sunlight. She glanced up at the ceiling and quickly glanced back. The ceiling depicted a Bacchanal scene, with many unclothed figures whose activity she dared not examine too closely.

Card tables were set up in the centre. Along the walls were hazard tables and faro banks, with gaily dressed women to run them. There were mostly gentlemen playing at the tables, but a few women players dotted the room.

A lady circulated among the card players. Not a lady, actually. Her bright red dress was cut so low, her generous breasts seemed ready to topple out at any moment. It made Emily's look like a Quaker's. Her lips and cheeks were almost as bright as her dress and her hair, also red, was a shade Emily was certain did not exist in nature. As the woman threaded her way through the tables, she rested her hands on the gentlemen's shoulders or patted their cheeks.

Surely she was a madam, Emily thought, in the baser use of the term. She could not help but stare, fascinated, as one stared at the oddities displayed at Bartholomew Fair. The creature in red glanced in their direction, flashed a white-toothed smile at Robert, and headed directly for them. Emily, still clutching Robert's arm, felt him fidget.

She nearly panicked. As the madam came nearer and nearer, Emily suddenly remembered seeing a stairway to an upper floor. What sorts of rooms were up there? Rooms for gentlemen to pass time with women such as this one? She gazed around the room. There were other women patrons playing cards, but no one she'd ever been introduced to. She'd landed in the world of the *demi-monde*. What was she doing in this place?

The riffle of cards and clink of coin brought her back to her senses. She was here to win money, as were the more respectably dressed ladies who dotted the room, playing cards or throwing dice. She would not flee back to Essex Court now.

She stiffened her back. The creature in red descended on Robert, taking both of his cheeks in her hands and kissing him full on the lips. Emily nearly dropped her jaw.

'Robert, darling,' she said. 'Where have you been? We have missed you.'

Robert blushed as deep a red as the woman's dress. 'Been busy.'

Emily contrived to look composed. It was somewhat of a challenge.

The woman eyed her. 'Who have you brought with you, *chéri*? A paramour?'

'Good God, no,' exclaimed Robert. 'She's my—'

Emily pinched his wrist. Hard. 'I am a mere friend, I fear,' she said, remembering in time to affect her mother's voice.

'That's the thing.' Robert pulled away and rubbed his wrist. 'Friend. Wants to play. Secret. Masked, you know. Call her Lady Widow.'

The woman extended her hand to Emily. 'I quite understand. I am Madame Bisou.' She laughed. 'Like your name, a description. "Little kiss", no?'

Madame Bisou's French accent was undoubtedly as affected as Emily's own speech.

She returned the handshake with a wide smile. 'I see you do understand.'

Madame Bisou turned back to her brother. 'Robert, *chéri*, if I do not know your…friend's name, how am I to know she will play an honest game? How will my loyal guests be assured she will pay her debts?'

'Uh,' said Robert. 'Vouch for her. Upon my honour.'

Emily flashed Madame Bisou another smile. 'I do not intend to lose.'

The woman laughed. She threaded her arm through Robert's and pressed the profusion of her bosom into his chest. 'I like her, *chéri*.'

Emily averted her gaze. Raising her voice, she said, 'I

would like to play whist, *madame*, if some gentleman present would be kind enough to partner me.'

Several gentlemen looked up. They stared at her with a boldness that would get them banned forever from Almack's.

One gentleman stepped forward, grasping her hand to actually kiss it. 'It would be my pleasure, ma'am.' He kept hold of her hand and caressed it with his thumb.

It was Sir Reginald, her recent card partner and Keating family friend.

Emily's heart banged against her chest. He would recognise her. Surely he would recognise her.

She laughed, as her mother would have done at such attention. 'I am called Lady Widow, sir. And you are?'

'Sir Reginald Roscomb at your service, Lady Widow.' He kissed her hand again, and she could swear she felt his tongue through the lace-mittened gloves she wore. 'You must call me Reggie.'

Trying not to appear as discomfited as she felt, she laughed again, but pulled her hand away. 'Such familiarity, sir? Don't be shocking.'

Another gentleman approached from behind. He spoke in a smooth, silky voice. 'My lady, you will surely lose, if Sir Reginald is your partner. You must partner me.'

'Oh?' she said, arching one brow and turning towards this new voice.

Her knees almost gave way from under her. Cyprian Sloane gazed down at her, his smoky grey eyes drinking in every inch of her with more blatant appreciation than when he'd eyed her in the Assembly room at Bath. Surely *he* would recognise her.

He bowed. 'Mr Cyprian Sloane.'

Her head felt full of cotton wool and all the air seemed

to leave the room. But no recognition dawned in Sloane's sleepy eyes. Had she fooled even him?

She curtsied, leaning over ever so slightly to show her low neckline to best effect. The gentleman's gaze riveted to that very spot.

When she rose, she forced herself to form a most charming smile. 'Mr Sloane. You may call me Lady Widow.'

'I would be delighted,' he said smoothly. 'But which of us do you choose to be your...partner? The older man...or the younger? I assure you, ma'am, I play a more stimulating game than Sir Reginald and will have more stamina when matters become...more heated.'

'Stuff!' interjected Sir Reginald.

Even with her limited experience, Emily caught the *double entendre* in Sloane's words. He, of all gentlemen, thought of her in that...that bedroom way? It was inconceivable. And Sir Reginald, old enough to be her father, did he too want to bed her?

It could not be so. She ought to be scandalised at this behaviour, repelled, but, oddly enough, she mostly felt a very satisfying feminine thrill.

These men desired her. What a novelty.

In a moment three others came to press her to select them. She tittered and giggled as her mother might have done, flirting with each of them. Robert, standing at the edge of her new admirers, wore a horrified expression. She caught his eye and made a face.

'Gentlemen, gentlemen,' she admonished, turning back to her flock. 'I intend to play all night. And if the cards are very good to me, I promise to return. You may all have a chance to play with me.'

While she spoke, the double meaning of her words dawned on her, every bit as shocking as Sloane's had been. She laughed at herself. What fun it was to say and do what one pleased.

All this masculine admiration, however, was not fattening her pockets. She had come to play cards.

She raised her arms to silence her new admirers. 'I will have Sir Reginald as my first gentleman,' she said, giving him a meaningful look that brought a huff of pride to his face.

She knew Sir Reginald to be a skilled player. She would not risk the little money she had partnering someone who had no card sense. Perhaps when she'd had an opportunity to observe the players, she would discover the best player, then she would know who her next partner would be.

She turned to Sloane. 'You may be my opponent, Mr Sloane. Do you fancy engaging in a contest with me?'

A seductive smile grew slowly across his face. 'I would fancy engaging you in any manner,' he said.

Oh, this was capital fun!

She searched her other admirers and picked a gentleman who had said he was with the East India Company, surmising he might have plenty of money to lose. 'Would you like to play as well, sir?' she asked.

'My pleasure,' the man replied.

Sloane assisted her into her chair, brushing his hand across her bare shoulders. Sir Reginald took his place opposite her.

As Sir Reginald dealt the cards, she spied Madame Bisou whispering in Robert's ear. A moment later, Robert left the room with her, disappearing in a blur of red as her skirts swished out the door. Emily felt her cheeks heat and hoped the gentlemen at her table did not notice. Her brother?

With all the artistry of a coquette, she charmed the gentlemen of her table to limit the stakes to suit her, ensuring her fifty pounds would be sufficient. She hoped in the future to have less need of limits. Their agreement was unanimous and immediate. They would do anything she desired. It was a heady feeling, indeed.

Winning came more easily than she'd dreamed, but she suspected Sloane and the East India man were conspiring to be kind to her. It wounded her pride to think they assumed she was not their equal at cards. Or perhaps they merely wished to court her favour. Sir Reginald, not to be outdone by the younger men, plied her with lavish compliments. So much so, she feared flushing with embarrassment.

In any event, her pile of counter pieces grew higher.

'La, gentlemen,' she exclaimed, 'you bring me such luck I dare renege on my promise to give others a chance.'

Protests sounded from all directions. She eventually allowed three other gentlemen to sit at her table, but the only contest seemed to be who could build her stack higher.

Sloane contrived to escort her in to supper and to seat her at a table in a secluded corner.

'You intrigue me, my lady,' he murmured to her, handing her a glass of champagne.

She sipped, and the bubbles seemed to sparkle inside her. 'I, sir?' She fluttered her lashes.

'I want to know who you are. Why you must hide such beauty under a mask.'

Such beauty? Now that was flummery, indeed. Still, her chest fluttered, and she felt the colour rise in her cheeks.

She took another sip. 'It is very simple, my lord. I wish to play cards and I prefer not to be spoken of for doing so.'

He peered at her from above his glass. 'So you are known in town?'

She gave him a sly smile. 'Isn't everyone?'

At that moment Robert walked up. 'Found you, Em—mmm—my lady.' His neckcloth was a dishevelled mess, and the perfect curls of his hair had been thoroughly disordered. 'Must leave. Getting late, y'know.'

'Not so soon,' protested Sloane. 'We were just becoming…acquainted.'

Emily pretended to sigh. In a bold move, she touched Sloane's cheek as Madame Bisou had done. 'Another time, perhaps,' she murmured. 'I should enjoy another round of whist with you.'

He lifted his glass. 'To another round, Lady Widow.'

She rose from the chair. Cyprian Sloane rose as well, capturing her hand and kissing it. Three more gentlemen, including Sir Reginald, kissed her hand before she made it to the door. Madame Bisou, waiting in the hall, gave Robert a full-on-the-lips kiss. Emily swore the woman's tongue was in his mouth before it ended. Surprisingly she felt a wave of sensation, remembering exactly how her husband's tongue had tasted.

Her husband.

Would her husband even care if another gentleman kissed her the way Madame Bisou kissed Robert? Any number of the gentlemen she met this night might kiss her that way if she allowed it. Emily ought to have been shocked at thinking such a thing, but somehow, as Lady Widow, she found it rather intoxicating.

When they were in the hackney, Emily pulled off her hat and mask.

Robert exclaimed, 'Zounds, Emily. Acting like a high-flyer. Not proper.'

'Look what pot calls the kettle black,' she countered. 'What were you and Madame Bisou engaging in while I was merely playing cards?'

She could almost feel him blush. 'Don't want to say, Em. Cost a bundle, though.'

She patted his arm. 'Do not fret about me. I am there to play cards, nothing else.'

'Not a proper place, Em,' he said.

'Oh, do not be a gudgeon. I won, Robert,' she cried, shaking him with her excitement. 'I more than tripled my money!'

He curled up to escape her revelry.

She ignored him. 'Will you come with me again? I think I can slip out tomorrow evening after the others are asleep.'

'Won't do it,' he said.

She pursed her lips and glared at him. What did it matter? She didn't need him. She would go alone.

When the hack left her off at Essex Court, she made the arrangements with the driver to pick her up the following night at the place they had agreed upon. She would sneak down the servants' staircase and cross the mews.

Emily leaned in the coach window. 'Thank you, Robert,' she said.

'Don't like it, Emily,' he responded, his voice gloomy.

The coach pulled away.

Rogers must have been watching for her, because he opened the door as soon as she walked up to it. She made her way up the stairs as quietly as she could. When she reached her bedchamber, the door to her husband's room opened.

She jumped. 'Oh!'

'I thought I heard you come in,' he said.

He was dressed in his shirtsleeves, the white of his shirt

glowing in the near darkness of the hallway, lit only by one small candle.

She gathered her cloak more tightly around her to hide her dress, glad it was too dark for him to see her face clearly.

'Yes,' she said. 'It is dreadfully late, I know, but—'

He rested one arm against the door-frame, high, so that his shirtsleeve slid down, revealing his bare skin. 'You went out with your brother?'

'Yes. To a…a card party.' *Please don't ask where*, she silently pleaded. Foolish of her not to have a ready story prepared, but who would have guessed anyone would be curious enough to ask?

'Did you enjoy yourself?' he said.

'Yes.' She felt weak with relief that he, this time as always, did not care where she had been.

He stood there staring at her. All the courage with which she'd faced the evening fled. No more giddy excitement. No heady sensation of feminine attraction. At this moment, she felt more like the Haymarket ware her brother accused her of being.

His voice crossed her gloom. 'I'm glad,' was all he said. 'Goodnight.'

He disappeared into his room. Emily expelled a long breath, but the glee at the night's success had suddenly left her.

Cyprian Sloane left the house on Bennett Street and stepped into the chill of the night air. No matter. He fancied a walk to his hotel.

Swinging his swordstick, he made his way to St James's Street, feeling more alive than he had in months, and all due to the mysterious Lady Widow.

Boredom had brought him to London, where the lure

of the gaming hells promised more excitement than Bath. What entertainment had been in Bath? Dull card games without a shred of excitement? The priggish Emily Keating? He needed more than the diversion of putting a milk-and-water miss to the blush.

London offered better sport. By Jove, hadn't he found it at Madame Bisou's? He'd expected at least a decent card game, maybe a toss in the blankets with one of her girls, but then *she* walked in.

Lady Widow. Arrogant and seductive and full of mystery. Desired by every man in the room. He'd be damned if he didn't become the first to peel off that mask of hers and to keep going until he peeled off the rest of her clothes as well. He'd wager on it.

Life was grand. He laughed out loud, startling the watchman sitting in his box. 'Good evening, man!' he called, thumping on the box with his stick.

The man grumbled a reply.

With another laugh, Cyprian set off again, whistling 'The Lass on Richmond Hill'.

Chapter Nine

Two weeks later at half past midnight, Guy sat near the bow window at White's, nursing a brandy. The card room was thin of players, a good excuse to relax with a drink before letting the cards perform their own manner of intoxication.

He would much rather have remained at home. He'd escorted his mother and Emily to the theatre this night and had not relished going back out after they both retired. If he did not play, however, he would not win. So here he was.

He swirled the brandy in his glass, idly watching how its spiral reflected in the light of a nearby lamp. It would have been pleasant to sit in front of a fire in his own parlour, sipping his own brandy, going off to bed at a decent hour. More pleasant than facing a stuffy card room with men whose luck and skill might exceed his own.

Even more pleasant would be to knock on his wife's bedchamber door. Enjoy the fruits of married life, but that was too soon to contemplate.

Maybe some day he could contrive a way to woo his wife, renew that intimacy they'd only begun to explore.

If he hadn't bungled everything, that is. If he could ever risk creating an heir.

He set the brandy to spinning again, eyes fixed upon its play, like a man in a trance. It would be very pleasant to mend that particular breach with his wife. In daylight so much distance loomed between them, but perhaps through that physical act of marriage they could forge a real union with each other.

Her response to his attempts at lovemaking had been sweet, really. Touching. Hopeful.

But hope could be sucked away in an instant. Sometimes it seemed to him that catastrophe loomed in every corner of the realm, perhaps in the whole world. Corn prices kept rising, riots were reported out in the countryside. People were starving. Whenever he walked down the street desperate men begged for pennies, the same men who had fought beside him on the Peninsula and at Waterloo. No winning at cards would ever be enough to stem this tide of poverty.

He raised the glass to his mouth, tasting the amber liquid, savouring the warmth it created as he swallowed.

Cards were a respite, he had to admit. When he was deep in play, he never thought of the world's catastrophes. Nor of his wife, his family, Annerley. He only thought of winning and losing. If he won a hand, he wanted to see how much more he could win. If he lost, he wanted to play until he reversed his luck.

It was a constant struggle to make his head control his play. To force himself to quit when ahead, to walk away when he lost. So far, he had won the struggle and had won more money than he had lost. He could credit himself with coming a long way towards saving Annerley and his family's future.

But he had not quite completed the battle. At the next seating, would he keep his head?

'Why, Keating!' a man's voice boomed from behind him. 'That is you, by Jupiter. I thought so.'

Sir Reginald clapped him on the shoulder and plopped his portly frame in the opposite chair.

'How do you do, Sir Reginald?' Guy said. 'Rare to see you here.'

'Yes. Yes.' Sir Reginald signalled for a drink. 'I don't fancy White's much at this hour. More tempting enticements in town.'

'Indeed?' said Guy, without true interest.

'Yes, indeed.' Sir Reginald nodded thanks to the footman who set a drink on the table. 'Just came in to collect on a small debt. I'm off to Madame Bisou's.' He took a sip. 'Come with me, lad.'

'Madame Bisou's?' he repeated automatically.

'Delightful place, I assure you.' Sir Reginald gave a jovial laugh. 'Games are honest. Women, pretty and clean, if you fancy a bit of sport.'

Honest games?

That caught his attention. He had considered venturing out to one of the gaming establishments that abounded on and around St James's Street. He'd been afraid to risk it.

Sir Reginald sipped his drink. 'Capital sport there, I tell you.' He leaned forward, speaking to Guy in hushed tones. 'There is a woman there I fancy very much. She is perfection. A piece of quality baggage. I'm about to offer her *carte blanche*. Called in a few vowels here to fatten my offer.'

Guy tried to sound amused. 'She sounds like a veritable Venus. What makes you think this Madame Bisou would let her go?'

'No. No. No.' Sir Reginald held up his hand. 'This

one's not in the business. No, indeed. She's a patron. Comes to play cards, she says.' He leaned closer. 'She is magnificent, Keating. Figure is perfection. And she wears this mask, you see—'

'To cover some imperfection, no doubt,' Guy interjected.

Sir Reginald looked wounded. 'I am sure there is not one part of her that is flawed. She just don't want anyone to know who she is, that's the ticket. All I need is one more run of luck and I shall have enough blunt to win her. Young blokes won't have a chance. There's a wager going, don't y'know, on who beds the lady first. I intend to win it.'

Guy smiled inwardly. Just one more run of luck? Just another big win? Sir Reginald repeated words that were constantly swimming around Guy's mind. One more round of luck and maybe Guy would win the lady, too, only the lady would be his wife.

He glanced back to the drink in his hand. If Sir Reginald's masked lady was the object of such a wager, she was probably out of the man's reach. Perhaps Emily was out of Guy's reach, as well. He'd certainly done nothing to win her.

'Come with me, Keating,' insisted the older man. 'One look at her and you will see what I mean.'

Guy glanced towards the game room. He'd not likely win his fortune there tonight. 'Games are honest, you say?'

'Depend upon it,' Sir Reginald said.

'Is the play deep?'

'Deep as you like,' assured Sir Reginald.

He shrugged. 'Very well. As you said, things are too tame here. Perhaps I should try my luck elsewhere.'

'Excellent. Excellent.' Sir Reginald rose, clapping him on the shoulder again. 'Let's be off.'

Emily rushed in to Madame Bisou's, later than usual. She'd waited until she was sure Lady Keating was asleep and her husband had departed. She hoped the card room would not be too full for her to play.

'Evenin', ma'am,' the footman said.

'Good evening, Cummings.' She was familiar to him now, a regular customer. She handed him her cloak and rushed up the stairs.

Cyprian Sloane was walking in the opposite direction. He gave her one of his most charming smiles. 'Why, Lady Widow, I nearly gave up on you. I was about to depart.'

She laughed at him. 'Mr Sloane, do not say you come here only to see me.'

He stood in her way, much too close. 'Very well,' he purred. 'I will not say it, for all that it is true.'

Sloane had become one of Lady Widow's most faithful admirers, singling her out, contriving to share supper with her alone on more than one occasion. It was flattering, even amusing, to watch his rakish technique, how he drew her in and tried to cast her under his spell. For two nights he'd seemed to ignore her completely. What an excellent ploy that had been. Without even realising it, she'd found herself wanting to seek him out.

This was a mere cat-and-mouse game they played, she knew. She doubted his intent to be any more serious than her own. Although he might relish a brief liaison, she definitely would not, as she told him when he asked her to accompany him to the upper floor. Several times.

'If I might pass, sir?' Emily kept her voice light.

He did not move.

'I must go, sir,' she said, irritated at him. 'I came to play cards. That is my passion, you know.'

He favoured her with the smile again. 'Are you sure you would not fancy other passions? Come above stairs with me. I will show you more excitement than a hand full of trumps.'

She spoke more firmly. 'Indeed not, sir.'

He leaned on the banister, but still took up too much space for her to get by. 'Why not?' he asked. 'Do you have some husband somewhere whose anger you fear? I assure you I am a match for any husband.'

'I will not tell you.' She made her voice light again. Matters went easier with him when she treated everything as a joke. 'So don't tease me, Mr Sloane.'

Again he leaned closer, his breath hot against her tender skin. 'Call me Cyprian. I long to hear my name on your lips.'

She placed her hands on his chest and pushed him away. The game had gone far enough for one night.

'Mr Sloane,' she said sternly, 'it would not be proper to address you so familiarly.'

He gave her a pained look, one she suspected was designed to melt a woman's resolve. 'You wound me mortally, my lady.'

'Gammon,' she said.

He grinned and stepped aside so she could go in the card room. 'Another time, perhaps?'

She tossed him an exasperated glance and hurried in to see who might play whist with her. Madame Bisou rushed up to her immediately.

'Lady Widow,' the woman said in her false French accent. 'Have you brought your…friend Robert with you?'

What did the woman see in her fribble of a brother? 'Not tonight, *madame*.'

The madam, dressed in a truly awful shade of purple, pushed her mouth into a moue and quickly lost interest in Lady Widow.

Several gentlemen leapt to their feet upon seeing her and begged her to play at their tables. It never ceased to amaze her. They treated her as if she were the most desirable creature in London. It was the mask, of course. It lent mystery. It also was curiously liberating. She could say and do as she pleased and no one knew who she was. No one could reproach her.

Thus far, Emily had confined her play to whist, no matter how strenuously she was urged to throw dice or turn cards at faro. Those were fools' games, too dependent on luck, a goddess her father and husband might revere, but she did not. Luck alone was too fickle. Skill gave her a winning edge.

Ironically, Madame Bisou's house gave her little opportunity to exercise her skill. Her counters might stack higher and higher in front of her, but the gentlemen who begged her company mostly contrived to let her win. She could tell. She'd watched their play at other tables, taking no time at all to recognise the serious players.

The women had no interest at all in playing whist with her. On the contrary, they often tossed her jealous looks when men clustered around her, acting like buffoons. These men played cards like buffoons as well, with the intent of currying her favour. Did they think she could not tell?

She supposed she ought not to complain, for her fortune grew steadily. The gamester in her protested, however.

A place was made for her at one of the tables, and she sat down with the son of a Duke, the East India man, and a much decorated naval captain. Men who had been deep in cards when she first walked in, now straightened in their seats, asked after her comfort, begged to get her a glass of wine. Lady Widow laughed at their solicitousness.

'Let us play cards, gentlemen,' she said.

The Duke's son dealt. She saw Sloane enter the room. He had not decided to leave after all. After her rebuff, would he finagle a chance to play at her table or was this a night to ignore her? It would be amusing to find out.

The hands went quickly and Emily's stack rose higher, as usual. In a fortnight, her fifty pounds had quickly ballooned into more than two thousand. How much she needed to live as an independent woman, she did not know, but it would require many more nights at Madame Bisou's. She did not mind. Life had become rather exciting.

Even if the card games lacked excitement. After several unchallenging games, other gentlemen begged her to change tables. Her stack grew higher. When Madame Bisou announced that supper was served, Emily was almost relieved. In spite of the exhilaration of Lady Widow's success, with any challenge lacking, she was beginning to get bored.

The East India man was the first to beg her company at supper. A glance at Cyprian Sloane showed he was not at all pleased. Emily grinned to herself. It was so easy to make a man jealous. She gave Sloane a saucy glance as she allowed the East India man to walk her to the door.

Sir Reginald appeared in the doorway, a huge grin erupting on his beefy face when he spied her. He strode towards her, another gentleman behind him.

With a face flushed red, Sir Reginald grasped her hand and kissed it. 'Lady Widow, you are a feast for my eyes.'

Emily laughed. 'I thought you had forgotten all about me, sir.'

'Never. Never. You are constantly in my thoughts.' He gave her a meaningful smile and squeezed her hand.

She pulled it away. 'You tease me, of course.'

'I was never more serious,' he said, 'But I've brought someone I wanted to meet you.' He stepped aside.

Emily froze.

Her husband stood before her. He would recognise her. He must. No one else who knew her had recognised her, but surely her husband would! A loud buzzing sounded in her ears. Everything faded from her sight except her husband, handsome as always, still in the evening attire he'd worn escorting her to the theatre.

Sir Reginald gestured him come forward. 'May I present Lord Keating to you, dear lady.'

He bowed to her. 'My pleasure, Lady Widow.'

When he rose from his bow, he looked straight in her face, shrouded as it was by her mask and the netting of her hat.

This is the moment, she thought. *He will know me.* Her knees turned weak. She thought she might faint.

But no recognition flickered in his sapphire blue eyes. Guy Keating, the man she married, looked at Lady Widow the same way every man in this room had done. With definite masculine appreciation.

'My very great pleasure.' He took her hand and raised it to his lips as Sir Reginald had done.

'Lord Keating, is it?' she managed to say.

He still did not recognise her. He smiled at her, that smile of unspoken invitation. She'd come to expect such smiles at Madame Bisou's. But not from her husband.

But he thought her to be Lady Widow, did he not? Lady Widow, who dressed in daring fashions. Lady Widow, who tinted her lips and cheeks. Lady Widow, who'd become the toast of one bawdy gaming hell. Her husband smiled at Lady Widow. Not Emily. Not his wife.

'You are going in to supper?' The gleam remained in his eye. 'Perhaps Sir Reginald and I might join you?'

The East India man huffed in disapproval. Emily ignored it, feeling an anger building in her so fiercely, she thought she might plant her husband a facer, pop his cork, draw some claret.

How dare he look at Lady Widow in this…this leering sort of way, when in his own home, he did not look at her at all? Is this what he was about when he went out at night? Was he jauntering through the London hells, searching for just such a creature as Lady Widow? A woman he might dally with? Goodness knows, he had no wish to dally with his wife.

Her throat constricted and a bitter taste filled her mouth. Why could he not look at Emily in that manner? Why could he not look at *her*? The jelly her insides had become now solidified into sharp-edged steel.

If her husband so desired Lady Widow, Lady Widow would lead him a merry dance. She would entice him and tease him. She would become everything he fancied. She would lead him to the brink and then she would push him over so hard, he would be knocked out of his senses. And when Lady Widow left him, he would know exactly what he had lost.

She leaned towards him to make sure he appreciated the low cut of the gold silk gown Hester had transformed. She lifted her hand and ran her finger slowly down his arm. He responded. His eyes darkened. Colour infused his face. His posture changed.

She smiled. 'Your company, sir, would give me great pleasure.'

Taking his arm, she pressed her bosom into his side as

she'd seen Madame Bisou do to Robert. He escorted her to the supper room, leaving Sir Reginald and the East India man to trail behind like two baby ducklings. Sloane glared at her from across the room.

Guy's gaze feasted upon the woman seated across from him in the supper room, his blood coursing through his veins. She had certainly roused his senses.

When he'd seen her stride gracefully across the room, her chin had been elevated regally. Her hips swayed gently. She'd moved with the knowledge that every man in that room wanted her in bed with him.

God help him, Guy was no exception. No wonder Sir Reginald was besotted. Guy was somewhat shocked that he'd reacted so physically. Every sense in his body was aroused. Every one.

Why her? He had certainly encountered other beautiful women on occasion. What was it about this one that stirred him so?

He had an uncanny notion he ought to know her, but that was nonsense. Surely he would remember. Lady Widow, masked or unmasked, could not be a female to forget. Still, the feeling of familiarity nagged at him.

She flirted openly with him, batting her eyelashes, touching his arm, pressing her knee against his. He was not immune. No, she'd whipped him into a vortex of sexual desire the likes of which he had not known since before he'd reached his majority.

When a droplet of wine rested on her lip and she slowly licked it off with her pink tongue, he was struck again with the feeling he'd seen this before, and reacted as strongly. At least the notion distracted him from his sudden raw sexual need.

'Why have you come to Madame Bisou's, Lord Keating?' she asked, music in her voice. 'To sample her lovely girls?'

He swallowed some wine. 'To play cards.'

'Indeed?' Her eyes widened from under her mask. 'That is why I attend as well. To play.' She paused and gave him a saucy look. 'Play cards, that is.' She was a seductress all right.

She swept her gaze over the other gentlemen at the table, lighting upon Sir Reginald, who puffed up like a rooster about to crow. 'The gentlemen here are not very good players, I fear.' Her eyes, looking golden like her dress, glittered with amusement. 'I seem to win almost every game I play. Perhaps you wish to partner me? You will win, too.'

He took another sip of wine, a bit wary of the effect she had on him. 'If you wish it.'

Her smile widened, and she shifted her attention to one of the other gentleman sitting with them, asking him something about trade with India.

A few minutes later, she declared supper over, and all the gentlemen rose in unison. Lucky Sir Reginald had the pleasure of escorting her back to the card room. Guy took up the rear.

He regarded her more dispassionately, an easier task with her back turned, even though that view of her was delightful as well. She flirted with him quite blatantly. Did he wish for a dalliance? Lord knew, he ached for release. Lady Widow was more temptation than his imagination could have conjured up, and he'd not lain with a woman since that night with his wife.

His wife. Emily, alone at home in bed. Always alone. And her husband could do nothing to bring enjoyment into her life, as her brother had so briefly done. Never her husband.

Lady Widow turned around, as if checking to be sure he followed her, smiling when she saw he did. Damn him, he could easily be hooked.

He blew out the breath he'd not been aware of holding. He had no intention of being unfaithful to his wife, no matter how much temptation a masked lady might be. Even if she could never discover it, his conscience would never allow it. He'd betrayed his wife enough.

Lady Widow led him to a table, directing him to be her partner and designating Sir Reginald and another man as their opponents. They all scurried to do her bidding, like bees buzzing around their queen.

She pointedly favoured Guy with her coy glances and flirtatious banter throughout the game. As she'd predicted, Sir Reginald and the other gentleman played like simpletons, putting down high trumps when low ones would do or leading with suits they knew she'd held. Lady Widow squealed becomingly at every trick she won. She grinned when the losing team pushed their counters to her side.

Guy gave Sir Reginald an amused glance. He'd watched Sir Reginald partner Emily in whist and knew the man to be a crack player. The love-struck old fool was merely tossing away money. Sir Reginald was a nodcock for letting his funds dribble through his fingers. He'd be better off playing at a high-stakes table and winning the fortune he said would entice the lady. The man could do it. He and Emily had been formidable opponents.

Sir Reginald and Emily.

Guy's head snapped up. He stared at Lady Widow as she regarded the hand she'd just been dealt. She tapped the cards against her fingertips, then snapped the cards into place exactly like a practised gamester.

Exactly like Emily. Guy's heart thudded in his chest. Could it be?

She looked up. He quickly averted his gaze for the moment, arranging his own hand. As the round commenced, he watched her carefully. When the cards were in play, her face held no expression. No smile, no frown, no clue to what she really thought or felt.

How many times had he seen that same lack of expression? Certainly in that game of whist more than a fortnight ago. He'd not thought about it, but, then, he'd glimpsed the same lack of expression every day when he said good morning at the breakfast sideboard.

By God, she was Emily. Lady Widow was Emily.

'Your turn, Keating,' Sir Reginald said.

He quickly put down a trump, winning the hand.

The game was theirs. Lady Widow's face lit with delight. 'Oh, thank you, Lord Keating! We have won again!' Smiling, she leaned over the table and scooped up the counters, giving all the gentlemen a good glimpse of her décolletage. 'Did I not tell you I always win?'

He wanted to throw his coat over her chest. This woman was nothing like his wife, but she was Emily all the same. He was very certain. 'Indeed you did, my lady,' he replied.

'You must play with me some more,' she teased, her eyes filling with mischief.

Would Emily speak so provocatively? No, she would not, but he heard the words coming from her mouth. 'The night is merely beginning,' he said.

She grinned wickedly at him. 'Do you mean to say you wish to spend the whole of the night with me, Lord Keating? I assure you, sir, other gentlemen will wish their turn.'

His body lit like a rushlight touched to flame, the heat of raw carnal desire. But before he went completely up in flames, he struggled to consider that this wife of his now spoke like a skilled coquette. What games was she playing here besides whist? Nothing yet, if Sir Reginald's tale of a wager was true.

By God, these gentlemen were wagering on bedding his wife! He had half a mind to call them all out. He had half a mind to drag her away from this place this very moment. Drag her to *his* bedchamber at least.

That would not answer, however, no matter how much he craved it. What was she doing here? Why was she dressed in this disguise? Why was she flirting with every man in the place—even her husband?

He'd never discover her purpose by prematurely tipping his hand. She did not know he recognised her. She believed he thought her to be Lady Widow. He could play along for a while, until he found out exactly what she was up to. And, by God, he would be here every night to make sure none of these men collected on that wager.

After winning the next game, she yawned, stretching her arms above her head and declaring she must retire for the night. All three men jumped to their feet as she rose from her chair, Guy included.

'Now, I do not need all three of you to escort me to the door, do I?' She swept her gaze over the three of them, letting it light on Guy longer than the others. 'I pick…Sir Reginald!'

'Delighted. Delighted.' Sir Reginald nearly knocked over his chair to give her his arm.

Guy's fingers curled into fists. By God, he didn't care if Sir Reginald was on the far side of fifty and an old friend of his father's, the man was asking for a duel if he led Guy's wife to a room above stairs.

Trying to appear calm, Guy wandered over to the door a bit behind Sir Reginald and *his* wife. If they turned to the stairway leading above, Guy would not be far behind.

None other than Cyprian Sloane waylaid him.

'No need to draw daggers, Keating,' Sloane said, sounding as slippery a cad as ever. 'She'll allow Sir Reginald help her with her cloak and walk her to her hack. Nothing more. He's no rival.'

What the devil was that fellow doing here? 'Sloane,' Guy said, pushing towards the doorway. 'Didn't know you were in town.'

As he reached the hallway, Sir Reginald's voice sounded from down in the hall. Guy heard the front door open and close. Apparently Sloane had been correct. Guy bit down on a relieved sigh and leaned against the wall.

Sloane, who had followed him, eyed him curiously. Of all people, why should Sloane show up here? He'd been in Bath, and here he was again. Was this an accident? Had Emily come to meet Sloane in this place? She'd hardly given him a glance, however. Or was that because her husband had walked in the door?

'Have a drink with me,' Sloane said, bending his head to the supper room.

Guy's eyes narrowed slightly. What better way to discover what kind of fast shuffle the man was playing with Guy's wife?

The supper room was nearly empty. They sat at a secluded table where no one would overhear their conversation. Sloane ordered whisky for them both. After the pretty maid delivered it, Guy sipped and waited.

Sloane lifted his glass as if in a toast. 'Congratulations, Keating. You seem to have won the regard of our Lady Widow. I commend you.'

Guy gave Sloane a shrug. 'What concern is this of yours?'

'I lay claim to her. I saw her first.' Sloane's voice

dropped into a more menacing tone. 'Consider yourself informed.'

'Indeed?' Guy kept his cards close to his chest, but he certainly did so with effort. 'She has your *carte blanche*?'

Sloane did not break off his gaze, but Guy perceived a fleeting look of uncertainty there. 'Not quite.' Sloane paused before continuing, 'She's a wily creature, Keating. Not an easy win. I intend to be the first to bed her, however.'

Guy nearly rose from his chair to plant his fist in Sloane's face. With difficulty he adopted a calm demeanour. Could Sloane indeed not know he was speaking of bedding Guy's wife?

'Why are you telling me this?' Guy asked casually.

Sloane took a swig of his drink. 'Damned if I know,' he said. 'Maybe to make the game more challenging. No cards hidden.'

'The game?'

Sloane smiled. 'The game of who wins the lady. Have you put your wager in the betting book? Stakes are at four thousand, I believe.'

Guy's fingers squeezed the glass in his hand. This was his wife Sloane spoke of! His wife the men had bet on! He silently fought for control. They could not know Lady Widow was his wife. Even a man like Sloane would not speak in this manner to a husband of his wife.

Guy believed he discovered the gentlemen's interest in Lady Widow, but he still did not know why Emily engaged in this masquerade. He'd discover nothing if he unleashed his temper. 'Who the devil is she, anyway?' he asked instead.

Sloane's brows rose. 'No one knows. Makes the game more interesting. The winner removes the mask!'

Guy let that one pass.

Sloane glared at him. 'The point is, Keating, *I* claim her. I aim to win. Do not waste your money on this wager. She's mine.'

No, Guy thought. *She's mine.*

The air vibrated with tension. The two men stared each other down, like two Captain Sharps, each daring the other to accuse him of playing a dirty game.

Guy figuratively threw in a stack of coins. 'Seems to me the lady decides,' he said. 'You play your cards, Sloane, and I'll play mine. We'll see whose hand wins the lady.'

Guy would play his hand, yes, indeed. He'd return to Madame Bisou's, every night if necessary, until he discovered why his wife came there in a mask, flirting like a demi-rep. He'd return to make certain Sloane failed in his plan to entice Lady Widow into his bed. He'd return to make sure all of them failed.

No one would bed Lady Widow. No one save her husband.

Chapter Ten

Emily slept late the next morning. Or rather, she remained abed, until certain her husband would not be about. It was his habit to go out in the morning, off on some jaunt in town. Perhaps he'd go to White's to boast of meeting Lady Widow.

She rolled onto her side, hugging her pillow. Silly. No one would speak of Lady Widow at White's. Lady Widow's renown confined itself to one gaming hell. Not very auspicious fame, but more than Emily had expected to experience. She had aimed merely to be considered above reproach in every quarter. Ironic that by being Lady Widow she risked every shred of her reputation. Emily would be mortified if discovered.

But even her husband had not known her. Lady Widow's mask proved to be an effective shield. She could say and do as she pleased.

Even flirt with her husband, if she chose to.

Emily sat up and pressed her fingers to her temple. Why had he, of all gentlemen, walked into Madame Bisou's? It changed everything. She must not allow him to ruin her plans. She would make sport of him instead, show him how his desires could be shattered just as easily as hers…

She drew her knees up and wrapped her arms around them. No, she must not admit to any foolish notion that she'd hoped for anything more from her marriage besides an escape from her parents. She'd known from the beginning it was a marriage of convenience. She merely had not known that the convenience her husband sought was a fortune to gamble away. She'd thought he sought an heir.

What a lovely idea. A baby. A robust boy with hair as dark as mahogany and eyes as blue as the sea. She sunk her head to her knees. This was indeed foolish in the extreme. Her husband avoided her bed. There would be no baby from this marriage.

Do not think of that, she scolded herself. *Think of how he looked upon Lady Widow. Think of the sweet revenge when she spurns him.*

The clock struck noon. Had she ever stayed in bed this long? Dragging herself from beneath the covers, she summoned Hester to help her dress.

'You have slept late, my lady,' Hester remarked.

'I was out very late.'

Would not Hester's eyes grow round as saucers if Emily told her the disguise she'd fashioned worked so effectively that Emily's own husband did not know her?

She and Hester had created a more dazzling creature. Lady Widow made his eyes glitter with desire. The reprobate.

'Did you win the card game?' Hester asked.

Oh, she'd won more than a card game. She'd won the favour of Lord Keating himself.

'Of course I won.' Emily opened a drawer and removed four shillings, dropping them into the maid's palm.

'Thank you, ma'am.' Hester curtsied and, with a wide grin, thrust the coins in a pocket of her apron.

'And your brother received his share as well.'

Still beaming, Hester skipped over to the wardrobe. 'What dress today, ma'am?'

Lady Widow would undoubtedly have picked something bright and gay, but Emily Keating owned nothing of that description. 'My green and brown stripe, I suppose.' The stripe was about as dashing as ever-so-proper Emily Keating could manage, which was to say, not at all.

Hester helped her into the dress, tying the laces in the back. The looking glass reflected back a drab young woman in a drab outfit. Emily sighed. It really was much more fun to dress in something like the gold confection that had captivated her husband the night before. For the first time Emily appreciated her mother's madness for the latest fashions.

Hester arranged her hair in a simple knot on top of her head. Emily wondered how Lady Widow would wear her hair if she went without her hat?

Probably in a becoming cascade of curls.

When she finished dressing, Emily made her way down the stairs. As she reached the first floor, the Dowager Lady Keating called from the drawing room, 'Is that you?'

Not, 'Is that you, Emily?', which would make some sense, but, 'Is that you?', which avoided using her name, and could be answered affirmatively by anyone.

She took a deep breath. 'It is Emily.'

Her mother-in-law appeared at the drawing-room door. 'You slept the morning, did you not?'

'My apologies, Lady Keating. Did you require me?'

Lady Keating walked back into the drawing room, no doubt expecting Emily to follow. 'I have several calls to make and I need someone to accompany me. I hope you do not have plans.'

The word *plans* was emphasised, referring, Emily supposed, to the one day her brother had called upon her.

Emily lingered at the doorway. 'I shall accompany you, if you wish.'

'Good,' said Lady Keating, 'because Guy has taken Aunt Dorrie and Aunt Pip out in the curricle, and I have no one else I might ask.'

He'd taken the aunts out? How nice of him. The dutiful grand-nephew.

'Indeed,' she said.

A tension inside her eased. She would not run into him after all. Inexplicably, this easing of tension closely resembled disappointment.

Lady Keating went on, 'Aunt Dorrie got a notion she needed air and ribbons, so Guy took them to the shops.'

Good for him, Emily thought. She hoped they would make him look at every ribbon and engage him in a quarter of an hour's discussion of whether to buy the yellow or the blue. And which shade of blue? Would this blue perhaps clash with the shade of her bonnet? It would, Miss Nuthall would say. Lady Pipham would insist it would not. Finally Miss Nuthall would choose green, because her sister said green would never do. Emily had been to the shops with the aunts.

'When do you wish me to be ready?' Emily asked.

'Well, not now,' Lady Keating huffed. 'I could not leave for another hour at least.'

'Then I shall go see how Mrs Wilson goes on.'

Emily continued down the stairs, finding the housekeeper in the passageway outside her sitting room giving instructions to the maid.

What crisis would Mrs Wilson report today? A tiff between the maid-of-all-work and the kitchen maid? No partridges for dinner? Mice in the cellar? No difficulty was too small for Mrs Wilson to lay at Emily's feet.

When she saw Emily, Mrs Wilson shooed the maid away. 'Good day, my lady,' she said.

'How do things go on, Mrs Wilson?' Emily asked.

The housekeeper launched into a long discussion about the coal porter, how he meant to cheat them, how she, not knowing what her ladyship would do, worried her head off, but finally gave the fellow what-for and he'd done just as he ought.

'What else could I do, my lady? You were abed and like to never get up,' she concluded.

Perhaps Emily ought to sleep late more often.

'You did very well,' she assured her.

She walked back to the hall where Bleasby approached, begging to ask how he might serve her. She'd managed to reduce his duties to the lightest of tasks, but the old butler felt remiss if he did not do as much work as he'd done thirty years ago. She spent some moments convincing him his services were perfectly adequate, trying all the while to salvage his pride.

The door opened. Guy and the aunts had returned, Lady Pipham's and Miss Nuthall's shrill voices, bickering as usual, echoing into the hall. With the quarrel in full swing and the door open to the chilly air, Guy urged each of them over the threshold. He stood ready to remove their pelisses, but Bleasby beat him to it, silently assisting while the two ladies barely drew a breath between angry words.

Emily could have made a hasty retreat, but instead watched as Guy removed his beaver hat and caped coat, moving as always with a masculine elegance totally without affectation. He continued placating the sensibilities of each great-aunt, and successfully cajoled them out of their huffiness, making them each feel they had won the point.

They were in perfect charity with each other as they made their way up the stairs. With any luck, their truce would last until they reached the upper floors.

Watching Guy's solicitude towards the aunts affected Emily as much as it had the first time she'd seen it. She watched him through the whole exchange with the aunts, as if in a trance, his kindness still able to touch that needy part of her she tried so hard to ignore.

She stepped forward to take his coat and hat, but he did not hand them over. Instead, he lay them on a nearby chair.

'Good day, Emily.' He gave her a smile.

It almost seemed as if he'd really looked at her.

'Good day, sir,' she responded.

'You were not at breakfast,' he went on. 'Were you feeling unwell?'

She felt herself blush, knowing she'd stayed abed merely to avoid him.

'I assure you, I am very well.' She heard the edge of anger creeping into her voice. Beware, she told herself. Do not give him anything to wonder about.

She composed her most colourless countenance, but it seemed his eyes almost twinkled in response, as if he alone knew the answer to a riddle and was keeping it to himself.

What was the reason for his sunny mood? He had won a great deal of money at Lady Widow's table the previous night. Perhaps that was the origin of his bonhomie. Or perhaps it was meeting Lady Widow herself.

Her mother-in-law emerged from above stairs. 'I am ready,' she announced.

Emily turned her blank expression on her husband's mother. 'I shall get my coat and bonnet.'

Lady Keating gave her a quick nod, then came over to her son's side.

'Where are you and Emily bound, Mother?' He kissed his mother's cheek.

It occurred to Emily then that he did not kiss her in greeting. A dagger twisted inside her. She'd wager he would kiss Lady Widow if she let him.

Lady Keating patted her son's cheek. 'The daughter of my dearest friend is in town awaiting the birth of her baby. I sent a note round asking if I might call on her and her reply arrived this morning.'

'How nice for you,' Guy said.

Emily tried to keep her tread light on the stairs, though she felt like stamping her way to the next floor. It should not bother her that this gambling husband of hers cared nothing for her, but lavished all his attention on his mother and his great-aunts. It should signify nothing to her. She would soon leave them all behind.

She paused a moment, straightened her back, and continued up the stairs with more iron in her spine. By next spring, she told herself, before the Season was underway, she should have winnings enough to walk out of the door and say good riddance to them all.

Guy's gaze followed his wife as she ascended the stairs, her spine straight, her step purposeful. She walked with Lady Widow's dignity, he thought. With Lady Widow's grace, but in Emily both were held back, controlled, contained. There all the same, however. How could he not have seen it before in Emily? He felt like a blind man suddenly blessed with sight. Everything became clear. Everything except why. Why masquerade as Lady Widow? Why hide Lady Widow's vivacity the rest of the time?

The cloth of her dress caught between her legs, for an instant clearly outlining her pleasing form. This sudden vision rekindled the desire she'd aroused the night before. He had half a mind to follow her to her bedchamber, putting an end to that infernal wager once and for all.

Be patient, he told himself. *Don't rush the cards. Play out the full hand.*

He turned back to his mother. 'I am glad you are taking Emily with you.' He gave a glance back to the now empty stair.

Lady Keating sighed. 'I would not upset you for the world, Guy, but I still cannot like her.'

His eyes narrowed. 'She tries mightily to please you. She tries to please all of us.' And underneath her pleasing manners was so much more.

'I know,' his mother admitted. 'But her parents, you know. They are such wretched people. I'm convinced she cannot be as utterly correct as she seems.'

If you only knew, Mother, Guy said to himself.

'Blood always tells, Guy.' She gave a knowing nod, obviously overlooking the blood of a wastrel father in his own veins.

Was that it? he suddenly wondered. Emily's father was a sad gamester, even more ruthless in his play than the elder Keating's had been. How much of Duprey's blood flowed through his daughter's veins? As much as his own father's flowed through his? If Guy were always a hair's breadth from falling completely into the lure of the cards, why not Emily?

Lady Widow's eyes had danced with every winning hand. Was Emily at Madame Bisou's for love of gambling?

Eventually the gentlemen at Madame Bisou's would tire of letting her win, especially if the wager about her were won. What would be the result? If her opponents played to win, how long before she must present her husband with her gambling debts? She would not be the only woman to have succumbed to the lure of the card table. The Duchess of Devonshire had been known to bet deep, owing everyone throughout London. It was said she sadly damaged the Duke's finances with her losses.

The Duchess was also known to have borne another man's child. Surely Emily would not go so far?

His mother broke into his reverie. 'Besides, she is utterly lacking in charm.'

Guy almost laughed aloud. If his mother only knew how much charm Emily could display when she so chose. 'Emily's is a quiet charm, Mother,' he told her.

His mother rolled her eyes.

His temper flared. 'Do not roll your eyes when I speak of her. She is my wife, ma'am. Treat her with the respect she deserves.' He leaned towards her to imprint upon her that he was entirely serious. 'One word from her and you could be away from here.'

Lady Keating put her hands on her hips. 'There is nothing I should more desire. I am perfectly content to make my home at Annerley. I pine for a spell in the country.'

A short time ago she'd longed for London.

He shook his head in frustration. 'Annerley is her house as well, Mother. But you know even the dower house at Annerley is unfit for habitation, and the main house needs total repair.'

The dower house was under repair, thanks to a fat pot won a fortnight ago, but it would be spring before work on it could be completed. Guy planned to live in the dower house while Annerley was restored. He wished to be in residence for spring planting and to oversee the renovations. First, however, he needed to win the necessary funds.

'Surely it is not as bad as all that?' his mother said.

His mother was not privy to the whole of their financial distress. He'd taken care that none of his family were.

Guy gave her a steady look. 'It would be a great inconvenience for you if you were not welcome in your daughter-in-law's house, would it not? There is nowhere else to live.'

She glared back at him defiantly. 'She would not dare to toss me out.'

He did not falter. 'No, she would not be so cruel. Do not be so certain of me.'

Her face paled. 'You?'

'I would send you off, Mother, make no mistake about it, but only if you force my hand, only if you refuse to be civil to my wife.'

She began to wring her hands. Guy stepped closer and wrapped his arm around her shoulder. 'Now, do not fly to pieces. It is not so difficult a request, is it? As I have said before, all you need do is give Emily a fair chance.'

She slanted him a wary glance.

He continued, 'We have all underestimated her.' How true a statement that was. Had he underestimated her love of cards?

His mother buried her face into his chest. 'Oh, I will try, I promise.'

Guy had been as remiss as his mother in attending to Emily. Was it his neglect that sent her off wagering into the night? Well, she would soon have an abundance of his attention, both she and Lady Widow.

Half an hour later, Emily and the Dowager walked the short distance to Grosvenor Square, Rogers the footman accompanying them a few steps behind. Her mother-in-law actually attempted conversation, in a petulant tone, perhaps, the topics forced, but conversation none the less. Emily could not have been more surprised had the squirrel in the square begun to talk. What led to this sudden volubility?

Emily, however, acted as if it were the most natural circumstance in the world, responding exactly as she ought and even making an effort to advance the conversation.

Grosvenor Square was such a premier address, Emily wondered exactly who they might be calling upon. Lady Keating had not informed her. Who might the Dowager know well enough to visit?

Emily, of course, did not presume to ask.

'Here we are,' Lady Keating said.

They had stopped in front of one of the finest residences, the one house on the square Emily did not wish to enter, not with her family's connection to this one.

'Who—who do we call upon here?' Emily stammered to her mother-in-law.

'The Marchioness of Heronvale,' Lady Keating said. 'Do you not know whose house this is? She is the daughter of my oldest friend.' Lady Keating gestured for Rogers to sound the knocker.

Perhaps there was no cause for worry. Perhaps the Marchioness would not even remember Emily.

They soon entered a spacious hall more than twice the size of the Keatings'. The gilt in this hall was not chipped. Indeed, the gilt-adorned walls were painted Chinese blue. Huge Chinese vases held fresh white, orange and yellow chrysanthemums.

After they were announced, a footman led them above

stairs to Lady Heronvale's personal sitting room, where she lay on a yellow giltwood chaise, a perfect complement to her blonde beauty.

'Lady Keating, how wonderful to see you.' She extended her hand. 'Forgive me if I do not get up. The doctor insists I rest.'

The ethereal Lady Heronvale was quite obviously with child.

She clasped the older Lady Keating's hand warmly before glancing towards Emily. 'Oh, Miss Duprey!' She blinked prettily. 'Forgive me, I ought to have said Lady Keating to you, ought I not? We all read of your marriage. My felicitations.'

Emily took the Marchioness's delicate hand. 'Thank you, my lady.' The Marchioness *had* remembered her. From the after-the-fact announcement of her marriage, she had also probably surmised the wedding to have been a precipitous one. Emily focused on remaining composed. At least on the outside.

Lady Heronvale invited them to sit, assuring them she had requested some refreshment.

'How do you go on, my child?' the Dowager Lady Keating asked with an expression of genuine concern.

The Marchioness laughed. 'Never better! I feel amazingly well, as if I could walk from here to Westminster and back, but the physician and my husband refuse to believe it.'

'The Marquess dotes upon you, does he?' Lady Keating said.

How nice for her, thought Emily, *to have a doting husband*.

'Pardon me, Serena.' A lady's voice came from the doorway behind her. 'I do not wish to intrude, but Barclay directs me to tell you that Cook is out of lemon cakes.

She is preparing another confection for you, which will take a little time.'

Emily remained perfectly still. She recognised that voice.

The Marchioness waved her hand and smiled. 'Come in, dearest. Come meet my friends.'

Lady Heronvale sat up on the chaise, while the lady approached. Emily still could not see her face, but there was no mistaking her lovely figure, the elegant length of her neck, the natural curl of her dark hair.

'Lady Keating,' the Marchioness said, gesturing to Emily who rose to her feet.

The lady who entered stiffened.

Lady Heronvale continued, 'May I present to you my dear sister-in-law, Lady Devlin Steele.'

Her sister Madeleine.

Madeleine turned and regarded Emily with her wide blue eyes. 'Emily,' she mouthed.

Emily extended her hand, hoping it did not tremble. 'Lady Devlin,' she managed.

Her sister Madeleine clasped her hand warmly, keeping hold of it until Lady Heronvale spoke. 'And the Dowager Lady Keating…'

Madeleine turned, 'My honour, ma'am.'

Emily's mother-in-law did not rise from her chair, but limply accepted Madeleine's handshake. Lady Keating probably thought, as everyone would, that Lord Devlin had married a woman beneath him, a common sort, perhaps.

Madeleine was far from common, however.

Lady Heronvale made room for Madeleine on her sofa. Madeleine sat facing Emily, looking every bit as uncomfortable as Emily felt.

Correct pleasantries were exchanged, to which both

Emily and her sister contributed, but soon the Dowager and the Marchioness lapsed into a more private conversation about mutual friends and family members.

Madeleine leaned over slightly. 'Do you like books, Lady Keating?' she asked Emily.

Such an odd question. 'Yes—yes, I suppose I do.'

'The Marquess has a fine library. Would you like to see it?'

Emily immediately understood. 'Yes, I would. I mean, it would be my pleasure.'

Madeleine interrupted Lady Heronvale's conversation. 'Lady Keating desires seeing the library. Do you mind, Serena?'

'If it does not displease you, ma'am,' added Emily.

Lady Heronvale smiled. 'Not at all, but we shall serve some refreshment shortly.'

As if they were two little girls bent on mischief, the sisters rushed down the hallway, Madeleine leading the way. When Madeleine shut the library doors, however, they faced each other with sudden reserve.

Emily longed to embrace her sister, longed to show her how dearly she loved her, longed for that affection to be returned. They had not parted badly last spring, but their encounter had been so brief and much lay unsaid.

'Madeleine—' Emily's voice cracked '—it is so good to see you.'

'Oh, Emily!' Madeleine rushed up and threw her arms around her.

Both produced a quantity of tears that would have made their sister Jessame proud. They finally pulled apart, still sniffling and groping for handkerchiefs.

Emily blew her nose. 'How are you, Madeleine? Are you well? Are you happy?'

Madeleine beamed at her. 'Very happy. I do not much

like being in town, but the Marquess insisted Serena come here for her confinement. I could not refuse her request for my company.'

'I read the announcement of your marriage, of course. Is...is Lord Devlin well?'

A dreamy look came over her sister's face. 'Yes, he is splendid.' She smiled again. 'But you are a married lady, too. You must tell me of your husband! How did you meet? Devlin said he knew Lord Keating in the Peninsula, but he'd not had the title then.'

Lord Devlin had known Guy? Had he known Guy was a gamester?

'I met him in Bath.'

'Bath.' Madeleine sighed. 'You must have seen the Cresent and the Circus. Did you meet in the Pump Room?'

'No,' Emily said. 'In the Assembly Rooms.' Though that first glimpse of him had been in the Pump Room.

'The Assembly Rooms,' Madeleine repeated in awe. 'The announcement did not say where you were married. Was it at the Abbey?'

'No.' Emily paused. How much ought she tell her sister? 'We had a Scottish marriage.'

Madeleine's eyes widened and her gaze lowered to Emily's waist. 'Are you—'

Emily felt herself blush. 'No, I am not.' *Far from it*, she thought.

Madeleine covered her mouth. 'Oh, I am sorry. I did not mean to offend... It is that I know how easy it...I mean, it could happen to...'

Emily grabbed her hand and squeezed it. 'Do not fret.' She spoke softly. 'I remember, Madeleine. I remember why Papa sent you away.'

Madeleine looked away. 'I am not saying you are like me, Emily. You and Jessame were never like me.'

Emily put her arms around her sister again. 'No, we were jealous of you, Madeleine. You were so beautiful, even though you were the youngest. We ought to have looked out for you better.'

Madeleine put her fingers to Emily's lips to silence her. 'That is all in the past, Emily. It no longer signifies.'

But it signified to Emily. She'd puzzled out what her sister must have been doing in Lord Farley's room that wretched night. Their father's wrath had been terrible. The next day, she and Jessame were told that Madeleine had run away and that Lord Farley had been summoned back to London. Emily thought Madeleine had run away with the gentleman, but then, after several days, their father had produced the body of a young girl.

When they buried that body under a stone with Madeleine's name upon it, her father had declared that Madeleine's wild ways had led her to destruction. If Madeleine's spirit and vivacity had led to her death, Emily knew she must suppress any such feelings in herself. She had vowed to always behave with perfect propriety.

What had all that propriety gained her?

'I ought to have protected you,' Emily said to Madeleine. 'I was older than you. I ought to have done something.'

Madeleine gave her another quick hug. 'It is past, Emily. Think only of the life we have now. That is what I do. And I am so very, very happy.'

More tears flowed, more sniffles and wiping of eyes with damp handkerchiefs.

Madeleine had married well, Emily realised. She had a good life, a loving husband, a darling daughter.

'I forgot to ask about your little girl,' Emily said.

Madeleine smiled again. 'She is very well. She is above stairs, napping at the moment.' She patted her stomach. 'Next spring she will have a sister or brother.'

'How lovely for you!' Emily exclaimed.

If wantonness brought death, propriety ought to have brought happiness. What had gone wrong? Her sister had been like a vine grown wild, almost lost among weeds, but she'd managed to flower notwithstanding. What had Emily's strict adherence to correct behaviour gained her? She had all but withered, blossoming only when pretending to be Lady Widow.

There was a knock on the door and both sisters automatically dabbed at their faces again and fussed with their dresses. 'Come in,' Madeleine said.

In walked Lord Devlin Steele, Madeleine's husband.

'There you are,' he said, giving his wife a loving glance. He came directly over to Emily and grasped both her hands in his. 'Emily, it is so good to see you.'

Lord Devlin was more handsome than ever, his green eyes sparkling, his smile showing the dimple in his cheek. He was taller than her husband, but just as dark. At one time his entrance to a ballroom had set her heart aflutter. Surprisingly, she felt none of that now.

'It is good to see you, too, Lord Devlin,' she said, meaning it.

'And I realise I must also wish you very happy.' He grinned at her. 'Lady Keating.'

Emily felt herself blush again.

'I served with Lord Keating for a bit. He is a good man, Emily. A very good man.'

A good man? Yes, yes, he might have been, but the knowledge did not make Emily feel happy.

Devlin released her hands and turned to his wife. 'Serena wishes you both to return to the parlour for tea.'

'Wait.' Emily faced her sister. 'Madeleine, I have told no one of…of your true identity. No one. But you must know Robert is in town. Do you wish me to tell him about you?'

'Robert? Oh, how is he?' Madeleine shrank back. 'Oh, dear! What if I run into him?' She gave her husband a reproachful glance. 'I knew I should not have come to town.'

'You are not likely to see him if you do not wish it,' her husband said.

She turned back to Emily. 'No one knows of me. Only you, Devlin, and the Marquess.' She nodded her head firmly. 'I think that is best. I…I would not wish any scandal to befall our family…'

Had not their parents generated scandal enough over the years? Why should Madeleine hide? Emily's brows knitted together. Of course, she herself had dread of scandal. Why else had she gone into the gaming hell in disguise?

Madeleine went on, 'We must continue the deception, Emily. Please.'

'Very well,' Emily said, depressed. It felt like losing her sister all over again.

Madeleine gave a tentative smile. 'But may not you and I be friends? As Lady Devlin and Lady Keating? Now we are introduced, may we not see each other a little? Or write letters to each other?'

Emily stepped forward and enfolded Madeleine in her arms again. 'Nothing would please me more,' she whispered.

Chapter Eleven

That night Guy departed the townhouse as usual, but waited nearby to see who might pick up Emily and drive her to Madame Bisou's. He waited near the end of the court for more than two hours, providing Emily with plenty of time to retire, dress and escape.

Through the night mist he heard the watchman's call, 'Eleven o'clock and all's well.' The damp chill seeped into his bones. Perhaps she would not appear.

He waited another half an hour. No carriage came. Either she was not attending the gaming parlour this night or her means of transport was more inventive than he'd supposed.

Guy shoved his hands into the folds of his caped topcoat and walked a few streets to where he could obtain a hack. If Lady Widow did not put in an appearance at Madame Bisou's, at least he could try his luck at the tables. He still had a fortune to restore.

He found a hack and directed the coachman to Bennett Street. He'd seen some players who might give him the sort of sport he needed. He could attend to that matter, even if his wife remained at home.

His emotions were much altered when he now saw Emily at home. Speaking quietly to the servants. Seated at his dinner table. Playing cards with his great-aunts. All he could think of was her transformation into Lady Widow. Because Emily and Lady Widow were the same, his desire for her had more than doubled. He wanted this chameleon wife of his with all the bone and sinew of his body.

Guy went straight to the game room. It took him a mere glance to see her, seated at a card table. All the candlelight seemed to shine directly upon her. All sound became mere harmony to the melody of her laugh. He could feel the smooth blue silk of her dress beneath his fingers. Could imagine the scent of lavender lingering around her.

She looked up and his heart beat faster. She tossed him a welcoming smile and immediately turned back to her cards.

He felt like a green lad receiving his first smile from a lady. Before this night was over, Guy would indulge in his craving for her company, try to discover if the gambling was her passion, try to discover if other seductions were her aim.

Sloane was also present in the room, Guy noticed, his eyes narrowing. Sloane collected winnings from a table of gentlemen who were all rising to leave. He saw Guy and beckoned him over.

'Do you fancy a game of whist, Keating?' Sloane asked.

'I came to play,' Guy said with some hostility.

Sloane laughed. 'Ah, cards or for the lady? I beg you, let us not be adversaries for the time being. Shall we find two well-breeched fellows and deprive them of their money?'

Guy shrugged his assent. He'd seen Sloane play. He could do worse in a whist partner.

Sloane called over to two gentlemen standing at the

faro table. They came across and Sloane introduced them to Guy as two merchants trading in fine goods throughout the Continent, goods that had once been the stock of the smuggling trade during the war. Perhaps these well-breeched gentlemen of Sloane's had been breeched on illegal trade. In any event, they looked wealthy, judging by the cut of their clothes and the heavy gold chains dangling from their pockets. What did the source of their money matter as long as they had plenty of it?

Both he and Sloane took seats that afforded them an opportunity to keep Lady Widow in sight. A sidelong glance was all it took to watch her charming the fortunate gentlemen at her table, the ones who gladly lost their money to her.

Once the game started, however, Guy's attention was held prisoner by the cards. These gentlemen were serious players. It would be the best sort of contest, one of wits and luck. Guy hoped both were with him. That familiar pounding of excitement drummed through him, that sense of being at the edge of a precipice ready to leap to the other side. He would either fall or land on his feet.

Guy, Sloane and the two merchants were closely matched. Each game became a close-run thing. Guy's euphoria increased when he won. His anxiety reined free when he lost. The stakes were driven higher and higher, none of the gentlemen flinching with each increase. It had become as much a contest of who would bet the most outrageous amount of money as who would win the game. Guy felt that same burst of energy he used to feel when charging into battle, that same driving hunger to come out alive.

He soon found himself at the brink, ready to wager all his cash. *Do it. Do it. See how much you can win. The cards will come. Luck is with you.*

He was about to push his whole stack of counters to the centre when he heard Lady Widow laugh. He glanced over at her, a vision in her blue dress, her face shadowed by the netting of her elegant hat. She returned his gaze, creating a different sort of heat from the card fever that had almost stolen his senses. At this distance, he could not see the expression on her face, but he could tell she did not smile.

This was his wife! This alluring vision. Would she wish her husband to bet the whole? Lady Widow might laugh off such a reckless act, but he was fairly certain Emily would not.

He took a few coins from his stack instead, throwing them in the centre of the table. At the end of the hand, his opponents were the richer.

Sloane signalled for drinks, and the pretty maid who set down the glasses gave him an inviting look. Guy studied the man while one of the merchants dealt the cards. Women were aware when Sloane entered a room. He'd noticed it in Bath when Sloane singled out Emily for attention. Emily had resisted his charms then, though Sloane had briefly been one of her suitors, but she'd had the constraint of public censure to impede her. With Lady Widow and her mask, there were no such constraints.

After the next game, Sloane signalled for more drinks. Guy drank as little as possible when playing cards and his glass had remained full. So had Sloane's. The maid brought fresh drinks for their opponents. After the fellows' third drink, the betting became even more reckless. Guy's heart raced, and the blood rushed through his veins, as it had when he'd engaged England's enemy, testing whose sword arm was the strongest, knowing either victory or death would result.

Guy and Sloane had handily won the third rubber when supper was called.

'I've had enough,' declared one of the merchants, standing on wobbly feet and rubbing his hands.

Guy had won more this night than in a week's play at White's. The two merchants merely shrugged off the enormous loss. 'Good game,' they bellowed, speech somewhat slurred. 'Good sport.'

Guy's emotions plummeted, as was always the case after a close game, no matter if he won or lost. If he'd lost this one, however, he would not be laughing it off like these gentlemen.

'It was the whisky,' Sloane said.

'What?' Guy looked up at him.

'You kept your head, Keating. I much admire that.' Sloane gathered up his counters to give to one of the girls to exchange for cash. 'Our late opponents liked their whisky. Been drinking all night. I would not have bet on our chances if they'd been sober.'

Sloane addled them with drink? It was less than sporting, true, but a device that had given them an edge.

'Remind me not to play against you,' Sloane added.

Guy stood as the maid brought him his cash. 'Thought we were in it deep already,' he said. 'For the lady.'

Sloane laughed. 'Dear me, I'd forgotten her in the thrill of fleecing some very clever sheep. Shall we find ourselves cut out in the supper room, I wonder?'

Sir Reginald, who sat at Emily's elbow in the supper room, mumbled something she did not hear. She'd just seen Guy and Sloane amble in together, looking very much like schoolboy mates. Her heart skipped a beat.

They looked well pleased with themselves, so perhaps they had won after all.

While her whist opponents had played their cards badly, she'd stolen glances at Guy and Sloane at their game. She'd been enough at Madame Bisou's to recognise the two gamblers at the opposing chairs as the genuine article, the sort who would never bother with Lady Widow, preferring to engage in real play. She'd watched her husband's stack of counters rise and fall and had held her breath for fear he would lose his last groat.

With cards in his hand, her husband had no time to spare for Lady Widow. That should have pleased Emily, but Emily could not abide him loving cards so well.

And whether she played Emily or Lady Widow, she resented him so easily dismissing her. Emily pressed her fingers to her temple, as if the gesture might keep the two sides of her together.

She managed to paste on a radiant smile as Sloane and Guy approached her table. The gentlemen seated around her grumbled and shifted positions. They were no match for these new rivals and they knew it.

Sloane flashed his perfect set of teeth at Lady Widow. 'You are looking remarkably beautiful this evening, my lady.' He took her hand and kissed it, as usual keeping hold a little too long.

Would her husband take her hand? Would his lips touch its bare skin? She scarcely attended to Sloane, glancing past him to where Guy stood. Guy's face, for one second, looked grim, but when he caught her eye, he smiled. Not as widely as Sloane, but with much more appeal.

'Pleasure to see you again so soon, ma'am.' He bowed and the corner of his mouth took an ironic twist. He did not touch her, however. He also nodded to Sir Reginald. 'Good evening, sir.'

Sloane, however, was heedless of Sir Reginald and Lady Widow's other admirers. He picked up a chair from a nearby table and set it beside her. Guy remained standing.

Would he sit with her? Would he walk away? What should she say to him to entice him to stay?

Emily's smile remained fixed on her face, hiding the muddle inside. It was not like Lady Widow to be at a loss for words. Once she'd launched this performance of hers, she'd never lacked for confidence. Each coquettish flutter of eyelashes, each pert comment, each trill of laughter had come naturally, almost as if she really were this mysterious creature who wore masks and flirted openly with gentlemen.

But in the presence of her husband, she suddenly felt she'd forgotten her lines. She became Emily again, who relied on silence when she did not know what to say.

Sloane, without realising it, came to her rescue. 'How do you do this night, my lady?' he murmured in his overly intimate fashion.

She shook herself back into her role as Lady Widow, who pretended petulance. 'How might I be? You and your companion have had no use for me all the night.'

Sloane's eyes flicked over her. 'I assure you, Lady Widow, I shall always have some use for you. Any night.'

Sloane's words were shockingly suggestive. Emily shot a glance at her husband, but he'd turned his back to speak to the maid and perhaps did not hear.

She could not allow it to pass. 'Goodness! Did you hear him, Lord Keating? I have never been so shocked in my life.'

Her entourage of admirers chirped up like a Greek chorus, Sir Reginald barking louder than the rest. They all avowed they'd certainly heard the fellow. Shocking. Shocking.

Guy turned to her, the hint of strain peeping into the

corners of his eyes. 'Forgive me, my lady. I was not attending.'

Sloane looked amused.

Emily fussed with the sleeve of her dress. 'Well, I suppose it was all flummery.' She sighed.

Sloane's smile fled.

Emily glanced back at her husband. His penetrating gaze had not left her, and she felt caught in it. Sloane might undress her with a glance, but a look such as Guy Keating gave could steal a woman's soul.

She lowered her lashes and tried to slow the rapid beat of her heart. He'd been looking at Lady Widow, she must recall. Not his wife. Still, her breath had quite caught in her throat.

'I thought to fix a plate, my lady,' her husband said, his eyes unwavering. 'May I bring you anything?'

Her flock of gentlemen all assured her they would be happy to bring her her heart's desire—as if they could.

She gave Guy her most appealing smile. 'More champagne, perhaps?'

The others were half out of their chairs, but sat back down when Guy bowed to her and left to do her bidding. She watched him walk away, and the gentlemen around her watched her watch him.

Sloane spoke, his voice low. 'You seem much taken with Lord Keating, my lady.'

Emily blinked and turned her gaze upon him. 'Do I?' She glanced back at Keating, pretending to study him thoroughly. 'He is a well-looking man, is he not?'

Jealousy flashed though Sloane's eyes. 'A paragon,' he said.

At least she had the satisfaction of making Cyprian Sloane jealous. But what about her husband? Could she make him care? If not for Emily, could she make him care for Lady Widow?

She forced a laugh at Sloane. 'Come now, Mr Sloane, you will convince me you have a *tendre* for me, which I know is a mere hum.'

'Have I not been attempting to convince you of this these many nights?' He glared at the men around her until they all shifted in their chairs again. 'I wonder if you gentlemen might give me a private moment with the lady,' he said in a deceptively smooth voice. 'You have monopolised her company quite enough.'

Amazingly, the gentlemen at her table all rose and bid her pretty words of farewell.

Only Sir Reginald hung back. 'Feel I ought not to leave you alone with this fellow,' he said. 'Say the word and I won't leave your side.'

'Don't be silly, sir!' she exclaimed. 'This is hardly a private place, and your friend Lord Keating will be returning any moment. I shall be well chaperoned, I assure you.' It was not that she wished to be alone with Sloane, but rather she wished to limit the distractions around her when her husband returned.

Sir Reginald clutched her hand, kissing it with much more feeling than was comfortable. 'I am at your service, always, good lady.'

When he'd left, Sloane drawled, 'Can't see how you tolerate that encroaching prig.'

She affected a deep sigh. 'He is my gallant.'

Sloane gave a snort. 'Enough sauce from you, my dear...'

Lady Widow's brows rose at that familiar endearment.

'I wish to speak with you before your besotted Keating returns.'

She feigned mild interest.

'I won a small fortune this evening. Was unusually lucky.'

As was her husband, then. What a relief.

He went on. 'I'll give all my winnings to you—'

'To me?' She toyed with a morsel of food left on her plate. 'Do not be absurd.'

Sloane moved his chair closer. 'I was never more serious. Come above stairs with me tonight and it is all yours. That and more delights than you can imagine.'

She gaped at him, her cheeks burning with deep shock. What he asked of her was no less than Madame Bisou's gaily dressed girls were paid to do each night. Walk above stairs with the gentlemen and dispense favours for money.

What did she care that he was reputed to be an ideal lover, an experienced pleasurer of women? He had cast her in the role of harlot.

He did not know, of course, that she was the respectable wife of Lord Keating, his recent whist partner. She doubted he would have made such an offer to Lady Keating, in any event.

She glanced at her husband still at the sideboard. Would he care that his wife had been so propositioned by Mr Sloane?

Not his wife. She forgot. Lady Widow had been propositioned.

Sloane said, 'I await your answer, my lady.'

She swallowed and made herself give him a direct look. 'You misjudge me, sir.' She spoke in a serious voice, not like Lady Widow, but not like Emily either. 'I come to this establishment to play cards. Nothing more.'

At that moment, her husband, his expression alert, walked up and handed her a glass of champagne.

How had this encounter with Sloane appeared to him? Emily's stomach fluttered in anxiety.

She covered it with Lady Widow's grateful smile. She accepted the glass. 'I thank you, Lord Keating. I was quite pining for more champagne.' She sipped, gazing at him over the rim of her glass.

Sloane slumped back in his chair.

'My pleasure, ma'am,' Keating said.

His eyes captured hers, with a questioning look at first, then darkening with all the carnal desire she'd perceived the previous night. If he'd considered Sloane a rival, with such a look he was certainly placing himself in the game. His way of informing her was vastly more subtle than Sloane's, however. And much more powerful.

Emily rubbed the edge of her mask, where it almost moulded itself to her face.

Though Emily might resent his clear desire for Lady Widow, Lady Widow was thrilled more than she cared to admit. The mask concealed who she was, but it offered no protection against her emotions. Instead, sensations that had only twice known life again poured through her. The desire to have him once more unclothed in bed with her, joining himself to her body, creating a paroxysm of pleasure she'd never before dreamed could exist.

The blatant sexual invitation by Cyprian Sloane held no appeal, but this one look from her husband laid raw the aching wish to couple with him once more. She'd not known such sensuality existed within her, that a look from a man could elicit it, making her feel alive, giving her spirit a flight to the heavens.

From deep within her came another emotion as passionate, as consuming. The searing knowledge that the man she married would never give his wife such a look. He looked at Lady Widow, not Emily. She made a bold decision. If Emily could not have her husband in bed with her, Lady Widow would. She would do more than toy

with his affections as first she'd planned. She would dev-
astate them.

She favoured her husband with one of Lady Widow's
most inviting looks. 'Mr Sloane tells me you won a great
deal of money this night.'

'Luck was with us,' he replied modestly. 'Though it
was a near-run thing.'

'Oh, I suspect you relish such sport,' she said, truthfully
enough. He would discover in time that there could be
something more enticing than cards. Lady Widow would
see to it.

'Perhaps you would fancy to play at my table.' She
fluttered her eyelashes and brushed her fingers across his
sleeve. 'As an opponent this time.'

'Perhaps,' he said, with a gleam in his eye. The gleam
of a gamester or a lover?

'You should like to conquer me, I fear,' she purred.
'Must I be afraid…?' Her finger drew a circle on the back
of his hand.

'I might wish to win, yes.' His eyes reflected the exact
seductive look she sought from him. 'I always wish to
win.'

She laughed, and rested her hand lazily on his.

Cyprian Sloane glared at this exchange between Keating and Lady Widow, one foot swinging up and down at
an irritated pace. She was definitely throwing out her lures
to Keating.

None of the other gentlemen posed any real threat.
Keating was his chief opponent. He had to admit Keating
had played this particular hand with skill. Keating had
kept his cards close to his chest, while he had impulsively
exposed his whole hand.

What a fool he'd been to use money to entice the lady,

rushing his luck, playing his best cards first. Keating's game was obviously more to her taste.

'I'd be honoured to play you, my lady,' Keating was saying. 'Either as your partner or your opponent.'

Honoured, repeated Sloane in his head, mocking the words. *Either as your partner or opponent.*

Bah! Keating would deal him out of the game, if he were not careful. Again. Not that he cared that, out from under his nose, Keating had married the Duprey chit. Served the man right to be shackled to such a colourless creature. It would be vastly more entertaining to free Lady Widow of her mask.

He'd be damned if he let Keating beat him to it.

Sloane pushed his chair forward, creating a barrier between Lady Widow and Keating.

'Why don't Keating and I play as your opponents, Lady Widow?' he said. 'I warn you, though, luck has been riding with us this night.'

She turned her smile on him, just as he'd wished her to. 'But you have much to lose, don't you?' Her eyes were cold. He'd made her angry with his proposal. 'Perhaps your luck will run out.'

He needed to intensify his efforts to charm her, since his own mistake had created a setback.

Sloane put on an expression of deep regret. 'I fear I have made my own ill luck tonight with my rashness. For that I am deeply regretful.'

One thing was certain. He would do anything necessary to win. Anything.

Chapter Twelve

It seemed to Guy that the gaming room hummed with excitement when the foursome sat down to the game of whist Lady Widow had dictated. Certainly envious gentlemen in the room looked up to see whom she had favoured, but the real excitement was inside him.

How often had he sat beside his wife at the breakfast table, at dinner, in the parlour? At such times he had been conscious of an aching regret, because he did not know how to heal the breach between them, but this temptress incarnate stirred his blood. To have her arm so near his, her skirt brushing his leg, her face almost kissably close—how was he to attend to cards?

She smiled like the hostess of a Mayfair ball. 'Sir Reginald, you shall shuffle the cards. You are so skilled at it. Mr Sloane, you may cut them to see who deals.'

On the other hand, perhaps she was more like his company commander.

Poor Sir Reginald was obviously in as sad a state as he. The man's colour was high, his eyes bright. Sloane was harder to read, but Guy had no illusion Sloane would abandon his conquest or forgo the gentlemen's bet. He had seen Sloane speak privately to her, had seen her respond. What had Sloane said to her? What had she replied?

A moment later he'd reached the table, and she'd turned her charm fully on him, her husband. Sloane was all but ignored. Was that part of her game, or had she truly dismissed the man?

Lady Widow won the deal.

Guy's first hands were unremarkable and he had no difficulty adhering to the unwritten rule that Lady Widow must always win. She and Sir Reginald took the first game. But the next hand! The ace, king, queen and knave of trump. Two other aces besides, and four other face cards. He couldn't be an idiot and lose this hand, even if Sloane played like a gudgeon. He could not help himself. At ten pounds a point, it was sure to be a heavy loss for the lady. But the money remained in the family, did it not? What harm was there?

Sloane shot him a sharp glance when he caught on to Guy's hand. Guy returned it with an impassive expression. Sir Reginald fidgeted in his chair. Lady Widow, however, remained engrossed in the play, watching every card thrown on the table. At the end of the hand, Guy had won the honours points. Once scratched, the itch to win took over. Guy played the rest of the hands to win.

At the end of the game, Lady Widow's eyes danced with excitement. 'Well done!' she exclaimed.

Both Sloane and Sir Reginald raised their eyebrows in surprise, but Guy knew what she was about.

His suspicion had been confirmed. His wife Emily, Lady Widow, was mad for cards. The more challenging the game, the more she liked it. She, like he, could become lost in that thrill of luck, that intoxication of wresting a win from what might have been a loss.

Guy also played the third game to win. Sloane glared

at him half the time, but went along with it, apparently not so willing to let the lady win if it meant crossing a partner. Sir Reginald became as caught up in the fever as Guy himself, and Lady Widow was delirious with the play. What parts of her face were visible were flushed with excitement. Her eyes had a sparkling clarity. She sat erect, economising her movements to what entailed playing the cards.

Guy and Sloane won the game and won the rubber.

'Oh, that was fun!' Lady Widow said, reaching into her reticule for more coin.

'Allow me to cover your losses,' said Sloane, pushing his stack of counters to her side.

'I would be honoured to pay your debt as well,' Sir Reginald piped up, clearly upset that Sloane had thought of it first.

'No, indeed.' She laughed them both off. 'How shabby would it be for me not to pay my own gambling debts?' She counted out coins to both Sloane and Guy. Sloane pushed the coins back at her, but she ignored him and left them on the table.

'Thank you, gentlemen, for much amusement.' She looked directly at Guy. 'Perhaps you will allow me a re-match another night?'

'My pleasure.' He inclined his head, but was not so certain he was happy to discover she could become as deep in cards as could he.

When the more serious gamblers in this room caught on how much she loved the challenge, she would certainly continue to lose. How long before her debts became unmanageable? In spite of that worry, the game had invigorated him as much as it had her, bringing no credit to either of them.

She rose. 'I must be leaving.' Before Sir Reginald or

Sloane could interject, she added, 'Lord Keating, would you escort me to my carriage?'

Yes, he would certainly like to discover who transported her back and forth. More so, he'd like the time alone with her.

'Another pleasure,' he said.

Knowing Sloane's eyes shot daggers at his back, Guy threaded his wife's arm though his and walked her to the hall. He directed the footman to bring her cloak and his topcoat, and placed her cloak around her shoulders, enjoying having his hands upon her again, even if through layers of cloth.

When he stepped out into the night air with Lady Widow on his arm, fog muted the street lamps and swirled at their feet like smoke over a cauldron. Guy fancied it was like a blanket wrapping around them both, blocking out the rest of the world. He would much prefer they be wrapped in a real blanket.

As they neared the end of the street, a hackney emerged from the mist, its driver holding the horses and nodding familiarly to Lady Widow as she became visible. Guy could barely see the man, and the hackney looked like a dozen others that might pass by in the space of an hour. How had she managed this arrangement?

'Allow me to accompany you, my lady, to see you arrive home safely.' It was worth a try.

'Oh, no!' she said in all seriousness. 'That would never do. You might discover where I live, and my secret would be out.'

Her secret had been out with him within a few moments of seeing her. He helped her in to the hack, amused by the irony of her statement. 'Would I know you, Lady Widow? Have I seen you before this?'

'No,' she said, with a confusing note of sadness in her voice. 'You have never seen me.'

The hackney driver flicked the ribbons and the coach moved down the street, soon disappearing into the mist. Her words seemed to float back to him on the droplets of moisture in the air.

You have never seen me.

Emily slept late enough to hope everyone had finished breakfast. She heard the aunts' voices in the back parlour as she went downstairs. With any luck, Lady Keating would be with them or in her own room. Guy's room had been very quiet. He was either still abed—and she did not wish to reflect much on that idea—or he was up and away. At least she hoped so. She said good morning to Rogers, who passed her in the hall, and made her way to the dining room.

At first glance it was blessedly empty, but as she entered, a voice came from the sideboard. 'Ah, good morning, Emily.'

Her husband. She nearly jumped in fright. 'Good morning, sir,' she mumbled.

She had no recourse but to stand at his side to fill her plate. He seemed inordinately slow, choosing this or that, picking at the slices of ham as if one mattered over another. She was forced to wait or lean over him for a bit of toast.

'Allow me,' he said, interrupting his interminable selection process and putting a slice of toast on her plate. 'Or would you prefer a fresh one? I'll call for Bleasby.'

What was this solicitude?

'No, do not trouble him,' she said. 'I'm quite content with what is here.'

She took her slice of toast and hurried to a seat, busying

herself with spreading the jam. Her husband whistled a Scottish air while he finished filling his plate. He sat in the chair adjacent to hers.

She poured him tea, knowing from other mornings how he liked it.

'Thank you,' he said. His whistle became a hum. 'Did you sleep well?'

This cheerfulness addled her. She glanced down at her plate to regain composure. 'Very well, thank you.'

His humming recommenced.

She did not think she'd ever seen him in such a jolly mood. He had won at cards, both with the gentlemen he'd played first and later from Lady Widow. Had the sum been so large to precipitate this good humour?

Or was he cheerful because Lady Widow had singled him out? Once planted, that idea grew like a bramble, wending its way through her insides, prickling wherever it touched.

'I have some errands on Bond Street,' he said, interrupting his infernal humming. 'Would you care to accompany me?'

She shot him a surprised glance. Luckily he was busy cutting his meat and had not noticed. She swallowed. 'If you desire it,' she said, keeping her voice steady.

He raised his head, smiled, and resumed humming.

This attention seemed too pointed to be due to winning. It smacked of…guilt. That was what it was. Guilt.

Whenever her father had done something particularly reprehensible, like staying out for days without a word then waltzing in big as you please, reeking of rosewater, he always fussed over her mother, bringing her trinkets, plying her with treats, escorting her to the theatre.

The door opened and Lady Keating entered. 'Ah, there you are,' she said to Emily, then, seeing her son, swished over to him and gave him a kiss on the cheek. 'Guy, I did not see you at first.'

'Good morning, Mother.' He stopped humming.

'Yes, to you too, my son, but I came in search of…of your wife. To see if she may accompany me on calls today.'

Emily opened her mouth to reply, but her husband spoke first. 'Then I suggest you ask her. She is right here in front of you, Mother.' His voice had hardened.

The Dowager went red. With anger, Emily supposed. Or embarrassment. 'What do you wish of me?' Emily asked in a mild tone.

Her mother-in-law looked almost grateful. 'I…I do beg your company this afternoon. To accompany me on my calls.'

Emily glanced at her husband whose expression remained stony. 'I would be honoured to come with you, ordinarily, but I am not entirely certain I will be available…' Her voice trailed off.

Guy could renege on his invitation to her if he wished. It seemed his practice to indulge his mother whenever possible. Emily was certain Lady Widow would not tolerate having her wishes come second to another's, but Emily would not risk causing a scene. She waited to see what he might decide.

'Emily is previously engaged,' he said.

His mother's lips pursed, and Emily's jaw nearly dropped open.

He added, 'She is to accompany me.'

Her eyes narrowed. 'Indeed,' Lady Keating said. 'And where do you go?'

'I have a few errands on Bond Street,' he replied.

His mother brightened, 'Oh, well, that cannot be so important. She would do better to come with me.'

His eyes grew stern. 'She accompanies me, Mother. That is the end of it.'

Emily observed this exchange with more astonishment. It was nonsensical that her husband and his mother would vie for her company.

'Very well,' the Dowager said with a huff. 'I bid you both good day.' She flounced out of the room.

Emily gaped at her husband, but he seemed absorbed in spearing a piece of ham on his fork.

A pleasing autumn breeze had swept the previous night's mist quite away, bringing back bright colour to the town.

As they stepped on to the pavement in front of the townhouse, Guy asked, 'Shall we walk to Bond Street?'

It was not far. 'Very well,' agreed Emily.

She had become accustomed to walking with her mother-in-law on their morning calls. Her mother-in-law was a great walker and, in truth, it was a pleasure Emily shared, although she did not so inform Lady Keating. Emily greatly missed long rambling walks in the country. Her sister Madeleine had been mad for riding, but Emily always preferred the sedate pace of her own two feet. An autumn day at Malvern, the family estate, would not see the smoke of London chimneys quickly erase the blue of the sky. One might walk all day in its beauty.

'What a glorious day,' her husband said expansively as they left Essex Court.

It was glorious for the moment, still clear and bright. He tipped his hat to a lady passing them, one who lived on the Court. Emily nodded to her. Might the lady remark to others that young Lady Keating had been seen out walking with her husband? It would be a novel *on dit*, indeed.

'What shops shall we visit?' Guy asked.

Another surprise. She was unused to any Keating asking her wishes. 'Wherever you wish,' she replied. 'You mentioned an errand.'

'Ah,' he said. 'Nothing significant. I thought to stop in Hatchard's. I've a fancy for purchasing *The Naturalist's Diary*.'

Naturalist's Diary? This seemed an odd choice for a gamester's library. She'd be less surprised if he were in search of a copy of Hoyle's book.

'Very well,' was all she replied.

He stopped as they were about to turn into St James's Street. 'Now, you also must select a destination. Do you fancy a visit to a draper's? A milliner? I am at your disposal.'

This solicitude was rattling. What had provoked it? Did he desire her to have a new dress? Perhaps something as daring as Lady Widow? After his win the previous night, perhaps he could well afford to purchase a new gown for his wife.

Her mother's wardrobe always expanded nicely when her father was philandering. Perhaps Guy Keating was anticipating similar recompense due to his pursuit of Lady Widow. Was he about to make Lady Widow a shocking proposition such as Sloane had made? How might Lady Widow respond?

Emily made herself gaze impassively at her husband. 'I would not impose upon you, sir. Your mother would, I presume, be happy to accompany me to such shops. I shall wait upon her.'

He gave her a crooked grin. 'You make it difficult for me to indulge you.'

She met the direct glittering blue of his eyes, eyes a woman could fall into and never, ever escape. What might it be like to have this handsome man bent on giving her pleasure?

She swallowed. No, she was convinced he meant to appease her as her father did her mother. The pleasure belonged to Lady Widow. 'There is no need to indulge me,' she said.

With a tiny shake of his head, he started walking again. They reached Piccadilly, where a ragged boy ran up holding a broom. Guy tossed him a ha'penny, and the boy swept the street in front of them as they crossed.

When they reached Hatchard's Bookshop, Guy went in search of *The Naturalist's Diary* and Emily was free to browse the shelves. She spotted *Glenarvon*, the shocking novel everyone knew had been penned by the scandalous Lady Caroline Lamb about her affair with Lord Byron. Emily would never have admitted to following the whole sordid sequence of events, but she had.

She opened the book, her eyes lighting on a passage.

...Oh I am changed, she continually thought; I have repressed and conquered every warm and eager feeling; I love and admire nothing; yet am I not heartless and cold enough for the world in which I live. What is it that makes me miserable? There is a fire burns within my soul...

She slammed the book shut and replaced it upon the shelf, closing her eyes on stinging tears. *A fire burns within my soul.*

'Would you like the book?'

She opened her eyes. Her husband stood before her, eyeing her quizzically. *A fire burns within my soul*, she thought again.

She shook her head. 'I was merely passing the time. I desire nothing.'

He cocked his head, regarding her for a long moment. He finally said, 'I will make my purchase.'

Guy offered his wife his arm as they walked out. She'd gone so pale in the bookshop. What had happened to her in there? He wished she would open up her thoughts to him, her hopes, her desires.

Emily, the mask you wear conceals more than Lady Widow's, he said to himself. He wished they could cease this masquerade and bring the fresh air of honesty into their relationship.

But he was not ready to be honest, not until he'd secured their finances and her future. He owed that to her. Still, it would be pleasant to give her some enjoyment on this lovely autumn day. He must be more clever.

'I have a notion Aunt Pip and Aunt Dorrie might fancy some sweets,' he said. 'Are you too fatigued to walk to Gunter's?'

'I am not too fatigued,' she responded, agreeable as ever.

They walked towards Berkeley Square, the day warming in the afternoon sun.

Another gentleman was entering the shop as they neared it. He smiled at them warmly. 'Lady Keating. Lord Keating. Delightful to see you.'

Guy recognised him as Lieutenant—no, Captain, he'd gained a promotion—Devlin Steele. He had a brief acquaintance with the man in the Peninsula, but not enough to warrant this friendly greeting. Emily's grip tightened on his arm. She knew him? And was distressed to see him? Another secret, no doubt? Guy extended his hand. 'Lord Devlin. Good to see you.'

Steele accepted the handshake and turned to Emily. 'How nice we meet again so soon.'

Soon? What sort of secret might this be?

The man went on, smiling at Emily. 'Do you come for an ice? The day is almost warm enough for it. I beg you will bear us company. Madeleine is in the carriage over there.' He gestured to a fine shining vehicle bearing the Heronvale crest. 'She will want to see you.'

She was acquainted with the wife! Guy felt more than a measure of relief. 'Would you desire it, Emily?'

With an odd light in her eyes, she responded, 'Oh, yes.'

Steele insisted upon procuring the ices and shooed them over to the carriage. Emily almost ran to it. As they approached, a pretty face appeared at the carriage window.

'Emily!' she exclaimed.

'We have come to sit with you,' Emily said, sounding happy.

Her friend opened the door, and Guy assisted his wife in.

As Emily took the seat beside her dark-haired companion, she said, 'My lord, may I present Lady Devlin. Madeleine—I mean, Lady Devlin, my husband, Lord Guy Keating.'

Guy remained on the pavement. 'My pleasure, ma'am.' He shook the lady's hand.

Lady Devlin regarded him intently. 'I am very delighted to meet you,' she said.

Emily smiled at her friend, and the smile reached her eyes.

'I shall leave to assist Lord Devlin,' Guy said, aware of a small pang of envy.

He bowed to them and walked to the confectioner's. He'd wished to please his wife this day. He had not known he would do so by giving her a moment alone with her friend, a moment away from her husband.

Cyprian Sloane stood in the shadow of the tall green shrubbery watching Keating leave the carriage and walk back to Gunter's. He'd caught sight of Lord and Lady Keating walking down Bruton Street and on a lark decided to follow them. One never knew what useful information might be unearthed if one seized an opportune moment like this.

He'd watched Keating and his wife meet up with Heronvale's younger brother and thought it mildly interesting. When he saw a lady's face at the window of the Heronvale carriage, hairs stood erect on the back of his neck.

Had his eyes deceived him?

He'd moved closer, selecting this vantage point amidst the shrubbery. All he need do was wait for the face to appear again to be sure.

If he were correct, he'd need some time to ponder how to use the information to further his aims. The connection appeared to be between Lady Keating and the young woman he'd recognised. He'd need to discover how she came to be in the Marquess of Heronvale's carriage, in the company of the Marquess's brother, and on friendly terms with the respectable Keatings. Then he'd find a way to make this knowledge useful.

Sloane grinned. He'd spent the war years bartering in information, not too dissimilar to what he thought he'd discovered here. It felt invigorating to exercise his skills once more. All it took was a talent for being in the right place at the right time, patience to wait until all facts were revealed, and a little luck.

It was all a bit like a card game. Sloane would wait as long as it took. Then he'd see if he'd just been dealt a queen of spades.

Chapter Thirteen

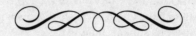

After spending almost the entire afternoon together, Lord and Lady Devlin persuaded Emily and Guy to come to dinner that evening, Guy's mother and the aunts included.

The evening was a very cordial one. Heronvale was a generous host, his wife a warm and welcoming hostess. Steele and Guy had much in common, and Emily and Lady Devlin were inseparable.

When it came time to leave, Heronvale insisted upon ordering his carriage for them. During the ride home, Emily was very quiet. Aunt Dorrie rattled on about how well sprung the Heronvale carriage was, how delightful the company had been, and how delicious the food. For once Aunt Pip agreed with every word. His mother repeatedly reminded them she was the Marchioness's mother's dearest friend.

For once his family was entirely in good spirits. Guy's heart felt light. He'd wished for this, worked for it, faced the gaming tables for it. He wanted them all to be happy.

While the three elder ladies were busily trying to outchatter each other, he leaned to his wife's ear. 'It was a pleasant evening, was it not?'

She turned, a startled expression on her face. 'Yes,' she said, her voice tightening. 'Yes, it was.'

His spirits dipped. None of his wife's happiness lay at his door.

When they were finally at home, Bleasby was there to greet them. His mother and great-aunts entered the town-house still clucking like chickens in a coop. Bleasby hurried to assist the ladies with their cloaks, his wrinkled face looking even more sunken than usual.

'Bleasby, what the devil are you doing up at this hour?' Guy asked. 'Where is Rogers?'

Arms piled with cloaks, Bleasby replied, 'I felt it my duty—'

'Duty—!' Guy began, but his wife interrupted him.

'Thank you, Bleasby,' she said kindly. 'It was good of you to take such care of us. You will retire now, will you not? And ask Rogers to take over?'

Bleasby bowed. 'As you wish, my lady.'

Guy stopped his wife in the act of removing her own cloak, assisting her himself. 'Thank you, Emily,' he whispered in her ear. 'That was much better said.'

She gaped at him with wide eyes. Her eyes looked grey this evening, he noticed, but he'd recalled them looking amber under Lady Widow's mask. Was her eye colour as mysterious as the rest of her, changing with her costume?

His hands lingered on her shoulders. He liked the air of mystery about her. It was frustrating, to be sure, but it also spawned more pleasurable senses.

Rogers rushed into the hall, a worried look on his face. 'Beg pardon, my lord,' he said in Guy's direction. 'Meant to be here before Mr Bleasby.' He quickly relieved Bleasby of the cloaks and waited for Guy to hand him Emily's.

Bleasby bowed and turned to leave, but stopped. 'I quite forgot, my lord. A note was delivered for you, and I was requested to put it into your hands tonight.'

He crossed to the marble-topped table and picked up a sealed paper from the silver tray.

Guy threw Emily's cloak on the pile in Rogers's arms, and took the note. He broke open the seal and read:

My dear Lord Keating,
Our wealthy sheep of last evening have begged for more shearing and are willing to increase the stakes. I beg you would attend Madame Bisou's this evening around midnight, where I have reserved a private parlour.
Your faithful servant, etc., C. S.

Sloane

His heart accelerated. Midnight? It was nearly midnight now. He read the note again and barely attended the good-nights of his mother and great-aunts as they started up the stairs to their rooms.

'Is it bad news?'

His head shot up. His wife stood before him, looking almost concerned. He smiled reassuringly. 'No, not bad news at all. I…I must go out again, however.'

Her eyes narrowed slightly. 'Very well,' she said impassively. 'I will bid you goodnight.'

She turned and quickly ascended the stairs. He watched her, wishing he could tell her the whole, and worrying that she would attempt to go out in the night herself as Lady Widow when he would be unable to watch over her. A private parlour meant serious play indeed, and his attention would be commanded by the game. In spite of his concern for his wife and the bevy of gentlemen who'd wagered on bedding her, a thrill shot through him. This game would test his skill, nerve and luck to their very limits.

He ought to pen a note declining the invitation. Playing this sort of high-stakes game was a rash and ill-conceived idea, but still his blood burned to test himself in such deep waters, the same blood that had flowed through his father and his brother. That reaction alone should warn him to beg off, but could he afford to pass up this opportunity? The night before, those gentlemen had dropped five thousand pounds without a blink of an eye. How much more were they willing to lose?

Rogers stood waiting for his coat and hat.

'I'm going out again, Rogers. I beg you not to wait for me. I will be late.'

He ran into the library and removed from his locked drawer the envelope of banknotes he'd intended to send to Annerley. Stuffing it into the pocket of his coat, he hurried back out into the night, already late and hoping the players had not found another to take his place.

From the first-floor landing, Emily watched her husband rush out of the door.

Only a card game could be so important, she suspected. A note from Lady Widow might be treated as highly, but, of course, Lady Widow had not penned that note.

She gripped the banister before spinning around to climb above stairs to her bedchamber. She had all but decided to stay home this night, content after her lovely long visit with her sister, but if her husband could end such an evening with cards, so could she.

She'd have Hester help her don Lady Widow's costume and she would stay out just as late as her husband, if she chose.

* * *

When Emily entered the game room at Madame Bisou's, several gentlemen turned welcoming faces her way.
Several, but not her husband. Holding her head erect, chin
up, she smiled Lady Widow's smile and glided across the
room with more feminine grace than she would employ
as her other self.

No, her husband was not present. Nor was Cyprian
Sloane, for that matter, but that was of no consequence.

Also absent were the two gentlemen who had played
cards with Sloane and Guy the previous night, but that
might be mere coincidence. Who was to say those men
had not gone elsewhere to play?

She barely reached the centre of the room before Sir
Reginald rushed up to her, grabbing her hand. Oh, dear,
she must endure another wet kiss.

'My dear lady, how good to see you this night,' he said,
planting his lips upon the back of her hand as moistly as
she'd feared. 'I do beg you to play at my table. Shall I
order you some champagne, or do you prefer something
else?'

She gave him Lady Widow's smile. 'Champagne, of
course.'

She might as well play cards with Sir Reginald as with
any of the others, but she would wager none of them
would provide the stimulation she'd experienced playing
whist with her husband. He was a true gamester.

She allowed the older gentleman to lead her to a chair.
Sir Reginald waved at one of the serving girls, who did
not hurry to leave the side of the gentleman so blatantly
ogling her cleavage. The East India man and the Duke's
son appeared at the table, begging to play.

Madame Bisou wandered over. 'We have your company again this night, Lady Widow,' she said, adjusting
the ribbons of a particularly atrocious salmon-coloured

dress. The matching plumes in her flame-red hair bobbed with every word she spoke. 'You have been excellent for business, I must say, but may I inquire if your friend Robert is…?' Her brows rose hopefully.

'Not tonight,' Emily told her with sympathy. This *tendre* for her brother taxed Emily's ability to refrain from a fit of giggles.

Would it not be delightful to share the tale with her sister and have a good laugh together? But what might Madeleine say about her scandalous masquerade?

'If I see him, *madame*, I will convey your regards.'

Madame Bisou cheered a little at her words. Emily knew the *madame* would, in due time, select another gentleman and disappear with him above stairs.

Emily turned her attention to the game of whist she was about to play. By the time the first game had come to a close, she discovered a slight difference in the quality of the play. The East India man and the Duke's son seemed bent upon a win, but as the rounds continued, their card-playing skills deteriorated and ultimately she won the game. It was as if they'd attempted to deal from both the top and the bottom of the deck, wanting to give her the challenge her husband had shown her the previous night, but not daring to take it so far as to give her a loss. What did they fear if they won? That Lady Widow would not pay her debt? That she would turn to other partners? That she would search for another gaming hell?

The gamester in her hated that her skills were not further tested as they'd been the night before. The practical side simply counted her money at the end of the night.

When supper was announced, she permitted Sir Reginald to escort her. The East India man and the Duke's son stuck with them like porridge on a spoon. They'd all seemed perfectly content to pass their losses on to her.

When the East India man brought her a plate and seated himself close to her, she casually moved her chair before commenting upon the excellent selections he had made. After a few minutes more of watching the door, she could stand it no longer.

'I notice Mr Sloane and Lord Keating are not present this evening.' She gave a coy smile. 'Have I lost two of my most ardent admirers?'

'No, indeed,' blurted the Duke's son. 'They remain in the game.'

'Remain in the game?' She blinked at him, truly not comprehending.

Sir Reginald quickly interjected, 'He means they are engaged in a private party.'

Her amused expression almost fled. The only private parties she knew to take place at Madame Bisou's were between men and women. If her husband had another assignation besides his precious Lady Widow, how would she abide it?

With great difficulty, she feigned a knowing smile. 'I see. They have abandoned me for the favours of some other ladies. I am desolated.'

'Not so,' said the East India Man, who tended towards pragmatical speech. 'They bespoke a parlour for a private whist game. Been at it since half past midnight.'

'That is what I mean,' she responded. The man's explanation still did not inform her there were no women present. 'I am certain they must play more than whist, or why be private?'

'I assure you,' the East India man went on, 'it is a card game. A deadly serious one. The two gentlemen who lost to them last night challenged them to another match. They wanted no distractions.'

She knew it. The gentlemen who had been so seemingly unconcerned about dropping a small fortune the night before were bent on revenge. They would ruin Guy. How foolish could he be? Unlike her father, why could her husband not be content with one big win? Why did men forever have to go back to lose it all again?

She paid particular attention to a small square of cake on her plate, picking at it with her fork, hoping she'd disguised her utter fury at her husband's foolishness.

After supper, she played another two games, but had great difficulty paying attention. Sir Reginald and the Duke's son almost took the game, and at the end, she forgot to call honours, until Sir Reginald pointed it out to her.

Guy and Sloane still had not appeared from their private room. Surely they would stop in the card room when the play was finished.

It was late, later than she usually stayed. She must leave.

When she was riding home in the hack, it occurred to her that Guy might have finished earlier and might at this moment be home. If so, would he be waiting for her? Would he catch her in the act of playing Lady Widow?

But he was not at home. When Hester let her into the house, commenting that she'd worried because her ladyship was so late, she confirmed that Lord Keating had not returned. Emily climbed the servants' narrow staircase to her room and changed out of Lady Widow's costume, donning her own nightdress. She crawled into her bed and wrapped herself in the blanket, warming her feet next to the hot brick Hester had placed there for her. She lay awake as the minutes ticked by. He did not return.

At dawn she fell asleep. At ten o'clock she woke with a start. Climbing hurriedly out of bed, she rushed over to the door connecting her room with her husband's. Pressing her ear against the wood, she could hear nothing. She carefully turned the knob and pulled. It was not locked. She opened the door and peeked into his room. It was empty.

Next to the wardrobe, his boots stood at attention like soldiers. His bed was neat as a pin. He had not set foot in this room since dressing for dinner. Her heart raced so fast she thought she could hear the blood rushing through her brain.

Had some danger befallen him? Had he been set upon by footpads? Or had there been a dispute over the cards and duels challenged? Did he lay dying on some grassy knoll somewhere, some corner of Hyde Park, his life's blood flowing into the thirsty earth? She compressed her lips into a grim line.

Or had he lost so catastrophically that he had shot himself, like his brother? Her hand flew to her mouth, and her breath came quicker. She paced the room, trying to calm herself.

It was possible he had won. Perhaps he was celebrating. She stopped pacing and narrowed her eyes. When the big winners celebrated at Madame Bisou's, the girls she employed flocked around them, sometimes throwing their arms around the men's necks and kissing them on the mouth.

At least he would be alive, if that were the case. She would prefer he be alive, even if the one way she could imagine it made her murderously angry—or jealous, she could not decide which.

She strode back into her own room and shut the door before summoning Hester to help her dress.

'Oh, my lady,' Hester said, her eyes round as full moons. 'Mr Rogers says his lordship did not return home all the night!'

Of course the servants would know. 'Yes, Hester, I realised that as well. I do hope no one spoke of this to Lord Keating's mother or to his aunts.'

'I do not think so, ma'am,' she said. 'Mr Bleasby said we was to keep mum until he spoke to you.'

At least that was fortunate.

'He did right.' Emily forced a smile and squeezed Hester's wringing hands. 'I am sure Lord Keating was merely…detained. Unavoidably, I am certain, but we must save the Dowager and her aunts any distress.'

'Yes, ma'am,' said the girl without conviction.

'Let us dress me quickly,' she went on.

A few minutes later she hurried down the stairs. When she reached the first floor, her mother-in-law stepped into the hallway.

'You have developed a habit of sleeping late,' the Dowager said by way of morning greeting.

Emily clutched the banister to stop herself. She took a deep breath. 'Good morning, Lady Keating. Did you have need of me?'

'No,' she said in a desultory tone. 'But I have not seen my son this morning either, and I had cause to wonder…'

Wonder what? Emily silently asked. Wonder if your son and his wife had slept late together?

'I believe Guy went out quite early,' she said. Which, she persuaded herself, was not a lie. He'd gone out when the clock marked the new day. 'Did you have need of him?'

'No,' her mother-in-law said. 'I merely wondered.'

'If you do not object, ma'am, I will take leave of you.' She took a step down the stairs.

'Where are you bound?'

Emily stopped again. 'To speak with Mrs Wilson and Bleasby. To…to check the arrangements for the day. That is all.'

'I see,' the elder Lady Keating said, turning away and walking back into the parlour.

Emily expelled a relieved breath and hurried to find Bleasby. He was at the silver closet, a worried frown on his face while he counted the silver and polished odd pieces.

When he saw her he said, 'Good morning, ma'am,' and gave her his usual bow. 'I have no wish to distress you, but Master Guy—I mean, Lord Keating—did not return…' He could not finish.

She placed her hand on his arm. 'I know, Bleasby. But you are not to worry. It is due to that note he received, you see.' That might be true, she thought. 'Please spread the word to the other servants. Tell them to say nothing that distresses Lady Keating or her aunts.'

'I have done so, ma'am, but, if you must know, Mr Guy does not do such things. I am certain a mischief has befallen him.' His eyes were filled with worry.

Poor Bleasby. It would not do for him to become ill over this. 'Perhaps you can send Rogers out to ask some discreet questions. If there is bad news, there will be talk of it.' She tried to give him an ironic smile. 'In fact, if there were bad news, we should have heard by now. It is always the way.'

Not always. Not if he were lying in some alley with a stab wound or some such, but she must not think so.

'Very good, ma'am.'

The idea of sending Rogers out appealed to her, too. Perhaps he could discover something.

Where was Guy? Was he all right? Her heart started pounding all over again.

Rogers returned with nary a word. He'd inquired at all the gentlemen's clubs and some of the shops. No one seemed to have seen Lord Keating.

When dinnertime came and Guy still had not come home, Emily felt near frantic. She assumed her most placid façade and endured the constant comments and questions from the Dowager and Lady Pipham and Miss Nuthall. She invented a fictitious note that she'd received saying Guy would not be home for dinner and would be out until very late.

Because they had received no invitation for the evening, Emily expected to endure more of the same comments throughout the evening.

After dinner Bleasby asked to have a word with her. She excused herself from the other ladies.

Bleasby looked as if he'd aged another ten years, though that seemed hardly possible.

He spoke in a low tone, leaning close to her. 'I confess, I am sick with worry, my lady. It is not like Master Guy to do such a thing.' She did not correct him for forgetting his master's title. 'His father or brother might stay out for days playing cards, but not Master Guy.'

She shared every bit of Bleasby's worry. It was, she agreed, not like him at all.

Which was why her mind conceived disaster after disaster. She'd even wondered if he'd been conscripted, taken off to sea, sold into slavery. Could it really be something so simple as a card game?

When the other ladies of the household finally retired for the night, Emily hurried Hester to dress her as Lady Widow. She was ready so early she had to wait for Hester's brother to drive up with the hackney coach.

When she arrived at Madame Bisou's, she rushed inside, remembering, in time, to appear as if she were the serene Lady Widow.

'Good evening, Cummings,' she said to the footman.

'Evening, my lady,' he responded in a voice that was always two octaves lower than anyone else's.

She did not usually engage the large man in conversation. 'What is it like inside tonight?' she asked. 'Who is playing cards?'

She hoped that was question enough for him to tell her what she wished to know.

'The usual sort,' he replied.

She abandoned the art of subtlety. 'Are Lord Keating and Mr Sloane still playing whist?'

'No, my lady.'

Her fledgling hopes were cast down to the depths. Visions of Guy bleeding in some alley returned. She handed Cummings her cloak and, with a step as leaden as her heart, climbed the stairway to the first floor.

When she reached the top step, a gentleman staggered out of the supper room, almost careening into her. His neckcloth was askew, his coat unbuttoned, his waistcoat stained. His face bore more than a shadow of beard and his hair stood on end.

It was her husband.

Chapter Fourteen

She grabbed the banister to keep from falling. Her husband swung around, tripping on the stair and winding up a step below her, his arms pinning her in place.

Her first thought was, *He is safe!* The second was, *He reeks of brandy.* While she'd been nearly sick with worry, he'd been here the whole time. Drinking.

He gave her a crooked grin. 'Em-m-m—Lady Widow!'

Trapped between his arms she could not move. He leaned into her, wrapping his arms around her and pressing her against the banister. Being a step below, his face was level with hers. He nuzzled her cheek with his stubble-covered one.

'Missed you, Lady Widow,' he said, chuckling as if he'd said something very funny.

'Unhand me,' she rasped, pushing against his chest. None of the gentlemen had ever pawed at Lady Widow. How dare he touch her in sight of anyone happening by? How dare he cause her to worry that he was dead somewhere, lying in the cold all alone?

'Don't want to.' He kissed her ear and, in spite of her fury, sent shivers of sensation riffling down her spine. 'Want to be with you, Lady Widow.' His lips warmed the sensitive skin of her neck. 'I did it,' he whispered, breath tickling her ear. 'I did it.'

She did not care what he had done. She pushed again. To no avail.

A laugh came from behind her. 'To think all I needed do was buy him a drink.'

She glanced up to see Sloane leaning against the door-frame of the supper room, looking as dishevelled and un-shaven as the man now rubbing his hand down her back.

Her husband was behaving even worse than Sloane had done, treating her like she was no better than one of Madame Bisou's girls. The thought that they might have had more than Madame Bisou's brandy made her push with new force.

He merely held her tighter.

'You might get him off me,' she said, casting Sloane an irritated look.

Sloane grinned, taking a step but steadying himself with a hand on the wall. 'Jus' when he's doing such a capital job of ruining his chances with you? Don't be a nodcock.'

Her husband tried to lift a leg on to the step where she stood. His foot missed the step and he almost unbalanced them both from their precarious perch.

'Oh, do something,' she demanded of Sloane, grabbing the banister to keep from falling. 'Before we both tumble down the stairs.'

Sloane did not wobble as he walked, but his gait was very, very careful. She'd once seen her brother walk like that when he'd broken into their father's wine stores.

Sloane took each stair carefully. He braced himself and grabbed Guy's shoulder. 'Come on, Keating. Time t'take ya home. I daresay y'r wife'll be at daggers drawn, but it cannot be helped.'

'You are as drunk as he is,' Emily accused.

'We had only one little drink. To celebrate. Promise…'
Sloane made a gesture with his thumb and finger, to show
just how little the drink had been. He gripped Guy's
shoulders and pulled with more force. 'Keating, get on
with it, man. Go home to your wife.'

Guy released Emily and wound around to Sloane, using
Sloane to keep his balance. 'Home to my wife?' he snick-
ered. His mirth escalated until he was shaking with laughter so intense, no sound came from his mouth. Sloane
needed to hold him upright.

Emily gripped the banister so hard her knuckles turned
white. He dared laugh about his wife? She was some mon-
strous jest to him, was she? What thanks these were for
the hours and hours of worry she had expended on his
behalf. If someone handed her a dagger at this moment,
she might indeed draw it.

Her husband's laughter died with one long sigh. His
expression changed to alarm and he quickly patted his
coat pocket. 'Must take care,' he said shaking his finger
in the air. 'Don't want to be set upon by footpads.'

'Indeed,' Sloane nodded his head vigorously as if Guy
had said something profound. 'Footpads.' Sloane slung
his arm around Guy. 'On our way, man.'

The two men stumbled their way down the stairs.

At the bottom, however, Guy turned back. He gazed up
at Emily with an expression on his face so raw with desire
it surely belonged only in a bedchamber. 'Goodnight,
Lady Widow,' he called to her in a voice suddenly steady
and clear.

He remained there, gazing at her, his eyes searing her
skin with a lick of fire. It thrilled her.

And sickened her.

How dare he look at Lady Widow in that way, when
his wife was nothing more to him than an object of laugh-

ter? How dare he touch Lady Widow as if she were a common harlot, when he did not touch his wife? How dare he arouse those senses in Lady Widow, when he could not bear to bed his wife?

He might look at Lady Widow all he pleased in that lascivious manner. It merely threw more fuel on the white-hot furnace burning inside her now.

So hot with anger she could not move, she glared at him as the men fumbled into their greatcoats and stumbled out of the door.

Lady Widow had one advantage over Emily Keating. Lady Widow could hurt him. Give him some measure of the pain he so casually inflicted upon his wife.

She tapped her fingers on the wood of the banister railing. She would do it. If her husband was so determined to be unfaithful, she would oblige him. She could also inflict a jest upon him. Would not it be worth a laugh to know he'd been unfaithful *with* his wife, rather than *to* her?

At that moment, the East India man walked out of the game room. Spying her, he said, 'Ah, Lady Widow! I beg you to sit down with me for a round of whist.'

Playing Lady Widow, even winning at cards, would give her no joy this night. The fawning attention the gentlemen showered upon her suddenly gave her a great disgust. She could not bear their compliments, their over-solicitousness. Not when her husband behaved in so horrid a manner.

She did not give the gentleman a glance. Glancing instead down towards the front door, she said more to herself than to him, 'I must leave.'

She did not wait to listen to his protests, but ran down the stairs, begging Cummings to get her cloak. Without bothering to put it on, she hurried out of the door, heedless of the night's chill. It would take more than cold weather to cool the fury within her. She ran down the street to where the hackney waited for her, calling for her driver to take her home.

Her driver made excellent speed, and she ran through the mews to the servants' entrance in the back, realising at the last minute that Hester would not be there to let her in. She rapped on the locked door.

It was opened by a startled Rogers. 'M'lady!'

She said a quick thank you, gave no explanation, and hurried off to the servants' stairway. She made it up the three flights of stairs to the hallway of her bedchamber's floor when noise from below stairs reached her ears. She tiptoed down to the first floor where she could see the hall.

Her husband stumbled in, greeted by an obviously frantic Bleasby, who was repeatedly exclaiming, 'Master Guy! Master Guy! Are you injured, lad?'

Her husband's laughter reached her ears once more, though he stepped out of her view. 'No, Bleasby, I could not be better. I've done it, you see! No more to worry over now.'

Oh, yes, he had done whatever it was he had done, but worry would not escape him. She intended to give him plenty to worry about.

'I'm devilish tired, Bleasby,' she heard him say. 'It was a hellish long game.'

Card playing as well as drinking. She ought to have known. It sounded like something her father would have done. That and more.

Rogers's voice was added. 'M'lord!' he exclaimed in much the same tone as his greeting to her.

'Ah, Rogers,' her husband said. 'Be so good as to help me to m'room. I'm devilish tired. Devilish tired.'

He might well be tired from playing cards and drinking and whatever else all that time. Let him sleep all he wanted. She would plot her revenge.

Emily ran ahead of them, reaching her bedchamber before their footsteps sounded in the hall.

Guy woke to daylight, but with no conception of what time it was or even what day it was. He was somewhat surprised to find himself in his own bed. His last clear memory had been of his two whist opponents, heads on the card table, sound asleep in the room where they'd spent almost twenty-four hours straight.

He bounded out of bed. Where was his coat?

He found it brushed and folded neatly in the wardrobe. Bleasby's dedication, he suspected, but his heart pounded until he inspected the inside pocket and discovered the packet of banknotes.

He spread them on a table. One note signed over to him the total sum of ninety-four thousand pounds. Other notes were in denominations of one thousand pounds. Still others in lower denominations. Guy was not entirely sure how much he had won, but he knew he had succeeded. He had won enough to rebuild Annerley, to fix the tenants' cottages, to pay for spring planting. And he had plenty left over to invest in the funds. He'd won enough to make his family and Annerley secure.

He'd done it!

After carefully replacing the banknotes in their packet, he walked to the bureau and poured water into the basin. Splashing it over his face, he caught sight of himself in the mirrored glass. He looked as if he'd survived a battle rather than a bout of cards. He rubbed his cheek, the stubble of his beard scratching his hand.

A vague memory of Lady Widow invaded his mind, of him rubbing his rough face against her soft, smooth skin. Had he seen her, embraced her, as his memory seemed to tell him, or was it a dream? She seemed to inhabit many of his dreams of late.

Lathering his bar of soap and wiping it on his face, he scraped his cheeks and chin with the razor and then quickly washed and dressed. Still unsure of the hour, he chose a brown frock coat and trousers. If there were still time in the day, he meant to call upon his father's former man-of-business. The man had been wise enough to sever ties with his father and brother when they did not heed his advice, but perhaps he would be willing to take a chance on another, luckier Keating. Guy meant to tie up his winnings in safe investments as soon as possible.

The house was quiet as he made his way downstairs. It was deflating he had no one with whom to celebrate, but he supposed that was the cost of keeping their financial problems to himself. He wanted to tell the whole to Emily, wanted to share his good fortune with her, to see her changeable eyes dance like Lady Widow's, to swing her around in total happiness.

But he'd never explained to her how badly he had needed that fictitious fortune of hers. At the time it would have been like rubbing salt in her wounds to tell her she'd married a man one step from Dun territory.

He found Bleasby napping in a chair in the hallway, his chin bobbing against his chest. Poor Bleasby. Soon he could have a small cottage of his own on the Annerley estate and he could nap all the days through, not needing to serve anyone's desires but his own.

Guy tiptoed by the old butler and went into the library.

The clock on the mantel said four-twenty. He might make it into town to complete his business, if he made haste. He gathered some of his other winnings from the locked drawer and put them all together in the packet, tucking it safely in the pocket of his coat. Proceeding quietly so as not to wake Bleasby, he collected his greatcoat and hurried out.

Guy returned at dinnertime, rushing above stairs to dress, his heart light now his shoulders were free of the burden of debt. He dressed quickly, and finding no one in the parlour, headed to the dining room.

His mother and the aunts all looked up when he entered. Emily was not at the table.

'Guy, where have you been?' his mother cried. 'We have all been so worried. You should have told us you had business away from home.'

He gave his mother a kiss on the cheek. 'My apologies, Mother, I ought to have sent word.'

'But your wife said you did send word,' the Dowager said.

Emily had lied for him? Of course. She would have known where he'd been.

'Where is Emily?' he asked.

His mother fussed with the sleeves of her dress. 'Oh, she pleads a sick headache. She has retired for the night.'

Guy frowned. She'd never been ill. 'Does she require a doctor?' he asked.

'She does not require a doctor,' his mother responded in a peevish voice. 'I believe she has the headache in order to keep from accompanying me this evening.'

'Young people have no notion of manners these days,' intoned Aunt Dorrie.

He gave his great-aunt a stern look. 'That is unkind, Aunt Dorrie.'

Aunt Dorrie looked chastised.

Aunt Pip almost smiled. 'Young ladies do get head-aches now and again. I am sure the poor dear needs a rest.'

From her late nights? Aunt Pip was correct. She must be exhausted with the hours she kept. He had not wished to postpone his interview with her.

Guy patted Aunt Pip's shoulder on the way to his seat at the head of the table.

His mother piped up, 'It is a wonder we are not all prostrate after the worry you gave us, Guy.'

'I do apologise, Mother,' he said again.

He let the rest of their conversation wash over him, mumbling occasional apologies for having worried them.

He wanted to see Emily. With the money safe and their future secured, he wanted to tell her the whole. From start to finish.

He wanted to tell her he'd known all along that she was Lady Widow. He wanted to tell her about the card game, how frightening it had been and how exhilarating. He wanted to confide in her his own weakness towards gambling and warn her to stop her own dangerous card playing before it ruined her like it had his father and brother. He wanted to confide in her what a shambles his father and brother had bequeathed to him, how many people would suffer if the estate went back into debt.

Most of all he wanted to beg her forgiveness and ask for an opportunity to begin their marriage again.

He was even willing to give up the intoxicating allure of Lady Widow. He wanted to put behind them Madame Bisou's and all it meant. No more secrets. No more masks.

But he should not inflict all this on her if she were ill upon her bed.

Guy stared at his plate, his appetite gone.

His mother's voice broke through his reverie. 'Guy? Guy!'

He looked up. 'Yes, Mother?'

'You were not attending to me,' she accused.

'Merely woolgathering a moment, what were you saying?' A change of subject might give a needed distraction.

'We are invited to a card party,' she said. 'And your wife has begged off. I am very desirous of attending.' She gave him a hopeful look. 'Will you escort me, Guy?'

He wanted to seek out his wife, not spend an evening at cards, but perhaps it would be cruel to inflict such a serious talk upon Emily if her head ached.

He might as well make one person happy this night. 'I'll escort you, Mother.'

It seemed he could not escape cards for even one evening.

Emily had arranged to arrive at Madame Bisou's early that night, departing before her husband and mother-in-law returned from the evening party. As soon as she handed Cummings her cloak, she asked to see Madame Bisou.

The madam attended her immediately, a hopeful look on her face. 'Robert?' she asked.

Emily shook her head. 'I have not seen him, *madame*.'

The henna-haired madam pursed her lips.

'I wished to request of you a private room,' Emily said.

Madame Bisou's eyes brightened. 'Ah, you have selected a fortunate gentleman? How very *superbe*!'

Emily affected her most haughty Lady Widow tone. 'I

wish a room in which to play a private game of cards. You have such rooms, do you not?'

Madame replied, still sounding amused, 'I do indeed. Will you follow me?' She grabbed a candle from the hall table.

Emily followed her to the floor above the game room, the set of rooms where Madame's girls took their gentlemen. Madame opened one of the doors and ushered her inside. She lit a colza oil lamp above a small card table.

'Will this do, my lady?' Madame asked.

Emily looked around. The card table would do nicely, but she also noticed a bed tucked away in the corner, swathed in curtains and piled with pillows.

'It will do,' she responded. 'I should also desire some refreshment. Some champagne, some brandy, and something to eat as well.'

'*Certainement,*' said Madame Bisou in her bad French. She started for the door.

'Another thing,' Emily said.

Madame paused.

'Would you please ask Lord Keating to join me?'

Madame's eyes lit up as brightly as her hair. 'Aha!' she exclaimed. 'So it is he! *Très bien.*'

'To play cards,' added Emily.

'Of course,' said Madame Bisou with a trill of laughter as she swept from the room.

Emily wandered around, touching the furniture, checking the fire in the grate, avoiding the bed.

She supposed it would be all around the premises that she had invited Lord Keating to a private party. It put her to the blush, but as Lady Widow she must remain cool.

She turned towards the bed and stared at it.

Nerves fluttered in her stomach. What had happened to her resolve? Did she not wish to carry off this new scheme? It was revenge she was after, was it not? What other reason could she have for seducing her husband?

Emily closed her eyes against an image of herself and Guy in that bed.

No, not herself and Guy. Lady Widow.

How much clearer could he have made his desire for Lady Widow than he'd done the night before, holding her and touching her in so familiar a manner? He had not come into his wife's bed, looking for that sort of intimacy, had he? No, he'd gone to sleep alone. He'd not even attempted to give his wife one word of explanation of where he had been for two full turns around the clock.

Her revenge would be to give him what he wanted. Lady Widow. Perhaps even this night she would entice him into that gaudy bed. Perhaps she would engineer a long sordid affair. When she was ready to leave him, she would reveal her secret. He would discover exactly what he had lost by chasing after a woman in a gaming hell and ignoring his wife. By then she would be gone, disappeared into a new quiet peaceful life somewhere.

Alone.

Directly after Guy returned from escorting his mother, he hurried up to his bedchamber. He strode immediately to the door connecting his wife's room with his. He had thought about it all evening. He ought not to have let her headache impede him. He ought to have visited her and asked after her health and informed her he wished to speak with her when she recovered. He hoped it would not be too late. He could see candlelight from under the door. She would be awake.

He opened the door.

Her maid gave a shriek and dropped the dress she'd

been holding in her hand. Guy looked around. Emily was not to be seen.

'I am looking for my wife,' he said to the maid.

She turned very pale and stood as still as a statue.

'Well, girl? Tell me where she is.'

The maid trembled. 'She's…she's gone out, sir.'

Out? To Madame Bisou's, no doubt. Without another word he slammed the door. Grabbing his hat and cloak, he hurried back down the stairs to the hall. Rogers sat attending the door.

'I'm going out, Rogers,' he said, not even waiting for the footman to open the door for him. He flung it open himself and ran down the street to secure a hack.

By the time he arrived at Madame Bisou's he'd calmed down somewhat. She'd not done anything out of the ordinary—*her* ordinary, that is. She did not know he wished never to see this establishment again. If her headache improved, why would she not go gaming?

He asked Cummings if Lady Widow were present and Cummings said, 'Aye.'

He looked for her first in the card room, but she was not to be seen there.

He wandered into the supper room and was waylaid by Sir Reginald, who begged him to sit down for a drink. Guy obliged his father's old friend, because he thought the man could give him news of Lady Widow. He ordered a glass of port and sipped while the older gentleman launched into his latest plan for winning the fair Lady Widow, shutting out all the younger bucks and winning the wager for her favours. It took all Guy's powers of self-command to refrain from planting a facer on this old gent, who rhapsodised about the delights he expected to find when he finally won the prize. Guy's wife. He might have punched him if not distracted by the notion that he had also not seen Cyprian Sloane about the place. Guy began to worry anew.

Madame Bisou waved at him from the doorway, potentially saving Sir Reginald's long straight aristocratic nose, and Guy's sanity. He excused himself.

When he reached the flamboyant madam, she took his arm and led him out into the hall.

'She awaits you upstairs, *chéri*,' Madame Bisou whispered, somehow sounding more like a mother giving her son a treat than a procuress.

'Who?' he asked. Madame Bisou had occasionally attempted to interest him in one of her girls.

'Why, our Lady Widow, of course.' She smiled. 'You have won, it seems.'

His heart skittered. Lady Widow? She had arranged a room and invited him there?

He bent down to Madame Bisou's ear. 'Tell me the room, but do not refer to the wager about her. I am not a part of it.'

She gave him a sceptical look and directed him to a room near the one where he'd spent twenty-four hours.

He knocked.

After a pause, he heard her voice. 'Come in.'

Heart now pounding, he entered.

She stood in the centre of the room facing him, her posture stiff, as if she were a fox that had suddenly discovered dogs trailing it. She wore the blue gown, with a matching cap. Her face was blurred by the netting and obscured by the mask, but she looked to him like some goddess down from Mount Olympus.

He ought to stop right now and tell her exactly what he knew about her. He ought to, but he could not make himself form the words. He saw the card table set up with decks of cards and stacks of counters. He saw the bed in the corner.

Closing the door, he turned the key in the lock, and leaned against it, waiting.

This was her game and to know what card he should play, she needed to toss hers down first.

'Good evening, Lord Keating.' She relaxed her body and spoke enticingly in Lady Widow's voice.

'Good evening, my lady,' he responded.

She walked over to the card table and fingered its green cloth. 'I understand you have a penchant for private card games.'

'Hardly a penchant, but I did very recently agree to one, as you well know.'

'Yes, I do know.' She cleared her throat and looked him directly in the eye. 'I fancy a game of cards, and you are the only gentleman of my acquaintance who will honestly challenge me.'

He glanced again to the bed. If this were merely an invitation to a game of cards, she could have met him in the game room. The rise of excitement he felt had nothing to do with gambling. He moved closer to her.

She walked over to a side table. 'Would you like a drink? I will have champagne, but I took the liberty of ordering brandy for you, since you like it so well.'

What the devil did she mean by that? He raised a brow. This game became more and more intriguing. 'I had no idea my likes and dislikes were of interest to you.'

Emily had never spoken to him in such a seductive voice, nor moved with that surety he was seeing in her. Those behaviours bore the seal of Lady Widow and he was enticed.

She feigned a small laugh. 'A good gamester studies

the opponent, does he not? If desiring to win, that is.' She
held up the bottle. 'Shall I pour for you?'

He gave a nod.

She poured brandy for him and champagne for herself
and carried both glasses to the card table, where she sat
down, her skirts rustling like the sound of bed linens.

He sat in the chair opposite her. 'What game do you
propose, Lady Widow?' he asked.

'Piquet?'

A difficult game. It required attention, computation,
memory and skill. And he was damnably rusty at it.

'As you wish,' he said.

She lifted her chin. 'What stakes?'

He took a sip of his brandy. If he wagered money and
she lost, it might eventually support his request that she
resist the lure of gaming. On the other hand, he could not
count on his skill in piquet. He'd not played since being
posted to the Peninsula.

She knew he would play in earnest. If she won from
him, would it not further fuel her passion for the cards?
He must choose stakes which would leave him at least
even, should he lose.

'If I win the partie,' he stated, 'you will remove your
mask.'

Her hand flew to her face, as if needing to ensure the
mask remained in place. She checked herself and slowly
lowered her hands to the table. 'That is too easy,' she
said. 'Not exciting enough by half.' She cocked her head,
her eyes suddenly brilliant from beneath the netting of her
cap.

Her eyes were blue this night, he noticed, reflecting the
blue of her gown.

She lifted a finger in the air between them. He wondered if it could gauge the palpable excitement in the air,

an excitement which had nothing to do with winning at cards. 'I suggest…' she began, but then left a pregnant pause. 'I suggest the loser of each round must remove a piece of clothing. If you play well enough, I might be forced to remove my mask.'

'And the winner of a partie?' The blood already surged through his veins.

She gave him a most seductive grin. 'The winner of a partie does the removing of the article of clothing.'

He was ensnared. He'd surely lose this game by virtue of being too addled by carnal desire.

He made himself answer as calmly as she. 'And does the winner of the partie choose the piece of clothing to remove?'

She laughed and shook her finger at him as if he were a naughty boy. 'No, indeed. You will not win my mask in that manner, sir.'

He lifted his glass and she raised hers to clink against his. They both drank, gazing at each other, as the fire crackled in the grate and the lamp flickered.

'Your deal or mine?' he asked.

Chapter Fifteen

By the time the clock struck the next hour, Emily sat at the card table without gloves, without shoes, and with only one stocking remaining. Guy had handily taken all five rounds, once with repique, earning sixty points before she'd even played a card. One round he took all the tricks, earning a capot. Fully dressed, he dealt the sixth hand.

Her third glass of champagne calmed her nerves somewhat, but her eyes suddenly went out of focus. Opening wider, she made out too many sevens and eights and not one ace. Holding her breath, she made her exchange. Luck was with her. She picked up the high spades, giving her a sequence of eight, and two more aces.

She made her declaration with confidence. For the first time, the round was hers.

Her husband grinned at her. With exaggerated drama, he removed one shoe, lifting it high in the air so she could see it was off his foot.

'Do not gloat, my lady. I won the partie, you know,' he said with a wicked grin. 'Your rules require me to remove an article of your clothing. What shall it be?'

She was so vexed at losing the previous rounds, she had not much heeded this part of their bargain.

No matter. It was merely the first partie. The rest would be hers. Her luck would change.

'You may remove my other stocking,' she said. How bad could that be?

He grinned and rose, twirling his finger to signal her to move her legs from beneath the table. She turned in her chair, but without a shred of graciousness.

He knelt at her feet, which suddenly felt very exposed without shoes. She tucked her bare foot under her chair out of his sight.

He placed her stockinged foot in the palm of one hand and covered it with the other, warming it in his hands. Then slowly he kneaded her foot, fingers digging into the sole and thumbs rubbing her arch. Not only did her foot tingle and throb and melt all at one time, but the sensations climbed clear up her leg, spreading a blanket of pleasure throughout her whole body.

'This…this is removing my stocking?' she managed, hoping her voice did not sound as breathless as she felt.

His clever hands moved to her ankle. 'No, this is for my enjoyment…and yours,' he murmured. His hands worked their way up her leg, higher and higher, warming, massaging.

Once, what seemed so long ago, he'd touched her even more intimately. The shock and the pleasure of that moment returned as if a mere hour had passed. She could not help but slide down in her chair, straightening her leg and giving him easier access. A long sigh escaped her lips.

Would his fingers reach that very private spot? Would he dare touch her there again? Please?

He fingered her garter, untying it. Perhaps all he meant to do, after all, was roll down her stocking and pull it off her foot.

His fingers reached underneath her stocking, touching her bare skin. With his palms against her bare flesh, he pushed the stocking along. No matter, Emily longed to be rid of the lacy white silk. She wanted his hands to never cease this delight.

But too soon he pulled the stocking from her skin and held it out to her. She grabbed it and threw it to the floor where her other one lay.

He rose with a bit of difficulty and stood with his back to her for a moment while it seemed her whole body vibrated with an incongruous mix of languor and longing.

Throat suddenly dry, she took a long sip of her champagne. It never occurred to her this weakness of hers towards him would ever recur. She'd trusted her fury to squelch it. She squeezed her eyes shut and forced herself to remember that Guy Keating, Emily's husband, touched not his wife's leg, but Lady Widow's.

How could she have known it would be so difficult to care about the difference?

He walked slowly to his chair and poured himself more brandy. 'Shall we continue?' he said.

She dealt the cards.

This partie was much more to her liking. She lost only one round, giving up her hat, hoping he was too enamoured of Lady Widow to recognise Emily without the netting that obscured her face.

He, on the other hand, had lost his other shoe, his stockings, neckcloth, and coat. She kept a sceptical eye on his play, alert for any evidence he was giving her the win, but his play seemed as serious as her own.

What did not appear to bother him, though, was the cost of losing. When he removed an article of clothing, he made a grand show of it, his blue eyes twinkling and a smile twitching at his lips. As Emily, she would have tempered her mirth, even registered shock, but Lady Widow need not be so missish. She laughed at his nonsense, and let herself enjoy the fun.

'Now the partie is yours,' he said, crossing his arms over his chest and leaning back in his chair. 'I wonder if I should ask you to remove my waistcoat, or my breeches?'

Her face grew hot, but she quickly covered her embarrassment. 'You must choose, sir,' she said coolly. 'I am sure it matters not to me.'

He stared at her, one corner of his mouth turned up. Make haste and decide! she thought. The sooner done with the task, the better.

'My breeches…' he began.

No… She swallowed.

He grinned. 'My breeches would leave me a bit chilled. You, ma'am, may remove my waistcoat.'

She tried not to have her shoulders slump in relief. As she rose from her chair, he stood. Walking up to him, coming so close with her feet bare, reminded her too much of her wedding night and their first night in Bath. She took a fortifying breath and reached for his buttons, but she was so aware of his eyes gazing down at her, his breath caressing her, the scent of him filling her nostrils, her fingers fumbled.

The moment she freed the buttons and parted the cloth of his waistcoat, he grabbed both her hands. 'My lady,' he groaned.

He wrapped his arms around her, holding her hips flush against him. His head bent not an inch from hers. 'Kiss me, Lady Widow.' It was more of a demand than a request.

She wanted to heed it. She could feel the strength in his arms pressing her against him, could feel the bulge of his desire for her. She wanted to kiss him, to taste of him again, to let herself be transported to the time when she felt hopeful. It was so very, very tempting.

No! a small voice inside her said. *He does not want you. He wants Lady Widow.*

She forced her anger forward. She would not be weak. She would have her retribution.

She gazed up at him, and made her lips curl into a cynical smile. 'Why, sir, that is not in the cards, is it? You are preventing me from removing your waistcoat.'

He released her, so abruptly she almost fell backwards. Somehow, winning this particular round of the game brought no delight.

It was not that she did not intend to bed him. She very much intended to do so. He desired that of Lady Widow and that is what she would give him. But on her terms, not on his.

He stood motionless, like a man awaiting his valet, giving no further hint of the passion that had previously provoked him. Surprisingly, his powers of restraint vexed her all the more.

She folded his waistcoat and put it on a side chair nearby, hanging his coat on the back of the chair as well. He watched her every move, standing there with his brilliant white shirt loose about him and his breeches moulded to his thighs. She realised too late that Lady Widow would have tossed his waistcoat carelessly aside, not caring where it fell.

'It is your deal,' she said, returning to the card table.

He dealt the cards.

She took another sip of champagne. Her fourth glass? She focused on her fury. She ought to be angry that he had attempted to kiss her, as though she were a common harlot. Never mind that it had been she who invented the stakes of the game for just such a purpose. He had started it, after all, with the silly notion she should remove her mask.

Lady Widow was of the quality, was she not? No man should trifle with her as if she were like whatever female company he and Sloane had entertained as part of their card party.

She gave a haughty sniff. 'I warn you, sir, I will not be treated like the other girls you've visited in these rooms.'

He glanced up. 'Other girls? There were no girls.' His voice was low and steady and his eyes fixed intently on hers. 'There was nothing but cards, I assure you. I have no interest in any woman but you.'

She could not look away. His gaze captured her and held her as securely as when he'd pinned her against the banister the night before. The fire she'd fed and stoked inside her, calmed to a soft glow. He wanted her.

No, not her. Lady Widow. The anger flickered back to life.

'Your exchange, my lady,' he said, breaking the contact and the spell.

Guy watched Emily as she arranged her cards. He ought to cease this charade forthwith, ought to inform her of his knowledge of her identity, tell her he had known all along. He no longer cared if he taught her a lesson about gambling. He no longer cared why she engaged in this folly.

He just wanted her.

By God, he'd almost taken her when she came so close, when she'd touched him. She was so alluring, so captivating in the back-and-forth struggle inside her. One moment she was cool and detached, the next as bound up in desire as he.

There was nothing stopping him now. He had the financial means to make up to her for tricking her into marriage. He had money enough for future generations to build upon. And he most definitely wished to risk conceiving an heir.

He finished the brandy in his glass, tried to pour another, but the bottle was empty. No, nothing impeded him from forging a future with his wife. Nothing but this masquerade. Devil take it, he wanted to bed Lady Widow, even if it were just this one time. He did not know why she, as Lady Widow, was intent upon taking him into her bed, but he wanted to experience this side of her just once.

He suspected, once the masquerade ended, Lady Widow would disappear.

She threw down five cards, picking replacements from the deck. Luckily, piquet had come back to him as effectively as jumping back on a horse after a fall. She wished for a challenging game and this had been one.

He exchanged his cards.

'Point of six,' she said.

'Good,' he replied. He did not have six cards of one suit.

'Quint,' she said.

She had five in sequence? 'Good,' he replied.

'Quatorze,' she said.

'What suit?'

She gave him a smug smile. 'Quatorze aces.'

All the aces? This hand was lost.

'Repique.' She grinned, automatically doubling her points.

He lost the round as was inevitable, but the loss might work in his favour. Perhaps she would play badly if required to stare at his bare chest. Slowly, knowing her eyes watched every flex of his muscles, he removed his shirt and tossed it to the chair where she'd placed his folded waistcoat and coat. Though bare-skinned, her eyes were heat enough. He felt no chill.

They played, speaking only declarations and points. Guy watched Emily drink the last of her champagne, her pink tongue licking a drop from her lips.

Dear God!

His breeches went next, removed without a flourish, best taken off under the table. His drawers, the only item of clothing left on his body, revealed too much from this arousing game.

He won the next round and his heart accelerated. Emily stood and seemed to unfasten her skirt, but only the top gossamer layer of cloth came off. Her modesty remained largely intact.

He won the next round as well, though he was amazed he could remember a knave from a ten. She removed a part of her bodice made of lace and ribbon.

Her hands shook as they played the next round and her voice quavered as she called out her scores. They were nearly even on tricks, but he won again by only five points.

She stood. 'I cannot remove my dress without assistance,' she said.

He went to her, forgetting his own dishabille. 'Allow me.'

She turned her back and he unbuttoned the row of tiny pearl buttons lining her spine. Her hair, swept up in a knot on top of her head, revealed her long graceful neck. It would be delicious to place his lips at the spot where her hairline met her neck, but it seemed like taking unfair advantage.

'All your buttons are undone,' he said, stepping back.

She let her dress slip from her shoulders and slide down

her body to the floor. She stepped out of the puddle of silk at her feet and turned to him, dressed only in corset and shift. From beneath her mask, her eyes beseeched him, but he knew not for what she pleaded.

'Do we continue to play?' he murmured.

She gave the ghost of a smile. 'One more hand.'

She played the next round badly, distractedly tossing down high cards when low ones remained in her hand. He could not say she intended to lose. Her choices seemed random; her mind elsewhere.

Perhaps her mind travelled in the same direction as his own, to the bed in the corner of the room.

The last card was played.

'I lost,' she said with little emotion in her voice. She lifted her head and steadily met his gaze. 'You may remove my corset.'

'Are you certain?' He found it hard to speak.

'Yes.' Her words were like a sigh. She smiled a Lady Widow kind of smile. 'We agreed upon these stakes, did we not?'

She rose and walked over to his chair and again presented her back to him. 'Undo my laces,' she commanded.

He stood. His fingers felt like clubs as he fumbled with the knot, finally untying it and freeing her of her garment. It seemed so familiar. He'd done the same on their wedding night, but without the emotions consuming him now. His feelings towards her were so altered, full of fascination, appreciation, gratitude.

She turned to him, that imploring, almost despairing look again on her face. Her sheer muslin shift revealed the shadow of her nipples, the dark triangle between her thighs. He gazed at her thirstily, wanting to plunder her, to take all his need of her in one glorious act.

But he could not. Was he not being as false to her in

this moment as he had been on their wedding night? He knew who she was. He must tell her.

'We must talk—' he began.

She covered his lips with her fingers and twined her arms around his neck. 'No talking, Guy,' she whispered. Her lips closed onto his.

Restraint vanished. Reason fled. He pulled her against him, deepening the kiss she offered, opening her mouth and tasting her with his tongue, savouring her sweetness, as effervescent as the champagne she'd consumed.

He ran his hands over her breasts, her abdomen, her back, wanting to explore every inch of her. He lifted her into his arms, while she rained his neck with kisses. He carried her to the bed.

She pulled the shift over her head and tossed it away. He made short work of his drawers, joining her on the bed, their naked bodies finally free of all barriers.

This was what he'd waited for, what he'd worked for all those nights at the gaming table, a prize he had not realised he wanted. This was something for himself. And for her.

He feasted upon the sight of her. 'You are beautiful,' he said.

Through her mask her eyes winced as if his words had injured her. 'Do not talk,' she cried, reaching for him.

This creature in bed with him was nothing like when he'd bedded her before. She had been quiet, passive then. Now she fully partook of the experience, touching him, kissing him, placing his hands where she wished him to touch.

He obliged her. Would do anything for her. His heart swelled with hope for their future. For countless nights like this one where their love could run free. He let her set the pace, let her climb on top of him and explore him, stroking and kissing. Whatever she wished, he would oblige.

His need grew with her every touch. Any coherent thought crumbled, until he felt only the desperate need to join his body to hers. He rolled them both over and rose above her. With her pliant and eager beneath him he entered her.

She gasped aloud and met his every move, catapulting him to the heights of ecstasy. With his last shred of will, he held back, waiting for her to reach the heights with him.

She did. With an impassioned cry she convulsed around him. He drove into her again and spilled his pleasure…and all his hopes…inside her.

Emily woke, tangled in bed linens and a masculine arm and leg. The clocked had chimed. What time?

She glanced at the room's window. It still appeared dark outside. Her husband was very soundly asleep next to her, his face as peaceful and untroubled as a young boy. As handsome as an Adonis.

What had she done? Somewhere in the last hands of the card game, things had gone awry. The more skin her husband exposed, the more her fury at him seemed to slip through her fingers, like so much water from a crystal pond. She had plunged in to their lovemaking as hungrily as a starving man would attack a long awaited meal.

No matter what, she could never regret making love to him, could never forget the glorious experience of being joined with him as one. Now she felt all at sea, no compass to guide her. What was she to do next? How could she return to being just Emily?

She slowly and carefully disentangled herself, wiggling out from under the arm and leg wrapped around her, freeing herself from the linens. She slipped out of the bed, the floor cool beneath her bare feet.

By the light of the dying colza lamp, she gathered her clothes and dressed hurriedly, buttoning what buttons she could reach, knowing she'd missed some. She stuffed her dishevelled hair beneath her cap. If she were lucky, no one would see her leave.

If she were lucky, her husband would not wake and profess his love for Lady Widow. She fingered the mask, still securely in place. This was the last night she would wear it. Lady Widow would disappear and somehow, someday, so would Emily.

Emily had already disappeared, however, and she, like Lady Widow, would never return. Who would appear in their place?

She smoothed her dress as best she could and tiptoed to the door. When she reached for the knob, she hesitated. Holding her breath, she glanced back at her sleeping husband, savouring one last look, saying a silent goodbye for what could never be.

She peeked into the hallway, glad to see no one there. She reached the stairs and hurried down the two flights, reaching the hall without encountering the night's clientele.

Cummings was at his post by the door. She begged him to quickly fetch her cloak.

He stared at her with a strange expression. 'Yes, m'lady,' he said and went off to do her bidding.

A moment more and she would be free of Madame Bisou's forever.

Cummings returned with her cloak. If he noticed her undone buttons while he assisted her into it, he gave no indication. She started for the door.

'Lady Widow!' a voice behind her called.

Reluctantly, she turned. It was Sir Reginald, looking painfully distressed. 'I beg a moment, ma'am.'

She did not wish to tarry, not even for a second, but she felt caught.

He rushed up to her and said, 'Let me escort you to your carriage.'

'Very well,' she agreed.

Once outside into the near freezing air, he fell to one knee, grasping her hands so tightly she could not pull away.

'Lady Widow, I know that Lord Keating has won the wager, but I beg of you—'

Her blood turned to ice. 'Wager? What wager?'

He gave her a look of chagrin. 'The wager of who would bed you first, but I beg you will—'

She jerked her hands away. 'You *wagered* about me?' Her voice escaped as cold as the night.

Guy and Sloane and Sir Reginald and the others took bets on who would get her into bed first? *Guy* did this?

He struggled back to his feet. 'A friendly wager, nothing to signify.'

'How…how…?' Words escaped her. She wanted to run. She wanted to know. Her voice dropped to no more than a rasp. 'Was it all about a wager?'

All the admiration, the flattery, allowing her to win at cards—that was all flummery? All aimed at getting her into bed, so one gentleman would win money?

Her husband's admiration of Lady Widow—was that, too, nothing more than…than…gambling?

'Don't quite get your meaning,' Sir Reginald said, dusting off his breeches. 'The odds favoured Sloane, to tell the truth, but, I must say, I retained my hopes. Would have won a bundle.'

He grabbed her hand again, but she quickly snatched it back and started for her carriage.

'Wait,' he called, hurrying to catch up. 'Want to tell you I have plenty of blunt to lay on you. Want to offer you *carte blanche*. A gentleman like me would be dashed more attentive than those younger fellows.'

She halted and spun towards him. He gave her a very hopeful smile. She swung her hand and slapped him across his cheek, the sharp smack resounding down the street.

Without another word, she ran to where Hester's brother waited for her with his hack.

Chapter Sixteen

Cyprian Sloane sat slumped in his chair in Madame Bisou's supper room, a whisky in his hand and three bottles on the table. He'd been there most of the night. He'd barely got in the door at Madame Bisou's when Sir Reginald accosted him and informed him he'd lost the wager. Keating at that moment was still occupied in a private room with Lady Widow.

That Greeking bounder.

T'think he, Cyprian Sloane, had taken the pains to invite Keating into that card game. Made the man's fortune, he had. Keating ought to have kissed his feet. Everyone knew the Viscount was nearly done up. Sloane had rescued him, plucked him out of Dun territory. This was his thanks?

Sloane downed another whisky. That bastard. That son of a whore.

Sloane laughed, the loud bark jolting the few other people in the room to look up at him. 'Son of a whore' best described himself, not Keating. No scandal attached itself to that paragon's birth, but everyone knew Sloane's father had not sired him. Nice gentleman, his *father*, saddling him with the name Cyprian lest anyone forget he was the product of cuckoldry.

Never mind that. Water over the dam. Water over the damned-if-he-cared. He laughed again, soundlessly this time, and placed his heels on the table. He folded his arms across his chest.

He'd told Keating how much this wager meant to him. Lady Widow was a tempting piece and the contest to win her had given him a vast amount of amusement. Until this night.

He cared nothing for losing the money. He had plenty of money, especially after that card game—the one into which he'd invited Keating. He was plenty rich, that was not to the point. He'd wanted to *win*, by damn, and Keating cut him out.

In his grandfather's time, he could have challenged Keating to a swordfight. He swished his sword arm through the air. A good fight would lift his spirits about now, especially if he could *win* it.

He crossed his arms again, staring dejectedly at the empty bottles on the table. No sense thinking of duelling. Only a fool risked his life for a bit o' muslin like Lady Widow. The way his luck was going, even if he won the duel, the scandal would run him out of England like that damned lame poet.

Curse the man! Keating, that is. Not the poet. At this moment Keating was fornicating with the prize when he, Sloane, was drinking bad whisky. He ought to have played his trump card. Not that he had any idea if the damned information was worth a farthing to Keating.

Discovering a drab of alcohol in one of the bottles, he poured it into his glass and downed it in one gulp. No sense staying in this damned place. He rose unsteadily to his feet. In his own rooms he could drink himself into oblivion with much better whisky.

Listing to one side, he made his way out of the room. As he entered the hallway, that devil Keating descended the stairs. 'Keating!' Sloane shouted. 'I'll have a word with you now!'

Keating scowled at him. In fact, the man looked dashed unhappy. How could any man not be happy after *winning* and bedding the mysterious widow?

Who the devil was she anyway? That was one piece of information he'd not yet discovered. Liked the mystery, frankly. Intended to peel that mask off her in a bedroom. Is that what Keating had done? Did Keating now know who she was? That would be another low blow.

'Well, what is it, Sloane?' Keating said.

That's right. He had something to say to Keating, if he had a moment to recall. Sloane wrapped his arm around Keating's shoulders and walked him over to a secluded corner.

Pointing his finger in the vicinity of Keating's nose, he said, 'The devil to you, man. You bedded her and you knew I had the first claim.'

'Do not speak to me of that wager of yours, Sloane. I will hear no more of it.' Keating shoved him aside.

Sloane grabbed the back of his collar. 'No, a moment, please. I have a plan.' He leaned into Keating's face, making the man wince. 'You...you tell them all it was a hoax. Just a card game, nothing more, and that the bet is still on. No one will be the wiser.'

'It is over.' Keating's voice rose. 'No more bets about the lady. I beg you would all forget her existence.'

'So you can have her?' Sloane gave a mirthless laugh. 'Mayhap I'll make a wager to be the man who takes her from you.' He raised a triumphant arm. 'Ha!'

'You are foxed.' Keating pushed him aside and headed towards the stairs.

'Tarry just a bit.' Sloane followed him down the stairs, grasping the banister to keep his balance. When Keating called to Cummings for his topcoat and hat, Sloane bade the man collect his as well.

'I'm going home,' Keating said.

'You will want to hear me out,' Sloane said, though he was not at all certain that would be true. In any event, sometimes you just had to throw a card on to the table and hope for the best. He trailed Keating out on to the street and kept pace, somewhat unsteadily, beside him.

'Speak up, Sloane, and allow me on my way.' Keating walked quickly. How could that be? He was half a foot shorter at least.

'Well, speak up,' Keating repeated.

'Give me a moment.' Damned soldiers always rushing to the charge.

They turned the corner before Sloane spoke.

'Your wife is acquainted with a lady, I believe,' he began. 'Sis…sis…sister-in-law to Heronvale.'

'What does that signify?' Keating slowed a bit.

'Patience, man. I'll tell you,' Sloane said, but paused, until Keating shook his head and resumed his pace.

'I met Lady Devlin some years ago,' Sloane finally said.

'I fail to see—' interjected Keating.

'Attend to me.' Sloane recomposed his thoughts into some semblance of coherency. 'I met Lady Devlin in a gaming hell run by Lord Farley. Remember him? Died earlier this year. Attacked by footpads, they say.'

'That means nothing—' Keating began.

'Nothing? She was Farley's prime piece, sir. She was the prize men won and plenty of 'em won her.' He rubbed his chin. 'Not me, you understand. Farley gulled his patrons. I didn't fancy being cheated.'

The information must be hitting a nerve. Keating had stopped walking. Luckily there was a lightpost to lean upon.

'Why are you telling me this, Sloane?'

Capital question. Why was he? Oh, yes... 'Well, I had the notion your wife's reputation might suffer if it became known they were so closely attached; that is, if the tale of Lady Devlin—the Mysterious Miss M, they called her—became the latest *on dit*.'

Keating stood his ground. 'And?'

'And this scandalous *on dit* might fail to reach the gossips' ears if...if you told the fellows at Madame Bisou's the bet is still on.'

As trump cards went, this one sounded more like a two-spotter, even to his ears. How much whisky had he consumed to induce him to think Keating would go for this lame nonsense?

Keating glared at him, illuminated by the gaslight. 'I took you for a different sort of man, Sloane,' he said, in a low even tone. 'We part ways here. There's a hack across the street and I'm off to hire him to drive me home.' Without another word, Keating crossed the street and, after a word with the driver, climbed in the hack.

Sloane watched him until the coach disappeared from his sight.

Guy leaned back against the cool leather of the hackney's seat. Curse Sloane for giving him one more thing to worry about. He needed to get home, to see Emily, and explain what he ought to have told her from the beginning.

When he woke and found her gone, he'd known he'd

erred by not telling her the whole. Now he realised he had managed to deceive her one more time. Would it be too late to explain? Would she understand that he'd merely wanted to play out her masquerade?

He hadn't needed Sloane's extra bit of information. If Sloane were willing to ruin that poor lady's life, the man indeed deserved his reputation as a scoundrel. To think Guy had almost come to like him.

But Sloane was a petty matter at the moment. He would deal with Sloane's threat later. Emily was more important.

The hack delivered him home and he hurried inside, rushing up the stairs to his bedchamber, and only then shedding his topcoat and hat. He went immediately to the door connecting his room with his wife's.

It was locked. She had never locked the door against him. Temptation had often driven him to test the door, though he stopped himself before entering her room.

He could knock. He could break down the door for that matter, but would either of those actions gain him credit with her?

No, he was done with forcing her into situations not of her choosing. He'd respect her desire to keep him out. Morning was time enough to speak to her.

He fell exhausted into bed, but sleep eluded him. The memory of Emily in his arms tormented him, again and again drawing his eyes back to the door that separated them. Would he ever unlock that door? Would he ever find his way to her side?

With their moment of pleasure lingering in his mind, he finally drifted off into a fitful sleep.

When morning came, Emily dragged herself from her bed. She'd heard her husband return a few hours before, listened to him checking the door between them. What had he thought? He could go from Lady Widow's bed to Emily's?

She grabbed the bedpost as the pain of it shot through her. She'd thought she could treasure that one moment with Guy, even if he had been with Lady Widow and not his wife. She thought she could hold the memory close to her heart, to warm her on lonely nights. A brief memory of love.

It was all illusion.

It had been a wager, nothing more. He'd bet on bedding her. They'd all bet on bedding her, as if her heart meant nothing more than a horse running a race, a man in a bout of fisticuffs, a cock fighting to the death.

She could not even hold that one moment as precious. How false men were. How easily they trifled with a woman's affections, the lot of them. She'd never return to Madame Bisou's. She'd been a fool to step foot in such a place from the outset.

Hester entered the room. 'You are awake, my lady.'

Awake. Had she ever been asleep? 'Yes, I'm awake.'

She accepted Hester's ministrations as if by rote, caring not which of her drab dresses she wore or how her hair was arranged. The walls around her seemed like a prison cell, but she could imagine no other place to feel less captive.

The idea of continuing as Emily, so correct, so compliant, so uncomplaining, felt akin to death, but what had Lady Widow's world brought her?

She watched herself in the glass as Hester put pins in her hair to keep it in place, fancying her image dissolving like fog after sunrise. She did not know who she could be.

'There you are, my lady,' Hester said with her usual cheer.

Emily took a fortifying breath. She could make it through the day. She could walk and talk and do whatever anyone required of her. She was well practised in that skill.

Trying to erect a tower around her heart with each step, Emily went down to the breakfast room. The staircase, the rooms, the hall all looked the same, but she felt so altered it was like seeing them in a dream. One from which she would never wake.

Her mother-in-law was the only one at breakfast. Emily was relieved she would not yet have to encounter Guy. The Dowager barely glanced up when Emily entered.

'Good morning,' Emily said, though it sounded like the words came from someone else.

'Hmph,' Lady Keating muttered.

Emily shrugged, selecting her slices of toast and sitting down to pour tea. Amazing how one could act with a modicum of normality when one's insides seemed shattered to bits.

'You have slept late again,' Lady Keating said.

Emily had been about to take a bite of toast. Her hand remained poised in the air for a moment before she returned the slice to her plate and clasped her hands in her lap.

'Not late enough,' she said, not quite under her breath.

Her mother-in-law seized upon her words. 'What is your meaning, not late enough?'

Emily took a breath before meeting the older woman's eye. She felt like a vessel, already filled to the brim, into which Lady Keating had poured another pitcher full. 'Lady Keating, please inform me. Why do you dislike me so? What have I done to deserve this constant disparagement?'

Her mother-in-law gasped. 'How impertinent!'

Emily kept her gaze level. 'Not impertinent, ma'am. I truly wish to know what it is you object to in me. I have endeavoured to be pleasing to you.'

Emily would not take another moment of this treatment from her mother-in-law. She was done with being agreeable. She doubted she could abide another second of being agreeable.

'I am sure I have never—' Lady Keating began.

Emily interrupted. 'I am sure you have never called me by name. Do you realise that? You have never once used my name.'

She was not a vessel overflowing, she feared. She was a dam bursting. 'Why is that, Lady Keating?'

'This is the outside of enough!' Her mother-in-law threw down her fork and started to rise.

'No,' Emily said. 'Do not leave. Let us have this out. Tell me why you despise me so.'

Lady Keating's eyes flashed. 'You tricked my son into marriage. You have ruined him!'

A denial flew to Emily's lips, but she held it back. 'How did I accomplish this feat?' she said, keeping her voice even. 'How did I trick him?'

Lady Keating averted her eyes for a moment. 'I do not precisely know, but I can think of no other reason to marry a woman like y—' She clamped her mouth closed.

'A woman like me,' Emily finished for her. 'Exactly what about me?'

'You have nothing to give Guy credit,' the Dowager spat out. 'You have no looks, no charm, no fortune…'

Emily laughed and her mother-in-law gaped in surprise.

'No fortune, you have the right of it. Do go on, Lady Keating.'

The Dowager's face flushed red. 'My son ought to have married a woman of consequence, someone with money, connections. After…after his brother's death—my dear boy! God rest his soul—all Guy could talk about was money. We have no funds for this. There is no money for that. He wanted to bring Cecily home from school! He made us leave Annerley and go to Bath. I thought he was in search of an eligible match, not marriage to you! With your shameful family—'

'My shameful family!' Emily cried. 'How is my family more shameful than this one? Perhaps you ought to consider who may have tricked whom into marriage. If you think I sought a gamester for a husband, you are mistaken!'

Lady Keating shot back, 'My son is not a gamester! How dare you!'

As the Dowager shouted these last words, Guy walked into the room. 'What is this?' he asked hotly.

'She has been saying shocking things to me, Guy!' his mother cried, choking on a sob.

Emily stood, shooting a glare at both her mother-in-law and her husband. 'I will leave you to discuss how shocking I can be!'

'Emily, wait!' Guy pleaded, but she pushed past him and ran from the room.

Guy swung around to his mother. 'What have you done this time?'

'Now do not shout at me!' his mother sobbed. 'She started it.'

He gripped the back of a chair to keep from throttling her. How was he to make things right with his wife when his mother made it her business to be thoughtless and

unkind? He did not need this from her! He needed to show
Emily he could give her a good life with him. Financial
security. A true partnership. Children. Most of all, children.

'Mother, I am going to end it. You have a fortnight to
find other accommodations. I will give you an allowance
and you may live where you please, but I'll not have you
interfering in my marriage or making my wife miserable.'

'Oh!' she exclaimed in a horrified voice.

He did not wait around to hear more. He hurried out
of the room in search of Emily. He met her in the hall,
in bonnet and pelisse, putting on her gloves. Her maid
was hurrying behind her. 'Emily…' he said.

'I am going out,' she declared. 'Hester will accompany
me.'

'I will go with you,' Guy said. 'Hester, stay here.'

Hester, appearing quite alarmed, halted in mid-step,
looking from one to the other.

'Hester will come with me,' Emily said.

'She will not,' Guy countered.

The maid glanced from one to the other.

'You will wait while I get my coat and hat.' Guy said.

As he turned to do so, she said, 'I will go alone.' She
walked briskly out of the door.

Guy ran to get his coat. He quickly put the hat on his
head and hurried after her, running to the end of the street,
still struggling into his topcoat.

He quickly caught up with her.

'Emily, I desire to talk with you.'

She walked quickly, not giving him a glance. 'About
your mother? I have no wish to converse on that topic.'

Her colour was high and her voice trembled with anger.
In spite of himself, something inside him felt a prick of

arousal. She was another new Emily. One he'd glimpsed that day when she threw the book at him.

'I am quite aware of my mother's ill-mannered behaviour towards you. I have spoken to her about it several times—'

'How well she heeds you,' Emily said with sarcasm.

He almost smiled, but thought better of it. 'I have asked her to find residence elsewhere.' If he'd hoped this would please her, he was mistaken. She stopped abruptly and faced him.

'And you think this improves matters?' She glared at him, the flashing of her eyes almost distracting him from what she was saying. 'What about your great-aunts? Your sister? Do you think I wish to be the cause of estrangement in the family? I think of my own family. Do you suppose I would be pleased to cause the same in yours?'

'What other recourse do I have?' he demanded. As difficult as it was to receive her anger, he was glad she did not mask it from him. 'My duty is to you, my wife.'

'Duty!' she said, as if it were a profanity. She started walking again.

He bolted to her side and kept stride with the brisk pace she set. They came to Piccadilly where the streets were busy with shoppers and tradesmen. This was not a place for him to engage in a private conversation. They had already received interested glances from passers-by.

Before he knew it, she darted through the traffic to cross the bustling street.

'Blast it, Emily,' he said, his heart still pounding in fright from seeing her nearly run over by a mail coach. 'Have a care. Where are you bound in such a hurry?'

'I have a fancy to call upon Lady Devlin,' she replied in a cool voice.

Oh, the devil, Guy thought. He'd nearly forgotten about

Lady Devlin. 'Emily, let us find a place to sit down a moment.'

'There isn't such a place,' she said.

'We could go to the park.'

Hyde Park was out of the way, but at least he could sit down with her in relative privacy and tell her about Lady Devlin. He didn't dare tell her the whole. That would have to wait until they returned home.

'I do not wish to go to the park,' she said.

He stopped this time and she kept walking several feet before resignedly stopping and turning back to him.

'Very well,' she said. 'The park.'

Though the day was chilly and rain threatened there was plenty of activity in the park. Soldiers exercising their horses. Grey-haired gentlemen taking constitutionals. The occasional couple looking more into each other's eyes than at the flora. He led her to a bench where she sat stiffly beside him.

'We are in the park,' she said unnecessarily.

He rubbed his face. How to tell her? He took her gloved hand and held it with both his hands. 'You should hear this information from me. I'll not risk you coming by it some other way—'

'Risk,' she murmured with a slight laugh.

'There is someone about who speaks of Lady Devlin's past,' he began.

To his surprise, she turned to him, her face turning pale.

'He…he says she used to be employed in a gaming hell—'

'No,' she gasped, rising.

He kept hold of her hand and pulled her back down. 'I thought you should know this. If this information becomes public knowledge, even being Heronvale's sister-in-law may not be enough for her to weather it.'

The distress on her face was much more than he expected. If he were not holding on to her, he was sure she would bolt.

'You may suffer by association to her,' he added.

'Are you forbidding me to see her?' Her voice was like ice.

'No,' he said, 'but you must take care. Our status could less stand such a scandal.'

She shot to her feet again and snatched her hand from his grasp. 'Our status? Do you think I give a moment's care for that?' Her eyes were wild, like a cornered animal looking for escape.

'Emily?' He regarded her with alarm.

People walking nearby stopped and stared at them.

'Who gave you this information?' she demanded.

'Calm yourself, Emily. Sit back down.'

'Who?' she repeated, looking wilder than the moment before. 'Who? Do not keep this information from me, I warn you.'

This was not biddable Emily who denied having any wants or desires. This was not the seductive Lady Widow, using feminine wiles to get what she wanted. This was someone entirely new. This was a mythological harpy—no—more like a mother bear protecting her cub.

'What is this, Emily?'

'Guy,' she pleaded, her whole body trembling, 'tell me who gave you this information.'

'It was Cyprian Sloane, but—'

'Oh!' She took off at a run, her skirts flying, and her bonnet blown off her head, held only by its ribbons.

Guy jumped to his feet and took off after her, heedless of the alarmed stares they received.

He caught up to her and grabbed her by the arm. Gripping her forearms, he held her firm.

'Guy, release me, I beg you. I must warn her, please.' She struggled to free herself.

'Not until you tell me why, Emily.'

They were both panting, but Guy was not certain it was due to the running or due to having her close to him.

She stilled. The surprise of it almost caused him to let go, when her struggles had not succeeded. She stared him directly in the eye. Her cheeks were flushed. Her eyes sparkled, but with pain. 'She is my sister,' she rasped.

He dropped his hands, but she did not run.

She held him with her eyes. 'Your mother called my family shameful this morning. Would you care to hear how shameful, Guy? Because, if you would, I will tell you now. I know you will keep what I say in confidence, because, having married me, you will not wish this to become known.' She gave him a haunted smile. 'If you think Sloane's revelation is a threat to the Keating name, you might wish to listen to me.'

She alarmed him. He had the notion that the walls she erected were tumbling down, but prematurely, before she was strong enough to do without them.

He reached over and put her hand into his. 'I am ready to hear you.'

Chapter Seventeen

He would despise her after this, Emily was certain. He would be even more regretful he'd married her than he'd been before. Not only did she have no fortune for him to gamble away, not only did she lack charm, as her mother-in-law said, but she also came from a family whose secrets could shrivel a person's soul.

She explained to him just how shameful her family really could be, leaving nothing out.

She told about her father bringing the body home, how she'd thought Madeleine had died alone outside in the cold. Tears flooded her eyes, and her voice caught on a sob.

To her surprise, he did not shake his head in disgust. He wrapped his arm around her and held her close against his chest until she was again able to speak.

'It is all right,' he murmured in a voice soft as kitten's fur. 'Your sister did not die.'

No, but that nagged at her too. Who was the poor girl buried in Madeleine's grave?

His arms held her close. The heat of his body warmed her, and the chill of the day disappeared. How was she to reconcile this kindness with all she knew of him? With all that had fuelled her anger?

Her mind refused to recall his wager on Lady Widow, refused to remember he'd tricked her into marriage, refused to accuse him of being like her father.

They continued on the park's path, her holding tightly to his arm. The trees in the park were already bare, their brown leaves scattered on the ground. Every so often the cold breeze stirred them into useless little whirlwinds.

She continued her tale. She told of encountering Madeleine in front of Lackington's Book Shop, on Devlin's arm, like seeing a ghost appear during the brightest part of the day.

She swallowed, her throat suddenly so dry she was unable to tell him she once had placed all her hopes on marrying Devlin Steele. This truth was too painful. She had been so eager to marry a good man. A man unlike her father.

Had she accomplished that goal by marrying Guy? Was he the good man he appeared to be at this moment, a man offering her no censure, no rebuff, merely comfort and understanding?

Whatever might happen in the days and weeks and years to come, she would never forget this moment with him. Her husband looked upon her with loving eyes. Her heart nearly burst with the joy of it.

In a halting voice she told him how thoughtless and selfish she'd been, and how jealous of the pretty Madeleine. If she had paid attention to her sister, guided her, looked out for her, Madeleine would have been safe.

'How could you have known, Emily?' he said. 'You could not have conceived of such events.'

Could she bear it? Could she believe it? She wanted to believe it. In this moment, walking with him and telling him the worst secret of her life, she wanted to believe she was not at fault. She wanted to believe he cared about her.

They left the park and walked to Grosvenor Square. She hated the thought of parting with him, but Madeleine would have difficulty enough in hearing the news from her. Besides, the longer he was with her, enfolding her in his kindness, the more foolhardy would the plan forming in her mind seem.

As they neared the Heronvale townhouse, she said, 'I wish to be alone with Madeleine when I tell her. I do not want you to be present. It will only distress her.'

Guy's blue eyes regarded her intently. 'Emily, I beg you not to tell her at all.'

'No! She must be warned! I insist upon it.' She could not keep this secret from Madeleine, not when her sister's whole future could be ruined by it. She would also tell Madeleine she would fix it.

His brow furrowed.

As Guy's wife she could do nothing for her sister. It would be scandalous for her to call upon Cyprian Sloane, even if she knew where to find him. Lady Widow, however, knew exactly where he would be that very evening. Lady Widow might be able to convince him to preserve Madeleine's reputation.

Her heart beat wildly with excitement. She knew she could resolve this! Lady Widow could convince Sloane, she knew she could! She could rescue her sister now as she had not done before.

She made her voice firm. 'Do not forbid me to do this, Guy. I have made no previous requests of you, but I am asking you now to allow me to warn my sister.'

They had reached the door to the Heronvale townhouse. He crossed his arms and bowed his head in thought.

'I will not forbid you,' he said at last. 'But it is a matter best resolved without her knowing of it, I am convinced. It would be far more effective if I spoke with her husband or with Heronvale.'

'No, Guy, you must not,' Emily begged. 'It is Madeleine's decision whether or not to tell her husband and the Marquess.'

She looked up at him, all turmoil inside. Wishing not to part with him. Not to become Lady Widow again. But excited and eager to rescue her sister.

'If this is what you desire…'

His eyes were warm and caring, their intense blue still having that melting effect on her bones and muscles. What she desired most was to throw herself into his arms and to feel his strength enfolding her, never letting go.

She must be realistic. She must take one more risk. For the sake of her sister. When she met his eyes, her gaze did not waver, even as the lie formed on her lips. 'I desire this above all things.'

What she truly desired above all things was for this moment with her husband to last forever.

He smiled at her and butterflies danced in her chest. He took her hand and lifted it to his lips. When he turned his back to her to sound the knocker, she rubbed where his lips had touched, her heart now aching with what she had decided to do.

For her sister, she would don Lady Widow's clothes one last time. She would wear Lady Widow's mask. She would return one last time to Madame Bisou's gaming hell and convince Sloane never to divulge this secret—no matter what it took. She would not fail Madeleine this time. She would right the wrong she had done, and her sister would be safe.

* * *

When a Heronvale footman opened the door, Guy watched Emily step over the threshold, and heard her ask for Lady Devlin. The door closed.

He had not wished to bid her goodbye. He turned away and stepped back on the pavement, remembering how it felt to hold her in his arms, to comfort her, to dry her tears.

The revelation about her family had been shocking in the extreme. He had not imagined how low her parents could sink. To abandon one daughter to such a fate. To treat the other like a mere encumbrance. Using them both as mere chattels to resolve gaming debts. Why, even his own father and brother had not been so lost to decency as that.

How had Emily come out of such a family with all her goodness? Her solicitousness of his mother, his great-aunts and the servants had been no pretence. If her father had passed on his love of gambling to her, Guy would help her conquer it. God knew, he understood all the temptations of a card table.

But first he must see her safe from this scandal. He must save her from the pain of seeing her sister ruined and banished all over again.

Guy turned towards Bond Street in search of a hack. He intended to stop at White's or whichever gentlemen's club might know where Cyprian Sloane could be found. He'd find Cyprian Sloane and do whatever was necessary to compel the man to keep his mouth shut. Then he would tackle all their other problems, including telling her he'd deceived her once more by pretending he did not know she was Lady Widow.

Guy spent half the afternoon searching before he finally located Sloane in a tavern near his rooms on Thornnaugh

Street. Sloane sat alone at a rough-hewn wood table, eating stewed partridge, drinking a tankard of ale, and looking like hell.

His bloodshot eyes only momentarily registered surprise before returning to their typical faintly mocking expression. 'Well, Keating. I must say, you are the last man I expected to see.' He added, 'Or wished to.'

'May I sit down?' Guy asked.

Sloane winced. 'Only if you promise not to shout. I have the devil of a headache.'

Guy signalled for the tavern maid to bring him some ale.

'To what do I owe this pleasure?' Sloane said with thick sarcasm.

Guy gave him a level stare. 'You shared some information with me last night. I am ready to discuss it.'

Sloane's brow wrinkled and he stared into his ale. Half a minute passed before the wrinkles cleared and he looked up again. 'Now I recall. Regarding Lady—'

Guy held up his hand. 'Do not say her name, if you please.'

Sloane shrugged. 'Regarding the "Mysterious Miss M".'

Guy gestured for him to be silent as the maid clapped down a tankard of ale in front of Guy and removed Sloane's dishes.

Guy took a sip before speaking. 'What would it take for you to agree to forget that piece of knowledge?'

Sloane's brows shot up. A slow grin came over his face. 'Did I not tell you what it would take? I want you to spread it around Madame Bisou's that you and Lady Widow merely played a private game of cards, and that the terms of the wager have not yet been met.'

Guy kept his eyes steadily on Sloane's as he again lifted the tankard to his lips.

Sloane continued, 'Then I want you to step aside, so I might have a chance with the lady.'

'I cannot do that,' Guy shot back. 'Tell me the stakes of the wager. I will pay you an equal amount.'

Sloane's brows rose again. 'Four thousand six hundred pounds?'

Guy did not move a muscle. 'Done. I will have a banknote in your hands tomorrow.' The amount would severely cut into the reserves he'd invested in the funds. It would strain his finances, and mean more years of pinching pennies so hard they would scream in pain.

Sloane laughed and shook his head, then pressed a finger to his brow with a wince. 'You miss the point, Keating. The money means nothing to me. I aspire to win the bet. Winning the bet is the important thing.'

Guy gave him a look of disgust. 'You would ruin that poor lady's reputation for the sake of a wager?'

'Well.' Sloane shifted in his seat. 'I confess not to have thought much upon that. I meant to induce you to my way of thinking by considering how your wife's reputation would suffer from the association. I thought preserving her good name would be the ticket.'

Guy slammed the tankard down on the table. 'Keep this matter of the wager between you and me. Why bring innocent women into it?'

Sloane leaned back, undaunted. 'Why, to compel you to agree to do what I want.'

Guy twisted halfway around, gripping the back of the chair so hard his knuckles turned white. He did not suppose a right hook to Sloane's face would persuade him to co-operate.

Sloane put on a horrified expression. 'Do not tell me you have developed a *tendre* for our Lady Widow?'

Guy glared at him.

Sloane took a drink and tapped his fingers against the pewter handle. 'Your heart is engaged. Fancy that.'

Guy ignored that statement. He leaned forward, putting his fists on the table. 'The point is, Sloane, why ruin the lady and her family? If you care nothing for her life, think of yourself. You would risk making powerful enemies. I dare say Heronvale's credit in the world exceeds your own.'

'I dare say it does.' Sloane laughed.

'Give me your word you will keep this damning information to yourself and never speak of it to anyone.' Guy looked him directly in the eye. 'I will pay you the money.'

Sloane did not so much as blink.

What would it take to make the man agree? Guy had no desire to challenge him to a duel, but it was beginning to appear that would be the next resort.

Sloane threw up a hand. 'Forget the money. You have more need of it than I.' He rocked back and forth on the hind legs of his chair. 'I'll give you my word, I shall never speak of the Mysterious Miss M.'

Guy peered at him, looking for any signs the man was not serious. He did not discover any. 'Thank you, Sloane.'

'Always felt sorry for her, to tell the truth,' Sloane added, draining the contents of his tankard. 'Didn't like that gulling bastard Farley by half. He got what he deserved.'

Guy signalled to the tavern maid. 'I'll buy you another drink to seal the bargain. What will you have?'

Sloane grimaced. 'Anything but whisky.'

A minute later they lifted two more tankards of ale.

Sloane eyed Guy suspiciously. 'Tell me, Keating. You accepted my word easily enough. Why? Why trust me?'

Guy smiled. 'I've heard you called many things, Sloane, but no man has ever said you do not keep your word.'

'What a shocking lapse.' Sloane took another sip. He put the tankard down and rested his elbows on the table.

A triumphant expression suddenly lit up his face. 'I have it, Keating!' He grinned like a harlequin. 'If you do not agree to deny bedding Lady Widow, I will inform your wife of her existence. How would that suit you?'

Guy laughed. 'Too late, sir.' He took a long swig of his ale. 'My wife already knows all about Lady Widow.'

Emily rode back to Essex Court in the Heronvale carriage. She'd stayed with Madeleine all the afternoon, but contrary to what she'd told Guy, she did not mention Sloane's threat. As soon as her sister's eyes glittered with pleasure upon seeing her, Emily knew he had been right. She could not burden her sister with this worry. Madeleine would be better off never knowing of the potential hazard to her happiness.

She and Madeleine spent a lovely afternoon together, playing with Madeleine's daughter, chatting with the Marchioness, catching up on each other's lives, though their conversations by necessity left much unsaid. Madeleine glossed over her time with Farley, and Emily glossed over her marriage. Nor did she mention Lady Widow.

One more night to wear Lady Widow's mask.

As soon as she entered the townhouse, Bleasby informed her that the Dowager Lady Keating wished to speak with her.

'At your convenience,' Bleasby said.

At her convenience? Was that a nicety Bleasby added? She went first to her room to make herself more pre-

sentable. Before she could finish tidying her hair, there
was a knock at the door. 'Come in,' she said.

Lady Keating entered. She had never visited Emily's
room before. She looked much altered, smaller, paler,
wringing her hands.

'Lady Keating!' Emily exclaimed.

'Am I disturbing you?' her mother-in-law said.

'Not at all.' Emily gestured to a chair. 'Do sit down. I
was on my way to see you.'

The Dowager sat in the faded brocade chair, one of a
pair that provided a nice place for comfortable chats. Emily had never had a use for the chairs before this time.

Her mother-in-law gazed off into the distance, looking
very distracted.

Emily went to her side, crouching down to her level.
'Ma'am?' Emily took her hand. 'Are you feeling unwell?'

Lady Keating's hand was cool to the touch. She
snatched it from Emily's grasp.

'I am not ill.' She took a breath. 'I came to beg you
not send me away. Where would I go? I have no wish to
be alone!'

Emily grasped both of her mother-in-law's hands this
time. She peered directly into the older lady's eyes, forcing her to look at her. 'You will not be sent away. That
is all nonsense.'

The Dowager's lips trembled. 'Guy says—'

Emily squeezed her hands. 'Guy will not send you
away! Now let us stop all this foolishness. We need to be
dressing for dinner soon.'

'I cannot eat a thing,' Lady Keating said dramatically.

Emily stood, giving a little laugh. 'You must regain
your appetite, then. Besides, if you do not appear at dinner, your aunts will worry. You do not wish to cause them
worry, do you?'

Her mother-in-law's eyes narrowed in suspicion, and her expression lost all its drama. 'Why are you being so agreeable to me?'

She had been fooled again, by a different Keating this time. She sighed. 'My lady, I have no wish to be your enemy. Nor do I wish to split your family. These are your decisions, not mine. But make no mistake. I am the lady of the house and I will brook no disrespect.'

The Dowager rose and raised her chin mutinously. Emily, however, did not miss the fleeting look of anxiety in her eyes.

Emily did not know if there was any chance for happiness between her and Guy. But she knew she would never leave her marriage. She would not be traipsing off to some other gaming hell to win money. She would not repeat such a folly.

If she indeed would remain in this household, as she must, she was determined not to be overrun by her mother-in-law.

Emily extended her hand to Lady Keating. 'Let us agree to be friends.'

Lady Keating stared at Emily's hand and lifted her head defiantly. Without a word, she strode past Emily and went out of the door.

Guy hurried in to the townhouse near the dinner hour. He and Sloane had consumed a third round before Guy had realised the time. He rushed to his room to change for dinner, all the time wondering if Emily were here, if her meeting with her sister had been difficult for her.

He tried to think of the best time to see her alone, hoping his good news about Sloane would earn him some credit in her eyes. He would need it if he was to tell her everything.

Unlike the previous night when he'd left Madame Bisou's, he was full of hope. Their afternoon, as difficult and emotional as it had been, had been a moment of unity between them. This night he hoped to strip off all the masks they wore and make love to his wife.

He found her in the parlour, standing by the window gazing into the street, now dark. His mother and her aunts were also present.

She turned her eyes upon him when he walked in. He met them briefly and smiled.

She smiled back.

His heart sang.

But for all that connection he felt with her, the room seemed to crackle with tension. He had forgotten the conversation with his mother that morning. Had his mother made things more difficult for Emily? He swore he would send her off by the morrow if she did not behave with more civility.

He glanced at his mother, who quickly averted her face. His aunts gave him the mildest of greetings and returned to their sewing. How much did they know? He hoped they had not been made a part of this discord.

The silence and tension in the room reminded him of a battlefield after the wounded and dead had been removed. Something of the horror always lingered. He glanced at Emily again and she returned a sympathetic look.

They were still attuned to each other! He nearly laughed with relief. The devil with the rest of them, he was happy to be in union with his wife. He took a step towards her, but, at that moment, Bleasby entered and announced dinner.

Emily walked over to him and took his arm. There was nothing impersonal in her touch. On the contrary, it stirred his senses as much as his hopes and he wished they could dispense with dinner.

He was eager for dessert.

When they were seated and the soup served, his mother said, 'You were gone all day, Guy.'

He glanced up. 'I had errands in town.'

The silence descended again. He ought to throttle his mother, who seemed unrepentant. With all their family had been through with his father and brother, she ought to jump through hoops like the horses at Astley's in order to achieve some measure of peace. The devil with her.

He turned to his wife. 'How was your afternoon, Emily?'

She gave him a meaningful look. 'I took your advice, Guy. I had a lovely afternoon with Lady Devlin.'

She had not told Lady Devlin then? Excellent! That was the best of all possible outcomes.

He smiled at her. 'I am very glad.'

'What d'you mean about Guy's advice?' Aunt Dorrie asked, pointing her soup spoon at Emily.

Guy opened his mouth to answer, but Emily spoke first. 'We walked through the park, and Guy suggested I call upon Lady Devlin.'

'Such a nice family!' sighed Aunt Pip.

Aunt Dorrie gave a huff. 'I should have liked to call upon the Marchioness.'

Emily gave her a kind look. 'Then we shall do so again soon.'

Guy's mother sat stiff and silent during this exchange.

To his surprise, Emily turned to her. 'Lady Keating, the Marchioness bid me to send you her very best regards.'

His mother glanced up. 'Did she?'

She returned to her soup, saying nothing more. Guy bit down on a scold. Rebuking his mother in front of them all would not improve the atmosphere. He'd not risk things worsening, when matters between he and Emily were looking up.

Rogers appeared to remove the soup bowls and to serve the fish. Side dishes were already on the table.

After a few moments, Guy's mother said, 'Emily, the menu you selected this evening is quite well done.'

Guy looked at his mother in great surprise.

Emily, however, seemed to take the comment as entirely natural. 'Thank you, ma'am,' she responded in a mild voice. 'I value your good opinion.'

Guy watched his mother favour Emily with a relieved, even apologetic smile. Guy felt like bursting into a triumphant song.

'Do we have any engagements tonight, Lady Keating?' Emily went on pleasantly.

'No,' his mother replied. 'The entertainments are getting rather thin. I expect many have returned to the country.'

Emily added, 'Have you read such announcements in the papers? There do seem to be many.'

Aunt Pip and Aunt Dorrie joined in the conversation, each declaring who they knew to be in town and who to be gone. Guy merely stared in wonder.

And in pride. Whatever had happened, he was proud of them all, conversing like one contented family. Just when he thought things couldn't be happier, something better transpired.

The good humour continued throughout the evening. Guy was loathe to interrupt it to request a private conference with his wife. He would wait until they all retired. He fancied, after all, talking with his wife in the solitude of her room, where they might be private, where they might go on as husband and wife.

She retired early, confessing to great fatigue. His mother and her aunts had insisted upon playing whist, and he was roped in to be the fourth partner. They were almost finished the rubber and he could beg off after that very comfortably.

The evening was still relatively young when he ascended the stairs. He would catch her before she gave any thought to dressing as Lady Widow.

He entered his own bedchamber and went quickly to the connecting door. Giving only one knock, he opened the door.

Emily's maid gave a shriek like before and dropped the dress she'd had in her hands. The girl was alone.

'Where is she?' Guy demanded.

She had never left the house so early. Surely she knew he wished to see her? Had he not sent enough messages with his inability to keep his eyes off her?

'I…I cannot…' stammered the girl.

'You can and must tell me,' Guy said, advancing on her.

He could not help his anger, it burned within him, trying to incinerate any hopes she'd gone to Madame Bisou's for a repeat of their night together. He tried desperately to cling to that slim, nearly ashen hope.

The maid took tiny steps away from him. 'I cannot.'

He backed her against a wall. 'You do not have to keep your lady's confidence,' he insisted, his voice firm and fierce. 'I know she goes to the gaming hell at night. I know she dresses in silks and wears a mask. Has she gone there early this night?'

The maid, eyes very wide, nodded.

Guy turned on his heel and stormed back into his room. Grabbing his topcoat and hat, he rushed down the stairs past a surprised Rogers, and out of the door.

Chapter Eighteen

Emily sat in the hackney coach as it clattered its way to Bennett Street. The risks she had taken before paled in comparison to this one. If Guy discovered her gone, what would he think? How would she ever explain?

She must meet Sloane. Once her sister was safe all her attention could turn to her marriage. And she would pray it would not be too late.

One worry teased her, but she tried to brush it away. What if Guy came looking for Lady Widow this night? What if his desire for Lady Widow had been more than to win a wager?

The idea made blood race through her veins, but it brought no comfort.

She hoped to arrive early enough at Madame Bisou's to catch Cyprian Sloane alone. Once involved in a card game, he might never speak with her. She must see Sloane tonight. After tonight, she would pack up her fine gowns and never appear as Lady Widow again. Her dress, the green silk she'd worn the first night she'd come to this place, seemed to chafe her skin, and the mask made her face so hot she wanted to rip it off.

Once she secured Sloane's promise not to divulge Madeleine's secret, she would run back to the hack and head home where she would try her best to build a life with Guy. To face whatever met her there.

Hester's brother dropped her off at the Bennett Street address. She knocked on Madame Bisou's door. It opened immediately. If Cummings was surprised to see her at this hour, he made no sign of it.

'Is Mr Sloane here tonight?' she asked.

'Not yet, ma'am,' Cummings replied.

'Be so good as to tell him I wish to see him.' Emily handed him her cloak.

'You wish to see Mr Sloane?' he repeated, with just a hint of curiosity in his deep voice.

'Yes,' she replied. 'I shall wait in the supper room.'

The first person she encountered was Sir Reginald. His hand leapt to his cheek, which still bore a red mark from where she had slapped it. 'Good evening, ma'am,' he mumbled, giving her a quick bow and a wide berth.

She refused to feel guilty for striking him. He had wagered for her and propositioned her as well. How would she ever act if again compelled to meet him as her mother-in-law's friend?

She peeked into the card room merely to assure herself Cummings had not been mistaken about Sloane. Her eyes swept the room. She jumped back out of sight.

Her brother Robert was wandering around the card tables, headed for the faro bank. Was he here looking for her? She certainly did not wish to see him.

At least Madame Bisou will be in transports, she thought wryly. She fled to the supper room, selecting a table as far out of sight as possible, but still affording a view of the doorway.

After a mere five minutes, Sloane sauntered in and scanned the room. When he saw her tucked away in her corner, he flashed his most charming smile and strode up to her.

'You wished to see me, Lady Widow.' He bowed, making the formality look ironic.

'I wish a private conference with you,' she said.

Interest kindled in his eyes. 'I am honoured to oblige,' he said. 'May I suggest one of the private rooms?'

Go into a private room with Sloane? She glanced away. Gentlemen walked in and out of this room. Serving maids brought them drinks. Someone might overhear them if they remained here.

She bit her lip. Stories of Sloane's conquests had abounded in Bath. It was said he had no scruples where women were concerned. Alone in a room with him, anything might happen, but what other choice did she have?

She lifted her chin, adopting Lady Widow's confident attitude. 'Very well, sir.'

He grinned. 'Let me attend to the arrangements.'

Sloane rushed out of the supper room, barely able to assimilate this unexpected turn of events.

He caught one of Madame Bisou's girls in the hallway. 'Procure me a private room and a bottle of your best champagne.'

She curtsied.

'Be quick about it,' he demanded.

She scampered away.

'Sir Reginald,' he cried, entering the card room. 'I have a wager to propose.'

Several gentlemen nearly knocked Sir Reginald aside as they hurried to Sloane's side and called for the betting book.

'One hundred pounds says I steal Lady Widow from Keating and remove her mask,' Sloane announced to the gathered throng. He had no difficulty finding takers, though he was a wee bit dismayed the odds were running against him succeeding.

More sweet the victory, he assured himself.

The girl returned with a room key, and Sloane left the men still arguing stakes back and forth. As he swiftly returned to the supper room, he caught Lady Widow looking unusually pensive. Well, if she were pining for Keating, he'd soon make her forget. Perhaps she was contemplating a comparison? If so, Sloane was determined to come out the winner.

He offered his arm, but she seemed not to notice. With a quick step, she ascended the stairs ahead of him. At the landing she tapped her foot impatiently until he caught up.

He opened the door of the room, extending his arm with a flourish to allow her to walk in first. He turned to lock it, but she said, 'I will take the key, please.'

His brows lifted, but he tossed it to her. What did he care if the door were locked or not?

She caught it and dropped it tantalisingly down between her breasts. *I'll retrieve that key later*, he thought smugly to himself.

She glanced at the bed in the corner of the room and, in a determined manner, turned her back upon it.

The champagne sat on the card table in the centre of the room. Sloane poured two glasses, handing one to her.

She took the glass, but placed it back on the table.

Did she wish to get right at it? Such eagerness. His luck was running high this night. He'd collect the winnings in no time at all. He took a step towards her.

She held up her hand, blocking his approach. 'I wish to speak with you, Mr Sloane.'

Not so lucky, perhaps. He sighed. Who would have

guessed she was the sort of female who demanded conversation first.

He folded his arms across his chest and attempted to look as if he had all the time in the world. 'I am your servant.'

She toyed with the stem of her glass, but did not pick it up. 'I will not mince words, sir,' she said finally.

Good! he thought.

She looked him directly in the eye. 'You have knowledge that could ruin Lady Devlin Steele. What will it take to induce you never to speak of it to anyone?'

He rolled his eyes. Not again.

He certainly had not expected this from Lady Widow. How many people knew this damned secret of his? Had Keating told her? If he had, it must have been after he'd left Sloane.

He tapped his fingers on his folded arms. Keating knew who she was! If Keating told her, he'd told her outside Madame Bisou's! Damnation.

'Well?' she asked, though her haughty voice quavered a bit.

Sloane peered at her through narrowed eyes. More had been going on with Lady Widow than he'd realised. This smacked of a mystery, and he hated mysteries. Much better to know all the answers. Unmasking her and revealing who she was would have been a particular treat. Second only to winning the wager, that was, but Keating had even ruined that moment. Blast the man!

One thing was certain. He would learn nothing if he scared her away. He'd play along with this game of hers. He gave her an engaging smile. 'I confess, I am astonished you possess this knowledge. I told only one person.'

She stood her ground, but her fingers left the glass and braced themselves against the table instead. 'Do not con-

cern yourself with how I came about my information. Answer my question. What do you want for your silence?'

Oh, what a card to open with! The game was surely to
be his if she played so recklessly.

He walked towards her, slowly, like a cat fooling its
prey into thinking it posed no threat. When she threw up
her hand again, he caught it in his and advanced so close
his body brushed against hers.

'Lie down with me,' he whispered. 'Let me show you
what delights I can offer, then let me peel that mask from
your face and—'

'No,' she said, in a voice not unlike one of his old
school masters. 'That is not acceptable.'

He was taken aback. She stepped away from his grasp
and put a chair between them.

'Not acceptable?' His powers of seduction must have
become rusty. From lack of use, no doubt.

'Such terms are not to be contemplated. I do have
money, however. How much to pay for your silence?'

He felt as if he were dreaming the same bad dream
twice in one day. 'Four thousand six hundred pounds,' he
said in a resigned voice.

She gasped. 'I…I can offer you three thousand.'

If he estimated correctly, that would be about the
amount she'd won at whist these past weeks, the amount
her foolish suitors threw her way. She was making a
sucker bet to wager all her money on one card.

He cocked his head. 'What is my silence to you, Lady
Widow? Do you know Lady Devlin?'

She blinked rapidly, glancing away. Finally she said,
'Yes, I do know her. It would do great harm for her past
to be public knowledge. It would be cruel in the extreme.'

'Which makes it information of value,' he added.

She looked at him hopefully. 'Will you accept the three thousand pounds?'

He stared at her, rubbing his chin.

Her confidence seemed to ebb. She nervously reached under the netting of her cap and adjusted her mask. The light from the lamp hanging above the table illuminated her face. He studied it.

It would make sense if she were Lady Devlin, but the hair colour was wrong. Lady Widow was taller and smaller-breasted, besides. But who the devil was she?

She seemed familiar, though that notion had never struck him before. That anxious look in her eye, that nervous gesture. Where had he seen her before?

She faced him again. 'You have not answered me.'

He walked a few steps to the side, examining her from another angle. He'd never really studied Lady Widow, he realised. He'd merely accepted her as a whole, delighting in a mystery yet to be solved.

He knew her. He just couldn't place…

She cleared her throat. 'Lord Keating told me you knew of Lady Devlin's past. It was kind of him to tell me, so I could try to make you see reason. To give your word—'

'My word?' Zeus. Where the devil had he gone wrong? It seemed the whole world believed he'd honour something as elusive as his word. He would, of course, but it rankled that it was so widely known.

'You know Lord Keating outside this place,' he stated, more as fact than question.

She did not reply, but she remained as motionless as a statue. He took a long sip of his champagne, watching her all the time.

Suddenly, he saw her. By God, it was so obvious he'd been a fool not to have recognised her right away! Did Keating know?

Of course, he did! It was all Sloane could do to keep from laughing. Keating had told him. His wife knew all about Lady Widow. Another mark on Keating's score-card.

'I…I know Lord Keating from here,' she said feebly. 'Nowhere else. But that has nothing to do with—'

He could not help interrupting. 'Surely you know him in the biblical sense, my lady.' *She's his damned wife!* He laughed to himself.

She glared at him and amazingly turned back into Lady Widow. 'Do not speak so crudely in my presence.'

'I beg your pardon.'

Oh, this is fun, he thought. He just hoped Keating did not show up and catch him with his wife. Sloane had no fancy for pistols at dawn. Besides, he'd started to like Keating.

'Tell me,' he said as casually as he could muster under the circumstances, 'does Keating know who you are?'

'He does not,' she said sharply and rather convincingly, Sloane thought. 'I have no intention of revealing who I am.'

He stifled another laugh. Difficult because this was too amusing. Her husband knew, but she did not know he knew. Delightful!

'Will you accept my money or not?' she demanded.

He waved a hand at her dismissively and dropped into a chair. 'The amount is but a trifle, and, I assure you, I do not need it.'

'I will not bed you,' she said.

Yes, that was certainly out of the question now, was it not? Another wager consigned to the dust heap.

'Then we are at a complete standstill,' he said, waiting to see what she would do next.

Her eyes bore into him, pained and fearful, like an animal caught in a trap. It made him consider abandoning the game.

She straightened her spine and her expression turned flirtatious. Good. She had recovered her bravado.

'But you are a gamester, are you not, sir?' She fluttered her eyelashes at him. 'Certainly you would not refuse the challenge of a game of cards?' She shoved the deck of cards towards him.

She certainly has my number, he thought. 'What stakes?'

She lifted her chin. 'If I win, I win your silence on Lady Devlin's behalf.'

Ha! She obviously did not know that prize had been secured earlier. Far be it from him to tell her and spoil the fun.

'And if I win?' he asked. What could she offer besides her body? And that was out of the question now as well.

'I shall remove my mask.'

He grinned. 'Name your game, Lady Widow.'

Guy pounded on Madame Bisou's door, his anger increased by winding up in the slowest hack in all of London. Cummings opened the door.

'Where is Lady Widow?' Guy demanded, thrusting his coat and hat into the man's arms.

'Supper room, last I knew of,' Cummings said.

Guy took the stairs two at a time. She was not in the supper room, he discovered. He hurried to the gaming room.

From the doorway, his eyes swept the room. She was not there. He looked again, more slowly and carefully. His gaze focused on one gentleman.

Robert Duprey hopped back with a shriek when he saw

Guy advancing upon him. There was no escape for him, however.

Guy grabbed him by the sleeve. 'I would speak with you, Duprey.' He nearly dragged Duprey out into the hall.

'Please, Keating...my coat...' Robert pleaded.

'Hang your coat,' Guy said. 'Where is Emily?'

'Em...Em...Emily?' he stuttered.

Guy grabbed the lapels of the young man's superfine garment and backed him into an alcove. 'Cut line, Duprey,' he spat. 'I know you are behind this Lady Widow business of hers. I ought to call you out.'

Robert struggled feebly. 'Oh, no! Not a duelling man. Not good at it at all.'

Guy shoved him against the wall and came within an inch of his face. 'Then why did you bring her here, you fool!'

'Made me do it,' shrieked Robert, his voice rising more than an octave. 'Forced me!'

'Emily?' Guy gave a dry laugh. 'My bet is you put her up to this charade and I demand to know why!' Guy let go of him with another shove and stepped back, waiting for Duprey's answer.

Robert cowered. 'Said...said she wanted money.'

Guy leaned menacingly towards him again. The young man raised his arms to protect his collar and neckcloth.

'Why did she need money,' Guy demanded. 'For gambling?'

'Y...yes,' stammered Robert. 'Fool plan, I told her. Couldn't win enough, I said. All of it yours anyway.'

'Explain yourself, man,' Guy said, again reaching for Duprey's lapels.

Robert tried desperately to protect his coat. 'Planned to leave you, she said,' he wailed. 'Told her it was not the thing!'

Guy dropped his hands. 'Leave me?'

Robert nodded vigorously. 'Said she'd buy a cottage where you'd never find her.'

The air filled with the pungent odour of too many hot-house flowers.

'There you are, *chéri*!' Madame Bisou's perfume had preceded her as she flounced in Robert's direction.

A relieved look came over the young man's face. Guy stepped away from him.

'I have pined for this moment,' Madame said, throwing her arms around his neck and crushing his coat and neck-cloth with her embrace. 'You will have time for me, no?'

'Y…yes.' Robert cast a wary glance at Guy. 'N…now if you wish.'

'I do wish.' She nuzzled his neck and pulled him towards the stairway.

Guy remained frozen. Emily had become Lady Widow in order to leave him. He ran a ragged hand through his hair, trying to reconcile the sweet, compliant, eager-to-please Emily with a woman plotting her escape. From him.

He could not blame her, to be truthful. It had been reprehensible of him to trick her into marriage in the first place, then to all but ignore her in his single-minded quest for money. But this day had offered hope for them, had it not?

He wandered absently to the doorway of the card room. The Duke's son nearly collided with him.

'The odds are three to one in your favour, Keating,' the man said excitedly. 'Have you placed your bet?'

'In my favour? What the devil are you talking about?' Guy asked.

The Duke's son smirked. 'Sloane proposed the terms. I suppose he did not like losing the other wager. The odds are three to one he will fail to win Lady Widow from you.'

'What?'

The man continued, 'But he's closed up with her in a room at this moment, so there's some chance the odds will change—'

Guy did not wait to hear the rest. He ran up the stairs, pounding on two locked doors, and receiving shouts from unfamiliar voices.

What did she think she was doing? Who was this woman that she could bed one man one night and another the next? Then it struck him. She was seeking Sloane's silence. Would she do so with her body?

The third door was unlocked. He did not bother to knock, but burst into the room. He saw the champagne. He saw the cards. He saw Lady Widow and Sloane seated at the table, each with a fan of cards in their hands. They were, he was relieved to see, fully dressed.

'Guy!' cried Lady Widow.

'Damn,' cursed Sloane.

'What goes on here?' Guy demanded.

Emily felt the air sucked from her lungs. Her legs trembled beneath the table. Her vision blurred.

He had come in search of Lady Widow after all. She could not speak.

Sloane answered him, his voice casual. 'Why, this is a friendly game of cards, Keating. A private one.'

'The devil it is,' Guy growled. 'I hear otherwise below stairs.'

The room grew dark and the men's voices echoed through her head. Emily fought the impulse to faint. She pressed her fingers to her temple. Of course, he would presume Sloane brought her here for seduction, would he not? The jealous rage inside him was palpable. Even a gamester did not feel so passionately about a wager already won. His attachment had been to Lady Widow all along.

Where did that leave her? *Where does that leave Madeleine?* she thought in a panic. How was she to win Sloane's silence now? She must keep her wits about her. She needed to win the card game. After this, Lady Widow would never return.

Would Lady Widow linger in her husband's memory? she wondered. Would she always stand between Guy and his wife? No. She mentally shook herself. She must think of Madeleine.

Forcing herself to stiffen her spine, she said, 'I resent your insinuation, sir!' Her voice was Lady Widow's. 'This is a private game of cards, and I ask you to leave.'

She could feel the rage flaming inside him, putting more colour in his face, more sparks in his eyes.

He strode over to the table and picked up her nearly empty champagne glass, lifting it to the light, then sweeping his eyes over her. 'Is it indeed a mere card game, ma'am? It must have just commenced, for I see you are completely dressed.'

Emily's cheeks grew hot. 'You wrong me, sir,' she murmured.

Sloane broke in, losing only a tad of his composure. 'I don't have a jot of an idea of what you two are talking about, Keating, but, I assure you, cards were the only game played in this room.'

'Do not take me for a fool,' said Guy, his voice like a sharp-edged sword. He did not take his eyes off Emily.

'Alas, it is true.' Sloane stood, adding, 'I give you my word.'

Guy shot him a look.

'Tell you what. You play out my hand. Lady Widow

may explain the stakes. Tell me later who won. I'll honour my part, my word on that, too.' Sloane ambled towards the door. 'I must go below stairs. I suspect there are considerable debts to settle.'

He gave an exaggerated sigh. With an equally dramatic bow, he fled the room.

All was not lost, Emily realised. To save her sister all she need do was win the game with Guy.

If she failed, however, she must remove her mask and he would see who really played tricks with him.

'We ought to replay this hand,' she said, feigning a casual tone so unlike the emotions churning within her. She collected the cards and shuffled them. 'It is your deal.'

Guy grabbed Sloane's chair and sat in it. When she finished shuffling, she handed him the cards.

'What game?' he asked gruffly.

'Piquet,' she replied.

He stared at her for at least half a minute before he spoke. 'What are the stakes?'

She met his eye. 'I shall tell you when we have finished.'

He dealt the cards.

Chapter Nineteen

The atmosphere was like in a dream, looking real but unreal at the same time. Sound echoed as if far away. Light seemed excessively bright. Guy felt as if he were in a dream, acting as if it all was perfectly ordinary, sitting across the table from the alluring creature who was his wife and who likely had been prepared to bed another man.

'What is the score?' he asked.

She answered in a voice without emotion. 'The first partie was mine by one hundred seventeen points. This is the first deal of the second.'

'Do you play for points?' he asked, in like tone.

'The most points after the third partie,' she said.

Guy sorted his hand, estimating what was likely in hers. He chose his play ruthlessly, his anger intensifying concentration, wresting every possible trick from his hand. He did not speak and neither did she, except to make their declarations and responses, call out their points.

The anger boiled inside him with every play of every card, though he was not certain which fuelled it the most. Sloane for trying to bed his wife? Emily for risking her virtue? Plotting to leave him? Or was he angered against himself for letting matters reach this moment, when he might have put a stop to them that first night?

At the end of six hands, he won easily. Guy burned to win the third partie, to discover if he were correct in what he feared she offered Sloane. She would be playing to win Sloane's silence about her sister's past, that was obvious, but had she wagered what he feared?

He dealt the cards. Damn Sloane for accepting her challenge when the man had already given his word to Guy. Perhaps Sloane was no better than his reputation suggested, placing a new wager in Madame Bisou's betting book. Sloane had lost the first bet about Lady Widow. Guy had no notion that the man would create a second one—the seduction of Guy's wife.

But Sloane did not know Lady Widow was Emily, did he? He thought the two of them were competing for a woman who frequented a gaming hell and toyed with its patrons. Lady Widow dangled the gentlemen from her fingers like puppets in a Punch and Judy show. She'd not improved Sloane's perception of her when she played her private game of cards with Guy. If Sloane believed she'd bedded one man, why not another?

She exchanged five cards. He exchanged three.

No, he, Guy, was not innocent in this situation. Plenty of blame could be laid directly at his door.

He'd fallen under her spell as well, even knowing she was his wife. He had not refused her lovemaking. On the contrary, he had revelled in every moment of it.

She led an ace of hearts.

They called out their points as she took several tricks, he others. At the end, the round went to her.

He glanced up at her. She breathed a long sigh of relief, not at all like the gambler he knew she could be. The lines of tension at the corners of her mouth eased slightly.

He shuffled the cards.

She sat stiffly in her chair, gazing down at the table, avoiding looking at him, he suspected. This was nothing like the playful, erotic game of piquet they had played the night before. Even though she wore the gown, the hat and the mask of Lady Widow, this was the woman he had met in Bath, the one who sat across from him at the breakfast table, the one who faded from one's sight, who hid behind her mask of mediocrity. All liveliness gone. All charm vanished.

Only now he knew what events had forged her need to disappear from everyone's notice. If she'd given her parents any reason to consider her value, she might have risked being sold as they sold her sister.

A muscle in Guy's cheek twitched. Her father had sold Emily, in a way, by inventing a way to use her for collateral. Guy had fallen for the ruse, because he'd sought to use her as well.

His anger ebbed suddenly, but was replaced by a tide of remorse. If he had been thinking of anything but his crippling debts he might have recognised how out of character it had been for the colourless, all-too-proper Emily to agree to an elopement. The desperation to escape her parents must have been intense indeed for her to take a chance marrying him.

What had he offered her in return? He was her husband, the man who ought to have cosseted her and protected her. What neglect of his caused her to risk everything at Madame Bisou's?

He passed her the cards.

Emily reached for the deck, her hand brushing her husband's. The touch jolted her as much as if a spark of static electricity had jumped between them. Her eyes flew to his, but she quickly looked back to the cards, getting ready to deal.

She would rather have studied him, drinking in every feature, every nuance of feeling revealed in his face. She longed to see his lips widen into a smile, lighting up his eyes with happiness, but this was impossible. He was lost to her, as surely as this card game would ultimately be lost. Luck had long abandoned her.

Blinking back tears she realised three good hands might give her an edge. The point spread after the first two parties was only slightly in Guy's favour, but he was playing his cards with uncanny skill. The gamester in her marvelled at it.

She tried to steel herself for the loss, though what could be worse than failing her sister and removing her mask in front of him? The thought of unlacing the silk covering her face, peeling it from her sweat-dampened brow, and seeing Guy's shocked expression when she revealed herself, made her stomach roil with nausea.

If luck returned, she might win, but that hope seemed suspended on a very thin thread. Even if she won, she must invent a reason for gambling on the fate of Lady Devlin Steele. How would she explain to Guy why Lady Widow would care about Emily's sister? Or how Lady Widow had been informed of the threat to Lady Devlin's reputation? No matter what happened, she would lose.

The deepest ache, like heavy metal scraping her insides, was the knowledge that his regard truly belonged to Lady Widow. Why else be so furious at finding Lady Widow with another man?

She glanced up while he pulled out cards to exchange. How foolish a woman's heart could be! Once she'd been so eager to leave him. Now, even knowing he loved an illusion, she knew she would stay. She would run his house for him. She would economise when his gambling brought losses and debt. She would endure a thousand cuts to her heart if it meant being with him.

He'd shown her he was the man she'd hoped he would be, a good man, a man she could depend upon, no matter his love of gambling. She remembered his arms around her earlier that day when she so desperately needed his strength. He might never love her like Lady Widow, but perhaps they could find their way to become friends. If she could just last through this one final card game.

Her exchange was reasonably successful, adding a third ace to her hand. If she could just guess in what order he would throw his cards, she might have a chance to earn good points.

In the previous rounds, he had worked out what cards she held and in what order she would play them. In this round, however, that talent appeared to fail him and she beat him by twenty points. Like withered flowers greeted by rain, her hopes revived. She forced herself to clear her mind of everything but the cards.

Three more hands.

She won again. And again! It was down to the last round. He dealt and they exchanged their cards. She declared her points and her score climbed. She won trick after trick, until her score reached thirty.

'Pique,' she said, the word catching in her throat. Her points doubled to sixty, and her heart pounded in her chest. She had won.

They played out the rest of the cards, but she already knew she'd amassed the points she needed. Her whole body trembled with relief. Her sister was safe! And she would not have to remove her mask.

'Congratulations, Lady Widow,' he said as he lay down

his last losing card. There was an odd, melancholy expression in his voice.

It took her several seconds before she could breathe in enough air to speak. 'You…you wished to be told the stakes.' Like a good gamester, she would fulfil her part of the bargain, knowing it meant more explanation than she knew how to make.

He stacked the cards neatly and stood. 'Since I lost, it is not necessary. Unless something is required of me?'

Another reprieve? She rose, too, but did not dare take a step towards him. 'Nothing is required of you.'

She could barely make her legs hold her upright. Having prepared herself for the worst, she could not conceive of escaping all of it. All she wanted now was to leave this place posthaste and never return.

She looked at her husband, who seemed as immobilised as she. 'Would you inform Sloane for me? Tell him that I won? It is he who must keep the bargain with me.'

'You do not wish to tell him yourself?' He returned her gaze with pain in his eyes.

She felt the pain reflected in her own body. He would still be thinking Lady Widow wagered her body, that she had been willing to lie down with another man.

A knife twisted inside her. In the morning she would wake up alone in her bed, knowing he lay in the room connected to hers wishing he could be with Lady Widow. He would not know Lady Widow was about to disappear forever. He would not even realise Lady Widow had been faithful to him.

She raised her eyes to him one more time. 'I have had enough of cards for one night.'

He looked resigned. 'I will inform Sloane of your win.' He headed towards the door, placed his hand on the knob.

She could at least spare him the pain of believing Lady Widow had betrayed him. 'Lord Keating?'

He stopped and turned back to her.

'I would have removed my mask. If Sloane had won, that is what I offered him. That is all I offered him.'

He stared at her a long time, his eyes unfathomable. Then he opened the door and walked out.

Emily waited until he would have had time to reach the floor below. She hurried out of the room and down the stairs, hoping to avoid notice. From the stairway she heard the hum of voices. As she passed the door to the supper room, she spied her brother, seated with Madame Bisou, holding that woman's hand, looking as relaxed and carefree as he'd been as a boy playing tricks on his sisters. She walked past the game room, where she glimpsed Guy leaning over Sloane, seated at a card table with Sir Reginald and two of the others. With the cards to distract them, she supposed that, in the space of a fortnight, none of the gentlemen would even recall Lady Widow.

Except perhaps her husband. Would he pine for Lady Widow? When he regarded his colourless wife, would he wish for the charm of Lady Widow?

She hurried down the stairs to the hall, retrieving her cloak from Cummings and fleeing out into the night to where her hack awaited her. As soon as she was inside, she pulled off her cap and mask.

In no time she was home, let in the house by a waiting Hester, and soon back in her bedchamber.

She could not wait to remove the green silk dress. Hester could pack the dress and cap away in the trunk, and Emily would never open it again. Perhaps she could ask Hester to sell the clothes on Petticoat Lane and keep the profits. As soon as the maid left the room, Emily would throw the mask into the fireplace and watch it burn to ashes.

Emily took the pins from her hair, letting it tumble to her shoulders. She held her hair aside as Hester unbuttoned the dress. Hester pulled it over her head and she was free of it.

As Hester held the gown in her arms, the door connecting her room to her husband's opened.

Her husband stood silhouetted in the doorway.

'Hester,' he said in a mild tone, 'be so good as to leave. I wish to speak with Lady Keating alone.'

Hester gave a quick curtsy, dropped the gown on the floor, and ran out of the room.

Emily, dressed only in her corset and shift, stood awaiting him, sick at heart, but almost relieved at the same time. She'd had enough of masks. When he asked her where she had been, she would tell him everything, no matter what.

But he did not ask her where she had been. He walked up to her and handed her a paper. In the candlelight, she could barely make out that it was a banknote made out to her, allowing her to withdraw a huge sum from his accounts.

'What is this?' she asked.

He looked so much like he had in that private room at Madame Bisou's, but also so different. So sad, so determined.

'Your freedom,' he replied.

She examined it again and glanced back at him. 'I do not understand.'

His eyes flicked over her undressed state, but she did not have the presence of mind to reach for her nearby shawl. He finally gazed directly into her face, but did not answer her. At last it dawned on her.

'Do you wish me to leave?' She could barely hear herself, her words came out so softly.

'Is that not what you wish, Emily?'

'No, I—' Once she had wanted nothing more than to escape him, but everything had changed.

With a grim expression he reached over and took the banknote from her hand, placing it on her dressing table. 'Come,' he said. 'Let us talk.'

He led her to the set of chairs her mother-in-law had used earlier in the day. It seemed a lifetime ago.

Emily had draped her paisley shawl over one of them. She wrapped it around herself before she sat down.

'First,' he began, 'I know everything. I've known most of it from the beginning, from the first time I walked in to Madame Bisou's.'

Her mind tried to take this in, while her heart thudded painfully in her chest. 'You knew?'

'I recognised you almost immediately—'

'You knew!' It was not possible. When he had gazed upon Lady Widow with such desire in his eyes, he knew she was Emily? When she peeled her clothes off for him, he knew? When he made love to her, he knew he made love to his wife?

'Yes,' he said quickly. 'And I do not expect your forgiveness for not letting on until now.'

Her forgiveness? Was it not the other way around?

His words came out in a rush. 'I did not know until tonight why you came to Madame Bisou's. I thought it was for love of gambling. I feared it was…for other interests, as well. Tonight I discovered you were desirous of money—'

'Robert.' Robert must have spilled everything.

'Yes,' he admitted. 'I saw Robert. I was rather harsh with him, I'm afraid, but he told me you masqueraded as

Lady Widow to win enough money to...' he paused and took a breath '...to leave me.'

A dam of pain broke inside her.

'I have the money to free you,' he said.

He wished her to go! Of course. She'd shamed him, seduced him at Madame Bisou's as though she were as common as one of the girls employed there. If it ever became known that Lady Widow was in fact Lady Keating—

'You need not return to Madame Bisou's. In fact, I wish very much for you not to return to that establishment or any like it. It is too dangerous.'

Would he believe she had already decided not to return? Never to be Lady Widow again? 'I—' she began.

He held up his hand. 'No, let me finish.' He shook his head. 'I wronged you from the start, Emily. I deceived you so often, but I have no wish for more secrets between us. Do not think I have not seen how good you have been to me and my family. I do not know what I would have done without you, if I'd had to concern myself with my mother, her aunts or the household. You were better to me than I deserved.'

He had valued her all this time? Noticed her efforts to care for his family? Why did that not please her? She wanted more from him. She wanted what she'd had as Lady Widow.

Heart bleeding, she touched his arm. 'No, please, do not say—'

His eyes flashed. 'I am not finished.' He glanced down to where her hand rested on his arm. His other hand reached over and grazed hers, but she was uncertain if he meant to remove her hand or hold it there in place.

He looked back at her and continued, 'I do not blame you for wanting to be rid of me and my family.'

Be *rid* of him! She opened her mouth to protest.

'We do not deserve you,' he carried on, apparently willing to send her away with at least some pride salvaged. 'But you must not take any risks. I can pay for your freedom now. I have enough money.'

The money he won at gambling, no doubt, but she would never forgive herself if she accepted his money and later learned he was in terrible debt.

'No, Guy, you must save the money,' she spoke earnestly. 'Do you not realise you will have a streak of losing some day? You must always keep money in reserve. If you wish, I will hold the money for you, so you cannot put your hands on it to gamble away.'

He looked puzzled now. 'Gamble it away? Do you think I would keep the money to gamble it?'

She grasped his hand and held it tight. 'Oh, you would not plan to, I am sure, but I know about this, Guy. From my father. When gaming takes hold, a gentleman will risk everything. Please let me stay with you. I can help you. I know I can.'

He gave a dry laugh. 'You would stay under such circumstances?'

His laugh wounded her, but he must be made to see she could help him. 'Yes. I know you are not like my father, but the gambling is so very hard to resist.'

He gave her a cynical look. 'Gambling is hard for you to resist as well, no doubt.'

She felt her cheeks go hot. 'I cannot deny I like a good card game, but I am content with private ones. I have no wish to enter another gaming hell in my life.'

Guy peered into her eyes, looking so full of resolution. Her hand was warm, clutching his so tightly it was almost painful. She continued to believe him a gambler, but was willing to stay with him? She'd conceded he was not like her father, but believed him enough like that disreputable man to require her help? What a model for comparison. In his single-minded quest to save his family and Anner-ley—and her—he had never thought how his gambling might have appeared to her.

He dropped to his knees in front of her, taking both her hands in his, making her look at him. 'I am not like your father, Emily, and I am not like my father, or my brother. I…I do not claim to be immune to the lure of cards, but I swear to you, I only played to win enough money to keep us all from the poorhouse.'

'The poorhouse?' She blinked down at him.

He blew out an embarrassed breath. 'Another secret I kept from you. From everyone. When I inherited, there was nothing left but debt. Not a feather to fly with. The estate was in ruins, its people near starvation. My mother, my great-aunts, my sister—and, then, you—how was I to feed all of you?'

She gave him an intent look. 'That is why you married me, when you thought I had money?'

'Yes. For the money, I admit.' He squeezed her hands. 'I panicked when you told me there was no money.'

'So you gambled?'

'I needed a great deal of money and I needed it as quickly as possible. I could think of nothing else to do.'

He let go of her hands and stood, moving back to the chair and collapsing in it. 'What a mess,' he muttered. 'What a mess I've created.'

She sat very still. He shot a glance at her, wondering what thoughts ran through her mind. Forgiving him would not be among them. 'I am sorry,' he said in a tired, hope-less voice.

'How much did you win?' she asked.

'Above one hundred and fifty thousand pounds,' he said.

She gasped. 'Above one hundred…' Her voice caught.

'Take or leave a little. I've got an accounting. Much of it has been sent to Annerley, and all the debts I could discover have been paid. The bulk of the rest are in the funds.'

'Above one hundred…' she said again.

He could not bear to look at her. Could bear even less that she deserved to walk out of his life. 'So you see, I can well afford for you to live handsomely. There is no reason to be trapped here with me.'

Once more she fell silent. For so long, he started to squirm, feet and hands refusing to keep still.

When she glanced up, she returned his gaze with the blank expression he'd seen so often. 'I assure you, sir, I would be comfortable with half the sum on the paper. When do you require me to leave?'

Guy shot to his feet. How had he caused her withdrawal? He wanted never again to see that retreat in her eyes. He leaned over her. 'I do not require you to leave, Emily.'

Before he walked in this room, he'd been intent on giving up the game, as he had given up winning Sloane's game of piquet with her. He had decided to throw in his cards and let her go without taking any further risks, telling himself he was being honourable, not cowardly. But suddenly, he needed to play this game to the end. To give it his all. If he lost after doing so, the pain might be worse, but she was worth this one last wager. It was worth everything to bring her back to life.

He kept his gaze steady. 'I do not wish you to leave. I want you to stay, Emily. I want a chance to make something of our marriage, but I will not force you to stay.

You must decide what you want. You. Not what you should or should not do. Not what is required of you. Not what *I* want.' His voice cracked, but he forced himself to finish. 'What *you* want.'

She glanced away, but he took her chin in his fingers and forced her to look at him again. 'What you want, Emily.'

He had not known he could risk more than Annerley. These stakes seemed higher than that for which he'd braved the gaming tables. He risked his heart. Their future.

He let go of her and stepped away. 'You do not need to decide now,' he said. 'You have the banknote if you choose to use it. I will leave you to your sleep and perhaps…perhaps we may talk more in the morning.'

She remained in her chair. After a moment she nodded slightly. He walked to the door.

'Guy?' Her voice halted him. 'You wagered on bedding me, did you not? They all did.' Her voice trembled, but at least there was some emotion in it.

He turned around to her. 'Not I, Emily. Good God! I knew you were my wife. That wager was abominable to me.'

She blinked at him. 'You did not bet on me?'

He shook his head.

'The gentlemen who did, their interest was in the wager, was it not? That is why they flattered Lady Widow.'

This was an Emily he'd not glimpsed before. Insecure, woefully fearing she'd not been the sensational Lady Widow after all. He folded his arms across his chest. 'Emily, they would not have made the wager if they had not been…attracted.'

'And were you…attracted? Did you…like…Lady Widow? You must have liked her…to…bed her.'

Her questions unsettled him. He spoke of her leaving him, and she, God help him, talked of his bedding Lady Widow. This was a dangerous hand to play without knowledge of the rules.

He closed his eyes for a moment, willing himself to be as honest in this as he'd tried to be in everything he'd said to her in this room, even if it felt like he was showing all his cards. 'I admit to being captivated.'

Her head drooped. 'I see.'

His spirits drooped as well, but he persisted. 'Lady Widow captivated me. She and you were one to me, though I could not sometimes reconcile the differences.'

She gave him a pained look. 'I am not Lady Widow. I only pretended to be her. It was like a role in a play.'

He held her gaze. 'I know that,' he said softly. 'Do we not all play roles, Emily? Was I not playing the gambler, when I sat down to cards? I pretended, too, you see. Were you not likewise playing a role as my wife? Making yourself so—'

'Drab?' She sprang to her feet, eyes blazing.

He cursed himself for his careless words. Still, anger was better than no emotion at all, though scant consolation.

'Would you have me tint my lips and cheeks like Lady Widow? Do you wish me to dress as she does? Talk as she talks?'

He faltered. 'You mistake my meaning—'

She shouted, 'I am not Lady Widow!'

He strode back to her, grabbing her by the shoulders. 'Just as I am not a gambler! But both of those roles are part of us, are they not? I do not wish for you to bury that part of you who is Lady Widow, who is confident and sure of what she desires. Neither do I want you to hide that part of you who would risk everything for your sister. Or the gambler inside you. Indeed, the gambler inside me would much like to challenge you to another game.' He squeezed her shoulders, aware of how delicate she felt beneath his fingers. 'I do not wish you to feel you must hide any part of you from me. Good God, Emily, do not hide yourself, no matter what your decision. You have so much beauty inside you, so much emotion. You allowed me to glimpse it when we walked through Hyde Park—'

'Hyde Park?' she snapped, nothing but scepticism in her voice.

'Hyde Park,' he repeated. 'I felt as if I were seeing you for the first time. Do you not know how fascinating it is to know you conceal so much? It is like opening a package and finding more prizes the deeper one goes.'

He looked into her face, but it had gone blank. She had retreated from him once more.

'You are hiding again,' he said sadly. 'Though I suppose that is precisely what I deserve. It is what I have done to you until this night. I have hidden myself from you just as thoroughly as you have from me. You and I do not know each other, do we? I would like to know you, Emily. I would like it very much.'

He released her and rubbed his hands, the hands that had so briefly held her. 'I know the blame is entirely at my door, from the moment I tricked you into marrying me—'

'Your regret at doing so has been no secret.'

He froze, seeking her eyes. 'But I have not regretted marrying you.'

She laughed, a pained, forced laugh.

How much he had hurt her! At least, difficult as it was for him to witness, she was not hiding now. He wanted to get her to look at him. She would not. 'You have tried to be a good wife. You have tried to please me. It is I who have not been a good husband. If I had, you would not have become Lady Widow. You would not wish to leave me.'

'No, I—' she said, her expression softening.

He held up his hand to silence her. 'I cannot regret meeting Lady Widow, knowing that side of you, but I value her no more or less than the woman who has put up with my uncivil family, who has run my household with skill and economy, who has asked for nothing for herself, but who deserves everything. I cannot regret making love to Lady Widow, but neither can I regret those times I lay with you as my wife, how sweet you were—'

Her eyes flashed again. 'No more falsehoods, Guy. Until that night with Lady Widow you have taken pains to avoid my bed.'

Her words stung as sharply as a slap across the cheek. Fool that he was, he'd no notion that this too had caused her such pain. Her forgiveness for all his slights seemed impossible indeed. He turned and walked slowly to the door, aware of the sharpness of the glare she aimed at his back.

He opened the door, but could not make himself step through. He had promised himself to be honest with her and he would be so, even if he appeared to be making excuses for his behaviour.

He turned. 'You are correct. Until I won the money, I could not risk begetting a child. It was not an easy sacrifice, however, knowing you were just on the other side of this door.'

She stared at him, her silence giving him no reward for his abstinence, nor respite from his conscience.

He took a breath and tried to make the corners of his mouth form a smile. 'Another matter I ought to have explained to you.' He bowed to her and crossed the threshold, closing the door behind him.

Chapter Twenty

Emily picked up a shoe from the floor and flung it at the closed door, but it fell short and he probably did not hear it. She collapsed upon the bed, tears stinging her eyes.

What a fool she had been. He put the blame upon himself, but she knew better. She had deliberately withdrawn from him, deliberately avoided challenging him about his nightly absences, deliberately avoided challenging him in any way at all. Merely hiding herself from him lest he discover the biggest secret of all.

She loved him. She wanted him. And had from the moment she had seen him in the Pump Room at Bath.

She jumped off the bed and paced the room, tripping over her other shoe, picking it up, and throwing it against the wall.

How stupid she had been, so sure of the superiority of her unfailing correct behaviour, so certain he would not wish to pay attention to a drab creature such as herself. She'd had to transform herself into another person in order to have the courage to make love to him.

Now everything was ruined. He'd given her the means of leaving him and perhaps, for his sake, she should do it.

Not what I want, he'd said. *What you want.*

Lady Widow would have no difficulty telling him exactly what she wanted. Lady Widow would insist on having her way.

But she could not be Lady Widow, no matter how much he thought Lady Widow a part of her. She could not be so bold, so sure of herself.

She picked up the emerald green gown, recalling how well it had flattered her figure and colouring. She threw it across one of the chairs. On the table she spied the silk mask. She reached for it, crumbling it into her fist and striding over to the fire. She threw it at the flames, but it fluttered to the hearthstone as if thrown back to her.

She snatched it up again, suddenly knowing what she wanted. With all her heart, she knew exactly what she wanted.

And she knew exactly how to get it.

Guy had kicked off his shoes and thrown his jacket and waistcoat on a chair. He pulled the knot out of his neckcloth, letting its ends dangle down his shirt.

It would be nonsense to think of sleeping. He rummaged around the room until he found the bottle of brandy he'd brought there the other night when desire and need clawed at him. Sitting at the small table, he poured himself a drink and downed it in one gulp. He poured another.

She'd be a fool to stay with me, he thought, and he thought her anything but a fool.

The branch of candles in his room fluttered. In the doorway connecting their rooms she stood fully dressed, with a paper in her hand. Had she decided to leave him so soon?

She walked towards him. The light revealed her wearing the green dress she'd worn earlier that evening.

Though her hair was still loose about her shoulders, she wore Lady Widow's mask.

In Lady Widow's voice she said, 'If you like gaming so much, Lord Keating, perhaps you would fancy another game of piquet. It is what I want. A game of piquet.'

'Piquet?' A glimmer of hope kindled inside him. He gave her a slow, careful smile. 'So sorry, ma'am. I have sworn off gambling.'

She sidled towards him, so close her skirt brushed his knees, and waved the paper at him. It was the banknote. 'You do not wish to play for money? Very well.' She let the paper float to the floor.

Every sense in his body came alive, and he had thought never to feel anything again but pain. 'What stakes do you desire, then?' he asked, his voice husky.

'As before,' she purred. 'You win a round, I remove one piece of clothing. I win, and you remove a piece of clothing.'

He stood, so close he already felt the warmth of her body. He combed his fingers through her unbound hair, every bit as soft as he expected.

She placed her hands on his chest, the touch of her fingers stealing his breath.

'One condition,' he said, brushing her hair off her shoulders and reaching around to the ribbons at back of her head. 'No masks.'

As the piece of silk fell from her face, her arms encircled his neck.

'No masks ever again, Emily,' he whispered, letting his hands run down her back, eager for a lifetime exploring every curve.

She lifted her hand to his face, her caress so soft and full of promise it claimed his heart forever.

'No masks,' she said, her lips smiling as they reached to touch his. 'You may wager on it.'

*   *   *   *   *

An Unconventional Widow

by

Georgina Devon

Georgina Devon has a Bachelor of Arts degree in Social Sciences with a concentration in History. Her interest in England began when she lived in East Anglia as a child and later as an adult. She met her husband in England and her wedding ring set is from Bath. She has many romantic and happy memories of the land. Today she lives in Tucson, Arizona, with her husband, two dogs, an inherited cat and a cockatiel. Her daughter has left the nest and does website design, including Georgina's. Contact her at www.georginadevon.com

Chapter One

Annabell Fenwick-Clyde, Lady Fenwick-Clyde, stood up, clenched her hands, pressed them into the small of her back and stretched. She looked skyward as she enjoyed the loosening of muscles made tight by bending over the shards of tiles found in this destroyed Roman villa she was excavating.

Clouds scuttled across the late April sky, promising rain later today. She would have to be sure the exposed portions of the villa were well covered before she left.

'Ah,' a raspy baritone voice said. 'A nymph, and a very interestingly dressed one.'

Annabell started, dropped her hands and whirled around. She had been caught up in her work and not heard anyone approach. A man stood not ten feet away, studying her. A very attractive man.

Tall and lean with long legs and broad shoulders, he let his gaze run over her in a way that made her blush. His brown hair was longer than the fashion and dishevelled, as was the brown jacket and white shirt that opened at the collar to reveal a light curling of brown hair. His eyes were a startling clear green and seemed to see through her clothing.

She took a step back, irritated at the heat suffusing her

face, but unable to stop it since he continued to look at her as though she were a tasty morsel he intended to devour. 'I did not hear you approach,' she said, her voice breathless, which added to her discomfort and ire.

He smiled and her knees nearly melted. His mouth was wide and well formed, the lips sharply delineated. His teeth were strong. He radiated a predatory interest.

'You were engrossed in something in the dirt. I was engrossed in something much more appealing.' His gaze dropped to her hips.

Her blush deepened. 'I beg your pardon, but a gentleman would not stare as you do.' Thankfully her voice was cold and pointed instead of the breathiness of seconds before. 'Nor would a gentleman continue to do so,' she added when his attention moved to her torso.

He shrugged. 'A lady does not wear clothing that is very similar to that worn by the women in an Arab sheik's harem.' He cocked his head to one side. 'Although it is a delightful contrast to the chip straw bonnet that is so very English and the starched and buttoned-to-the-ears shirt. Which, unless I mistake the tailoring, is a man's garment.' His gaze moved to her face. 'Altogether charming.'

Her skin flamed, the heat spreading down her neck. Drat the man and drat her response to him, a reaction she could not explain. She was used to meeting men head on and holding her own, even dressed as she was. Her two brothers, Guy, Viscount Chillings, and Dominic, had first been scandalised by this mode of dress, then vocally adamant that she was to wear the clothing of an English lady and then, when she continued to go her own way, *nearly* indifferent. A smile curved up one corner of her mouth. Now, when they saw her dressed this way, all they did was glare.

This specimen of the species, however, was doing much more than glaring. He was mentally undressing her, unless she missed her mark, which she did not think likely. Her deceased husband had taught her what it felt like to have a male undress you with his eyes. But instead of the nausea the previous Lord Fenwick-Clyde had always made her feel, this man made her as unsure as a Miss just out of the schoolroom.

'I have had better compliments,' she said tartly, the words out before she considered them.

He took several strides towards her, his well-muscled legs encased in buckskin breeches eating up the distance. 'I am sure you have,' he murmured.

She clamped her lips shut before she said something else suggestive. Her eyes narrowed as he took another step in her direction.

The sun chose that moment to break through the clouds and shine down on them. She noted that his eyes were deep set and heavy lidded, with lines of dissipation radiating from the outside corners. He looked to be in his late thirties, a man who had lived a hard life. And noting the gleam in his eyes as he watched her study him, he had enjoyed every minute of his dissipation. Most likely, he was a rake of the highest magnitude. Well, that was nothing to her and nothing she had not encountered before. In fact, her younger brother was a libertine and she handled him quite well. Of course, Dominic's interest was never aimed at her.

'Now that you have studied me like one would a specimen pinned to a board, please be on your way. I,' she said pointedly, 'am busy.'

His eyelids drooped over speculative eyes and his mouth turned sensual. 'I warrant you are.' He closed the distance between them. 'But you are busy on my property, and I think, what with life's trials, tribulations and…' his voice turned husky '…temptations, you owe me a forfeit for trespassing.'

'I owe you nothing,' she said indignantly, moving to one side. 'If you are Sir Hugo Fitzsimmon, your steward has given me permission to be here.'

His smile lost none of its anticipation as he moved to

block her. 'Then he did not ask me before granting you leave.'

'That is your problem,' she said sharply. 'Not mine.'

She dodged to one side as he continued to close the distance between them. Sir Hugo or not Sir Hugo, she did not know him. No matter that her body screamed she did know him and wanted to know him better, her mind was adamant. She did not know this man.

She was too slow. He caught her and drew her inexorably toward him. Her face inches from his, she noted that he had the swarthy complexion of a man who spent much of his time outdoors. The muscled strength of the arm holding her pinned to his chest suggested that he was a sportsman, possibly a Corinthian.

All of this observation, she knew, was a wild attempt on her part to ignore the tension that started in her stomach and was spreading outwards through her body in waves. There was something about this man that ignited sensations she had never known she possessed. But no matter what that something was, she did not appreciate her body doing things her mind did not want it to do.

His smile widened as though he could read her thoughts and found them amusing. With his free hand, he caught the cherry-coloured satin ribbon tied into a bow beneath her chin and pulled. Her wide-brimmed bonnet toppled off the back of her head.

'How dare you.'

His grin turned wolfish. 'I dare a lot. As you shall see.'

Then his mouth was on hers. She expected him to be rough. She was prepared for rough. He was persuasive.

His lips moved provocatively over hers as his free hand burrowed into the hair at her nape, and held her still for his exploration. His arm around her waist tightened so her breasts pressed against his chest, making her aware of him in ways she had never experienced before.

When his tongue glided along her bottom lip, skimming

her skin so lightly that he was like a treat held just beyond reach, she wondered if she would disgrace herself by following his oh, so clever tongue with her own. He saved her that indignity by taking her small gasp of surprise and using it to slip inside her mouth.

Sensation coursed through her, sensual and warm and arousing. Her eyes closed slowly, as she sank into his embrace. A shudder of delight rippled down her spine.

She gave herself over to his seduction without conscious thought. Her body reacted as her mind slid away.

'Ahh…' he breathed, taking his lips from hers, his voice a rasp. 'You have rewarded me well.'

Her eyes snapped open, and her mind seemed to get back into working order. What had she done? She had acted like a wanton, like a loose woman. And she did not even enjoy the carnal relationship between a man and woman. Her past husband had told her that frequently enough—and she had agreed wholeheartedly with him.

She splayed her palms against this stranger's chest and pushed. Hard.

'Let me go.' Her former blush returned with a vengeance.

He laughed, but did not release her. 'And what will you give me if I do?'

Her eyes sparked. 'What will I give you if you do not, is the better question, sirrah!'

His laugh deepened, so that lines carved into the skin around his mouth. His hair, too long and too long from a razor, lifted in the breeze.

'Threats or promises?' He leaned back and gazed down at where their bodies still met. 'I choose to believe promises.'

'You are no gentleman. Nor are you very intelligent.' Annabell tried desperately not to sputter in her anger at his arrogant assumption of her willing compliance. Although, in all honesty—and she always tried to be honest with herself—he had every reason to think she would succumb to him.

'No?' he drawled, his eyes narrowing dangerously, all hint of humour gone. 'I think I understand you perfectly. Shall I prove it again—to your satisfaction and mine?'

'You have gone too far already.' She sputtered in her fury. 'I may have let you kiss me—'

'Let me? You kissed me back.'

'Let you kiss me, but I was not willing.'

He laughed outright. The sound was full and rich with resonance. It sent shivers cascading down her spine. But enough was enough. She pushed hard at him and hooked her lower leg behind his knee. He released her waist just before he fell to the ground like a stone. Surprise widened his eyes seconds before they narrowed.

Instead of jumping to his feet as she had expected, he rose up on his elbows and studied her with an insolence that made his countenance cold. 'I see you are a woman who can defend herself.'

She returned his appraisal, hands on hips. 'I learned early with two brothers that sometimes fighting unfairly is the only way a woman can protect herself.'

A twinge of guilt narrowed her eyes. Guy and Dominic had never abused her as her husband had. If truth be told, the late Fenwick-Clyde had taught her more about unfair fighting than either of her brothers. But that was something only she knew or needed to know.

The man who called himself Sir Hugo got to his feet in one lithe movement that told her clearer than words that, if he really wanted to do something to her, he could. Instead, he carelessly straightened the handkerchief knotted at his neck, similar to those worn by prizefighters.

'Women are not the only ones who often need an advantage to protect themselves. But that is neither here nor there.' He slid out of his loose-fitting jacket and shook it to get off some of the dirt from the excavation. Instead of putting it back on, he folded it across his arm. 'You are on my land without my permission. I could have you arrested for trespassing.'

Annabell's deep blue eyes sparked in a way both her brothers would recognise as the first warning of a verbal attack. 'If you are unaware of my presence then it is the fault of your steward, who agreed to our excavation.' Her mouth thinned. 'Perhaps he could not reach you. And furthermore, you could try to arrest me for trespassing, but you would be unsuccessful. Everyone around here knows who I am and that I am invited.'

'Perhaps.' His voice grated.

She smiled sweetly while venom dripped from her words. 'I assure you, Sir Hugo, I have a letter from your man authorising me to be here.'

His jaw sharpened. 'I am sure you do, Miss—'

She notched up her chin. '*Lady* Fenwick-Clyde.'

For an instant only, his pupils dilated. He made a curt, mocking bow. '*Lady* Fenwick-Clyde.' He waved his long-fingered hand to encompass her work area. 'Until I check into this further, please feel free to do with my land as you please.'

She ignored the sarcasm in his voice. 'I shall do just that, Sir Hugo.'

He gave her one last, long look. This one did not go below her neck. It was as though he were reassessing her. Then he spun on his well-shod heel and strode to where a chestnut mare stood patiently waiting, eating the vibrant spring grass.

It was not until he walked away that she noticed his limp. The catch in his gait was so minor as to be nearly indiscernible. Nor did it mar his natural predatory grace.

She watched him mount the horse and disappear into the smattering of trees separating the site from the nearby dirt path that substituted as a road. He rode with the same easy grace that he moved. No wonder he had a reputation with women.

He was one of the handsomest men, albeit in a disreputable way, she had every seen. Her brothers were considered very good specimens, but to her mind Sir Hugo surpassed them.

Unconsciously, her fingers went to her lips. She could still feel the tingle of his mouth on hers. Ridiculous.

She had things to do. This was a valuable site of Roman occupation. Her goal was to preserve it for posterity. She had thought she had months to do so. With Sir Hugo in residence, she had very little time. Not even a widow's reputation was safe when linked with the Wolf of Covent Garden.

A rueful grin twisted her mouth. Funny she should remember that name for him. Her younger brother Dominic had thrown it at her in one of his tirades when he discovered exactly where the Roman villa she was excavating was located. He had called Sir Hugo dangerous. He was probably right.

She unconsciously rubbed her still swollen lips.

And the way the man had looked at her. It had been nothing short of indecent. She might be dressed unconventionally, but she had every right to wear what she chose. Men did.

But, perhaps, with him in residence, it would be better to dress more conservatively. Much as she had denied the attraction he exuded, she had been unable to resist him. What if he chose to take advantage of her again?

Her body heated and she sank to the ground.

Tomorrow she would wear a proper English skirt. Her spine stiffened and she pushed herself back up to her feet.

No, no, she wouldn't. His bold disregard for the proprieties would not make her skittish. She would do as she wished and was practical. As she always did. No man, and especially not one as disreputable as he, would alter her actions.

That settled, she bent back to her work, forgetting that her bonnet lay in the dirt several feet away where it had fallen.

Hugo moved easily in the saddle despite the twinge in his left thigh and the sharp pull that radiated to his groin. He was not a man to pity himself. He had taken a musket ball during Waterloo. Many others had taken worse.

He had even been given a knighthood for bravery. His mouth twisted. He had only done what needed to be done. Still, he had accepted the knighthood for his father's memory. His father had spent his life trying to get a title bestowed on his only child and failed. Hugo knew logically that his father was gone and the knighthood bestowed too late to make his father feel better, but his heart had told him to accept and trust that somehow his father knew.

He resisted the temptation to look back at Lady Fenwick-Clyde. He was not sure if he would feel desire or pity, and did not want to find out. Instead, he urged Molly into a canter.

He remembered Fenwick-Clyde as a lecherous old sot with a reputation for roughness among the less privileged prostitutes. He scowled. No sense sugar-coating it to himself. Fenwick-Clyde had been abusive. He had heard rumours the man was the same with his young wife. He had been repulsed by Fenwick-Clyde and so never met the wife who had kept to herself and avoided most of the *ton*'s activities. He wondered if she still stayed away from society now that she was widowed.

It was none of his concern.

He noticed the ground change. They were on the fine gravel driveway leading to Rosemont, named for the profusion of roses that came into bloom during the late spring and summer. Hugo urged Molly into a run for the remaining distance.

Minutes later they came to a halt, dirt and rocks flying behind the mare's back legs. With a laugh of pleasure, Hugo slid to the ground. Home at last. It had been nearly a year.

He breathed deeply of the fresh air, redolent with growing life—freshly scythed grass, flowers and the hint of stables. His mouth twisted into a wry smile. He had missed this place more than he cared to admit.

In front of him were the steps to the entrance, situated in the middle between two wings. Rosemont was an H-shaped Elizabethan manor house, built from red bricks and thick oak beams. He had been born here in the housekeeper's room thirty-six years ago.

The front door opened and Butterfield came out. The old butler was tall and stick thin, holding himself with more dignity than anyone else Hugo knew, with the possible except of the Iron Duke. Wellington was well-known for his good self-image. And Hugo knew it well. He had served as one of Wellington's *aides-de-camp* for the past year. He had been one of the few to survive that duty.

'Butterfield,' Hugo said, hugging the butler in spite of the old man's attempt to hold himself aloof.

'Sir Hugo,' Butterfield said, his voice warm even through the tone of censure. 'You mustn't do that.'

Hugo took pity on his old retainer and released him. 'You did not always feel that way.'

Butterfield's old rheumy eyes softened. 'Aye, but you were a young buck in leading strings then. Now you are the lord here and a man with a reputation for bravery, too.'

Hugo waved him to silence. 'None of that.' He strode forward. 'The carriage with my baggage will be here later. We ran into rain and, subsequently, muddy, pocked roads.'

He strode past the running stable lad come to fetch Molly. The boy pulled his forelock and grinned from ear to ear. Hugo smiled, but kept going. Now that he was here at last, he wanted nothing more than to be inside, seated in the library with a snifter of good French brandy that had not been smuggled. The Lord knew he and others had fought long and hard to defeat Napoleon and gain access once more to a France under Bourbon rule. He hoped they would never forget all Britain had sacrificed.

He entered the foyer, unconsciously absorbing the presence of the wooden plank floor and various suits of armour and the accoutrements that went with them. Shields of every shape and size hung from the oak-panelled walls. Muskets alternated with lances. Everything was polished to mirror brightness. He expected nothing less from his staff with Butterfield in charge. But the butler was ageing. He would have to hire a housekeeper soon, whether he wanted to or not. He had never wanted another housekeeper after his own history. Not that he would repeat his father's indiscretions.

Hugo waved off a footman who had come to get his jacket. 'No, Michael, I will keep it with me.'

The young man, short and thin, the antithesis of most footmen who were often hired for their looks so as to enhance their employer's standing, stepped back. A smile curved the youth's mouth at being remembered. Unlike some of the aristocracy, Sir Hugo always knew the names of his servants and called them by their given names. Some of his peers named their staff for the jobs each servant did, regardless of the servant's actual name.

The footman bowed. 'Yes, Sir Hugo.'

Hugo continued to the library. It was the room at Rosemont where he felt most at home and relaxed.

With a sigh of satisfaction, he entered the room. Huge multi-paned windows covered the outside wall, allowing the late afternoon sunlight to enter in myriad prisms. Colours danced off the polished wood floor and flashed from the glass that enclosed floor-to-ceiling bookcases. A fire roared in the massive grate. Even this late in the year it was cold inside a house this old.

He went to his desk and picked up a full decanter of brandy and poured himself a healthy portion. He drank it down in one long, satisfied gulp.

'Ahem,' a female voice said. 'I don't believe you belong here.'

Hugo swallowed a less than gracious retort. Instead of looking in the direction of the voice, he poured himself another brandy. He had a feeling he was going to need it.

'This is a private home, young man, and the owner is not about.' The woman's voice was sharp yet breathy, as though she struggled for oxygen. 'I suggest you leave before I call a footman and have you ousted.'

Taking another long drink, Hugo pivoted on his heel and faced the woman. She was tall and thin to the point of near emaciation. Her chin was pointed and her brown eyes seemed too big for her face. Pale blonde hair, streaked with grey, was pulled back into a tight bun. Her mouth was pinched with irritation at the moment.

'I don't believe I have the pleasure of your acquaintance, ma'am,' he drawled, finishing the brandy.

She drew herself up. 'Nor do I have yours. Nor do I wish to.' She crossed to the pull by the fireplace and yanked the velvet strip.

'You must be here with Lady Fenwick-Clyde.'

'Yes.' Her back was ramrod straight in its pale lavender kerseymere.

He set the empty glass down, resigned to another confrontation and one not nearly as pleasant as the last. He made her a short bow. 'Allow me to introduce myself then, since I doubt I will be seeing the last of you for some time.' He ignored her indignant gasp. 'I am Sir Hugo Fitzsimmon—your host.'

Her pale blue eyes widened and a scarlet flush mounted

her cheeks. 'Oh, dear. How very inconvenient,' she muttered.

Hugo choked back a laugh, grateful he was not drinking the brandy. It would have spattered over everything.

'How gracious of you,' he replied. 'You must be Lady Fenwick-Clyde's companion.'

'Yes, I am, and I can tell you, sir, that we certainly did not expect you to return as you have.' She shook her head. 'Your reputation is such that not even a widowed lady with a chaperon is safe with you in attendance.'

He shrugged with true indifference. 'Then you must relocate to the inn nearby. Their rooms are clean and their food passable.'

'You could much easier go back to where you came from for a while.'

Hugo wondered if his hearing was going bad or if she had just attempted a joke. One look at her serious, clearly affronted countenance told him neither was correct. She meant exactly what she had said.

'We, after all,' she continued, 'have express permission from your steward to lodge here and be at liberty on your land for as long as it takes Bell and her team to excavate the Roman villa.'

Hugo wondered if he had actually died at Waterloo and gone someplace that was not heaven. This situation was surreal.

'I think not,' he said, pouring another glass of brandy and gulping it down. 'I shall leave you here while I go to my rooms. When I come back, I shall expect you to be gone.'

Before she could do more than open and close her mouth, he was out of the room. His one refuge in this house, the one place he felt completely at liberty, and she had invaded it.

'Sir Hugo,' Butterfield said, coming toward the library. 'Oh. Miss Pennyworth must be in there.'

Hugo halted. 'Miss Pennyworth? A tall, thin woman who thinks she owns Rosemont?'

Butterfield nodded.

'I am going to my rooms, Butterfield. Get Tatterly and tell him I expect him to meet with me on the hour. In the library. Without Miss Pennyworth or anyone else for that matter.'

'Yes, m'lord,' Butterfield said to Hugo's back.

Chapter Two

Annabell strode into the foyer to the sound of male voices raised in irritation. They came from the library, her favourite room. Much as it pained her to admit it, she recognised one of the voices as belonging to Sir Hugo. A meeting lasting only minutes, and his voice was now imprinted on her senses. What was happening to her?

'Tatterly,' Sir Hugo said, his tone low, 'see that Lady Fenwick-Clyde and her chaperon are out of here by tomorrow. Tonight if possible.'

Hearing her name, Annabell did the unthinkable. She moved closer. Better to know in advance what was being said about her than to find out when it was too late to do anything about it. She all but put her ear to the oak panel.

'Yes, Sir Hugo, but—'

'No buts. I am home and intend to stay here until I decide to leave, not until some rumour-monger forces me to leave in order to save that woman's reputation.' There was an ominous silence. 'And that chaperon. She would drive me to mayhem.'

That was enough! How dare he speak that way about Susan. Annabell found herself fully as angry as Sir Hugo. She marched through the library's open door and stood just past the entrance, feet apart.

'You, Sir Hugo, should ensure the doors are closed before you go on about unwelcomed guests.'

The object of her censure turned slowly to face her. 'I should not have to pay attention to what I say in my own home, Lady Fenwick-Clyde.'

He was right and she knew it, but still… 'You may not have expressly invited me, but Mr Tatterly said it would be acceptable for Miss Pennyworth and me to stay here as long as necessary to excavate the Roman villa.'

Sir Hugo took one step towards her and stopped as though he did not trust himself any closer. 'As long as I was on the Continent it was. I am not there now. Nor do I intend to move into a room at the village inn. So, you had best go. Your reputation won't be worth the breath used to shred it if it becomes known you are sleeping under the same roof as I am.'

She notched her chin up. 'I am a widow. Widows may do as they please.'

His eloquent mouth nearly sneered. 'Widows of a certain ilk, certainly. Somehow…' he ran his gaze insolently up and down her body '…I don't believe you want to be in that category in spite of your unconventional dress. But correct me if I am wrong.'

'Leave my clothes out of this,' she said, barely able to contain her ire at his insinuations. 'Until you arrived unannounced, my reputation did not need preserving.'

He shrugged and turned his back to her. 'I am here now, this is my home, and that is that.'

'Sir Hugo—' Tatterly said, his strong, solid face agonised.

'Not another word, Tatterly.'

Annabell took pity on the man. It was not his fault. 'Mr Tatterly, don't worry. You are not to blame for any of this. None of us believed Sir Hugo would forego his pleasures so quickly to rusticate.'

Sir Hugo's shoulders shook and Annabell heard what

sounded suspiciously like a snort. Yet, when he turned around, his face was unreadable. 'I take my pleasures where I find them, Lady Fenwick-Clyde. For the moment, I find them here.'

Annabell bit her lip, a bad habit she had when confronted with a problem to which she did not like the solution. 'Very well, Sir Hugo. Miss Pennyworth and I shall move to the inn.' She turned her brightest smile on the steward. 'If you would be so kind as to procure us rooms, Mr Tatterly, I would be forever in your debt.'

Mr Tatterly turned brick red. 'Of course, milady. It would be my pleasure.' He started for the door where Annabell still stood, but stopped in time to ask his employer, 'May I be off, Sir Hugo? The sooner this is done, the sooner everything is solved.'

Sir Hugo nodded. 'By all means, Tatterly. We wouldn't want to inconvenience Lady Fenwick-Clyde any more than necessary.'

Annabell stepped to the side so Mr Tatterly could pass. She pointedly did not look at Sir Hugo, who had moved to stand by one of the many windows. His sarcasm in dismissing Mr Tatterly had increased her irritation, which was decidedly unlike her. All the years of her marriage she had managed to ignore Fenwick-Clyde's snide remarks and disparaging words. Although, in all truth, Sir Hugo was not disparaging or snide, he was sarcastic and sensual and hard to ignore.

'Do you have a maid?' Sir Hugo asked without taking his attention from the scene outside. 'If not, I will have a maid sent to help you pack.'

'That won't be necessary. I can take care of myself, Sir Hugo.'

He turned and gave her an appraising study. 'I believe you can, but why would you when it isn't necessary?'

She raised one black brow. 'Because it makes me self-sufficient.'

'As you wish.'

She thought his mouth thinned, but if so it was so slight she immediately decided she had been mistaken. And even if she was not, it did not matter. After life with Fenwick-Clyde, she did not care what a man thought of her or her need for independence.

'I won't impose on you a moment longer than absolutely necessary.' She pivoted on the heel of her boot and stalked from the room. The sooner she was gone, the better for all of them.

Hugo watched her stride from the room and shook his head. She looked cool and composed in her outrageous clothing—a woman who thumbed her nose at the world—but in truth she was anything but cool. She was a spitfire for all that her hair was as silver as the full moon. And undoubtedly a bluestocking, determined to prove she did not need a man for anything.

Before he realised it, his mouth curved into a devilish smile. It would prove interesting to show the very independent Lady Fenwick-Clyde that men were good for many things. His smile deepened and his green eyes darkened. His body responded.

His laugh filled the empty library. Oh, yes, it was good to be home.

Annabell turned to her travelling writing desk and made sure the quills were in place and the ink securely stoppered. Without her volition, her fingers strayed to the leather writing portion. Many years of use had made the fine cowhide smooth as satin. In one corner was an ink stain. In another were initials she'd carved into the mahogany wood years ago. She could still remember when.

She had been married several years and miserable. Guy, her older brother, had given her the money to get away from Fenwick-Clyde not knowing she intended to go to Egypt. He had thought she just wanted to go to Scotland or Ireland or even Italy, places acceptable for a married woman with a chaperon to go. Guy had been furious when he learned where she had really gone, but it was too late by then. She was at her destination and fascinated.

The Egyptian desert with its exotic heat and plants had intrigued her, but the pyramids had caught her imagination. It was the start of her love for antiquities. Prior to that she had been interested, but it had been academic. Now it was nearly a passion.

Her Egyptian guide had been a native of the region who taught her to enjoy strong coffee and to appreciate the harsh beauty of the desert. If she concentrated hard enough, she could still imagine the feel of the dry, hot winds against her skin.

The trip had been a turning point for her.

She had always been interested in everything ancient, since first studying the classics with her brothers when they prepared for university. This trip showed her she could participate in the discovery of the past, not just read about it.

Fenwick-Clyde had threatened to banish her to the country when she made her first trip to Egypt against his orders, but she had not cared, she had gone anyway. A wife who openly defied her husband—he had made her pay in ways polite society would never know about. Fenwick-Clyde had died shortly after that, overtaken by too much drink, women and general dissipation.

Annabell snapped shut the lock on her portmanteau as someone knocked on the bedchamber door. 'Come in.'

'Lady Fenwick-Clyde,' Tatterly said, his tone slow and stolid, yet managing to draw her back from her reverie. 'Excuse me, but there is a problem.'

Still fiddling with her packing, she looked at him. 'Yes?'

His large fingers played slowly against the smooth wood of the doorjamb. He was a wide man, not particularly tall, but solid. Like a man who made his living at physical labour even though he was a gentleman and had been educated at Oxford.

'Yes, my lady.' He took a deep breath. 'The inn is filled completely. There is a prizefight in the area this coming weekend.'

'Does Sir Hugo know?'

'No, my lady. He is riding the grounds, letting the tenants know he is back.'

In spite of herself, she was impressed. Very few men of her acquaintance would take the time immediately upon arriving home after being gone for nearly a year to reacquaint themselves with their landholders.

'He is a conscientious man.'

'Very much so, my lady.' Tatterly still stood on the threshold of the room, his stance tense. The problem of her quarters was not resolved. 'What do you want me to do, Lady Fenwick-Clyde? There is another small village, but it is more distant and would take you at least an hour in travel each way. And that is if the weather is good.'

Annabell frowned and stopped what she was doing. Things were definitely not getting any better. 'Tell Sir Hugo I would like to meet with him immediately upon his return.'

'Yes, my lady.'

She smiled at the still-tense man. 'And thank you for everything you have done, Tatterly.'

'You are welcome, Lady Fenwick-Clyde.'

He stayed where he was, radiating uncertainty. Now his fingers were motionless against the door. Annabell glanced at him and raised one brow.

'Yes, Tatterly?'

'Um…if you permit, I thought I would tell Miss Pennyworth you won't be leaving immediately. I saw her in the morning room.' His fair skin turned russet. 'That is, if you don't think she would mind.'

Annabell smiled. The man was transparent. 'Please do

that for me. I would appreciate not having to stop what I am doing to inform her.'

He cleared his throat so that his Adam's apple bobbed. 'My pleasure.'

I don't doubt that, Annabell thought, watching him leave without closing her bedchamber door. If they stayed here too long, she might lose her companion. She and Pennyworth had been together a long time. They met on Annabell's first trip to Egypt, on the ship coming back from Gibraltar. Miss Pennyworth had been escorting a young girl from India back to England for school. Annabell had offered her the position of her companion when her commitment to the girl was finished. Miss Pennyworth had accepted. Now Tatterly, unless Annabell missed her guess, was interested in offering Miss Pennyworth a new position as wife. If that was what Pennyworth wanted, she would not begrudge her the chance for happiness, even though she would miss her sorely.

But for the immediate future, she had other problems. She was not travelling an hour each way every day in order to excavate the Roman villa. And longer if the weather turned bad.

She started unpacking.

Hugo breathed deeply of the cool air, filled with the hint of moisture. The scent of live things permeated everything. He heard the sound of movement in the underbrush and saw the flip of a wing overhead. He had missed England. He had missed Rosemont. He had not expected to miss either.

His hands tightened on the reins so that Molly shied. 'Easy, girl,' he murmured, leaning forward to stroke her glossy neck. 'Nothing is wrong. Not really.'

He reined Molly to a stop. The remains of the Roman villa stood in stark contrast to the green grass and trees surrounding it. He could make out bright shards and pieces of earthenware pottery. She had done a good job of preserving the site. Antiquities had interested him since his Oxford days. It was intriguing that she was fascinated by them as well.

He might not want her in his home because of all the problems her presence would create, but he did want to see this villa preserved. If possible, he would like it restored to its former glory, or as near as possible without compromising its integrity.

That was why, when Tatterly had written to tell him one of the farmers had dug up a Roman antiquity while ploughing near the orchard, he had told his steward to arrange for someone qualified to come and excavate the site. He had thought the expert would be male.

His mouth quirked. Never in his most fantastical dreams would he have imagined a woman interested and qualified to do what Lady Fenwick-Clyde was doing.

This interest was a strange thing to have in common. But his concerns over the excavation were not enough to allow her to remain in his home, given the possible ramifications. She could easily be ruined, or he could be pressured to marry her. Neither possibility was acceptable.

Unless she chose to stay, understanding that, no matter what happened, marriage was not an option.

Annabell found him once more in the library, his legs propped on an ottoman, a book in one hand and a brandy in the other. He looked perfectly content. For a man of his reputation, he seemed to spend a lot of time in a quiet room. She would have thought he would be gambling or wenching in the nearby tavern, the one he had wanted her to relocate to.

When the footman moved to announce her, she waved him away. Better to have the advantage of surprise. It had always worked when dealing with her brothers—no matter that it had not been effective with Fenwick-Clyde. Somehow she thought Sir Hugo was more like her younger sibling than her previous spouse.

'Sir Hugo,' she said firmly, entering the book-shrouded room. 'I need to speak with you.'

He said something she could not make out. He did not bother to stand or to even look back at her. He ignored her.

'I said I have something to talk to you about.'

She stopped to the side of where he sat and scowled down at him. It was a mistake.

His hair was tousled from his ride, the heavy curls falling across his wide forehead. His eyes were greener than she remembered and held a hint of emotion she could not name. His mouth, that generous yet firmly moulded mouth, caught her attention.

She knew what his lips felt like pressed to hers. She knew his mouth was as skilled at kissing as it was beguiling to look at. The urge to reach out and trace the curves of his lips nearly undid her. She curled her fingers into fists and held them securely at her sides. Better to look anywhere else than at his mouth. It made her remember sensations better forgotten.

Her gaze dropped. His shirt was loosened at the neck and the handkerchief that had been knotted around his throat earlier was gone.

He was a very disturbing man.

He laid down the book he had been reading, one of Jane Austen's. 'I thought you would be gone by now.'

'The inn is full.' She made it a flat statement of fact, unarguable.

'That is too bad.'

She waited, but he didn't say anything else, just sipped his brandy. 'You drink a lot of that.'

She was trying to be deliberately provoking. For some reason he brought out the worst in her.

He nodded. 'Yes, but not as much as others. Where are you going to stay now?'

Her mouth opened to tell him in no uncertain terms that she was staying here. She clamped it shut so hard her teeth clicked. This was his house. He could order her out even if she had nowhere else to go. She had been on her own and answerable to no one for too long when her manners went begging like this.

'May I have a seat?' She kept her voice mild and reasonable.

He waved a negligent hand at the nearest chair, a big, stuffed chintz she often sat in. There was nothing nicer than sitting in here before a roaring fire, having tea and reading a good book. Sometimes eating buttered toast. He had an extensive collection, everything from the classics to Jane Austen. She wondered if he had read them all, but doubted it because there were so many.

She sat down and ran her hands down her lap, smoothing the skirt of the high-waisted kerseymere she had changed into. 'The next closest inn is at least an hour's ride each way. That will make it very difficult for me to have a productive day.'

He turned to watch her, but said nothing. She found his perusal unsettling, to say the least. It made her flush and her stomach twitch. She wanted him to look elsewhere—anywhere but at her, which made her uncomfortable.

'Have I a smudge on my nose or chin?' Her voice was more tart than she had intended.

His mouth curved into a rakish grin. 'Not that I can see, and I am looking very hard for flaws.'

Her eyes widened and she leaned away from him. 'I beg your pardon, Sir Hugo.' Embarrassment was a wonderful cure for self-consciousness, she found. All thought vanished of trying to talk reasonably in order to convince him to let her stay here. 'I did not come here to be flirted with.'

His smiled widened. 'No, I imagine you didn't. You came to wheedle me into letting you stay here at Rosemont.'

'I didn't come here to *wheedle* you. I came here to explain why I need to stay here at least until the village inn has room, which should be early next week after everyone who has come for the prizefight has left.'

'Ah, I understand now.' He took a long drink of his liquor. 'You don't much care about your reputation. You think that being a widow with a chaperon will protect you from the gossips. You are more concerned about your convenience and comfort.'

She eyed him with dislike. Her body might respond to him and her eyes might take pleasure in looking at him, but she did not have to like him as a person.

'I am an adult woman. I can do as I choose. Men do it all the time. I choose to stay where it is convenient for me to accomplish my work.' She took a deep breath. 'Were you in my position, you would do exactly that.'

He laughed outright, but it wasn't a mirthful sound. 'You are either naïve or delusional. Women, *like men*, should value their good name. For you, much of your good name is locked up in your reputation. Nothing would protect your reputation—or any other woman's for that matter—from the gossip-mongers. Particularly since my conduct among the fairer sex is disreputable to say the least, as you so willingly informed me this afternoon.'

'You were insufferable,' she retorted without thinking. When his smile became self-satisfied, she knew she had played right into his hand. 'Not that I can't handle you.'

A different look moved over his face. 'I am sure you can.'

Now she'd made the situation worse. And he did have a valid point. In many ways, she knew him to be right, which only increased her irritation with the entire situation. It was the way of their world to constrain women and to put name and background before individual happiness. She had done that once by entering into an arranged marriage. Never again. She was tired of the world she came from. She wanted freedom to be herself, hard as that might be.

Her voice was waspish as a result of her thoughts. 'Let us not mince words, Sir Hugo. You are a rake and a libertine. I know that, and I am prepared to take the risk of ruining my reputation.'

He shook his head and set the empty glass down. 'Is this excavation so important that you can't wait a couple of days? Move to the distant tavern or go back to London until the village inn has room.'

She raised her chin up and squared her shoulders. What he said had merit, but not for her. 'I could do that, and that would be the reasonable thing to do. But I don't choose to do so.'

'May I ask why?'

'You may, and I will even tell you.' She took a deep breath. 'I choose not to do the respectable thing because I am sick of what society says is acceptable for a woman. Men may do as they damn well please, but women must do as they are told. Well, I will do as I see fit. If that ruins me in the eyes of the *ton,* then so be it. It is a small price to pay for being able to decide what I do, when I do it and with whom I do it.'

She stopped, realising she had very nearly launched into a tirade. Ever since Fenwick-Clyde had dominated her in every way possible, she had taken every opportunity to defy anyone and anything that tried to dictate to her. And, truth be told, she had always been rebellious. That trait had just worsened after her marriage.

He refilled his glass, picked it up and saluted her. 'I believe I understand perfectly. You are a bluestocking and a revolutionary. I congratulate you on your courage. Make yourself at home. It does not matter to me if it does not matter to you.'

She gaped. Her victory was too easily won. But then they had not been in battle.

'Why have you changed your mind? Earlier today you were adamant that I was to leave.'

'Earlier today I felt like following society's dictates. Now I see you do not care, so I leave the responsibility for your welfare to you. I came home to rest and recuperate, not fight with a woman I don't even know.' He drank the brandy in one long gulp, his Adam's apple moving just above the white collar of his shirt. 'Besides, I admire your courage.'

She nearly fell over from shock. 'Admire my courage?'

He nodded, a mysterious gleam in his green, green eyes. 'Yes, courage. That is a rare commodity in any person and one to be preserved. If you are not afraid of anything, then so be it.'

'You are letting me stay because you think I have courage?' He nodded and she blinked. 'I also have stubbornness.'

He shrugged. 'That too. Besides which,' he added, 'my stepmother has written to inform me that she and my brother and sister will be here shortly. She started from London as soon as she heard I was in the country.'

'Ah.' That explained his change. 'An impeccable chaperon.'

He shrugged. 'Perhaps to some.' He slanted a speculative look at Annabell, his gaze traveling from her smooth hair, which she had pulled primly back into a bun, to her lap where her hands lay still. 'I believe she is your age or younger. My father married late in his life.'

'Hah! Yes, she will be the perfect protection for my honour. How like society to determine that your stepmother, even though she may be younger than me, can be depended upon to be a buffer between your lascivious urges and my widowhood. That is exactly what I meant about freedom.'

'You are right, but that is the way of things.'

He continued to watch her as he said the irritating words. Annabell wondered if he said them merely to goad her, to see what she would say. Her brothers would have. But she had been on her high horse long enough, and it was late and she wanted to take one last look at the site before finishing for the day.

She stood abruptly. 'Well, now that we have resolved everything, I will leave you to your pleasures.'

He nodded. 'Yes, I do like my pleasures.'

She gave him a narrowed look, suspecting him of innuendo, but saw his countenance was noncommittal. 'Yes, you do, Sir Hugo.'

She looked pointedly at a nearby brazier that added its warmth to that from the fireplace. Then there was the fine cashmere rug he had over his legs and the supple leather slippers he wore that seemed soft as a second skin.

He smiled up at her, not in the least discommoded. 'Life is short. I live it to the fullest and the devil take the hindmost.'

'A hedonist.'

He smiled, thinning his lips. 'Exactly.'

'Someday you will tire of living only for pleasure.'

'I doubt that.'

'Wait and see.'

She was always one to give as good as she got and she never backed down from anything. She had often confronted Fenwick-Clyde, usually to her regret in the long run. But she had been determined to stand up for herself, even when performing the duties expected of a wife. She shivered.

'Are you feeling unwell?' Sir Hugo stood so that he was nearly touching her. 'You suddenly paled.'

She blinked and realised her hands were clenched. It had been ages since she thought of what Fenwick-Clyde had required of her. Why now?

'I am fine. Just old memories.' She would have sounded more convincing if her voice hadn't trembled. Sometimes she disgusted herself. 'Perfectly fine. I must be on my way.

Thank you so much for allowing Miss Pennyworth and my-self to remain here.'

He watched her, the look in his eyes telling her as clear as spoken words that he didn't believe her. But he said nothing further about that.

'One last thing,' he drawled, his voice stopping her. She looked back at him. 'If your reputation is shredded, Lady Fenwick-Clyde, don't look to me to remedy the situation.'

She stared at him, not sure she understood. 'Exactly what are you trying to say?'

He sipped his brandy. 'That I won't marry you to pre-serve a name you are determined to sully.'

The urge to stalk across the room and slap him for his arrogance was strong. Somehow, she managed to resist.

'Be assured, Sir Hugo, I won't require that sacrifice from you. Ever.'

Annabell made her exit before he could reply. Goodness only knew what he would say given the opportunity. And goodness only knew what she would do if he continued to goad her.

Sir Hugo watched her go and wondered if he had made a colossal mistake by allowing her to stay. Her slim hips swayed in spite of how stiffly she held her shoulders. Wisps of her blond, nearly silver hair escaped the severe bun and wafted behind her like moonbeams. He scowled. He was not a poet and had no aspirations to be one, yet here he was describing her in flowery words. Sometimes his libido got the better of him.

He sank back into his chair.

Juliet might be coming and bringing his half-brother and half-sister, Joseph and Rosalie, but he doubted they would make good chaperons. Still, society would be appeased. He would nearly have a house party.

His mouth curled into a sardonic grin. The perfect setting for a seduction.

And he had warned her that he would not marry her, no matter what happened. His conscience was clear.

Chapter Three

Hugo sprawled leisurely in his chair and watched the other three people at the dinner table. Lady Fenwick-Clyde sat on his right, Miss Susan Pennyworth on his left. Beside Miss Pennyworth was Tatterly, still as a church mouse as he listened attentively to every word Miss Pennyworth uttered, which was many. The man was transparent, but Miss Pennyworth seemed unaware of his infatuation. Of course, Hugo decided, Miss Pennyworth was a ninnyhammer and very likely unaware of many things.

'Lady Fenwick-Clyde, was your archaeological site safe when you checked it earlier?' He had to find conversation of some substance or banish the nattering companion from the room.

She looked at him as though she suspected him of teasing her, which he was. He found her interest in scientific matters fascinating. He also enjoyed watching the emotions flit across her face. She was totally unaffected. For an instant, he wondered how she had ever survived Fenwick-Clyde. Then he pushed the thought away. It was none of his concern.

'Yes, Sir Hugo. Tomorrow I shall start removing the top layers of dirt and debris in the area I was exploring today. I believe there is a nearly intact mosaic.'

'Really,' he drawled, more interested in her than her words.

The play of enthusiasm and interest across her delicate face caught him, made him wonder how she would look beneath him, with him buried inside her. An interesting possibility.

'What do you intend to do with your find? It is, lest you forget, on my property.'

She blinked and bit her bottom lip. The actions made her eyes sparkle and her mouth blossom a deep, rosy hue that beckoned to him. He doubted she realised how enticing she was. But she would know if he stood up. His reaction to her was strong and intense, unlike anything he had experienced in these last ten to twenty years.

'Well, I had thought you would preserve it. It is a fine example of Roman life here. A wonderful bit of history. Otherwise, why would you have commissioned the dig?'

He wondered what she would do if he continued to bait her. The urge to find out was irresistible. He had always been curious, even as a child. The trait had often ended with him covered in mud or dirt, or finding himself in a situation that was potentially dangerous. Like the time he had found a colony of bees and decided to get a piece of their honeycomb on his own. At ten, he had considered himself nearly a man. Instead, he had got badly stung, but he had also got the honeycomb. He always got what he wanted.

'Curiosity. I go to great lengths to satisfy it.'

She looked stunned, her scholar's heart shocked at such an answer. 'Curiosity? Is that all this is to you?'

He shrugged, enjoying her reaction. 'I am not sure that preserving an archaeological site of Roman occupation is the best use of my land, Lady Fenwick-Clyde. The area you are exploring is excellent farming land. I believe it is also in the middle of one of my orchards.' He turned to Tatterly, who was looking at his plate, his tongue tied by the proximity of his goddess. 'Is that not so, Tatterly?'

Tatterly started. 'What? Pardon me, Sir Hugo, I was not attending.'

Hugo swallowed his laugh. There was no sense in making his steward feel even more awkward than he already did. And Hugo did not enjoy making other people uncomfortable. Teasing and provoking, yes, but Tatterly was on the thin line between heaven and hell.

'I was telling Lady Fenwick-Clyde that her Roman dig is in the middle of one of my best orchards. Is that not so?'

'Yes. Yes, it is.' Tatterly's pleasant tenor was slow and solid no matter how uncomfortable he might be.

Hugo shook his head. The poor man was besotted. 'So you see, Lady Fenwick-Clyde, I must weigh economics against the preservation of history.'

He waved his hand to one of the footmen for more wine to be served. 'Thank you, John.'

The young man smiled with pleasure, ignoring the butler's frown. Footmen were to be seen, but were to keep a bland countenance. It was hard to do so when Sir Hugo was always friendly and always remembered names.

Annabell watched the byplay with interest but said nothing. Hugo decided to gratify her obvious curiosity. And a part of him wanted to see how she would react. He wanted to see if she was the woman he was beginning to think she might be.

'Once I would have been lucky to grow up to be a footman. I never forget that. So I always remember they are human beings the same as I am, only not so lucky in their birth.'

Her attention snapped back to him but she said nothing, even though her face held an arrested look. He had truly piqued her interest. Satisfaction was a sensation he hoped to experience with her in other ways as well as this.

'Surely you jest, Sir Hugo,' Miss Pennyworth said, waving away the young man with the wine. 'A man of your position and lineage would never have been at risk of being a servant. I mean, after all…' she waved her thin, white hand to encompass the elegantly appointed room '…you have all of this and more. Why would you want to spend even a short amount of time as a footman—or worse? I mean, it is inconceivable.'

Hugo considered the woman and her words while John poured him more wine. He thought he heard Lady Fenwick-Clyde groan but she said nothing. Wise. Miss Pennyworth was not only silly and a woman who rattled on, but was insensitive to the feelings of the people who worked around her. The truth would be a rude awakening for her to the realities of life and possibly make her more considerate of others' feelings. He could hope it would curtail her nattering, but he doubted that.

He took a long drink, set the glass down and relaxed back into his chair even more than he had been. 'No, ma'am, I don't jest. Not about that. I am surprised you have not heard my story. At one time it was on the tongue of every wag in London.'

Miss Pennyworth's pale blue eyes widened like saucers, seeming to take up her entire face.

'My companion and I do not frequent London salons,' Annabell said coolly. 'We also do not follow gossip.'

Hugo slanted her a look that spoke volumes about his doubt on the last. 'You are to be commended, Lady Fenwick-Clyde. Very few people have your discretion.'

'Indeed,' she said, her tone nearly a huff.

'Back to my story.' He turned his consideration back to Miss Pennyworth. 'My father, the late Sir Rafael Fitzsimmon, was not married to my mother.' The companion's mouth dropped open before she managed to snap it shut. 'Yes, it is true. A scandal had my mother been of good birth, but she was the housekeeper. A liaison like that is not all that unheard of. Particularly when the servant is comely, as everyone assures me my mother was.'

He heard Annabell Fenwick-Clyde's sharp intake of breath. For some reason, which he did not intend to explore, her reaction disappointed him. He had hoped that with her pointed disregard for polite society she would be more accepting of his past. An emotion he could not name made him curt.

'To make a long story short, I was given a baronetcy after Waterloo. My father had already willed me the part of his fortune not entailed. My half-brother will inherit my father's title and all that goes with it when he comes of age. Until that time, his mother and I are his joint guardians and trustees.'

Miss Pennyworth's complexion went from the red of embarrassment over his origins to white with discomfort. Hugo wondered if it would modify her attitude towards servants. Possibly, but probably not. He forced away the irritation that made him want to add something more shocking to the story.

'What happened to your mother?' Annabell asked so softly he barely heard her.

He shifted to look at her. Her eyes were soft with compassion, their deep blue nearly as black as a starless night. Perhaps he had been too quick to judge her. She seemed more concerned than repelled.

His gaze dropped to her lips. He had kissed them briefly, too briefly. He regretted that lapse. She had tasted of fresh air and sweet enticement. He wanted to touch her. Hell, he wanted to do a whole lot more than just touch her.

'She died giving birth to me.'

'Oh, I am so sorry.'

He waved off her concern. 'Don't be. I never knew her to mourn her and my father adored me. I never really missed having a mother. Unlike most men of his generation, my father spent a great deal of time with me.'

'But still,' she murmured.

He watched her, amazed to see her eyes fill with unshed tears. How had she managed to survive Fenwick-Clyde when his own far-from-sad story made her melancholy? It was a miracle.

'But enough of my tale.' Hugo stood. 'Can I interest the three of you in a game of whist?'

Annabell looked at her companion.

Miss Pennyworth smiled in delight. 'I so enjoy whist, or any card game. Many's the night Annabell and I have entertained ourselves with a deck of cards while she was on one of her travels. Isn't that so? Why, I remember the time we were caught in—'

'Susan,' Lady Fenwick-Clyde interrupted firmly. 'I am sure no one is interested in our boring lives. Shall we go?' To emphasise her words and determination, she rose and started toward the door.

Hugo smiled to himself. She obviously did not like her life discussed, or perhaps just that particular incident. He would have to pursue that story. Another challenge. They kept life interesting.

Tatterly stood as well. 'I...'

'Come along, Tatterly, you used to play cards with the best of them. Why, I remember one night in London—'

'Yes, Sir Hugo,' Tatterly interrupted. 'I would like to play whist.'

Hugo laughed. 'Good.'

He moved to follow Lady Fenwick-Clyde and touched her lightly on her gloved elbow. She jerked as though he had touched her with a hot coal. He smiled.

'And how about you, Lady Fenwick-Clyde?' he said, his voice intentionally pitched seductively low. 'You have not agreed or disagreed.'

She stayed far enough away that he could not casually touch her again, but he could see the pulse beating rapidly at the base of her throat. The light scent of honeysuckle wafted from her.

'I am outvoted. So, for the time being, I would be delighted to play whist.' She did not smile and her eyes held the sardonic acceptance that some things must be done for politeness.

'Gracious of you,' Hugo murmured. He made her a short bow. 'To the—'

'Library,' she said.

He smiled. 'But of course.' He turned to Butterworth. 'Please bring tea and more brandy. I fear I drank the last of the brandy earlier today.'

'Immediately, Sir Hugo,' the old retainer said.

'After you, dear ladies,' Hugo said.

Miss Pennyworth smiled broadly and Tatterly followed her from the room. Lady Fenwick-Clyde was slower, casting him a questioning look.

'Yes?'

'You don't have to entertain us, Sir Hugo. I am sure we are not the company you are used to keeping.'

'How do you know the company I keep?'

'Rumour.'

He smiled, but it did not reach his eyes. 'Rumour is a two-headed beast. It speaks with one mouth and turns around with the other and contradicts itself.'

She took a deep breath, making her full bosom rise and fall seductively, although he doubted she was aware of that. 'I insisted on staying to be near my site, not to spend the evenings with you.'

'Blunt. How delightful.'

Sarcasm edged his last words, but he could not help it. She irritated him at the same time as she intrigued him. Pursuing her would be interesting. Bedding her would be worth every minute of time and every ounce of energy it took to accomplish.

'But I am outvoted, as I said before. So, cards it will be.'

She turned and swept from the room. Hugo watched her with pleasure. She was a tall woman and well-endowed, with hips that swayed enticingly and made him long to feel them moving beneath his.

It would be some small satisfaction to beat her at cards. A start.

The library fire roared, sending golden and orange light to the game table set in front of it. A face screen was nearby for the person next to the fire to situate to protect his or her face. Several small braziers held lit coals that added to the warmth. Expensive wax candles surrounded their playing area. A serving table held tea, brandy and an assortment of sweetmeats.

Sir Hugo enjoyed his comforts, Annabell thought.

She sat farthest from the fire and was still comfortable. Her shawl was just enough. She watched Susan sit across from Mr Tatterly, her thin frame angling unconsciously toward the fire's heat. It was a good thing her companion would not be Sir Hugo's partner. Susan enjoyed cards, but she was not a good player. She tended to talk rather than pay attention to her hand. To finish settling in, Susan adjusted the fire-screen to shield her face from the direct heat.

Mr Tatterly gave Susan a hesitant, yet warm smile. Annabell barely kept from shaking her head. The two were such opposites, yet they seemed drawn to one another. Strange.

Sir Hugo sat with his back to the fire and picked up the cards. He fanned them on the table for every one to draw to see who was high card and dealer. His fingers, long, white and impeccably groomed, drew Annabell's attention. He might be the son of a housekeeper, but every part of him was elegant and refined. His nails were short and clean, his hands smoothly muscled. In a previous age, a fine fall of lace would have covered his supple wrists.

She shivered. What was she doing, admiring his hands?

But they moved with such grace. He flipped over a card. The ace of spades.

She shook her head slightly to clear it of unwelcome thoughts about her host and picked a card. The two of hearts. Sir Hugo won the draw and picked up the cards. With a manual dexterity that, for some reason she could not fathom, was mesmerising to her, he shuffled the cards and dealt them. The game began.

Annabell considered herself a competent player. Sir Hugo was better. They won the first rubber in spite of not always having the best cards.

'Tea?' he asked, watching her with an intensity that made her uncomfortable.

'Please.'

'Miss Pennyworth?'

'Please, Sir Hugo.' She laughed, her pale blue eyes sparkling. 'I cannot remember when I have enjoyed playing whist this much.'

'Really?' Sir Hugo's voice held a hint of sardonic amusement.

Annabell gave him a sharp glance, but he met her look without expression. Even so, she sensed he was not impressed with her companion, not that it was any of his concern.

He poured the tea for both of them, adding sugar and cream without asking. 'Brandy?' he asked Tatterly. 'Since we did not stay behind the ladies and drink ourselves under the table with port, we might as well drink ourselves under the card table with brandy.'

Mr Tatterly gave his employer a censorious look, but nodded.

They changed partners. This time Annabell played with Mr Tatterly. It was a débâcle. Miss Pennyworth, more interested in conversation, bid wrong then played wrong. Mr Tatterly had not cared. Annabell noticed Sir Hugo was not made from the same cut of cloth. Sir Hugo was competitive, nor was he enamoured of the lady. Annabell and Mr Tatterly won easily, but not soon enough for her comfort.

She rose immediately. 'I believe it is time for me to leave. I hope to be at the dig very early tomorrow.'

Sir Hugo stood more slowly. 'Of course. I will walk you to your room.'

'There is no need. I am a grown woman and can find my own way.'

'You are most decidedly a woman, Lady Fenwick-Clyde.' His gaze held hers with a hint of something warmer than appropriate, which was typical for him she knew. 'And a very independent one as you have gone to great lengths to prove, but I am going that way and wish company. And...' he gave her a mocking smile '...it will save on my candle bill. We will be able to share one instead of each of us carrying our own.'

'Hah! As though you care about such small economies.' She waved a hand in a semi-circle to take in the three small braziers burning brightly and warmly nearby. Not to mention the multitude of candles lighting their play area.

'Annabell,' Susan said, her voice holding mild reproof.

Annabell sighed. Obviously Susan had not sensed Sir Hugo's growing irritation, but then Susan was always happily ensconced in her own world.

Still, the last thing Annabell wanted was his company. After the fiasco at cards, she was not sure if she was afraid of his sensuality or angry at him for his barely concealed disgust with Susan. Either way, she did not want him escorting her anywhere. But it seemed she did not have a choice.

Her acceptance was grudging. 'If you insist, Sir Hugo.'

His smile mocked her. 'Oh, I do, Lady Fenwick-Clyde.'

Rather than stay and continue to play this game of words, she pivoted on her heel and moved into the foyer and from there to the stairs. Footmen, dressed in crimson and gold, stood their ground near the banister. She nodded at them and heard Sir Hugo address each by name and wish them a good night. He was a contradiction. He baited her and barely concealed his contempt for Susan, yet treated his servants as people in their own right. Of course, as he had told them at dinner, he had nearly been one.

They climbed. She could hear his shoes on the glossy waxed steps and sense his closeness. Then he was beside her, offering her his arm.

'No, thank you,' she said, hoping her voice was reasonably polite.

'As you wish,' he murmured.

The last thing she needed was to feel that sharp, disturbing jolt his touch created in her. It was bad enough that her entire being seemed on alert. Besides, she was still upset with him over the card game.

They left the stairs and walked down the carpeted hall. Now he was closer to her, if that were possible. The hall, while wide, was not nearly as wide as the stairs had been. Annabell felt as though his hips brushed hers, although she knew that was not so. There was at least a foot between them. Cinnamon and cloves filled her senses, a very unusual combination for a man to wear. But she found she liked it.

'You are an intelligent woman.' He spoke to her for the first time since leaving the library.

'I have always thought so.' She made no attempt to modify her haughty tone.

'And not overly modest.'

She glanced sharply at him, wondering where he was headed. 'I believe in knowing one's abilities. If that is being unmodest, then so be it.'

'Very practical.'

'I think so.'

'Then why do you saddle yourself with a companion who is so obviously inferior to you?'

She bristled. 'Susan is compassionate and kind. I could not hope for a better companion and friend.'

'Possibly,' he drawled. 'But she has not a thought in her brain. Let alone interesting conversation.'

She stopped dead in her tracks. 'How dare you speak of her like that? Just because you don't seem to appreciate her finer points doesn't make her worthless.'

'True,' he murmured.

She stared at him. 'Why did you bring this up?'

'To learn more about you?'

He watched her the way a wolf very likely watched the lamb it had decided to devour. She edged closer to the wall.

'And why would you do that?'

'Because you are my uninvited guest and because you intrigue me. I have never met a woman like you.'

She edged away. His attention made her feel decidedly uncomfortable. 'Well, you must have led a more sheltered life than I had thought.'

He laughed. *'Touché.'*

She moved forward, eager to be away from this disturbing situation he had created. Even so, she felt his gaze on her back like a flame. She shivered in spite of the warmth provided by her practical dress and shawl.

He chuckled low in his throat so that the sound came out like a growl. 'I promise not to attack you out here where anyone going about their business can see.'

She glanced over her shoulder. The glitter in his eyes was unnerving.

'Just promise not to attack me at all,' she muttered, forgetting he was close enough to hear anything she said.

He laughed. 'I can't promise that. Nor would I even if I thought I could control myself.'

She paused, taken aback by his response, before forcing herself to keep walking. She picked up her pace.

'You are a self-indulgent man.'

She kept herself from looking at him to see his reaction to her censorious words. Very likely he did not like her blunt speaking—most men did not—or she had provoked him into doing or saying something outrageous. She seemed to have that effect on him.

'I am a hedonist.' He kept pace with her. 'I take my pleasures where I find them. Life is too short to deny oneself.'

She snorted. 'I believe I heard that explanation earlier.'

'Because it is true.'

Something in his voice caught her. She stopped and looked at him. He met her scrutiny without reaction.

'You truly do mean that, self-centred as the philosophy is.'

He nodded. 'If I did not, I would not have said so this afternoon, let alone just repeated it. Remember that.'

He lifted a hand to her face. She stepped back, but the wall kept her from going far enough. One long, elegantly strong finger touched the bow in her upper lip. Her reaction to him was swift and intense. Her legs weakened, and she was thankful the wall supported her back and kept her from slipping to the floor.

He closed the already too-small distance between them. 'Why should I deny myself life's physical pleasures? Particularly when they don't harm anyone else.' He paused and his eyes met hers with a hunger that made her senses whirl. 'And even give another person equal or greater pleasure?'

She swallowed hard and wondered fleetingly how she had got into this situation. Then his finger fell away from her. The hunger that had sharpened his face seconds before fell away also and was replaced by another emotion she couldn't read.

'You are leaning on my bedchamber door.'

She jumped, her eyes wide. 'Your door?'

He nodded. 'Very close to yours.'

She stood mute, chills chasing flames down her spine.

'No comment?' His voice was low and provocative, with a hint of barely concealed sardonic amusement.

She made herself shrug. 'What is there to say, Sir Hugo?

You are on the same floor as I am. That is not unusual.'
She wished her voice sounded as blasé as her words.

'True.'

He stepped back enough for her to slide away from his
door. She took a deep breath of relief, ignoring the sudden
urge to turn the handle to his room and look inside. As
decadent as he was, his rooms were likely opulent and seductive. A silly thought that had no relevance to her. Silly
it might be, but her stomach did somersaults at the thought.

She forced herself to continue down the hall to her chamber. She sensed him behind her and could swear he laughed
at her, but she could hear nothing.

She reached her door and kept herself from dashing inside to safety by squaring her shoulders and reminding herself she was a woman who met life's challenges head on.
To do otherwise was to be weak and usually at the mercy
of someone who was physically or emotionally stronger.
She had been in that position. She would never be there
again.

She turned and faced Sir Hugo. 'Thank you for walking
me here.'

He stopped, one brow lifted. 'Polite now that you are
about to get rid of me?'

She refused to let him embarrass her. 'Rudeness has not
deterred you.'

'Nothing keeps me from a goal, Lady Fenwick-Clyde.'
He studied her, his gaze travelling from her eyes to her lips
and lowered. 'Nothing.'

'Nothing?' She met the challenge of his study.

He watched her with an intensity in his green eyes that
made her jumpy. She felt breathless and hot and excited
and nervous and all manner of things that were not comfortable and yet were not uncomfortable either. He aroused
emotions in her she had never experienced. It took every
ounce of determination not to turn the handle and bolt into
her room.

He continued to watch her, his gaze lingering on her lips. 'I didn't kiss you for long enough.'

'What?' What was he talking about? What was he doing?

'I didn't kiss you for long enough earlier today.'

She felt the heat rise up her neck and stain her cheeks. 'You shouldn't have kissed me at all.'

'That's a matter of opinion. Mine happens to differ from yours.' His voice lowered to a husky rasp. 'I should not have stopped kissing you.'

She shook her head. 'I can't believe you are saying these things, Sir Hugo. You are much too forward.'

He smiled, slowly and seductively. 'Then go into your room, Lady Fenwick-Clyde. I won't follow unless you invite me.'

She gasped. But she didn't turn the handle. She wasn't sure why not. He fascinated her, even in his aggressive pursuit of her. She belonged in Bedlam, surely, or worse, Bedlam in a straitjacket.

'Be assured, Sir Hugo, I won't invite you.'

His smile turned predatory. 'Not tonight.'

'Not ever.'

He reached out and she flinched, afraid of what he intended to do, but more afraid of what she would do. When he laid a single finger on her jaw and nothing more, she remembered to breathe.

'We shall see about that.'

It was a challenge and she rose to meet it. 'Yes, we will.'

He chuckled low in his throat. 'Spitfire. Lady Spitfire.'

He continued to look at her, his gaze going back to her mouth. Was he going to kiss her? Here in the hall where anyone could see? Was she going to be able to resist him? Did she want to? This was crazy.

His finger traced up her jaw before falling away. She took a deep breath. He chuckled again. Without another word, he left.

Annabell stood rooted to the spot and watched him saunter down the hall and enter his room without looking back at her. She wasn't sure whether to be hurt that he'd put her from his mind so easily or glad that he'd done so. If he wasn't thinking about her then she was likely to be safe from his dangerous advances. Even if he was dangerous only because she was susceptible, it was the same danger.

She sighed and slipped into her room, no longer sure of anything. She needed a good night's sleep—with no dreams of her disturbing host.

Hugo resisted the temptation to look back. She had already tempted him too much this night.

He entered his room and went to a large, comfortable leather chair pulled in front of a roaring fire. He sank into it.

'M'lord, do you wish to prepare for bed?'

He had not seen Jamison. The valet had a knack for being unobtrusive. 'Very proper tonight, aren't we?'

He smiled as he said the words. The two of them had been through a great deal and forged a bond that went beyond employer and employee.

The valet came to stand near the fire. Jamison was a short, bandy-legged man with a bald pate and a twinkling eye. He didn't carry an ounce of extra weight and, Hugo knew very well, could handle himself in any fight.

'I'll put myself to bed, Jamison.'

'That's a shame, sir. But, for meself, there's a new barmaid at the Horse and Donkey. If you don't need me, I'll make my way there.'

Hugo laughed. 'You old reprobate.'

His valet, who had been his batman during the wars and before that had been a sergeant in Wellington's Indian army, grinned. Jamison was a farmer's son and believed in ploughing any field he encountered.

'Like I always said, sir, it takes one to know one.'

Hugo shook his head. 'It's a good thing for you I appreciate frankness.'

'That it is, sir.' For a moment only he sobered, then the look was gone as though it had never existed. 'Well, I'll be on me way then.'

'But,' Hugo said to his valet's disappearing back, 'I will be needing hot water tomorrow morning to shave. It was a little lacking this morning.'

Jamison almost looked sheepish. 'Didn't feel up to snuff after courting the lady last night. I'll be sure to do better tomorrow, sir.'

Hugo shook his head. If the water wasn't here, he'd ring and have some brought up. That's what he paid good wages for to the house servants. Jamison, he owed more than money could buy. Jamison had saved his life at Waterloo.

'Enjoy yourself, old man.'

'I'll try, sir.'

Hugo laughed. Nothing like a bout with Jamison to put everything into perspective. Miss Pennyworth might drive him to the consideration of murder, and Lady Fenwick-Clyde—Lady Spitfire—Annabell—might drive him to the point of physical pain, but both were something he could deal with. He could hand Miss Pennyworth over to Tatterly, and he could join Jamison at the pub and find a willing wench to ease the ache caused by Lady Fenwick-Clyde.

He rose and shook his head as he made his way to the bed. No, he couldn't ease this particular ache with anyone but the woman who created it. He was experienced enough to realise that about himself.

With nimble fingers, he undid his clothing and stepped out of them. From force of habit, he laid them neatly across a nearby chair. He added the nightshirt to the pile. He enjoyed his luxuries, but required that they be neatly compartmentalised. Clutter was as uncomfortable as being cold.

He snuffed the bedside candle and climbed between the satin sheets with nothing between him and them to diminish the pleasure. The smooth silky material slid along his skin. They were cool, but the warming pan had made them tolerable. Soon the hot water bottles and heated bricks would make them nearly toasty. Jamison might be rackety in some areas, but he knew to warm the bed.

Hugo rolled on to his back and stared at the ceiling of his canopied bed. Lascivious cherubs frolicked with sylphs, doing things no innocent could imagine. He imaged himself doing those things to and with Annabell Fenwick-Clyde. He was instantly, painfully aware of how much he wanted that.

Soon.

Chapter Four

Annabell woke the next day with an aching head and shoulders that felt as though she'd been carrying the weight of the world on them. She closed her eyes and wished she could go back to sleep, but that would solve nothing. Sir Hugo Fitzsimmon had figured prominently in the dreams she hadn't wanted to have.

He had done things with her and to her that made her blush to remember. Things her husband had forced her to do with him, which she had not enjoyed. With Sir Hugo—Hugo—she had revelled in the sensations. She scowled. Sir Hugo had not bound her.

To put paid to the unwelcomed thoughts, both memory and dream, she clambered out of bed. The sooner she moved about, the sooner she would be at the site and the sooner she would forget the disturbing dreams that were becoming nightly visitors.

She dropped her nightdress to the floor, planning to pick it up later. She dressed without help, a skill she had mastered in her travels. Then she went to the dresser and rummaged around the bottles and vials, looking for her brush. She knew she had left it here, but…

She found it on a table beside the chair where she normally read. A copy of Jane Austen's latest book lay beside it. She brushed her thick, silver-blonde hair quickly and secured it in a long braid, which she wrapped around the back of her head. Now it would stay out of the way while she dug.

She moved to the mirror to examine herself. She wasn't fashionable, but she was practical. That was more important.

The sound of wheels on gravel drew her to the window. She pulled back the heavy blue-velvet curtain and peered through the many-paned glass.

A post-chaise stopped in the circular carriage drive and two young children erupted from the vehicle. The boy's head glinted like a newly minted penny. The girl's shone like summer sunshine. They must be Sir Hugo's half-brother and half-sister. It had been some time since he had told her they were coming. Presumably, they had stopped someplace for the night on their way here.

Seconds later, a woman emerged, moving more sedately than her offspring, but still with a buoyancy that made Annabell think she must be a happy person. She wore a royal blue pelisse with epaulets in the military style that was all the rage since Waterloo. She was much shorter than the footman who helped her.

The woman entered the front door and passed out of Annabell's sight. She turned from the window. Likely, she would meet the three of them at dinner.

Things would be less strained with more people. Sir Hugo wouldn't watch her as carefully as he currently did. Somehow, that thought did not comfort her no matter how she told herself it should. She was not interested in him, or only a little. She couldn't help that her body desired his, she could only make sure she did not give into temptation.

Having his stepmother and two young children around them would help.

* * *

Hugo strode to greet his stepmother. 'Juliet. Welcome.'

Two whirling dervishes attacked him before Juliet could reply. He grabbed the smaller package and lifted her high.

'Hugo,' Rosalie Fitzsimmon squealed.

Hugo laughed. 'Rosalie!'

The larger of the two slowed down so he wouldn't get hit by his sister's feet as Hugo swung the girl around. 'Hugo,' Joseph said more sedately, but with the same thread of excitement his sister had exhibited. 'Put her down.'

Hugo smiled at his half-brother, catching the unspoken *and pay attention to me*. He set Rosalie down in spite of her pout.

'Joseph, I am glad to see you. It will be nice to have another man around here.' Hugo extended his hand.

Joseph took Hugo's hand and broke into a smile that nearly split his face. 'Hugo, can we go talk about Waterloo?'

Hugo glanced at Juliet, saw her frown and said, 'Perhaps later we can discuss some of it, but right now I wish to speak with your mother.'

'You *always* talk to her.'

Hugo ruffled the boy's fine hair. 'Not always. Sometimes I talk to Rosalie. You have to learn, Joseph, that women are worth talking to.' He grinned at the boy's unconcealed disbelief. 'I know it's hard to believe at your age, but trust me.'

Joseph scowled. 'I will accept what you say, but I do find it hard to believe.'

Hugo laughed at the look on Juliet's face, the mingled humour and resignation. 'You will.'

The young governess made her way through the entrance, saw them and realised it was time for the children to go to their rooms and the nursery. 'Come along,' she said, nodding her head shyly at Hugo's smile. 'We must get ready for our nap.'

'Oh…' Joseph complained.

'Don't want to,' Rosalie protested.

She herded them anyway.

'Would you like refreshments?' Hugo took Juliet's cape before the footman could reach them. He handed it to the strapping young man.

'I would die for a hot cup of tea.' Juliet undid the bow of her chip bonnet. 'In the library?'

'Where else?' Hugo smiled and waved his stepmother ahead.

She smiled back and made her way to the familiar room. She settled into her favourite chair, the one Lady Fenwick-Clyde always sat in. Hugo wondered what it was about overstuffed chintz.

He sat beside her. 'Why did you pick that chair?'

Juliet gave him a quizzical look. 'What brought that up?'

He smiled and shook his head. 'I am curious. It seems to be a favourite with the ladies.'

She took off her bonnet and set it on the table beside her seat. 'What a queer observation, Hugo. Are you sure you aren't ailing?'

He laughed. 'Not in the way you suggest.'

She sobered. 'Really?'

Tea arrived and they spent several quiet moments while Juliet prepared herself a cup. He declined any.

'I have two women here, Juliet.'

She choked, nearly spilling her tea. 'Hugo! How could you dare?'

He frowned. Even Juliet thought him an unprincipled rakehell. 'They are not my mistresses.' Honesty made him add, 'At least, not yet.'

Her expression went from relief to alarm. 'Yet?'

'That is why I am especially grateful to have you here.'

'You are?' She took a hasty sip, as though she needed it to fortify herself.

This time his smile was that of a wolf, anticipating a very good meal. 'That is what I tell myself.'

She shook her head. 'You are talking in riddles.'

'Miss Pennyworth must be rubbing off on me.'

'Hugo?'

'Lady Fenwick-Clyde and her companion, Miss Pennyworth, are staying here while Lady Fenwick-Clyde excavates a Roman ruin.'

Juliet paled, then flushed, her fair complexion coming as close to mottled as it was capable. 'Lady Fenwick-Clyde?'

Hugo watched the emotions flit across her face and wondered how she even knew Annabell Fenwick-Clyde. He had moved in the *ton*'s rarified stratosphere as a crony of Prinney's, and he had not met Lady Fenwick-Clyde until he kissed her on his property just days ago.

And what a kiss. Her lips had been soft and yielding, drawing him into an inferno he had not known existed. Now it was hell every time he saw her and couldn't kiss her. Even now, sitting in front of the roaring fire in his favourite room with his stepmother, just the thought of that kiss aroused him to the point that he was grateful to be sitting down and not standing in front of Juliet. He was many things, but he had never flouted his interests before anyone but the women who created them. Until now.

He snorted. 'Yes, Lady Fenwick-Clyde. It seems she is something of an amateur antiquarian.'

'Does she have a stepson?' Juliet's tone was innocent, but there was an intensity in her gaze that told Hugo the question meant more to her than she wanted to divulge.

'I believe so. At least I know the late Fenwick-Clyde had a son by his first wife. Don't remember the boy's name.'

Juliet's blush deepened. 'Timothy. His name is Timothy.' Her fingers twisted in her lap. 'And he isn't a boy. He is a widower. His wife and babe died in childbirth over a year ago.'

'My mistake.' Hugo watched his stepmother with great interest. 'Do you know him well?'

'No. That is, some. We met during the Season. The children like him.'

Hugo caught himself before he frowned. He did not like the sound of this. Fenwick-Clyde's son was not someone he wished his sweet stepmother to associate with. In his experience, the apple never fell far from the tree.

'Are you seeing him?'

Juliet's fair skin got fairer. Her hand stilled. 'Not exactly.'

'Do you wish to tell me what that means?'

'No, Hugo. I don't. At least, not yet.' She took a deep breath. 'But that is not why we are in here. You were going to tell me about your guests.'

'Bravo, Juliet. You have put me in my place, which is not to question you about the men you see. But I do worry.'

She smiled gently at him. 'I know you do, Hugo. But things are not that way.'

He would have believed her if she had not blushed again. But he chose not to comment.

'Back to my problem. As a bachelor, and one with a reputation to maintain,' he said, tongue-in-cheek, 'it did not seem like the best thing for everyone involved to have Lady Fenwick-Clyde staying here. Although she is a widow and has a companion, I didn't feel her good name could withstand the consequences of being here alone with me.'

Juliet's violet eyes widened. 'Since when have you cared a tuppence for that?'

This time Hugo reddened, a fact that irritated him. 'Since I am not in the habit of ruining respectable women.'

'You are in the habit of forming liaisons with widows.' Her point was pertinent and the look of disbelief she wore told him she was not sure she believed his concern.

He shrugged. 'Widows of a certain ilk. Lady Fenwick-Clyde is not in that category.'

'Really? I look forward to meeting her, for I vow, Hugo, I have yet to meet the woman who can resist you or even wants to. Most fall willy-nilly into your arms and are glad of it.' She cocked her delicate head to one side. 'There is something about you. Your father had it.'

His eyes narrowed. 'Then why didn't you succumb?'

She dropped her gaze for a long moment before looking back at him. 'Because Rafael married me for convenience. He had decided you needed a woman's hand. What he failed to realise was that you needed the hand of an older woman who could be a mother to you.' She took a deep breath. 'Still, I was wise enough to know better than to lose my heart to him. He did not want it.'

Hugo was taken aback, but hid it. She had never told him this. He had known the marriage was one of convenience, but he had not realised she had cared for his father beyond that of a dutiful wife.

He did let his sympathy show. 'I am so sorry, Juliet.' He reached across the small table separating them and took one of her hands. 'I did not realise or I would not have pried.'

She smiled. 'It is in the past, my dear. I don't dwell on it. And I have Joseph and Rosalie. I could not wish for more, yet I have it. I have your love and concern and a very generous widow's portion.' Her eyes turned mischievous. 'What more could I want?'

Hugo did not say the word that came instantly to mind. He was not even comfortable thinking it. Yet, it had sprung forward without his conscious thought. *Love.* Damn, he was getting maudlin and for no good reason.

'Well,' she said briskly, looking away from the concern in his eyes, 'I must go freshen up. I want to look my best when I meet this paragon who can resist temptation.'

Hugo stood and drew her up with him. He closed the distance between them and kissed her lightly on the top of her head that barely reached his shoulder.

'You are an angel, Juliet. Thank you for coming.'

She grinned. 'From what I've just heard, I would not miss this for the world. A woman who can resist you. Will wonders never cease?'

He watched her glide from the room. Better she think Annabell Fenwick-Clyde could resist him than she know that both he and the lady shared an awareness of each other that was like dry wood ready to burst into an inferno. Even better that she not know he intended to seduce Annabell. Juliet being here provided respectability—it did not prevent anything from happening.

Annabell stood in the salon gazing up at Sir Rafael Fitzsimmon. Sir Hugo had a look of his father. Both were tall and well formed with rich chestnut-coloured hair that fell rakishly across their broad foreheads. But where Sir Hugo's eyes were a startling grass green, his father's had been deep brown. Both men shared Sir Hugo's erotic mouth.

'He was a handsome man, even in middle age,' a light, female voice said. 'As is his son.'

Annabell jumped and turned to face the speaker she had not heard enter the room. A petite woman with masses of waving Titian-coloured hair smiled at her. Sir Hugo's stepmother was dressed in the latest fashion of pale muslin with an embroidered ruched hem. Pearls circled her wrists and throat and dripped from her tiny, shell-pink ears. She was a Pocket Venus, unless Annabell missed her mark, which she doubted. Her brothers would describe Lady Fitzsimmon as a diamond of the first water.

'Pardon me,' the lady said. 'I did not mean to startle you. I am Juliet Fitzsimmon, Hugo's stepmother.'

Annabell smiled and introduced herself. 'It is not your fault. I was engrossed in studying your husband. As you said, he was very attractive. Even his picture radiates a sense of power and charisma. I can imagine that when he spoke to someone, he gave them his complete attention.'

Lady Fitzsimmon's violet eyes, heavily fringed with pale red lashes, watched Annabell. 'You have described him perfectly. One would almost think you knew him.' She cocked her head to one side and her little Cupid's bow mouth quirked into a smile. 'But you know Hugo. It is very nearly the same.'

'Not really,' Annabell said, hoping to avoid a discussion about her host. 'That is, I don't know Sir Hugo well at all.'

She had not realised, until Lady Fitzsimmon said it, that she had attributed Sir Hugo's traits to his father. It was disconcerting, to say the least, and had been totally unconscious.

'I see you two have met,' the object of their discussion drawled, entering the room.

While Annabell and Lady Fitzsimmon had dressed formally, Sir Hugo was his usual casual self. He wore a loose bottle-green coat and black pantaloons, a style only beginning to be popular but normally never worn in the evening. They were considered casual, daytime wear. His shirt points were moderate and he wore a loosely knotted cravat. He was dressed up for himself. Still, he radiated presence and...

Annabell took a deep breath. All he had to do was enter a room and her blood warmed. What was wrong with her? She did not love the man, yet she was intensely aware of him. She shivered.

'Are you cold?' Sir Hugo asked, his voice solicitous. 'We must move closer to the fire.'

'Thank you, no.' Annabell silently berated herself for the breathiness of her voice, especially when Lady Fitzsimmon gave her a quizzical look. 'I will go get a shawl.'

'No,' Sir Hugo said. He moved past Annabell and pulled the sash to summon a servant. 'By the time you returned it would be dinner, and I don't wish to push it back.' His eyes warmed with something Annabell didn't think was caused by the thought of food. 'And I am hungry.'

Annabell closed her mouth on a retort telling him she would do as she pleased. There was no reason to be rude even if his action struck her as high-handed, even if his gaze on her made her uncomfortably aware that he was a man and she was a woman. She would not give him the satisfaction of knowing he disturbed her. She could be stubborn to a fault, but sometimes it was to her advantage.

'Hugo tells me you study antiquities,' Lady Fitzsimmon said.

Annabell studied the other woman's face for a hint of what she felt. Most females were not the least bit interested in what Annabell did. To her surprise, Lady Fitzsimmon seemed to actually care or was a very good actress.

'I like to find and preserve pieces of the past. That is why I am here. There is what appears to be a Roman villa on Sir Hugo's land—in one of his very productive orchards.' She cast him a look, daring him to say something. He kept quiet. 'But I won't know for sure until I uncover more of it.'

'Hugo mentioned something about that. However did you hear about it?'

'I was visiting the Society of Antiquaries, or rather I was there listening to one of the members give a talk about his discoveries. It turned out to be this site.'

'That explains how you found out,' Sir Hugo interrupted, his voice dry, 'but not why you are the one here instead of a man.'

'Hugo.' Lady Fitzsimmon's voice was low.

He glanced at his stepmother before turning his attention back to Annabell. Annabell took a deep breath, telling herself not to explode. This was his house, his Roman villa and his money was funding the dig. He could tell her to leave, now, this instant, and very nearly had already.

She took a deep breath. 'I was the only one present who was not already committed elsewhere. Besides—' she met his gaze defiantly '—I am as well qualified as anyone else—male or female.'

As though realising Annabell was a power keg just waiting for the right spark, Lady Fitzsimmon intervened. 'How long do you expect your work to take?'

It took Annabell a second to appreciate that Lady Fitzsimmon was trying to direct their conversation away from a volatile area. Only the lady did not know that this was equally risky. Annabell wanted to say not long at all, but honesty forbade her. She knew Sir Hugo wanted her gone quickly and feared if he knew how long she really thought the excavation would take he would order her out of his house immediately. That would be very inconvenient for her. He had made it abundantly clear he did not want her under his roof for long, and her digging was going to be longer than he would like. When his stepmother left, which she anticipated would be before she was finished, she would have to relocate. And that would be the least evil.

'Many months.' She sighed. 'Or possibly even years. It is very hard to gauge.'

'That is a long time. You did not tell me that.'

Sir Hugo's deep voice startled her. She had been thinking so hard about her dilemma she had not realised Sir Hugo had come up beside her.

Annabell shrugged, trying doggedly to ignore the jump in her pulse. Cinnamon and cloves engulfed her. He smelled good enough to eat. The image that provoked made her face flame.

When she spoke her voice was rough. 'I…I didn't think it mattered. And, as I said, I could not give you a definite time. It just depends on what we find. And how thoroughly we excavate, and a host of other things I can't begin to see at this stage.'

'Mama!' a light-pitched voice yelled.

'Hugo!'

All three adults turned simultaneously. Relief flooded Annabell. For the moment she would be off the hot seat.

She watched with pleasure as two whirlwinds swept into the room and launched themselves at Lady Fitzsimmon and Sir Hugo. Naturally, the girl went for Sir Hugo. Annabell could understand perfectly.

'Easy, or you will knock me down.' He caught the bundle of white muslin skirts and guinea-gold hair and swung the girl into the air. 'You just saw me this afternoon, Rosalie. Why all this excitement?'

The girl giggled. 'Because I missed you. You were gone to the Continent for ever so long.'

Sir Hugo set her gently on her feet. 'Yes, I was. Too long. I missed you and Joseph, but the Duke of Wellington needed my help.'

He said it so solemnly that it took Annabell a minute to realise he was teasing about his importance to Wellington. Although from the way he continued to hold the child's hand, she knew he meant what he said about missing her.

The boy's eyes turned wide as saucers, and he wiggled out of his mother's hug and rushed to Sir Hugo. 'Jolly well done, Hugo. To be important to Wellington.'

Sir Hugo smiled and put his arm around the boy's shoulders. 'Actually he had plenty of help. I left early. Many are still with him.'

'Ah, you were teasing us,' the girl said.

The boy frowned. 'I thought you were serious, Hugo. I am quite old enough that you should not tease me about important things like Wellington and Waterloo. I know we defeated Napoleon and kept him from conquering the world.'

Sir Hugo's face turned solemn, even the gleam disappeared from his eyes. 'You are right, Joseph. I should not talk down to you. I won't in the future.'

'Thank you, Hugo.'

Joseph's smile lit his face and accentuated the trail of freckles that started at the outer corner of one cheek and marched across his snubbed nose to the corner of the other cheek. He had the former Baronet Fitzsimmon's dark brown eyes and enticing mouth. Otherwise, his colouring was his momma's.

The girl, on the other hand, had the deeper olive skin

tones of Sir Hugo and his father. Her eyes were the clear violet of her mother's, and her mouth was a sweet Cupid's bow. She would be arresting when she was older, her snub nose and light dusting of freckles only adding to her appeal.

'Joseph, Rosalie, you need to meet Hugo's guest.' Both children immediately quietened and turned to face Annabell. 'Rosalie, Joseph, this is Lady Fenwick-Clyde.'

The girl curtsied and the young man bowed. Both looked serious and curious all at once.

'How do you do?' Joseph said, obviously hoping she would treat him as the adult he considered himself to be.

Annabell smiled. 'I am pleased to meet both of you.'

She saw some of the tension leave the boy's shoulders at her formal reply. The girl cocked her head to one side and smiled widely.

'You are very tall,' Rosalie said.

'Rosalie!' Lady Fitzsimmon groaned in gentle exasperation. 'Children. No matter how you try to drum manners into them, they will leave them behind.'

Annabell chuckled. 'No matter, Lady Fitzsimmon. I was much worse at their ages.'

'Really?'

'Somehow I find that not surprising,' Sir Hugo drawled in a dry tone.

She shot him a minatory look before focusing back on the children. 'I was the despair of my poor mother. But I believe all children are that way, usually through no fault of their own.'

'How interesting,' Sir Hugo said, ruffling Rosalie's fine hair so that wisps escaped out from its braid. 'I dare say most parents are not so sanguine.'

Annabell laughed. 'Neither were mine. I spent plenty of time in the nursery with no dinner. But then, so did my brothers, so it was not at all bad.' She winked at the children. 'The nursery maid would sneak us up food.'

'Well, enough of this before they decide to emulate you,'

Lady Fitzsimmon said, a laugh in her voice. 'Miss Childs is come to take them up to supper and bed.'

The governess moved shyly into the room. She was of medium height with a pleasing figure and dressed demurely in grey wool. Her hair was light brown with gold highlights, and her nose was a trifle long. But her eyes were striking. They were grey with long straight lashes that made them appear to droop at the outer corners, giving her an exotic, sultry look. But she did not move like a siren, she moved like a young woman out of her depth.

Annabell smiled at the governess and noticed Sir Hugo did the same. Instantly, to her shame, jealousy tightened her stomach. This was awful, this envy of a woman she didn't even know simply because Sir Hugo Fitzsimmon smiled at her. This was not like her, nor did she like this reaction. She made her smile wider in an effort to compensate for her thoughts.

'You must come back and join us for dinner,' Sir Hugo said.

'Yes, Melissa,' Lady Fitzsimmon added. 'We would enjoy having you.' She smiled. 'And I am sure the sound of adult conversation would be welcomed.'

'Mama,' protested Joseph.

His mother smiled down at him. 'Joseph, I know you are maturing, but you are not a man yet. Just as Rosalie is still a young girl. Melissa should mingle with adults, if for no other reason than to have a reprieve from your demands.'

Before the children could protest again or Melissa accept the invitation, Miss Pennyworth arrived with Mr Tatterly in tow. Both smiled and were introduced to the governess and children.

'Remember,' Lady Fitzsimmon said to the governess, 'I expect you back shortly.'

Hugo smiled. 'We will hold dinner until you return.'

Miss Childs blushed, but looked pleased with the invitation and the attention. 'Yes, my lady,' she murmured before shooing the children from the room.

'What a delightful young woman,' Susan Pennyworth said. 'She must be wonderful with your children, Lady Fitzsimmon. Why, I remember when I was a governess in India. Hot, nasty climate, but I enjoyed the children.' She caught Annabell's raised brow. 'All but the last. She was the devil in child's form. Fortunately for me, Annabell rescued me and I have never looked back.'

Everyone politely listened, but Annabell noticed a sardonic curve to Sir Hugo's mouth. She frowned at him. Even when Susan made perfect sense, he chose to see her as frivolous.

Thankfully for her increasing temper, Miss Childs returned quickly and Lady Fitzsimmon led them into dinner. Now, if only they would eat as quickly and she could retire.

Chapter Five

Annabell watched Sir Hugo dance around the music-room floor with the governess, Miss Melissa Childs, and wondered why she was not enjoying herself. Probably because she had wished to escape to her room after dinner, but had been put to the blush when she had suggested it. Now she was here against her will, but a guest often did things she did not wish.

She knew for a surety that her discomfort was not caused by Sir Hugo smiling at something Miss Childs was saying. In order to reaffirm her conviction, she looked at the other people in the room.

Lady Fitzsimmon sat at the pianoforte, playing a lively country tune. Susan blushed and tittered as Mr Tatterly carefully swung her around, mindful not to step on her feet. The servants had rolled back the Aubusson rug so that the highly polished oak planks provided more than enough room.

There! She knew she did not have to watch Sir Hugo. She was perfectly happy watching everyone else.

The music came to a rousing finish and Annabell clapped, glad of another diversion. 'You play very well, Lady Fitzsimmon.'

Lady Fitzsimmon laughed. 'Please, call me Juliet. If we

are to spend the next couple of weeks—or more—together, let us not stand on formality.'

Annabell smiled and wondered why this quick affinity between them seemed so right. 'Only if you will call me Annabell.'

'Most certainly.' Juliet cast a conspiratorial glance at Annabell. 'Shall I play a waltz? It is all the craze.'

Annabell shrugged. 'If you wish. You are, after all, the musician. The rest of us are at your mercy.'

'Fie,' Susan said, coming to a breathless stop by the two women. 'Do not be so ungracious, Annabell.'

There were times when she wondered why she tolerated Susan. Immediately she regretted the spurt of irritation. She tolerated her companion because she loved her. They had been together a long time and had gone through a lot of things together. And she had been churlish. The thought of Sir Hugo waltzing with Miss Melissa Childs had not been a pleasant one, no matter how she had tried to mislead herself. Which only made her feelings that much more unacceptable.

'You are right, Susan.' She smiled down at Juliet. 'Please, give us the pleasure of a waltz.'

Juliet smiled back. 'Do you waltz?'

Before she could reply, Susan answered for her. 'She will not learn it. I have implored her to do so, for it is vastly entertaining. Like flying free. But she refuses.'

'Perhaps I can persuade her,' Sir Hugo's deep, honey-rich voice said from too close to Annabell's back.

She willed herself to calmness and pivoted to face him. 'Better men and…' she cast a glance at Susan '…women than you have tried, Sir Hugo.'

'A challenge?' He raised one mahogany brow.

'No, a refusal. Nothing more.' She forced herself to laugh lightly. 'But I am sure you can find a willing partner, even from so limited a supply.'

He made her a mocking bow. 'I would ask Juliet, but she must play the tune—unless you also play the pianoforte.'

'Unfortunately, Sir Hugo, that is not one of my accomplishments.'

Only after the words were out did she realise how defensive she had sounded. He seemed to bring out the worst in her.

He gave her a knowing look before turning to the governess. 'I fear you must do me the honour once more, Miss Childs.'

She smiled timidly at him before her gaze dropped. 'I should look in on the children, sir.'

'No, no, Melissa,' Juliet Fitzsimmon said. 'You deserve to have some fun. Dance with Hugo, for I swear he is very graceful.'

Miss Childs blushed to the roots of her ash-brown hair. 'I don't know how to waltz.'

'Is that all?' Sir Hugo held out his hand. 'I will teach you.'

'Oh, dear. I could not.'

He smiled. 'Yes, you can. You are light on your feet and have a good sense of rhythm. You will learn quickly. Juliet, if you will.'

Juliet turned back to the keyboard, flexed her fingers like a maestro and began with a flourish. Music filled the room.

Mr Tatterly bowed to Miss Pennyworth, who laughed delightedly as she moved into the stiff and very proper circle of his arms. They waltzed away.

Annabell watched from the side and told herself it did not matter if Sir Hugo's arm was around another woman's waist. It did not matter at all. Absolutely not.

But she knew better.

He moved with consummate skill, leading his faltering partner with grace. One would never know he had suffered a war injury in his left leg. He bent down to say something to Miss Childs, who smiled and blushed wildly. He was charming the girl.

Annabell gritted her teeth against the urge to offer herself for the next waltz, if there was one. Better judgement said the less she had to do with her host, the better off she would be. Still, she was sorely tempted.

To distract herself, she watched Susan and Mr Tatterly. They made a very disparate couple. She was tall and lean while he was just barely her height and solid, although not fat. Yet, each wore a look on their face that spoke of wonder, as though neither had thought they would ever find someone to care for and who would care for them in return.

Annabell smiled wistfully. Her oldest brother had found that happiness with Felicia. There were times she envied him, but, for the most part, she was content going on as she was.

The music stopped with a flourish, drawing her back to the picture of Miss Childs in Sir Hugo's arms. He escorted her back to the pianoforte, his attention on her heart-shaped, upturned face. The young woman was besotted. Annabell found herself feeling sorry for the governess. Sir Hugo would break the girl's heart and not even realise it.

'Perhaps,' Juliet said, a worried look on her face, 'you would do me a favour, Annabell, and dance with Hugo next. While I know he has no designs on my governess, I do not wish to see the chit hurt.'

'I agree, Juliet. That would not be fair to her.' Annabell sighed. 'Perhaps we should stop for the night?'

'Never say so,' Susan said, hurrying over and pulling Mr Tatterly with her. 'We are having so much fun, aren't we, Mr Tatterly?' She turned adoring eyes on her escort, who reddened with pleasure.

He returned her look. 'I do not generally enjoy dancing, Miss Pennyworth, but tonight is an exception.' He smiled, a tiny thing, but one that lit his brown eyes. 'I would be sorry to have it end so soon.'

Annabell shifted so she did not look at the couple. If she left, the gathering would likely break up. If she stayed, she had to save Miss Childs from Sir Hugo's unconscious charm, which would end with the chit sitting or standing by herself, and her in Sir Hugo's arms. Neither was ideal. Nor was the flush of heated anticipation that seared her senses from just the thought of having Sir Hugo holding her. She was behaving like a ninnyhammer, instead of the independent woman she had worked so hard to become.

Sir Hugo and his partner reached them. The warmth that had plagued Annabell just seconds before intensified. She scowled at her nemesis, wondering what it was about him that aroused her so. He flashed a rakish smile that showed strong white teeth and hinted of things done in the dark. Her pulse jumped, and she knew this was still another thing about him that appealed to her. He was a rebel who went his own way. His path was hedonistic pleasure. Hers was independence, but neither of them played by society's rules.

'Changed your mind?' His voice, so deep and enticing, made her decision easier than she would have liked.

'Yes, Sir Hugo, I have.' She looked at Miss Childs. 'If you don't mind, I would like to learn to waltz as you are doing. You seemed to enjoy doing it and to have learned rapidly. I find myself curious to experience it.'

The girl blushed so her face mottled. 'I am not very good.' She cast a surreptitious glance at her partner. 'And I stepped on Sir Hugo's feet more times than the floor, but I enjoyed it immensely. It is…' she paused, searching for the right word '…it is exhilarating.'

Sir Hugo made Miss Childs an elegant leg. 'For your first time, you did very well. It was my pleasure to teach you, and I will be delighted to do so again.'

Annabell watched with sardonic amusement as the young woman's blush deepened to a shade closely resembling the flames in the nearby fireplace. She was more susceptible to Sir Hugo's charms than a puppy to a kind word.

'Well, Juliet,' Annabell said firmly, 'I am ready when you are.' Juliet gave her a startled look, and Annabell realised she had sounded like a martyr going to the stake. 'I am truly not a good dancer,' she added in an effort to lighten her words.

Juliet gave her one last considering look before starting. Sir Hugo stepped toward her and smiled his predatory smile that did nothing to ease the butterflies beginning to flutter in Annabell's stomach. Dimly she was aware of Mr Tatterly asking Miss Childs to dance and Susan sitting in the chair beside the pianoforte. But only vaguely did she notice what the others were doing because Sir Hugo chose that moment to encircle her waist with his arm.

Her mouth was suddenly dry.

'It is customary for the woman to put her left hand on the man's shoulder,' he murmured with just a hint of amusement.

'Yes.'

She did as he instructed and nearly recoiled. Even through the fine kid of her gloves and the weave of his jacket she felt his muscles. There was a casual dissoluteness about him that had misled her into thinking he was soft. She had been vastly wrong.

He took her right hand in his left. 'By the time we are through positioning our hands and arms, the music will be over.'

He was needling her, but he was right. She was behaving strangely, even to herself. And why? He had already kissed her and invited her to his bedchamber. She should be immune to his nearness. But she was not. The waltz would be much longer than the kiss. They would be farther apart, but he would still be touching her.

She took a deep breath and he whirled her away.

She did her best to follow his lead, but she was so focused on his closeness that she found it hard to concentrate on her steps. He radiated heat and the scent of cinnamon and male muskiness. The muscles under her left hand flexed with a strength she found exciting.

'You must relax in order to waltz well.' His deep voice penetrated to her core.

Instead of answering, she concentrated on ignoring her reaction to him. *This is just a dance,* she told herself. *He is not going to kiss you. He is not going to seduce you. He is merely holding you at arm's length and twirling you around the floor. Nothing more. This means nothing.*

She swallowed a groan at her inability to discipline herself. She might as well be inebriated on the brandy he drank so liberally for all the good her will-power was doing.

He swung and dipped her in one smooth motion. Annabell gasped and would have stumbled if not for the iron band of his arm around her waist. He steadied her.

'You did that on purpose.'

His dangerous smile was firmly in place. 'If you would relax, you would enjoy it when I do that to you.'

She grimaced. 'I am sure I would enjoy any number of things better if I relaxed. Unfortunately, it is not in me.'

He moved back, drawing her with him. 'Take a deep breath and let it out slowly. If you concentrate on that, you won't be so aware of dancing.'

She laughed a short burst of sarcasm. 'I doubt that. It is very difficult to ignore your arm around my waist and your hand at the small of my back.'

He raised one brow. 'Really?'

She bit her lip. Why had she said that? It was true, for his hand felt like a hot brand that seared through clothing, skin and bone and into a part of her she had never known existed before now.

When he inched her slightly closer, she went. She told herself she did so because resisting him would make it even more difficult to learn the dance. In truth, she did it because his warmth, his masculinity, called to that part of her that was uniquely female.

He bent his head down to whisper in her ear, 'You smell of honeysuckle and mystery.'

Her short, abrupt laugh, meant to cover her embarrassment at his unexpected compliment, failed. She felt breathless and titillated, as though she balanced precariously on the edge of a precipice and to fall would be the end of everything she had worked so hard to achieve. Her susceptibility to the man was frightening.

He twirled her around, his face intense as though he put his entire being into this dance. Somehow she managed to follow him. He was very skilled at this, just as Juliet had said.

He pulled her still closer. She went.

Her breasts grazed his chest and lightning shot through her. She looked up to see if she was alone in this storm. She was not.

His eyes were like twin green flames. They caught her gaze and threatened to burn her to ashes in his passion. He no longer smiled. His beautiful mouth was the only soft thing in his face. His cheeks and jaw were razor slashes.

'I want you,' he said softly.

She stared, not sure she had heard correctly, or that he had even spoken, for she could not imagine him saying what she thought he had. Even for him the words were brazen. He had implied as much when he invited her to his room, but she had been able to tell herself the offer was something easily ignored. This blatant statement was so much more.

'I want to do things to you in the dark.'

She gulped hard. 'You should not be saying things like that to me.'

'I know, but if I don't, how will you know I desire you?'

She forced herself not to look away from his green eyes. They were filled with a hunger that quickened her pulse. But she would not succumb to temptation.

'If you don't stop talking such nonsense this instant, I

will be forced by your rudeness to stop right now, calling attention to us that neither of us wishes.'

If only she hadn't sounded so much like Susan, she would have been proud of her defiance. He did that to her intelligence. He banished it beneath a desire so hot and thick it threatened to smother her.

'For the moment, but only for the moment,' he murmured, a satisfied look on his face.

He swung her into a circle that took her breath away and she was glad for it. She closed her eyes to the invitation he made no effort to hide and focused on her steps. Only then was she able to ease some of the tension from her shoulders and—other areas. For the moment.

To her chagrin, Annabell did not hear the music end. She had been too caught up in the spell Sir Hugo had wrapped around them. When he stopped, she staggered.

His arm tightened until she rested against his chest, their mouths inches from each other. Her pulse beat painfully at the base of her throat. She fought to take in air.

He stared down at her. 'If I kiss you, will you slap me?'

Her eyes widened. 'I don't know.'

'Come to my room.' The words were low and spoken in a husky whisper no one else could hear.

Unable to answer for fear she would accept without realising it, Annabell shook her head.

He released her and stepped back.

She swayed, but managed not to wobble. Nothing like this had ever happened to her. She felt vulnerable and raw.

'Hugo,' Juliet Fitzsimmon's voice intruded. 'Stop flirting with poor Annabell and bring her over here. We are taking a vote to see if we continue or if we stop for the evening.'

Annabell flinched. She had completely forgotten there were other people in the room. Somehow she managed to walk to the pianoforte, although she didn't remember doing so. She was too conscious of Sir Hugo moving at her side.

'I say we stop,' she said, angry at herself because her

voice was breathy and weak. 'I need to get up early to finish uncovering a mosaic. The longer I dally, the longer I will be obliged to impose on Sir Hugo's hospitality.'

'Come, Annabell,' Susan said. 'Just one more.'

Annabell looked at her companion. Susan's cheeks glowed with happiness and her eyes sparkled. She had rarely seen her friend like this. But she had to leave. Another dance with Sir Hugo would put her very being in jeopardy. The man called to her like a siren called to unwary sailors. He was everything she did not need or want in her life.

'No, Susan, I am sorry, but I must get some sleep.' She pasted a smile on her face and looked around at everyone, skimming over Sir Hugo. 'Surely the rest of you can continue without me. After all, you will be two couples to dance and Juliet to play the music.'

There was grudging acceptance. Miss Childs had a wishful look on her face, and Annabell realised the young woman wanted very much to dance again with Sir Hugo. For a moment jealousy raised its ugly head once more, but she would not let that awful emotion keep her from escaping. She just hoped Sir Hugo didn't break the girl's heart.

Susan said, 'I will be up early to go with you. I imagine you will want the mosaic sketched as you uncover it.'

Annabell smiled. 'That would be perfect. I will see you then.' She looked at everyone else. 'And thank you, Juliet. I enjoyed myself very much.'

'I am glad to hear that, Annabell. For a moment, when you first stood up with Hugo, I thought you were going to change your mind.'

Annabell kept the smile on her face. 'I am made of stronger stuff than that, Juliet.'

Juliet laughed. 'Go to bed.'

Annabell did not wait any longer. The way her good-nights were going, she would be here for ever if she didn't leave. To her chagrin, she sensed Sir Hugo close behind her.

She reached the door and paused. 'I am perfectly capable of going to my room alone.'

'Fleeing?' Sir Hugo's tone was sardonic in the extreme.

'You?' She lifted her chin. 'I think not.'

'The waltz. You found it to be much more intoxicating than you had anticipated.'

She glared at him. 'Only a prude would not enjoy the dance, Sir Hugo. I am many things, but I am not a prude.'

He smiled, but it was not amusement that shone in his eyes. 'I imagine you aren't.'

She caught her breath, conscious of the other people who still grouped around Juliet and the pianoforte some distance away. 'If you will leave me alone, I am going to bed.'

His eyes narrowed, his jaw sharpened, but he said nothing. Instead, he made her a mocking half-bow.

She snapped her mouth shut, heard her teeth click in irritation, and whirled around. She could not get to her room any second too soon. She was fit to explode from irritation and something she refused to name.

Instead of going directly to bed, she paced the spacious room, her speed increasing until she fairly whirled around. When she finally burnt off some of her energy, she started undressing. She left the clothes where they landed. Tomorrow would be soon enough to put them away.

She fell into bed and an unrestful sleep, where her host twirled her around a massive ballroom that looked suspiciously like an inferno. No doubt, she had succumbed to him and they were in Hades.

The next morning, Annabell walked to the excavation. She needed the fresh, cold air to clear her head. She was becoming strange and unfamiliar to herself. It was all because of Sir Hugo. She kicked at a rock, her harem pants billowing out around her legs.

Birds twittered and she caught a glimpse of a russet tail. The foxes were coming out of hibernation. Then there were the wild flowers poking up from the ground and the pale green shoots of new grass. She stopped and gazed at the beauty. This was a rich, verdant land, something the Romans had known or they would not have settled here.

She resumed walking and reached the site quickly, only to find Molly, Sir Hugo's mare, munching on the tender spring grass. Sir Hugo had to be nearby. Annabell frowned as she searched the area for him. Movement caught her eye and she angled to watch him saunter toward her.

He moved with athletic grace, only a slight hitch betraying his bad left leg and then not with every motion. Funny, she had not even noticed it last night when he danced. He was very adept at concealing any hardship the wound might cause.

'I forgot you were wounded.' The words were out before she realised she had said them. Awkward even for her bluntness. 'You move so gracefully.'

He waved his arm as though pushing away her comment, but his eyes darkened as though he remembered a past pain. 'It was nothing. Many others were hurt worse.'

'Many were killed,' she said softly, 'but that does not make less of what happened to you.'

She was nearly as surprised at her gentle words as she had been at her blunt ones. He made her erratic. Not a good thing for someone who prided herself on her sensibility.

He looked carefully at her, as though seeing something that had not been there before. Perhaps he did. She had not felt compassion for him until this instant and, even so, it was quickly gone. He might have been hurt, but he was still dangerous. To her.

'Tell me exactly what you do here.' He closed the distance between them.

She studied him for long minutes, trying to decide if he really wanted to know. He wasn't laughing.

'I am carefully, and consequently quite slowly, uncovering this villa.' She edged away from him and glanced around the area. 'I believe I told you that much before.'

He nodded. 'I am more interested in how you are doing it and how it was discovered and how Tatterly chose you. Antiquities are not his area of interest, and his letter explaining everything was brief to the point of uninformative.'

'One of your tenant farmers found it after ploughing up the field that runs with your orchard and hitting a large stone, which turned out to be a water basin in one of the rooms. As I said last night, I heard about it quite by accident.'

She walked to where a cloth lay over a large expanse of ground. She lifted the corner and pulled the cover to one side. 'I contacted Mr Tatterly.' She paused, even now discomfited by how she had misled the man. 'I wrote to him through my man of business, offering a specialist in antiquities free of charge to excavate the newly discovered site. I told him I came highly recommended by the Society of Antiquaries.' She glanced up to see what he was thinking, but his face was noncommittal. 'I believe Tatterly was relieved to have the matter so easily resolved.'

'I believe he was. His letter to me on the solution was briefer than the first.' His words were as dry as the Egyptian desert.

She knelt down, took a nearby brush and began to carefully sweep away dirt from the mosaic that lay beneath. 'It was not his fault. By the time he knew I was a female, I had already arrived.'

'He should have sent you packing.'

She paused in her cleaning to look up at him. 'As you would have?'

He nodded curtly.

'He has not your determination and coldness.' She brushed back a strand that had come loose from her braid and slipped out of her bonnet. 'Besides, I gave him no choice. Just as I gave Susan none when she would have left, particularly after she learned whose house we would be staying in.'

'She was not happy? That doesn't surprise me.'

'No respectable woman would be happy.'

'Except you.'

'I have an overriding purpose for being here.'

'Ah, your calling.'

'Sarcasm will not deter me, Sir Hugo.'

'I believe that.' He ran his fingers through the thick locks that fell over his forehead. 'Shall we change the subject, Lady Fenwick-Clyde? This is getting us nowhere and keeping you from your work.'

It was her turn to nod curtly. The man always distracted her from her goal. No matter that they were discussing how she came to be here. If he didn't distract her with his masculinity, he distracted her with his questions that implied doubt of her abilities.

'Why don't you hire someone to help you?' He squatted down beside her.

She blinked. 'I intend to do so, but I thought we were changing the subject.'

'This is. We are talking about the present, something we have the power to change, not the past, which is done.'

'A hedonist and a pragmatist.' She angled her head to study him. His mouth was still sensually mobile and his clothing comfortably loose. He had not changed, yet... 'Somehow I had never put the two together in one person.

'I am eminently pragmatic, as you will see.'

His eyes spoke of actions that were far from practical for her to be doing with him. She ignored them.

'Back to your question, Sir Hugo. I did not want to spend your money freely, and I wanted to get a better idea of what is here. Now that I'm nearly positive it's a Roman villa, and probably belonged to a very prosperous farmer, I will have a better idea how to tell a crew to go on. I also intend to pay the workers myself.'

'This means a lot to you, doesn't it?'

She paused in the act of carefully scraping mud from what appeared to be a woman's face. 'Is there anything wrong with that? Just because I am a woman doesn't mean I don't have a brain or that I don't find the past interesting and worth preserving.'

He shook his head. 'I never said it did. You are very sensitive.'

She bit her bottom lip. 'I am very independent.'

'That too. But I will pay for the workers. This is my property and…my villa.'

She scowled. 'Yes, it is your…villa. And the more help I have the sooner I will be gone. You are right. You will pay for the workers.'

'Of course.' There was an underlying rumble to his voice, as though he laughed at her to himself. 'And what if I get tired of all this and decide you must stop? After all, this Roman antiquity is on my property. I might not like all the activity.'

She set the brush carefully down and twisted to face him. 'If you meant to do that, I believe you would have already done so.' She quirked one brow. 'Do I misjudge you?'

'Probably not, but it is still on my property. Doesn't it bother you to spend time and a great deal of effort digging on someone else's land? Particularly when I might not pre-serve it as you would wish.'

She twisted into a cross-legged position, which she al-ways found comfortable, for this conversation seemed to be expanding. 'Of course that bothers me. But what can I do about it? Not excavate it at all, or let someone else do it?'

'Some people would likely do that.'

She snorted. 'Well, I cannot. No, I will do whatever it takes to uncover and preserve the thing and then I will leave it to you and hope you will take care of it.'

'Aren't you afraid I might not?'

She looked into the blue sky and let go some of her tension before replying. 'You cannot be all play and no responsibility. After all, you rode out to inform your tenants you were home the very first day you arrived. Not many men of my acquaintance would have been that diligent. So, I have to hope you will feel the same about this when I am done and you see what a beautiful thing it is.'

She gave him a sly look. 'And besides, you could earn quite a bit of money from this, you know.'

'Really?' He smiled as though he did not believe her.

'Really. I have seen it done not far from here. The owner is still excavating, but he has already opened it to the public for a small entrance fee. He seems to be doing very well.'

Sir Hugo laughed. 'Very good, Lady Fenwick-Clyde. An antiquarian and a business woman. What else have you dipped your interesting head into?'

She was not sure whether to feel complimented or insulted. He implied she was intelligent and interesting, but he had also laughed as though he found the entire situation amusing and not very serious. This was not funny to her.

'My affairs are none of your concern, Sir Hugo. I merely mentioned a way you might turn this to a profit when all is said and done.'

He stopped laughing. 'So you did. But I've an aversion to strangers tramping my land, and you already said this will take months or years. Just the thought of people mucking all about leaves me unenthused.'

She sighed. 'Very likely. But I don't intend to be involved that long. I find there is never a shortage of gentlemen willing to come in and finish a project or share the work involved.'

He looked intrigued. 'You have done this before?'

She smiled in remembered pleasure. 'I didn't start it. I was one of the latecomers who helped finish the project. It was in Egypt. The pyramids. Totally fascinating. A strange land with a stranger past. Imagine, embalming your dead royalty.'

'I imagine Prinny would not be adverse to that. He has already built himself a temple. That monstrosity at Brighton. The only thing it lacks is a gold and jewel-encrusted sarcophagus for his mummified body.'

The image his words conjured was too much for Annabell's sobriety. She started laughing. 'How naughty of you to suggest such a thing. And rumour says you are an intimate of the Prince Regent.'

He laughed with her. 'I am, but that does not mean I am blind to his faults. He can be generosity itself, and he may single-handedly preserve the finest of English arts and crafts, but he is also vain and prone to spend money he doesn't have.'

She nodded. 'So true. His minuses are as big as his pluses.'

'But enough of him.' Sir Hugo stood. 'What can I do to help you? After all, I stand to profit from all of this, so the sooner it is finished the better for me.'

She shook her head at his levity, but rose with him. 'I imagine you have plenty of other things to occupy you, Sir Hugo. You don't need to help me, and I will even be glad to see you get the entrance fees.'

'I want to help.'

She looked away from him. He was too intense in spite of the half-smile curving his tantalising lips up at one corner. She did not want him here. He muddled her thoughts, made her think of things that had nothing remotely to do with the excavation.

She arranged her refusal carefully, determined not to say something he could interpret as encouragement. 'I appreciate your offer, Sir Hugo. But at this point, as I said before, it is much easier for me to work by myself. I know exactly what I need to do and can do it quicker if I don't have to direct someone else.'

'Really?' He brushed at a speck on his loose-fitting country coat. 'You can do all the work here by yourself? Surely you are overly optimistic about your time.'

He had her there. She fully intended to hire people from the nearby village, and they would not constantly disturb her peace of mind and make her wish for things she had determined not to wish for. But she was not about to tell him that.

'You are not dressed to be grubbing in the dirt. Your buff pantaloons, while the height of fashion, would be ruined after less than an hour here. Surely you don't want to destroy them when you don't have to.'

He shrugged. 'It doesn't matter to me, and I doubt Jamison would care either. He's a better soldier than a valet.'

She angled away so he wouldn't see her mounting frustration. She had work to do and he was a distraction.

He closed the distance between them and touched her arm to make her look back at him. 'Surely I can do something you don't need to supervise.'

The contact made her jump. Her entire body felt suddenly, gloriously alive. This was exactly why she didn't want him here.

She scowled. 'There is nothing you can do that I don't have to keep an eye on while you do it. Is that clear enough?'

His eyes widened slightly before narrowing. 'Are you sure the fact of the matter isn't that you just don't want me here? If that is so, then at least be honest about it.'

'Right. That is exactly it.' She pulled her arm away and stepped back.

He watched her move, but did not follow. 'Honesty will get you a lot further with me than polite subterfuge.'

'I don't want to get far with you. I want to be left alone by you.'

His face took on a dangerous sharpness. 'Really? I don't

thing so, Lady Fenwick-Clyde—Annabell. I think you are afraid of the way I make you feel.'

'Nonsense.' But the breathiness of her voice ruined her denial, and she inched further away.

'I think you want me to touch you. I think you want me to be around you.' His voice was low and raspy, the melody normally in it gone.

'You are absurd.' She jerked her head to one side. 'Absolutely delusional.'

Good, she told herself. She sounded definite. Her voice had been firm, and she had not edged away. She had hit just the right note of dismissal. So what if her heart pounded and her palms were moist? She was merely uncomfortable because of his confrontation.

'No,' he murmured. 'I am honest.'

She watched him carefully, wondering if he was really as dangerous as he looked this instant. He reminded her of a stalking lion she had seen at the Tower some months back. He watched her with the same predatory gleam the lion had directed at its dinner. Sir Hugo was many things, but she doubted that he intended to eat her.

'So am I,' she said in her haughtiest tone.

He laughed, but it was not an amused sound. It was more of a challenge. 'No, you are lying to me…and to yourself.'

She shook her head.

'Yes,' he said softly. 'Your body was alive and tingling last night when I held you in my arms. You even moved closer when we danced.'

'I did not.' She was affronted by his forward words and assumption that she was that type of woman.

'Yes,' he murmured. 'Your face was soft and your lips were swollen. You swayed in my arms as though you belonged in them.'

She shook her head again. 'No.' But her rejection was barely a whisper.

'Prove it to me,' he said, closing the distance between

them. 'Resist me when I take you back into my arms and kiss you and…' He trailed off, leaving the rest to her imagination.

She shivered and stepped back more from instinct than any intentional decision to avoid him. Her foot hit a rock and her ankle twisted. She gasped. Her arms windmilled, and he caught her around the waist.

Before she could regain her breath, she found herself pressed to his chest. She stared into his eyes and wondered where this would lead, how far he would go and how far she would let him.

'Annabell.' Susan Pennyworth's voice penetrated the haze of desire that enveloped Annabell. 'I know you're here. I've come to finish my drawing of the Zeus mosaic.'

Annabell pushed hard on Sir Hugo's chest. He released her with a sardonic twist of his lips. She stepped away, feeling dizzy and lost. Something she had wanted very badly had just been taken away from her.

In a voice she barely recognised, Annabell called, 'I am over here, Susan. Behind the bush near the geometric mosaic.'

'There you are,' Susan said, rounding the barrier. 'Oh, Sir Hugo. I didn't know you were here.'

He made her an abbreviated bow. 'I am just leaving.'

'Oh, dear,' Susan said, 'don't leave on my account. I am sure you are interested in what we are doing. I don't mean to chase you away. I am merely here to draw the mosaic. Nothing more.'

A pained expression moved over Sir Hugo's face. 'Rest easy, Miss Pennyworth. I am leaving.'

Annabell watched him with relief and regret as he made true his words. Susan had come just in time—or had she?

Chapter Six

Annabell peeked into the library. The last thing she wanted was an encounter with her host. Their interlude at the site was enough to last the rest of her life, or so she told herself. She shivered and wondered why she felt suddenly cold. It was as though something had been taken away from her. She shook her shoulders, told herself not to be fanciful and entered the room.

Even with summer nearly upon them, there was a fire in the grate to keep the chill and damp from the air in this old house. Several lit candles cast a golden glow. The room was always ready for Sir Hugo. For a man of his licentious reputation, he was very bookish. She could not fault him for that trait.

'Come in,' his deep voice said from behind a large, leather wing-back chair pulled close to the fireplace.

She started briefly. 'I should have known you were here by the half-full glass of brandy on the table.' And she should have. He seemed to have a particular taste for the drink.

He looked around the chair. 'Had you been more observant, you would have.'

'You are right, but a gentleman would not be so blunt about the fact.'

He laughed. 'But I am not a gentleman. I thought we had settled that.'

'True.'

She entered the room, pulling her paisley shawl tight around her shoulders. The fire might be roaring, but there was a cold snap, as though winter wanted one last fling.

'Come sit here.' He indicated a large, fat-cushioned chair near him. 'The warmth will reach you.'

She hesitated. 'I did not come here to socialise.'

He raised one brow. 'Really. Did you come for a book?'

She nodded. But the shabby, chintz-covered chair was inviting, as was the roaring fire. They were cosy, a word she would not have associated with Sir Hugo Fitzsimmon, the scourge of London's fairer sex—and the man who had nearly seduced her this afternoon.

She cast a glance at him. He appeared perfectly at his ease, as though he had never invited her to his bed.

He beckoned her. 'Come, Lady Fenwick-Clyde, I won't bite.' His lips curved wickedly. 'Not unless you ask.'

She shook her head at him. 'Innuendoes, Sir Hugo?'

'Always.' He took a drink of brandy. 'Particularly when I have sampled something I long to know better.'

A faint blush mounted her features. 'You are being deliberately provocative.'

He took another sip and eyed her speculatively over the rim of his glass. 'Not nearly as much as I would like to be.'

A *frisson* ran her spine and she stopped. Danger lurked here. 'Perhaps I should leave.'

Unfortunately, her voice was breathy, which ruined the effect she had tried for of haughty coldness. But it was hard to be cool when your blood was starting to heat. He always had this effect on her. It was unnatural as well as unseemly.

'No,' he said. 'I will mind my manners—unless you invite me to do otherwise.'

She took a step back.

'No, I meant it. Sit, and I will pour you a glass of brandy.'

'I don't drink. I watched my brothers consume whisky the way you swig brandy. Inebriation doesn't appeal to me.'

She recognized the disgust in her voice that she always felt when her younger brother, Dominic, had come home, barely able to move. He was much like Sir Hugo—a womaniser, a drinker, and a charmer no member of the opposite sex seemed able to resist. She should leave now before her attraction to her host allowed him to lead them into deeper waters.

Instead of moving to the door like her mind directed, she moved toward the chair. She was like a moth drawn to the flame of his masculinity. He burned with an energy that never failed to excite her in ways she had previously never experienced. He was very dangerous indeed.

'You drink sherry,' he said, a curl to his mouth. 'This is much better.' When she sank into the opposite chair without accepting his offer, he added, 'Trust me.'

She laughed. 'Trust you? I don't think so, Sir Hugo. And I never drink more than a small glass of sherry.'

He smiled. 'Well, at least try the brandy. A sip. If you don't like it, you needn't finish it. Here,' he said, holding out his glass, 'I will even let you drink from mine. That way you won't feel as though I am pressing a great amount on you.'

She eyed his outstretched hand holding the goblet of liquor in the way she might eye a dangerous cobra poised to strike. On one level, his offer seemed perfectly innocuous. But on a deeper level, he was asking her to put her lips where his had already been. When thought of like that, his offer was temptation in the extreme.

She appreciated that he was flirting with her. It was oddly appealing. But then, so was the mesmerising sway of an aroused cobra.

'Perhaps a little.' When a slow, sensual smile intensified

the harsh angle of his jaw, she added, 'Just to make you hush about it. I am sure I won't like it.'

She stared at him for a long moment, wondering how far he intended to take this, and then wondering how far she wanted him to take it. He said nothing, but his gaze was intense, as though he found her fascinating. In its own way, that look was more seductive than anything else he could have done. Even more so than the anticipation of putting her lips to the glass he held out to her—his glass. Annabell found herself wishing he would reach across the table and touch her. Anywhere. Just touch her so she could feel his flesh against hers.

She settled for touching his fingers with her own when she took the brandy. Her reaction to him was swift and strong. Her stomach clenched in pleasure and her fingers trembled. He held on to the glass even though she also held it. He leaned forward so she could put the rim to her lips. Somehow she knew he meant for her to sip from the very spot he had just drank from. She shivered in anticipation.

She took a sip of the brandy and fire welled up her throat. Fortunately, he still held the goblet. She barely managed to swallow before a coughing fit took her. She gasped.

He knelt in front of her before she realised he had moved. 'Easy, Lady Fenwick-Clyde—Bell,' he murmured, using her family's pet name for her. He set the glass on the nearby table.

'Oh,' she gasped. 'I didn't conceive it could be so strong.'

'It isn't. You gulped it. That will make anything seem overpowering.'

She hadn't noticed that he had moved again until his knee nudged hers. She shivered and tried to shift so they didn't touch. He shifted so they did.

Her eyes watered, blurred his image. His hand cupped the side of her face, his touch warmer than the fire. With his thumb, he wiped away the tear trailing down her cheek.

It was a gentle gesture, yet her body reacted as though he had crushed her to him. There wasn't enough air for her to inhale. Her mouth opened.

He leaned into her and his lips touched hers.

He did not hold her or in any way confine her. She could pull away, and she knew it. But she didn't. She was caught, like a butterfly pinned to a board. Only she didn't want to escape.

Her eyes drifted shut, and she sank into his caress.

His mouth drank from hers. She tasted brandy on his lips and tongue. It was sweet and strong and intoxicating. He sucked at her, nipped at her and made her want him with nothing more than his kiss. He barely touched her.

When he finally broke the contact, she sighed in regret. She opened her eyes slowly to see him watching her carefully.

'Will you come to my room, Bell? You want me as much as I want you.' His voice was low and raspy, his hands clenched on his thighs. He still crouched so their knees met.

She swallowed her need. 'No, Sir Hugo. I... That is not what I want from life.'

He rocked back so they no longer touched, his face blank. 'What do you want?'

She had to look away from him in order to think straight since, seeing him so close, all she wanted was him, but in her saner moments she knew she wanted more. She wanted freedom to do what she wanted when she wanted to do it. Marriage to Fenwick-Clyde had taught her well that a wife has no freedom. She was subject to her husband's every whim.

'Independence,' she whispered and wondered why it hurt to say that.

'You can have that and still come with me,' he said, his offer sweet and beguiling.

She shook her head. 'No. What if I became pregnant? What then?'

He frowned, his beautiful mouth turning down at the corners. 'I am not some callow youth with no experience, Bell. I would protect you.'

She tilted her head to the side and studied him. He was not classically handsome. Her brothers were more attractive. But there was a magnetism about him. And his body was firm, broad in the shoulders and lean in the hips. He had an athlete's body, a body that belonged on a Greek marble.

And he intrigued her.

'How would you protect me? I don't believe there is any such thing for the woman when she and a man make love.'

'Of course there is,' he said gently, still not touching her. 'Your husband was a cad or he would have shown you.'

Her eyes widened slightly. 'You malign someone who can't defend himself.'

He held her gaze without flinching at her criticism. 'Could he defend himself? I don't think so.' His voice hardened. 'What I find hard to believe is that your parents gave you to him.'

She was instantly defensive. 'They did not know.' He raised one brow in doubt. 'They didn't. They did not go about in society. He came from a good family. Besides…' she sniffed '…it was a marriage of convenience. They had made one and found they fell in love. They thought the same would happen to me.'

He snorted. 'They were fools.'

She felt her shoulders begin to bunch. They were skirting uncomfortable memories. She wanted to be angry with him for bringing this up, but instead she found she wanted to discuss Fenwick-Clyde. She wanted to find out what another man thought of her husband. She had never been brave enough to discuss her husband with either of her brothers. She had sensed that his actions would have infuriated her brothers to the point where they might have done something everyone would regret.

'Who are you to say that?' The question was as close as she could come to asking him what he thought of Fenwick-Clyde.

'Do you really want to know?'

She clenched her hands and wondered if she really did. How could she even contemplate discussing what Fenwick-Clyde had done, and to someone she barely knew? Yet, she sensed she could discuss this with him. Strange. She even trusted him, at least in this.

'Yes,' she finally said.

He settled himself more comfortably on his knees as though sensing this conversation would be long. 'I knew your husband.' When she started in surprise, he held up his hand. 'Not well, but we often ran into each other during the course of a night. We frequented many of the same places.'

She bit down hard on the urge to make some scathing comment. She had not asked him to talk to her so that she could denigrate him or accuse him.

As though he sensed her disapproval, he said, 'I am not going to ask you to understand. I am a man and I do as I please. And what I please is to enjoy my life as I see fit. For me that is often women, gambling and drink.'

She nodded, trying desperately not to show him how his words hurt. She was being silly and knew it. What he wanted from her was sex, not love. She knew from watching her brothers that for a man the two were often mutually exclusive.

'Your husband obviously felt the same.' His face hardened. 'The only difference between us is that I believe in making my encounters enjoyable for everyone involved. Fenwick-Clyde did not.'

She jerked. Her nails dug into her palms, but she said nothing. He was absolutely right.

'There were rumours about him. Unsavoury ones. After

a while, many of the women refused to service him. From what I heard, I didn't blame them.'

The memories rose inside her, memories she had tried so hard to bury so deeply they would never surface again in her life. She stared, not seeing the present. Her breathing increased.

'Annabell!'

Sir Hugo's firm voice called to her, but the memories would not stop. Once Fenwick-Clyde had tied her, spread-eagled, to the bed. He had done things to her she had never imagined possible. That had been their wedding night.

'Annabell, stop!'

This time Sir Hugo's voice penetrated her misery. She blinked and focused on him. Her breathing eased.

'I'm sorry. I didn't mean to do that.'

He laid a hand over one of hers. 'I wish he had not misused you.'

She blanched and started to pull her hand away from his, then hesitated. He was warm and strong, and his touch made her feel safe. She stared at his concerned face and realised she cared for him. Cared for him a great deal.

'It is in the past,' she finally said, wondering how she was going to deal with the man kneeling in front of her now that she appreciated the fact that he meant more to her than he should or than she wanted him to. 'He is gone and cannot touch me ever again.'

'Nor can any other man because of what he did to you.' His tone was bitter. Not at all like him.

'You have certainly touched me,' she said with more irony than necessary.

He studied her. 'I kissed you. That is only the beginning. But you keep who you are locked away.'

He was much more perceptive than she would have thought. It must come from his experience with women.

'Why do you care?' she asked without thinking and instantly regretted it. 'I'm sorry. It is none of my business. Please ignore that question.'

He held her gaze with his. His tone was rueful. 'Because I find myself intrigued by you. I want to know more about you and at the same time my body aches for you.' When she gasped, he added, 'Is that sufficient reason?'

Shocked, she nodded.

His smile was wry. 'Surely, I've told you enough times how I feel for you that you should not be surprised.'

'Well…' She noticed that he still held her hand. She pulled free. 'Yes, you have been very forward in regard to your physical wants, but this is the first time you've indicated an interest in anything else.'

He leaned back, as though deciding that more distance between them would help prove his attraction was more than skin deep. 'In all honesty, this is the first time I realise that I want more from you than physical pleasure.'

He stood and moved back to the chair he had vacated what seemed eons ago. He sprawled with his slippered feet nearly touching the fireplace grate. He was relaxed and enticing all at once. A heady combination.

'Are you serious?'

He turned to her. 'Regretfully, yes.'

'Regretfully?' She was not sure if she was offended or amused.

'Yes, Annabell, regretfully.' He picked up the glass of brandy and drained it. 'I don't normally become interested in the workings of my lover's mind. Usually I am more than satisfied to understand how her body responds to mine.'

The image conjured by his last words sent tingles through her spine. He was being prosaic, and she was finding him seductive. No wonder she found him nearly impossible to resist when he set out to entice her. She wanted him to make love to her, and she went cold with the realisation.

She licked suddenly dry lips and tried desperately to find

a subject to scintillate him with and take her thoughts from the image that seemed lodged in her mind. Nothing came to mind.

'I can't image what you find interesting,' she finally said. 'All I can think about is y—' She stopped herself, her fingers shaking at her near admission. 'All I can think about is antiquities. I can't image that interesting a man like you.'

He watched her from the corner of his eye. 'Why?'

'Because you are a rake,' she blurted out.

'Rakes have more than one interest,' he answered, his voice sardonic.

'Gambling?'

'More than two.' He turned to face her full on. 'Are you flirting with me?'

'I…' She had not intended to. He was making her lose control of herself. This was unacceptable. 'No.'

He laughed, a short bark that wasn't really amused. 'I didn't think so. More's the pity.'

'It is time I left.'

She stood, no longer able to withstand him this close. One minute he was trying to seduce her, the next he told her he admired her brain, and now he was being charming. He was as multifaceted as she was confused.

He got to his feet. 'Wait a minute. I have something you might want to take to bed with you.'

She paused, wondering if he had meant to be provocative. The blade-sharp angle of his jaw told her he had.

He went to one of the shelves and pulled two books down. Handling them carefully, he came to her. 'You probably already have these, but, if not, they will make for interesting reading.'

She looked at the top book. 'William Camden's *Brittania*.' She looked up at him. 'This is considered the first book to give topographical descriptions of monuments in Britain. It was written in 1585.'

'I know. This copy is from the early 1700s.' He lifted

that one and put it underneath the second book, which was actually a bound manuscript. 'This is part of John Aubrey's *Monumenta Britannica.*'

She gaped. 'That is extremely rare.'

'I know. But I also know you will handle it as though it was a relic.'

She glanced sharply at him. Was he being sarcastic? She couldn't tell from the neutral expression he wore.

'I will certainly treat it with the respect it deserves,' she said more tartly than he deserved. 'But where did you get this?'

'One of my ancestors must have been friends with the man. Who knows?'

'Spoken like a man who isn't interested in the contents.'

'Take them and enjoy them. I read them a long time ago.'

She took them with reverential care. 'I am sorry for implying that you hadn't read them.'

He shrugged. 'It has been a long time. I studied antiquities at Oxford and read them then. I have forgotten most of what I learned.'

She doubted that. She was fast learning that Sir Hugo was a very intelligent man with a superb memory.

'I imagine you remember everything you intend to remember,' she said drily.

'Perhaps.' He stepped back. 'Goodnight.'

She gave him a hesitant smile, wondering if he was going to add an invitation to his bed as he had already done several times. When he said nothing further, she turned and left.

Sir Hugo watched her leave the room. She was tall and elegant and intelligent, all attributes he valued and admired. He would have a difficult time leaving her when the affair he intended to have with her ended.

Which reminded him that there was still Elizabeth. She must have reached London by now and would be expecting to hear from him. A task he was no longer looking forward to fulfilling.

He returned to the chair and sank down. He poured another full glass of brandy and lifted it to his lips. For a fleeting moment, he remembered Annabell putting the glass to her mouth. He shifted the glass to where he imagined she had sipped from it and downed the contents. The liquor burned all the way down.

The hairs on Annabell's nape tingled as though someone watched her. She looked up to see Sir Hugo in the morning-room entrance. He didn't look much different from last night in the library. And he still aroused feelings in her that she didn't want to experience.

She felt a fleeting sense of embarrassment caused by the memory of their talk last night. She also found herself glad to see him, something she did not want to be happening. But it was.

'I see you have invaded my breakfast room as well as my library and my orchard with my Roman villa.' He sauntered toward her. 'I am curious to discover what other areas of my property you intend to inhabit.'

She thought instantly of his bed and blushed a bright pink. The idea had been unbidden and unexpected. He always took her by surprise.

'Good morning to you too.' She ignored his leading statements. Some things were better left unaddressed. 'You are up early.'

He came closer. 'I see you are going to ignore my comment. Never mind. You will show me sooner or later. I am a patient man.' Before she could think of a retort, he gave her a mock frown. 'And you seem to have a jaundiced opinion of me. I am often up this early.'

'Really?' She put all her doubt into that one word. Still, she would rather this conversation than his original one. She felt mildly safe discussing this. 'I thought you drank and gambled the nights away. It has been my experience with my brothers, particularly my younger one, that when a man does such, he doesn't get up early the next day.'

He reached the dainty desk she sat at. 'I didn't drink and gamble the night away.' His voice deepened to a rasp. 'Nor did I entertain anyone in my rooms.'

Instantly what safety she felt evaporated. Leave it to him to turn any conversation in a dangerously erotic direction.

She had thought at her advanced age and previous marital status that she was beyond blushing at implied improprieties, but she was not. Her fingers froze in the act of shifting a paper.

'You are very bold for so early in the day.'

'True.'

He spoke as nonchalantly as he was dressed. He had no coat on and no cravat or belcher tie either. His shirt was open at the neck to reveal curling brown hairs, and his buff breeches were like a second skin. Even his less than perfectly polished Hessians called to her. Annabell suddenly found herself trying desperately to ignore a heightened awareness of him, which wasn't helped by his cinnamon-and-musk scent. This was unacceptable.

'What can I do for you?' she asked with more asperity than he deserved. But she was battling for her sanity, and the sooner he left the sooner she would return to normal.

His eyelids drooped suggestively. 'Now that you ask...'

His deep voice trailed off, and she found her irritation mounting with her growing arousal. 'You are behaving beyond the pale. Stop it this instant or I shall leave.'

He shrugged and his voice returned to its normal melodic baritone. 'You bring out the worst in me, I'm afraid.'

She looked at him in surprise. 'I do? I thought you behaved like this as a matter of course.'

'Not with every woman I meet.' He gave her a rakish grin that told her was completely unrepentant.

He grabbed a nearby ladderback chair and pulled it close to the desk. He straddled it and crossed his arms over the back of the chair, much like her younger brother always did. She found herself softening toward him because he reminded her so much of Dominic.

'You are so much like my brother.'

'Should I be offended or flattered?'

'It depends on whether you want to be known as a libertine or an upstanding man.' She eyed him. 'Which will it be?'

'Libertine, I think.'

'Then you should be flattered.' Her tone was acerbic with disappointment.

Although they were teasing each other, there was a seriousness about his demeanour that told her he meant every word he spoke. The knowledge saddened her. Libertines were not the type of men she wished to become better acquainted with. Her brother was enough.

'What are you studying?' All trace of seduction had left his voice.

She blinked. 'One minute we are talking about your unsavoury proclivities and the next you are quizzing me on my work. You are a conundrum.'

'I try. It keeps the ladies on their mettle.'

She shook her head. 'Now we are back to that. Well…' She pushed the top sheet closer to him. 'I am studying these drawings taken from the excavation and labelling them as I go.'

He studied the finely drawn pencil illustrations. 'These are excellent.' He looked up at her, his eyes alight with renewed interest. 'Did you draw these?'

She laughed in an effort to chase away the thrill caused by his piqued interest and the following disappointment at realising the look would fade from his eyes when she told him the truth.

'No. Susan did. She is a superb artist.'

His mouth opened as though he wanted to speak but was speechless. He looked back down at the drawing, then back up at her. 'Surely you jest.'

She shook her head, a tiny spurt of irritation forming at his obvious disdain for her friend and companion. 'She is good enough to illustrate for any antiquarian. Not many people have that talent.'

'But she has not a coherent thought in her head,' he muttered. 'She speaks one inanity after another ad nauseum.'

'Shame on you for thinking so uncharitably of her.' She pulled back the picture as though by taking it from him she was protecting Susan from his criticism.

'I'm only calling a spade a spade.' His lip curled sardonically. 'Just as I am doing when I call her artwork some of the best I have ever seen. The woman is a contradiction.'

'Well...' Annabell huffed in spite of her effort to let go the irritation his denigration had caused '...I believe artistic talent does not have to be accompanied by perfect sense. *I* always understand Susan perfectly.'

A small twinge of conscience caught her. She might always understand her companion, but that did not mean Susan's sometimes empty chattering didn't upset her or make her impatient with the other woman. But she was not about to admit that to Sir Hugo with his smug face.

'I am sure you do.' He stood. 'But I'd also wager you sometimes wish she would stop chattering so that you can hear yourself think.'

She dropped her gaze from his penetrating study and gathered the sheets of paper and carefully straightened them into a single pile with all the edges lined up. She glanced up at him from the corner of her eye. He stood patiently waiting for her reply.

She let out a huff of air. 'All right. You are correct.' She hastened to add, 'But not often.'

'I thought so.'

She picked up the papers and stood abruptly. 'If you will

excuse me, I need to put these back in their portfolio and get out to the site.'

'By all means.' But he didn't move to let her go around him.

She frowned. There was only one way to go. The other end of the desk abutted the wall. 'Will you move?'

His mocking smile returned accompanied by a half-bow. 'Of course.'

He stepped aside, but it was slow and infuriatingly provocative. She gathered the papers close to her chest as though they were a shield and edged by him, ignoring the slow grin he gave her as though he knew exactly what he was doing to her.

She scowled at him. 'You are the most difficult man, Sir Hugo.'

His smiled widened. 'I aim to please, Lady Fenwick-Clyde.'

Her heart skipped a beat, and she hugged the papers closer. In spite of the unease he created in her, she managed to keep her voice cool. 'I imagine you do.'

He laughed outright. 'I've been told I do.'

'Insufferable,' she muttered, making her escape to the door and into the hall.

He could be so irritating. He even used the same word to describe Susan's incessant talking: chattering. She shook her head. He was beginning to have altogether too many similarities to her. It was uncomfortable for her peace of mind.

Chapter Seven

Annabell stood, hands on hips, and surveyed her handiwork. A large, nearly intact mosaic stood out. It was geometric, with all the colours of the surrounding rocks from which the small tiles had been made. But it was unprotected and a storm threatened. Hopefully the men from the nearby village would arrive with the poles and large awning she had commissioned last week.

She heard a horse's hooves and turned, anxious to get the cover up. 'Oh, it is you.'

Sir Hugo sat astride Molly just where the road passed by the clearing Annabell stood in. His hair was wind blown, accentuating its unfashionable length. It was suddenly difficult to breathe. And she had seen him only several hours before in the breakfast room.

Eyes narrowed, he said, 'I'm sorry to disappoint you, Lady Fenwick-Clyde. You were expecting someone else?'

'I was expecting the men from the village with the cover.'

'Ah.'

He dismounted with only a small hitch in his fluidity to show that his healed wound pained him. Funny, she had not noticed him limp earlier today. Probably because, honest with herself for once where he was concerned, she had been more interested in the way his shirt had been open at the neck and his breeches had hugged his muscles. Ladies were not supposed to notice those things about a man, or, if they did, they simply said he had a fine figure.

She watched him from the corner of her eye. She did not trust him—or herself. Not any more. The more she learned about him, the more she liked him in spite of herself. With a start, she realised she had been looking at the lean musculature of his hips and thighs—again. She bit her lip and turned away. It was better not to watch him at all than to ogle him. This was so unlike her. But everything since he came into her life was so unlike the way she normally was.

'Is something wrong?' There was a glint in his eyes that told her he knew exactly what was wrong.

Her entire body flushed, making it nearly impossible for her to answer him with even a modicum of nonchalance. She tried anyway. 'No. Nothing.'

'Of course,' he murmured.

He spoke in such a way that she knew he knew she was having difficulty continuing to resist him. She supposed a man of his experience sensed when women were near to succumbing. That was what would make him so successful a rake—and rumour said he was very successful indeed.

He moved past her with only a cursory glance that took in her flushed face and loose hair. His gaze slid down her body to her harem pants. 'You look wicked and enticing in those. But I suppose you know that.'

She hadn't thought it possible to feel more uncomfortable, but he had made her so. 'I don't choose my clothes to look any way. I wear what is practical for clambering over rocks and working in dirt.'

He gave her the smile she was becoming too familiar with. It said he believed her but it was time for her to learn about reality. She glared back at him.

He stopped just short of where the mosaic started. 'You have the mosaic completely uncovered. Very impressive.'

She took a moment to digest the fact that he had changed the subject. Then she nodded, before realising he couldn't see her with his back to her. 'Yes.'

He looked over his shoulder. 'You truly enjoy this.'

She felt like shaking her head. His habit of flitting from one subject to another was disconcerting.

'Yes, yes, I do,' she finally managed, her pleasure warming her voice. 'I have always been intrigued by the ancients. This gives me a chance to see how they actually lived, perhaps even tells me a little about how they thought. Much more satisfying than reading about them.'

'Tell me about it.'

She met his eyes with hers. 'Do you really want to know?'

He laughed, his rich baritone sending shivers down her spine. 'I believe you have asked me that before. The answer hasn't changed. Yes, I am interested. I may be a debauched rake, but before travelling down this dissolute road, I studied antiquities at Oxford, as I told you last night. I just never pursued my interest as you have yours.'

She digested his words. 'Still another side to you.'

He shrugged. 'Most people have many facets.'

'I suppose they do.'

She moved closer to him, still careful to leave a safe distance. Last night and the intimacy of shared experiences was too fresh. He was becoming more than a one-dimensional rake. He was becoming an interesting human being.

He laughed. 'You say that as though you wish it weren't so.'

One corner of her mouth inched up in a rueful smile. 'Sometimes it is easier to deal with people on a more simplistic level.'

He sobered. 'Are you talking about us?'

She nodded, wondering how he always seemed to know

what she was thinking. It was unsettling and appealing and made resisting him all that much harder.

To change to a safer topic, she waved at the mosaic and adopted her most prosy voice. 'What you are looking at was the floor of the triclinium or dining room. It was not heated, so probably was only used in warm weather. I imagine if there is more here, which I suspect there is, we will find other rooms where the floors were heated by lead pipes laid beneath through which hot water circulated. The Romans were very sophisticated.'

'In many ways, more than we are today.'

'True,' she said.

In moments like this, her affinity with him was frightening. He could seduce her with his mind as easily as with his body. She shivered.

'You are cold. Your harem pants are not as warm as skirts and petticoats.'

'They are perfectly warm. I should have worn a pelisse.'

She had left Rosemont in a hurry, eager to be away before he accosted her again. And here she was with him in spite of her effort.

He shrugged out of his greatcoat, and before she could protest, threw it over her shoulders. Warmth and his scent engulfed her, a dizzying combination that made her sway. He was at her side immediately, his arm around her waist, his face inches from her own.

'I am fine,' she managed to say in spite of the dryness that made her tongue feel thick. 'Nor do I need your coat.'

He did not release her. 'You shall keep my coat and I shall keep my arm around you.'

She licked her lips. 'Please, Sir Hugo—Hugo, don't do this.'

'Do what?' His voice was a challenge. 'Make you desire me?'

She turned away from the twin green flames that were his eyes. His musky scent combined with the fresh smell of a fine winter day permeated her senses. His arm around her was security and threat. A small breathy laugh escaped her.

'What?' His gloved fingers caught her chin and gently forced her face up. 'What is funny?'

She took a deep gulp of air and turned her gaze back to him only to be caught by the passion in his face. His lips were curved, their well-defined outline begging to be traced by her finger…by her tongue.

'Funny?' he reminded her.

'You. Me. The feelings you create in me.' The words tumbled from her mouth, making no sense. 'Both safe and yet scared.'

'As though this is completely new?'

She nodded. Was he going to kiss her? Would he stop with just a kiss? Did she want him to? She no longer knew what she wanted.

'I am going to kiss you, Annabell. If you don't want that, then tell me now.' His voice was low and urgent.

Her eyes fluttered shut. Fool that she was, she wanted his kiss, his touch. 'Please.'

He scattered gossamer kisses across her cheeks. 'How do you feel now?'

Her breath caught as his lips paused to caress the curve of her jaw. 'Safe in your strength. Scared of my reaction to you.'

'Scared?' He lifted his face from hers and one thick brow quirked up.

She nodded. 'You are so thoroughly comfortable with who you are and your appetites. It can be frightening.'

'No more frightening than the need you create in me, Bell.'

He had used her family nickname last night too. Then, as now, it created a sense of homecoming in her. As though he had a right to use it, although she knew intellectually that he did not.

He lowered his face until his lips skimmed her cheek. He barely touched her, and she felt as though she would erupt into molten desire. Nothing in her life had prepared her for this response. Nothing.

She sucked in tiny gulps of air. 'Don't, Hugo.' She turned her face away and closed her eyes as though doing so would close out his warmth and nearness. 'I've changed my mind. I don't want this.'

'Liar.' But he let her go.

She felt bereft, silly, weak creature that she was. The warmth that had engulfed her seconds before was gone as though it never existed. Suddenly she was more aware of the sharp wind and chill in the air than she had been all morning. She stuffed her hands into the pockets of her pants.

She wanted to continue lying to him and tell him he was wrong. She did not want to become his lover, but the same innate honesty that had always made her confess to any infraction of the rules—even if it meant a night with no dinner while her brothers made faces at her and had their fill of every sweet—forbade her from compounding her un-truths.

She faced him and spoke some of the most difficult words she had ever had to utter, simply because she did not want to want him. But she did.

'You are right…I am a liar.' Her hands clenched. 'I do want you. I want you to kiss me… I want you to do more…but that would be the worst thing for me.'

He ran his finger along her jaw, but made no move to take her back into his arms. 'Why? You are a grown woman, an independent woman who fully understands what we would be embarking upon.'

She caught his hand to stop the caress. 'And I do not want any of it.' She sighed and moved his hand from her face. 'That is not true, and yet it is. I don't want to be your lover because of all the complications and ramifications.

Yet, at the same time, I want you to make love to me.' Her brows knitted in frustration. 'Can you understand that?'

He raised her hand for his kiss. She would swear she felt the soft firmness and heat of his mouth even through her glove.

'Yes. Would you feel any better if I told you I feel the same?'

She laughed, a weak disbelieving sound. 'You? You have done this more times than you can probably remember. I have never done this.'

His grip tightened painfully. 'No matter how many times I have done this with other women, Bell, I have never made love to you.'

'True.'

His hold loosened and he chuckled ruefully. 'Until I tell you why you are different, you will think I am splitting hairs.'

She nodded. More than anything she wanted him to tell her she was special, different from the others. A vain wish, she knew, but still hope twisted her stomach. She did not want to be just the latest in a string of mistresses.

He sat on one of the nearby recently uncovered stones and pulled her down on to a second one so they were eye level. 'You are different from the others.'

'I'm sure,' she said sarcastically, unable to help herself. She felt so vulnerable.

He scowled. 'See. You want me to tell you why making love to you won't be as simple for me as you think it will, but when I try you immediately belittle what I say.'

She notched her chin up. 'I find it hard to comprehend that you are willing to talk to me about this. It has been my experience that men don't talk about their feelings. They talk about horse flesh or their sporting pursuits and even politics—but never their emotions. So, why now?'

'Because if I don't, you will never believe that I find you different from the rest. You won't understand that you are special to me.' He shrugged. 'Women like to talk about their feelings. I am trying.'

'Another skill in your arsenal?'

Anger tinged his words. 'You are very cynical for a woman who wants reassurance.'

She sighed. 'I can't help it, Hugo. I am new to this and you are an old hand. I can't help but think you have more practice. It makes for an uneasy melding.'

He nodded. 'But not impossible.' She tried to pull her hand from his, but he held tighter. 'No, don't break this contact. If you do, the next thing you will do is stand and then you will walk away. You will escape this conversation and avoid me.'

'You know me too well,' she murmured, conscious that he was not going to let her ignore what was between them. 'You are determined to bring our response to each other out into the open.'

'I will do whatever it takes to get you into my bed.'

His simple statement took her breath away. Somehow, she managed to say, 'You are moving too fast.'

'Not fast enough.'

She yanked her hand free and jumped up. 'Too fast for me. I don't care how much you talk about your feelings, I need time to adjust to what you are telling me. I am…' she took a deep breath '…I am not used to this openness with a man.'

He rose slowly. 'I have always considered myself a patient man when it comes to getting what I want, but with you my patience is fraying.'

She eyed him askance. 'You make the assumption we will become lovers. Assumptions frequently do not become reality.'

He caught her and pulled her to him even as she splayed her hands on his chest to stop him. 'This one will.'

This time his kiss was hard and demanding. His lips forced hers to part and his tongue invaded her mouth. She gasped, but her body responded immediately. A soft warmth started in her abdomen and spread outward. Her hands crept up his chest and wrapped around his neck.

All thought of escape fled as she sank into the inferno he created in her. Her inhibitions disappeared. Her body wanted what he was doing to her. She angled her mouth to give him better access.

His hands roved up and down her back, pressing her closer to him so her breasts were crushed against his chest. Her nipples tingled with tight awareness. She wanted him to caress them.

As though he had heard her thoughts, one of his hands slid to the front and cupped her aching flesh. He kneaded and massaged her bosom until she thought she would scream if he did not do something, but what? She didn't know what she wanted from him, just that she wanted more than this.

She clung to him and drank in the taste, feel and smell of him. He intoxicated her.

His free hand skimmed down the length of her hip and thigh, slid back up, the fabric of her harem pants caught in his fist. He splayed his fingers and slid around to cup her derriere. He drew her against him so her breasts flattened against his chest.

'Feel what you do to me?' His voice was low, nearly guttural, yet…

He pressed against her abdomen. He was hard and long and enticing. Desire, hot and aching, welled in her, just as it had last night. Just as it did every night since she met him. She wanted him inside her, moving with her. The realisation that she was a breath away from giving herself to him shocked her. She shook her head, more at her reaction than what he was doing.

He increased the pressure until he pushed into her. 'Don't deny this, Bell.'

She shook her head again. 'This is not like me. I'm not like this. Passion doesn't rule me. Never.' Only now it did.

His eyes deepened. 'Don't challenge me.' His lips curled into a smile that would have been cruel if it had not been so seductive. 'It only makes me more determined, and I am already convinced I must have you.'

She stared up at him, her stomach doing funny things. Her entire body felt strange, lethargic, while at the same time she felt edgy, as though something was just beyond her reach.

His mouth lowered…

The sound of wagon wheels intruded. He released her and Annabell jumped back, her pulse skyrocketing.

'The awning,' she said, unsure whether she was relieved or regretful. Much as she knew it would only create problems, she was drawn to him in ways she could not explain.

He stepped away, leaving his caped greatcoat around her shoulders. She reached up with shaking fingers and fumbled with the button.

'No,' he said, his voice harsh. 'Keep it for now. You will be here for some time while they set the contraption up and it is only going to get colder.'

'I can't. What about you?'

'I am going home. To a warm fire and a stiff shot of brandy.' His voice turned rueful. 'I have things to get under control.'

She flushed, knowing he meant his body's reaction to her. For that matter, her stomach was still a knot of desire and her legs felt weaker than normal.

Without answering, she watched him mount Molly, noting, as always, the slight hitch in his otherwise graceful movement as his wound caught. It was as though he forgot about it until it reminded him that it was always there, always a reminder of Waterloo.

She forced her attention from him to the lumbering wagon, driven by a labourer with his hat pulled low to protect him from the wind. She had been so caught up in what was happening between her and Sir Hugo that she had failed to notice the storm was nearly upon them. She would be thankful for his coat before she got back to his house.

'We must move quickly,' she said to the driver.

A second man jumped down and secured the mules pulling the wagon. Then the two set to work erecting the awning and tying down the poles to withstand the oncoming storm.

Annabell entered the hall late that afternoon. She was tired, her back ached and the last person she wanted to see was Hugo. So, of course, he was the first person she saw.

'Ah, Lady Fenwick-Clyde,' he drawled, closing the distance between them.

His hair was mussed and his shirt was open. She was beginning to expect that of him. Her heart skipped a beat. She was beginning to expect that of herself when she saw him.

'Sir Hugo,' she replied, trying her hardest to sound as though it didn't matter a jot to her that he was here, that they might have made love if the workers hadn't arrived when they did.

He smiled. 'You were gone a long time today.'

She nodded. 'The men took longer than either they or I had expected. And the women were late.'

'Women?'

She eyed him narrowly, wondering if his voice held censure or if she was over-sensitive, a fault she sometimes displayed. 'Yes, women. I hired a number of females from the village.'

'How very independent of you.'

She would swear he was trying to needle her, and he was succeeding. 'As I have told you repeatedly, I am nothing if not independent. And women can uncover the villa as well as any man. Many times better. They tend to be more patient, which I attribute to sewing, knitting and weaving, all of which require concentration and agile fingers.'

His smiled widened. 'I imagine you are right.'

It was on the tip of her tongue to say something scathing.

'Hugo,' a young voice shrilled. 'Watch me.'

Annabell looked up and Hugo whirled around. Rosalie sat perched precariously on the edge of the ornately carved wood banister. Her hair rippled unbound down her back, and her skirts were hitched high enough so she could comfortably slide down sideways. Coming around the upstairs hall corner was the governess, Miss Childs, but she would be too late.

'Rosalie, don't!' Hugo said in a tone that brooked no nonsense.

'Oh, my goodness!' Annabell took a step forward just as the child launched herself downward.

Hugo lunged for the stairs. The child teetered precariously on the banister, nearly falling backwards. Hugo altered his course. Annabell saw him lurch and pain lanced across his features, then he was beneath Rosalie, who lost her balance and plunged over the edge. He caught her, going to his knees from the force of her impact.

'Oh, Hugo, Hugo,' Rosalie sobbed, fear making her childish voice higher than normal. Tears streamed down her face.

Annabell reached them as Hugo stroked the wild hair from the girl's face. 'Are you all right?' she asked, more concerned for him than she wanted to be.

He glanced at her, his green eyes dark with pain. 'Fine.' Turning his attention back to the child, he crooned, 'It's all right, Rosalie. I have you. You aren't hurt, are you?'

She shook her head, but the sobs continued.

Miss Childs rushed down the stairs, her eyes wide with shock. 'Rosalie, dear, let me see you.'

The girl shook her head. 'Stay with…hiccup…Hugo.' She burrowed into his arms.

Annabell understood perfectly. Hugo was a man who would keep a child—or a woman—safe.

Still holding Rosalie, he stood up, wincing as he shifted so that his weight was on his good leg. 'Hush, now, Rosalie. The more you cry, the worse you will make yourself feel. You are scared, not hurt.'

She nodded and hiccupped.

Juliet rushed into the hall from outside. 'I heard a scream.' She saw her daughter. 'Rosalie!' She hurried to the group and held out her arms for her child. Hugo handed Rosalie to her mother. 'Are you hurt, Rosalie?' After the girl shook her head, Juliet looked at Hugo. 'Thank you so much, Hugo. She slid down the banister, didn't she?'

'It is tempting,' he said with a grimace.

'You are hurt,' Annabell said to him, finally having seen enough. 'You should take care of yourself.'

He gave her an inscrutable look. 'A little. Nothing that won't heal.' But when he tried to walk, he winced again and stopped. 'Perhaps a little more than I thought.'

Butterfield, who had been hovering in the background, stepped forward. 'I have sent for Jamison, sir.'

'Thank you,' Hugo said, standing perfectly still. 'Why don't you take Rosalie upstairs, Juliet?'

Juliet frowned at her daughter, who still snuggled in her arms. 'I think Rosalie needs a lesson.' The child looked up, apprehension clear in her violet eyes. 'Yes, a lesson. I have told you repeatedly not to slide down that banister, haven't I?'

Rosalie nodded.

'But you did it anyway.'

'Yes,' the child said in a tiny voice.

'You could have been hurt very badly.'

Rosalie hung her head.

'I think you can spend the afternoon inside today and think about what you have done.'

There was no protest from Rosalie as Juliet carried her

up the stairs to the nursery. Annabell watched them go and sighed.

'I suppose you slid down the banister,' Sir Hugo said drily.

Annabell looked at him ruefully. 'Many times.'

'But you did not fall backwards.'

'No.'

'Sir Hugo,' Jamison said, interrupting them, 'what have you done this time?'

Hugo grimaced. 'I think I pulled the muscle the ball went into.'

Jamison clicked his tongue. 'Let's hope that's all you did. The last time you attempted some fool stunt, you were laid up for a month. Wounds like them don't ever completely heal back to normal.'

'Don't I know that,' Sir Hugo said.

'You've done this before?' Annabell asked, impressed that he had moved so quickly to save his half-sister despite knowing what it would do.

Jamison gave her a sour look. 'More times than he should have, my lady.'

'I do what I must,' Sir Hugo said in a flat voice that brooked no argument.

'That you do, sir,' Jamison said, putting an arm around his employer's shoulders. 'Lean on me and we'll get you into the library. I think a poultice is called for.'

Sir Hugo's fine mouth was a thin line by the time Jamison had his shoulder under Sir Hugo's arm. It thinned even more when they began moving. 'If you will excuse us?'

Annabell nearly laughed at his drollness, but sympathy quickly kept her from doing so. He was so obviously in a great deal of pain. 'Of course.'

She watched Hugo hobble away, supported by his valet. The man never ceased to amaze her and intrigue her. She had thought him too self-centred to jeopardise himself like

he just had. And he had done it without a thought for himself. He would not have caught Rosalie if he had hesitated.

Her liking for him and attraction to him took on a deeper
dimension. She admired him. This was not good. Not good
at all unless she left here soon. Otherwise she feared she
would weaken and do something about her feelings for him.

But what? Make love to him as he had already suggested
so many times? Her stomach did somersaults at the idea
and her heart pounded painfully against her ribs.

Perhaps?

Dinner was a desultory event. Hugo was in the library
with a tray and Juliet, feeling badly that she had had to
discipline Rosalie, had chosen to eat in her rooms. Susan
and Mr Tatterly carried on a lively conversation, but Annabell didn't bother to follow it. Her thoughts were on her
host.

As soon as dessert was served, she rose. 'Please excuse
me. I want to look in on Sir Hugo and see how he is
feeling.'

'He is in some pain, but I believe he said the poultice
Jamison applied is helping,' Mr Tatterly said, standing
while Annabell made her way to the door.

'Oh, dear,' Susan murmured. 'He was such a hero, saving
poor little Rosalie, it is too bad he hurt himself.'

'True,' Mr Tatterly said, 'but that is the way he is. That
wasn't the first time he's risked himself for someone else.'

Annabell paused, arrested by Mr Tatterly's words. 'Really?'

He nodded. 'Oh, yes, Lady Fenwick-Clyde. That is how
he got the wound in the first place. He won't tell you.'

'But you will, surely,' she prompted.

He turned a dull red in embarrassment. 'Probably
shouldn't. He doesn't like the story told, but—' he gave her
a speculative look '—I will.'

She moved back to the table and took her seat so he could sit. 'Please do.'

'Oh, yes,' Susan added her encouragement.

'Right.' Mr Tatterly took a deep breath. 'It was at Waterloo. You know he was shot there.' Both women nodded. 'Well, he was shot by a Frenchie while he, Sir Hugo, stood guard over Jamison. Jamison had been knocked unconscious by the concussion of a cannon blast and Sir Hugo had been determined not to leave him and several other men. But Sir Hugo was alone, his horse having thrown him and bolted because of the same blast, and he couldn't carry all three men to safety. So he stayed until help arrived. He ran out of ammunition and a Frenchman shot him in the leg. Fortunately for us, the Frenchman came in for the kill and Sir Hugo is more than handy with a sword. Ran the man through and took his ammunition.'

Annabell's mouth rounded in admiration and awe. 'That is incredible.'

'Oh, my. Oh, my,' Susan said. 'I would have never thought it of him.' She realised what she'd said and blushed. 'That is, I believe him capable, but he is such a hedonist that one doesn't think of him putting himself in danger for someone else. That isn't very comfortable.'

'No,' Mr Tatterly said. 'It isn't comfortable, but that is Sir Hugo. He likes his creature comforts all right, but he also has courage. Don't ever try to mistreat someone when he is around. He will put you down with a word or with his fists. He believes in standing up for what he believes in.'

Annabell realised her chest felt tight and her eyes burned. There was so much more to Sir Hugo—Hugo—than she had seen or even imagined. She rose slowly.

'Thank you for telling us, Mr Tatterly. It was very enlightening.'

He gave her a grim smile. 'I hoped it would be, my lady.'

Something in his tone made her look closely at him. If

she didn't know better, she would think he had done it on purpose to show her another facet of Sir Hugo. The expression on his solid face implied that he had done it for that reason.

She smiled at him. 'I am even more interested now in seeing how Sir Hugo is doing.'

'Give him our regards,' Susan said. 'We will be in there shortly. He would probably like a good game of whist to occupy his time, don't you think, Mr Tatterly?'

Annabell didn't hear what Mr Tatterly replied, but she picked up her step. She would warn Sir Hugo of the treat in store for him.

Chapter Eight

Annabell entered the library expecting to see Hugo in his favourite chair. She was not surprised. The only difference was that his bad leg was propped on an ottoman.

'How are you feeling?' she asked, moving toward him.

He eyed her. 'About what I expected.'

She reached him and choked. 'What is that awful smell?'

He grimaced. 'That is the poultice Jamison put on me.'

'What is in it?'

'The same thing one would use for a horse's sprain.'

'Certainly you jest?' She dug her handkerchief from inside the small puff sleeve of her dress and held it to her nose. 'That is barbarous.'

He smiled wryly. 'Perhaps. But Jamison's philosophy is that if the medicine is good enough for the horse then it is good enough for me.'

'I find that hard to believe.'

He shrugged. 'Have it your way, but it is true nonetheless.'

She gave him a lopsided grin. 'It definitely does not do anything for your appeal.'

His face took on an arrested look. 'Do I take that to mean you find me appealing?'

She felt heat creep up her neck. The urge to evade his

question was strong, but that was not what she really wanted. She had come in here to tell him how much she admired his earlier actions. She was not going to let her nerve fail her.

She licked her dry lips. 'I… Yes, that is what it meant. What you did earlier was remarkable.'

'And until then I was just a rake?'

There was an edge to his voice that told her he was not all that happy to hear the reason for her reversal of opinion about him. She tilted her head and studied him.

'I suppose that was rather arrogant of me to assume you would be happy to know my opinion of you is improving.' She paused before adding, 'Or that it took such a painful action on your part to bring it about.'

He shifted as though his leg irritated him. 'I had hoped you were interested in me before this afternoon. I am not any different than I was yesterday or the day before.'

'No, you aren't.' He was not making this easy. It was almost as though he resented her thinking better of him because he had saved Rosalie. 'But yesterday and the days before, I didn't know this side of your personality.'

'I believe we have had a similar discussion before,' he said drily. 'You seem to continually find it amazing that I am more than a drunken wastrel.'

She sighed, beginning to take affront at his belligerence. 'Perhaps you are in great discomfort and that is why you are behaving like a boor.'

He snorted. 'No more pain than earlier today. I am merely curious that you can change your opinion of me so readily.'

She stood. 'Well, so am I. Still, I am willing to admit that I might have misjudged you. You could at least give me credit for that.'

His eyes softened. 'You are right. I have not portrayed myself in the best light. Suffice that I wanted you to know the worst.'

'Before…'

But she could not finish the sentence. She could barely finish the thought. *Before we become lovers.*

She shivered in the heated room. Just the thought of making love with him scared her at the same time that it excited her.

How had she come to this? Just because she had seen him put another before himself?

She stood abruptly. 'I am tired, Hugo—Sir Hugo. I will see you in the morning.'

She fled the room before he could follow up on her unfinished statement. She was not ready to deal with the progression of their relationship. Not yet.

Hugo watched her escape the room and smiled. He knew what she had left unspoken, and he knew that soon they would be lovers. He only wished the idea did not cause the breath to catch painfully in his throat.

Annabell reached her bedroom, locked the door behind herself and wished she could as easily lock away her burgeoning feelings for Sir Hugo Fitzsimmon. She tossed the key on to a table in passing and paced to the end of the room before turning and retracing her steps.

Tension ate at her spine. She wanted to make love to the man. She was half in love with the man. She froze.

Surely not. Desire and love were not the same thing… only for her they seemed irrevocably intertwined.

What was she thinking? She was crazy, a Bedlamite to have even intimated they would become lovers—to even be considering it. Where was her vaunted freedom from involvement with the opposite sex? Where was her sense of self-preservation?

Gone up in the flames Hugo always ignited in her body. And her mind must have gone with it.

She threw herself on to a chair and stared at the wall.

Her emotions were raw and on the surface. Her need for

what Hugo offered was to the point where she knew if she walked away from him, she would always wonder what she had let go. A silly, stupid idea, but there it was.

She wanted to make love with Hugo Fitzsimmon. She wanted to have the memory of him touching her, loving her. More than anything, she wanted him to erase the memory of Fenwick-Clyde, something she knew he could do.

She jumped to her feet, determined to seek him out before she changed her mind and lost her courage. It was now or never. Or wait until the next time he tried to seduce her. But she did not want to wait.

Annabell took a deep breath that did nothing to calm her trepidation. What if he sent her away? How mortifying. Even worse, it would mean he didn't want her. Not only mortifying, but so painful that the possibility of his rejection did not bear thinking upon.

Funny, that a woman with her independent streak could contemplate giving her body to him even as she tried to keep her soul free. She was not sure she could give one without the other. Yet, she did not want to love Sir Hugo, to have him mean more to her than her freedom.

She only wanted to share his bed. Just once.

She had given Fenwick-Clyde her body because she had had no choice. They had been married and she had been under law to provide him whatever he wanted of her physically. Nothing in the world would have induced her to give her dead husband that which she contemplated giving Hugo… Her heart?

Her heart.

The enormity of what she was about to do swamped her. She stopped. She shook. Her pulse thundered in her ears.

How could she think she was giving Sir Hugo her heart? She was only giving him her body. She did not love him. Could not love him. Could she? Did she dare?

Her shaking increased. Her chest rose and fell in rapid, shallow breaths. Surely not.

Enough. He wanted her. She wanted him. That was all that mattered.

She went to her door, opened it and slipped outside. The hall was cold and dimly lit. Everyone must have gone to bed. She had spent more time pacing and agonising than she had realised. She moved forwards.

Minutes later, she stood motionless in front of his door where anyone passing by would see her. She smoothed her moist palms down the fine satin of her evening gown and told herself to stop overreacting. Everyone had gone to bed. She raised her clenched hand to knock and paused. What if someone heard? Did she dare enter without announcing herself? Did she dare risk someone else knowing what was happening? Neither choice was good.

And if he answered? Would that be any better? All her doubts and fears swept over her like a tidal wave crashing to shore. She swayed in indecision.

'Hello?' Hugo's voice came from the other side of the thick oak door.

His words were like being doused with a jug of ice water. She heard the discomfort he now took no effort to hide. He was in no condition for what she contemplated, even if what she had come here for was something they should be doing. And he was not alone. And she was a fool.

As though awakening from a dream where she had seen paradise and then had it taken away, she turned away. She had been right earlier. She belonged in Bedlam, not Sir Hugo's bed.

She was a widow and he was a rake. They had no future together. She had never engaged in a relationship just for the pleasure. She had never slept with any man but her husband.

This was too huge a step for her to take.

She retraced her footsteps. She locked her door once more, and this time she put the key to her room on the very top of the wardrobe. Perhaps if she had to make an effort to let herself out, she would stop and think more clearly. She could only hope.

But he was a great temptation, and she was learning just how weak she was.

Annabell woke with the sun the next day. She had barely slept, tossing and turning, until she dozed. Now she felt exhausted and had a headache that she knew would be with her all day. She dragged herself from bed. The maid would be here with hot chocolate soon. The way she felt, a tot of Sir Hugo's ever-present brandy would be welcome.

She ran her fingers through the tangle of her hair, having forgotten to braid it the night before, and told herself that succumbing to Sir Hugo's brandy was nearly as bad as succumbing to the man himself. The maid chose that moment to knock.

Thankful for the interruption to her disturbing thoughts, Annabell called, 'Come in.'

The doorknob twisted, and only then did Annabell remember she had locked herself in and put the key on top of the wardrobe. She pulled the chair to the piece of furniture, climbed on top of the cushions and found the key. Before letting the maid in, she put the chair back in its spot. No sense the entire household knowing where she had hidden the key. Coupled with her locking the door in the first place, that would precipitate more talk about her eccentricity than there already was.

Unlocking the door, Annabell said, 'Thank you, Sally.'

The young maid bobbed a curtsy as she entered. She cast a look around. 'Here, my lady. I'll just pick up your gown, if you please.'

The gown was the mauve silk she had worn last night and left lying on the floor after coming back from Hugo's room. She had never been neat except in her antiquities work. She sighed. 'Thank you, Sally.'

The girl smiled. 'Shall I help you dress, my lady?' She

flushed at her temerity. 'I ain't a fancy French lady's maid, but—'

'You will do just fine. I've never had any use for a lady's maid to begin with. If you will just help hook the dress in the middle of my back where I have difficulty reaching, that will be more than enough.'

'Yes, my lady.' Sally bobbed another curtsy.

After the girl was gone, Annabelle quickly twisted her silvery blonde hair into braids and secured them on her head before studying herself. Her dress was serviceable. Grey kerseymere cut loosely. She had not put on her harem pants because… She frowned at herself. Why had she not put them on? She had not made a conscious decision not to, she just hadn't thought to. Was this another example of her indecision about Hugo, not being able to dress in her normal working attire?

She twisted away from her reflection. She was totally confused about what she wanted.

She stalked to the door and threw it open just in time to see her nemesis leaving his room. He turned to look at her, his gaze catching her attention and holding her captive.

'What a fetching gown.'

His murmured voice seemed to caress her even though the upward curve of his sensual lips told her he did not think the dress was fetching at all. Yet his eyes told her he didn't care what she wore.

She frowned, as irritated with him as she was with herself. 'I dare say you tell all the women that, regardless of how they look.'

He shrugged. 'Why not? Anything else only hurts their sensibilities.'

'Honesty.'

He raised one dark brow. 'Sometimes it is better to compliment than to denigrate.'

She moved toward him. 'You are the one always harping about honesty.'

He watched her. 'In emotions and intent. I never lie about what I plan to do or how I feel about something.'

She stopped near enough to him that she could see the fine lines of dissipation that radiated from his eyes and the slight tension around his mouth. Suddenly their bickering was not worth the energy and ill will.

'Are you still in pain?'

He laughed. 'Changing the subject?'

She shrugged, but returned his smile with a small one of her own. 'I suppose I am. It just suddenly seemed so trivial to be arguing about a compliment when you are likely still in pain from yesterday.'

'We are back to my heroism, I see.'

'Is that so bad?'

'No.'

He spoke so softly she only knew what he said by the movement of his lips, lips that could move so expertly over her own. Her eyes widened even as his narrowed.

'Did you come to my door last night?' His words were barely a whisper, meant only for her.

Shock erased her arousal of seconds before. 'Of course not.'

'No?' That eyebrow rose again. 'I thought I heard a sound outside my room. It was too late for a servant and Jamison was with me.' He continued to watch her.

She felt a flush rise from her neck to her cheeks. 'I am not so craven as to come that far and then retreat.'

'Aren't you?'

The collar of her gown was suddenly too tight, and she could no longer meet his eyes. 'Oh, very well,' she said ungraciously. 'I did come to your door. I meant to see how you were doing.'

'But you had seen that just hours before in the library.'

She studied him and wondered how long she could skirt his questions, or if she even wanted to. Just as she wondered how long she could continue to deny her own attraction to him. She was in uncharted territory and didn't know what to do.

His eyes darkened. 'You came to my room for a different reason, didn't you?'

She continued to look at him, knowing she should say something, but not able to. This was all so much more complicated than she had ever imagined. She did not plan the words that tumbled from her mouth.

'Yes. I wanted… I wanted…' She twisted away so she would not have to see his face. 'I don't know what I wanted.'

His hands touched her shoulders, his fingers warm and firm through the kerseymere dress. He did not try to turn her, only spoke gently to her. 'You want me to make love to you, Annabell. You want to know what it is like between a man and woman who desire each other and want to give each other pleasure.'

She took a deep shuddering breath, aware on a bone-deep level that she felt as though a great burden had been lifted. His words, so blunt and truthful, spoke directly to the core of who she was. He understood her.

She nodded, still unable to turn back to him. 'Yes. More than I ever imagined possible.'

The sound of a heel on the carpet came from behind them. They jumped apart and Annabell whirled around. Desire still etched furrows in Sir Hugo's cheeks. Annabell felt like a small child caught doing something unspeakable. Her breath wheezed through a painfully tight throat.

Juliet Fitzsimmon rounded the corner from the stairs and stopped. 'Good morning, Annabell. Hugo.' She looked searchingly at her stepson and then her guest. 'It seems I came along at an inopportune time, but that will happen when private matters are discussed in public places.'

'So true.' Hugo's voice was dry, his gaze on Annabell.

Mortified at how close they had come to being discovered, Annabell spoke hastily. 'I must be on my way.' She paused. 'I am sorry for having put you in the position of having to find us this way.'

Juliet looked at her. 'Sometimes the heart is stronger than our sense of caution, Annabell. I am glad I was the one to come around the corner.'

'You are a true friend,' Annabell murmured as she left.

Hugo watched Annabell walk away before turning to Juliet. 'It seems we are becoming indiscreet. My apologies.'

Juliet put her slender white fingers on Hugo's arm. 'Do not break her heart, Hugo. She does not deserve it.'

He scowled down at his stepmother. 'I have no intentions of doing so.'

'Then your intentions are honourable?'

His scowl deepened. 'Lady Fenwick-Clyde is a widow and knows what she is about, Juliet. Just as you are.'

His stepmother's pale complexion pinkened. 'You always know exactly what to say, Hugo, to stop someone from prying when it is none of their business to begin with. I hope you know what you are about this time.' She walked away without waiting for his reply.

Hugo watched Juliet disappear down the hall that suddenly seemed to lead to everyone's bedchamber. Much as he did not like to agree with what she had said, Juliet had spoken truly. He just was not going to let her words influence him. This was between him and Annabell and to hell with everyone else.

Annabell reached the front hall, feeling as though she had just escaped from mortal danger. Emotional danger. Her mouth twisted. She had never considered herself fanciful, but the things Hugo made her feel were frightening to someone who never wanted to be controlled by another person.

'My lady,' Butterfield intoned. 'A letter.'

Annabell jumped, not having seen him approach because she was too engrossed in her worries. 'Oh, thank you.'

She managed to smile and take the letter, thankful Hugo had not witnessed the incident. He would know her pre-occupation was because of what had just occurred between them. She glanced down at the letter, the delicate writing and franking telling her it was from her new sister-in-law, Felicia, Viscountess Chillings.

Eager for news about her family, Annabell moved instinctively to the library where she could read in comfort and privacy. Sitting in her favourite chintz chair, she peeled off the wax seal and unfolded the single sheet of thick vellum.

Dearest Bell,

I would not write this, but I need to share my thoughts with someone and I do not think Guy could easily deal with my worries. He was too afraid of losing me and the babe from the beginning.

The breath caught in Annabell's throat. Something horrible must have happened for the normally calm Felicia to write this. And the next words were blurred by what had been tears.

Adam is sick. The physician says it is merely croup, but my baby coughs day and night and is not eating well. I know I am being silly, but seeing him this way makes me worry that something will happen to him. Absolutely silly. Absolutely. But…

The rest of the letter was about other family matters, the disreputable Damien and what a wonderful husband Guy was. Annabell smiled. Felicia understood so much about the two brothers. Her sister-in-law ended with love and a request for a reply.

Annabell set the paper down and gazed at nothing. Croup was not unusual in babies, and the physician they called would be the best. Probably Prinny's own, and what was good enough for the Prince of Wales should be good enough for the future Viscount Chillings. And Felicia and Guy would give their son all the love and attention a baby needed. Likely, Adam was perfectly fine by now since Felicia had written the letter two days ago.

Still, Felicia's worry made Annabell's heart hurt. Felicia had lost her two children from her first marriage because of an ice skating accident several years ago. Although Felicia had had amnesia when she first came into their lives and had not remembered who she was or the children she had lost, she had been consciously aware of a deep hurt. Annabell understood how something, anything might make Felicia worry about this child. And she had been right in saying Guy would have difficulty if his wife openly worried because it had been constant torture for Guy during the delivery, having lost his first wife and heir in childbirth. Life was so fragile, and sometimes too short.

Annabell took a deep breath, surprised at her last thought, and felt unexpected tears well up. She wiped them away, appalled at her maudlin reaction. Her emotions were all twisted up. She had not consciously thought about how long life was or wasn't since her parents' untimely death in a boating accident.

But life was short.

The library door opened and closed, and, without looking, she knew Hugo had come in. There was a sense of electricity in the air—and his scent of cinnamon.

She folded the paper and made herself smile as she stood to face him. 'I was just leaving.'

He studied her, not moving from the door so that she could exit. 'What is wrong?'

Her gaze skipped away. He was too perceptive. Would he understand her upset when she didn't really understand it herself? She sighed and looked back at him.

'I have a letter from Felicia—my new sister-in-law.

The…' She stopped to clear the catch in her throat. 'It seems baby Adam has the croup and Felicia is worried. Not that there is really anything to worry about,' she added hastily. 'Croup is so much a part of being a baby. I dare say Felicia isn't getting enough sleep and the tiredness is making her more emotional about the situation.'

Instead of the cynical curve of lips she expected, Hugo crossed the room to her. 'And you are worried too.'

He was so close that cinnamon seemed to surround her, and she could feel the heat from his body. She wished he hadn't got near enough that a step—just a tiny little step— would put her in his arms. He did not want to comfort her in his embrace, as she wanted right now, he wanted to seduce her. Two totally different goals.

'Yes. Silly as it seems, her letter made me think how short life can be.' Her voice became little more than a whisper. 'She lost her two children by her first husband in an accident. Felicia will never forget.'

'No mother would.' Hugo's voice was as quiet as hers, and his arms gathered her in.

She went, knowing it was a mistake, but no longer wanting to resist. He was gentle, his hands cradling her back. He made no move to kiss her, only held her.

She revelled in the feel of him and the security his solid chest gave her. For a brief moment, she let herself sink into his warmth before pushing away.

'And I am not even a mother, just a silly woman who has let her emotions get the better of her. Adam is not even in danger. I am merely reacting to Felicia's worry.'

He let her go, but did not step away from her. He made her do that. 'You are the furthest from silly that I have ever encountered in a woman. You let your head rule your emotions nearly all the time. You must be tired.'

Her eyes narrowed, wondering if he was jesting with her or serious. 'Why would I be tired?'

He shrugged. 'I don't know, Annabell. I only know I've never seen you distraught over anything.'

She moved, realising she had not put any real distance between them. 'It is past time for me to be getting to work. I have much to do and the sooner I do it, the sooner I will be out of your way.'

He stepped aside for her with an ironic bow that made him grimace. 'As you say.'

Concern lined the space between her brows. 'You are in no condition to be making bows yet.' She sniffed. 'And where is that nasty-smelling poultice Jamison made to help you heal faster?'

A smile hovered over his full lips. 'He is making me a fresh one.'

'A more potent one.' She shuddered. 'Do not come near me when you are wearing it, please.'

He laughed outright. 'Obviously, Jamison's ministrations do nothing for my appeal.'

She shook her had. 'Absolutely nothing.'

He sobered instantly. 'That is unfortunate.'

Her eyes widened as she realised his mood had changed instantly, like a storm that had hovered in the distance and finally blew in without warning. No longer comforting, he was now flirting.

'I must be leaving.'

This time, she did not wait or hesitate at the pinching around his mouth created by his movement as she skirted past him. He was too dangerous to her sensibilities. First he seduced her with desire, then he seduced her with concern for her feelings. He was too skilled for her.

Hugo watched her escape, for that was what she did, and smiled. She was much more susceptible to him than she wanted to admit, and it was making her emotions raw. Like her, he knew croup was likely not dangerous to the baby, and he believed that normally she would not have been so upset. But he also knew she was undecided about what to do about him and the sensations he created in her.

He limped over to his favourite chair and sank gratefully into the cushion. He lifted his injured leg with a sigh, wondering briefly if he would be up to making love to Annabell when she finally decided their joining was inevitable.

He only wished she would realise soon that they were meant to be together. Or did he? He grimaced as his old wound knotted. Kneading the muscle, he knew he hoped it would be soon and be damned to his injury.

Chapter Nine

Late that night, exhausted by an intentionally long day digging, Annabell took refuge in her room from the activity still going on in the drawing room. Susan and Mr Tatterly had got Lady Fitzsimmon and Sir Hugo to play cards. The last thing Annabell felt like doing was watching Hugo try to control his exasperation with Susan, who was blithely unaware that she constantly irritated the man.

Annabell dug her portable writing desk from the trunk where she had packed it when it had seemed she was to relocate to the inn. It seemed eons ago, but was only days. Sinking into the nearest chair, she settled the desk on her lap and took a thick sheet of paper from under the hinged top and dipped her quill in ink.

She wasn't sure what to say to Felicia. Her first inclination was to make light of Adam's problem and tell Felicia not to worry, but she knew that would not help her sister-in-law. Felicia had written because she had needed someone to share her fears with, not someone to tell her they were unfounded. The woman had already lost two children—any threat, serious or not, to Adam would be enough to cause near panic. And Guy would be no better than his wife if Felicia tried to confide her fears to him because of his previous loss.

Annabell sighed and laid her quill down. Who was she to say Felicia was overreacting? Life could be too short. She had seen that often enough. Her parents. And even Hugo. He might have died at Waterloo instead of becoming a hero and knighted for his bravery. Many men had died during that battle.

Hugo. What if something happened to him? Not that anything would, but what if? What if he were thrown by a horse? That wasn't uncommon, and his thigh often caused him to hesitate just as his leg went over his mount's back. It might also cause him to land badly.

Her heart clenched painfully. *Stop it!* She closed her eyes, trying to close her mind to the possibilities.

The mantel clock struck the half-hour. Annabell opened her eyes and stared at the timepiece. Hugo would be in his chambers by now. He would have escaped the cards as soon as possible.

She wanted him. She wanted what only he could give her.

As though walking in a dream, her actions already planned, she set the writing desk on the floor and stood. She took a deep breath and ran her damp palms down the sides of her dress. She would go to him. It was what she wanted to do, what she had nearly done last night.

She moved to the door and inched it open, belatedly worrying about someone being in the hallway. Life might be too short to deny herself and Hugo the pleasure of loving one another, but it could be all too long if her reputation were ruined.

Not seeing anyone, she slipped into the hall. The sconces were still lit, throwing her shadow against the wall. She moved swiftly and quietly.

She stopped at Hugo's door. Breathing deeply, wondering if she was going to faint from nervousness, she raised her hand and tapped lightly with her knuckles. Her heart pounded so loudly, a herd of horses could have come down the hall and she would not have heard them. When there was no answer, she gripped the door handle, telling herself he had invited her to his room so many times he would not mind her letting herself in.

She slid inside and shut the door behind herself, her chest rising and falling like a bellows. Her gaze darted around the room until she located the bed. It was empty. She scanned the room slowly this time. It was empty. He wasn't here.

She slumped against the solid wood of the door at her back. The butterflies that had rioted through her blood disappeared as though they had never been. Disappointment was a rock in her stomach.

She sighed. All her trepidation, all her strength of purpose needed to come here, and he was still playing cards. She giggled at the release of tension and to keep herself from crying. Until now, feeling this keen disappointment, she had not realised just how much she truly wanted to make love with Hugo. She had known she wanted to, but this bone-aching, heart-wrenching need seemed too big for her body to contain.

She took a deep shuddering breath and pushed away from the door, intending to leave. She stopped and turned back around. She could wait for him. There was no place else for him to go at this time of night. He would be here eventually.

So would his valet. She did not want the servant, or anyone else, to know she was here. She shook her head sadly. No, she couldn't wait for him. If he had already been here and the valet dismissed, that would have been different. She could have left before daylight and no one would have been the wiser. She had to go.

She took one last look around his room, as though a part of her thought Hugo might be hiding somewhere. The walls were golden, the furniture finely carved and heavy. The carpet under her feet was thick and well cushioned. The fire roared in the grate and a small brazier stood by the bed to heat that area. Everything was neatly in its spot or folded. She knew from her own experience that not even the best servant could keep a room this immaculate if the person who lived here wasn't fastidious.

A smile lifted one corner of her mouth. She was such an untidy person, who left things lying where they fell or where she last put them. She looked once more around his room, noting his dressing robe folded neatly over the back of the chair nearest the fire so it would be warm when he put it on. Several books lay on a table near the same chair. Each spine was centred on the one below it. In some ways, Hugo was her exact opposite.

A gilt Louis XIV clock chimed the hour, its high tinkle disconcerting in the quiet room. Annabell started. She had been here too long.

Still bemused by her discoveries, of herself and Hugo, she cracked open his door, made sure no one was about and slid into the hall. She ran to her own room, heart pounding, and slipped inside.

She collapsed onto the chair she had climbed on just the night before to hide her bedchamber key atop the wardrobe. Her hands shook. Her chest rose and fell as she dragged in air, more winded by her emotions than her exertion. She was also exhilarated.

She realised with no real surprise that she was going to go back to Hugo's room. She was going to make love with him. She was going to take this chance to be happy, to be a woman experiencing one of life's greatest pleasures. Life was too short not to. But he wasn't there yet. She would reply to Felicia's letter while she waited.

Once more she gathered her writing desk and set it on her lap. She took a deep breath to calm herself and dipped a quill in ink and started.

Dearest Felicia,
I hope this finds Adam much better. I will not make light of your fears. I know how you love him and worry about him, as does Guy. I also know you will not leave him alone and that he will receive the best care possible and your love will surround him, giving him strength. My thoughts are with you. If you need me, I can be there in a day.

Love, Bell

She had written from the heart. She sanded the paper and quickly folded it and sealed it. She would ask the butler to see that it was posted. She set her desk on the floor and stared at the fire.

Annabell thought about what she had written. She had written about love and its power to make even the toughest situation somehow bearable. We give love to others no matter what the risk to ourselves. She had loved her parents and lost them. She loved Guy and Damien and now Felicia and Adam. She would risk anything for them.

But why was she risking her reputation to go to Hugo? Because she desired him? Because he made her blood course hotly through her body until she thought she would burst into flames for the want of him?

Because as she got to know him better, she found she liked him better? She sighed. She even admired him. He was a rake and a womaniser, but he was not callous about it. Nor did he lie. And he risked himself for those he loved, as he had demonstrated with Rosalie. And even more amply when he had stood guard over his valet at Waterloo.

If she denied herself this opportunity for happiness with Hugo, she feared the chance would never come again.

The mantel clock that had chimed hours ago chimed again. It was one in the morning. Surely Hugo was in his room by now—and alone?

Suddenly calm for the first time in days, Annabell rose. This time she would not turn back. With a determined tread, she went to her door and into the now-unlit hall. The candles in the wall sconces had been snuffed. Even the servants were abed.

She made her way as quietly as possible across the small distance that separated her room from Hugo's. Her breathing was the loudest noise in her ears. She grimaced. Though she had made this journey twice already, she was still scared.

He had asked her to his room and to be his lover often enough that she should feel confident. But she did not. She had never had a lover. And she was the one making the final move.

She stopped, but only for an instant. She wanted this. Either she went to him tonight or she waited for him to ask her again. She did not want to wait. She covered the rest of the distance to his room.

Annabell took another shuddering breath and reached for the doorknob. Her fingers shook as she twisted the brass lever. Her entire body trembled as she slipped into Hugo's bedchamber.

The fire still simmered in the grate, giving the room a warmth that normally was not present during this time of year. Hugo pampered himself.

The curtains at the window were open and the full moon spilled through the tiny diamond glass panes in a river of silver prisms to the floor. Light fell across the bed where Hugo lay, raised on one elbow watching her. His eyes met hers.

She shifted her gaze, unable to meet the intensity of his. Half his face was in shadow, the other was outlined in harsh angles of cheek, jaw and enticing mouth. His shoulders and chest rose from the bed in firm delineation against the dusky sheets beneath him.

The linens draped dangerously low on his hips. His lean, muscular hips. She swallowed.

'Annabell?'

His voice was deep and raspy and made her insides turn to lava. Then he threw aside the sheet and rose. He was naked. Somehow, she was not surprised.

Annabell reached for the back of a nearby chair to support her suddenly weak legs. He was everything she had ever imagined a man could be. More.

The fire turned his right side to burnished copper. The moon silvered his left. His muscles rippled with each movement. He was magnificent.

Dark hair fell over his forehead in waves of reckless abandon. His shoulders swayed just a little, just enough to draw attention to how broad and well formed they were. His torso tapered into narrow hips, leading to strong, muscular thighs and calves that needed no padding for their shape.

'Annabell?' he said again, moving inexorably toward her.

'Hugo,' she managed to say around the constriction in her throat.

She collapsed into the chair she had recently used for support. What was she doing here? She belonged in Bedlam. And yet…

He reached her and squatted down in front of her. His face level with hers, his bare knees brushing hers through the fabric of her dress, she saw him wince. His wound.

'Oh, Hugo,' she said, her voice a hoarse whisper, 'I should not be here. You are still hurting.'

His firm lips formed a seductive, wry smile. 'Only a little, Annabell.'

'Are you sure?' She barely got the words out, her throat was so tight. He smelled of cinnamon and brandy and desire.

She glanced to the inside of his thigh, where the wound was, and her hand reached instinctively to touch the scar. But it was too close to another part of his body, a part that was more than ready for her visit. She felt a rush of hot blood.

'What are you doing here?' He had seen her glance, and now his voice was hoarse.

There was a look of hunger in his eyes as they met hers without wavering. His mouth, that temptation that haunted her dreams, quirked up at one corner. She reached out without conscious thought and lightly, oh, so lightly, touched the left corner of his lips with her right index finger. This was much safer than touching that other part of him, no matter how she longed to do so. Carefully, she traced the outline of his mouth. He let her, the only evidence that he felt her touch being the sudden stiffness of his jaw. The need in his gaze intensified.

He caught her hand and held it away from his face. 'Annabell, don't start something you have no intention of seeing through to the finish.'

She let him keep her hand in his. 'I know what I'm doing, Hugo.'

'Are you sure?'

'If you are sure the pain from your wound will not be too much.'

She did not want him to hurt when he made love to her. She wanted him to enjoy it as much as she knew she would.

His mouth twisted. 'Look at me, Annabell, where you did before.'

Aghast at his bluntness, she hesitated. But only for a second. She wanted to do more than look at him there, she wanted to touch him there. She licked her dry lips.

'And?' she managed to ask.

'Do I look like a man who cares about anything other than you being here?'

A small laugh of sheer surprise and something else escaped her. 'No, you don't.'

Instead of answering her, he rose, pulling her with him. His gaze never left her face as he bent and lifted her into his arms.

'Your leg.'

He shook his head. 'To hell with my leg, Annabell.' He carried her to the bed and laid her down.

She watched him, nearly paralysed by what she was doing, what they were about to do. She had wanted this for weeks, since the first time he kissed her. Yet, the enormity of what she was about to do nearly overwhelmed her.

He laid on his side beside her, propped up on his left arm, his bare flesh gleaming in the pale light from the window. She turned to face him, still fully clothed.

'We'll go slowly.' His voice was thick with desire and his eyes were nearly black with his arousal.

'Not too slowly.' She did not think she could bear to have what they were about to do take forever. She had been anticipating it too long already.

He smiled. 'Eager?'

She couldn't smile. 'Yes.'

He traced the line of her chin to her jaw and up to her ear with one finger. Shivers chased down her spine. No man had ever touched her so gently, so erotically. Then his hand slipped into her hair and she felt him pull the pins out one by one and saw him toss them to the floor.

'You have beautiful hair,' he murmured. 'I want to bury myself in it.' He dug his fingers into her curls and spread her hair out on the pillow behind her head. 'Lovely.'

Unable to lay passively, Annabell followed his lead. She took hold of his waving hair and combed her fingers through the thick satin.

He grinned at her. 'Shall we play follow the leader?'

'Yes,' she whispered.

He laughed outright, the sound joyous and sexy and incredibly arousing. 'Who is the leader?'

'You,' she said without hesitation.

'My pleasure.' His eyes turned slumberous. 'This time.'

His hand left her hair and travelled down her neck to the edge of her bodice. The fine linen of her nightdress was nearly transparent and cut just below where her breasts began to swell. He traced the line of fine fabric with his finger, followed with his tongue, then with his lips. She felt alternately hot and cold as his mouth caressed her sensitive skin. Her fingers flexed in the thickness of his hair, holding him to her.

He moved to a nipple and nipped it through the thin material of the bodice. She gasped as lightning jolted to her loins. As though he sensed her reaction, he took the sensitive nub into his mouth and sucked long and strong until she thought he pulled a string that directly connected her breast to her womb.

He looked up at her, a knowing gleam in his eyes. 'This is just the beginning,' he promised.

'Just the beginning,' she said so softly she barely heard herself.

Her fingers fluttered along the smooth expanse of his shoulders. She wanted to dig her nails into his muscles and urge him closer, but she knew he intended to take this slowly. Agonisingly slow. She closed her eyes with a sigh.

His hand cupped her left breast, his mouth still caressing the other one. The fine wool of her robe and finer linen of her chemise were all that separated his flesh from hers. She could feel his heat like a brand. Or maybe that was her skin that burned because of his touch. His thumb found her nipple and flicked across it, creating a friction that made her want him to do other things to her. Deeper, more penetrating things. He squeezed and rubbed until she felt as though the centre of her being was intimately connected to her bosom and that what he did to one would be instantly, crashingly felt by the other.

He moved on. She felt as though paradise had been instantly taken away.

'Oh,' she breathed, 'don't stop.'

He chuckled low in his throat. 'That was only the beginning. I have much more to show you.'

She released a shuddering breath and came back to hover

on the edge of sanity. Vaguely she knew it was her turn. She was to do to him whatever he did to her, but his hand was smoothing down her hip, kneading and caressing as it went, leaving fire in its wake down her outer thigh. His fingers caught at the thin material of her gown and pulled it inexorably up until she felt the warm air of the room on her bare skin.

She licked suddenly dry lips and opened her eyes. He stared at her, his gaze intense and questioning. Without his saying so, she knew he was giving her one last chance to flee, to stop this madness they were embarked on.

She lifted her face to his and caught his head with her hands and pulled him to her. His kiss was fire and ice and heat and passion and everything she had ever imagined it would be, everything it had always been and more. But it was not gentle. The gentleness was gone now that need rode them like a demon.

She met his demand with everything in her. Her tongue darted out to meet and dance with his. Her lips slanted to give him better access to her moist warmth. She revelled when he accepted everything she offered and gave her back more in return.

She could feel his heart beating hard and fast against hers. She felt his chest rise and fall with each ragged breath he took. His fingers clenched against the skin of her outer thigh.

'Help me,' she muttered. 'Too many clothes.'

He chuckled and his fingers were everywhere. Before she could appreciate how skilled he was, her robe was on the floor with her nightdress beside it.

He rose above her before easing himself down so his chest crushed her breasts. His skin was hot and rough against the tender flesh of her bosom. Looking down at her, his eyes slumberous with passion, he began to rub against her. The wiry hairs that spread across his chest scraped and tickled her nipples, making the buds harden in exquisite delight.

When she was hot and needy and thinking she could take no more, he lowered his mouth to hers and hungrily took her lips and her moans. She wanted him to never stop. His hands spread her legs apart and she wanted him to sink completely into her.

'Please, now, Hugo. Now.'

She wanted this more than she had ever wanted anything. She lifted her legs to give him access. She shifted her hands to his hips and pulled him to her.

He deepened the kiss and slid into her. She gasped and he swallowed the sound. He moved slowly and he swallowed her moan of desire. He lodged fully inside her until it felt as though he touched her very soul.

He released her mouth and rose up on his hands to look where their bodies joined. She felt him spasm.

'Ah,' he murmured, 'I have wanted to see this for so long and to feel it for longer still.'

He turned his attention to her face and began to move slowly again. He teased her with mounting pleasure, never taking his gaze from her face.

She watched him with equal avidity. The angles of his jaw were razor sharp. His beautiful mouth was pulled back against his teeth as though he was in great pain, but she knew differently. His pupils dilated until the clear green of his irises was nearly gone. And still he moved slowly, yet each thrust was full and penetrated to the point where she gasped from tiny bursts of delight.

With each steady, slow entry he moved his hips so her pleasure increased. She thought she would explode.

She gasped and let out a low scream of release. He stayed motionless inside her until she relaxed. Then he slid out and reached for something on the nearby table.

'What?' For a second apprehension held her. For the first time in her life she had enjoyed making love, but Hugo had stopped. She remembered her husband had used many toys in his bedroom games, none of them to please her.

In the act of picking up whatever it was he wanted, Hugo glanced at her. He left the object.

'What is wrong, Bell?'

'Nothing.' Her throat was suddenly dry, all her previous delight gone as though it had never happened.

'Don't lie to me.' He rolled off her, but did not take his hands from her. 'That is not how we are to deal with each other. Ever.'

She realised he was upset with her. But she did not want to tell him the truth. What had happened to her before was the past. Still, she had been the one to flinch.

'What were you reaching for?' She couldn't keep the apprehension from her voice.

He frowned. 'Protection.'

'Protection?' What was he talking about?

'Yes,' he said patiently, 'protection. To keep you from conceiving my child.'

She blushed. How incongruent. He had just made very thorough love to her, exploring her body with an intimacy that had held her enthralled and she had not been embarrassed. But the talk of carrying his child made her feel vulnerable as nothing before had.

'I…I did not know there was such a thing. I thought…' how very, very uncomfortable to talk of these things '…I thought you would just withdraw or I would use something afterwards.'

He gave her a rueful grin. 'I would like to think I have the control to withdraw in time, but I am not sure. This is safer. Safer than you douching afterwards.'

Her blush deepened at his frank talk.

'But that is not why you were scared when I reached for the condom, Bell.' His voice held a firm determination she had not heard before. 'Tell me what frightened you.'

She rubbed her eyes, feeling suddenly tired. 'Fenwick-

Clyde used to stop, but he did so in order to find his latest toy.' She sighed. 'I had hoped loving you would erase that memory.'

Compassion darkened his eyes and a bone-deep anger clenched his jaw. 'I promise to do everything in my power to make you forget that man. I promise, Bell.'

She looked at him and knew he meant what he said. 'Thank you, Hugo.'

He came back to her and made good his word.

Chapter Ten

Hugo took the proffered billet-doux from the silver tray Butterfield held and strolled to the library. The paper smelled strongly of tuberose, Elizabeth Mainwaring's favourite scent. He scowled and ran his fingers through the unruly wave of hair that always wanted to spill down his forehead. He should have been expecting this, but he had completely forgotten his arrangement to meet her in London.

He sat down in the chair near the desk so that the morning light fell on his former mistress's handwriting. *I am in London. Come immediately, my dear. E.* Sweet and brief, not at all like Elizabeth. Normally her words overflowed the page. Something was wrong, or she thought something was. Very likely the fact that he had not been in London to welcome her. He had meant to be.

Things had changed drastically since he last saw Elizabeth.

Hugo wadded up the expensive paper and held it in his fist, staring out at the grounds. The last of the daffodils formed yellow carpets across the garden. Soon the roses would begin to bloom and their scent would perfume the air. But not yet. It had snowed lightly last night.

He had made love to Annabell last night, their passion

keeping them warm in spite of the cold outside. He still smelled of her, honeysuckle with a hint of woman. He wondered if his scent remained with her. She had taken one of his shirts back to her room with her, saying she wanted the smell of him near her. When she had explained why she wanted the piece of clothing, he had responded instantly. They had made love until it was nearly too late for her to get back to her room without meeting a servant doing early morning tasks.

And now this.

'Damnation!'

He rose and went to the grate where a fire roared. He tossed the note into the flames and watched it burn, the smell of tuberose mingling with the acrid bite of smoke.

He had not ended his liaison with Elizabeth, even though he had known she was seeing another man as well. He had even known who her other lover was. St. Cyrus, another one of Wellington's aides. It had not mattered to him that Elizabeth was sharing her favours. He had enjoyed her company and revelled in the lushness of her body, but that had been all. He had not loved her.

He would have to go to Elizabeth. His honour dictated that he end their connection face to face. And, she would like an expensive bauble to ease her disappointment at receiving no more—from him.

He returned to the desk chair and swivelled it around so he could gaze once more at the grounds. The bright sun had already started melting the dusting of snow. The roads would be a quagmire.

He had to tell Annabell.

He didn't think she would appreciate him leaving her to visit his former mistress, no matter what his reasons. His hands clenched in white-knuckled fists. And, damn it, he could finally understand why. All these years he had been doing whatever took his fancy, loving women with no thought for the future. And now there was Annabell.

She was so independent. What if she left him over this? Surely not. He had not proposed marriage to her, wasn't sure he would. Nor did he think she would accept if he did. But he didn't want to lose her. Not yet.

He was a selfish bastard.

A knock on the door broke his reverie. 'Come in.'

'Hugo,' his stepmother's high, sweet voice said, 'I need to speak with you.'

He turned to face her and stood up. 'Come in, Juliet, and have a seat.'

She glided into the room and sat down in the chair he had indicated. Her strawberry-blonde hair curled around her heart-shaped face, but her complexion was so pale that the faint dusting of peach freckles stood out in stark relief. Something bothered her.

He smiled and put aside his own problem. 'Come, Juliet. What has upset you so?'

She returned his smile, but it was forced and didn't reach her sherry-coloured eyes. 'Oh, Hugo. I have a request, but it is an awkward one at best.'

'Why?'

She sighed and wrung her fingers. 'I don't wish to inconvenience you and I would return to London, but then you would have no chaperon for Annabell. I don't want her reputation ruined. But I fear what I am about to ask will make her very uncomfortable here.'

Hugo quirked one brow. 'How so?'

Juliet's gaze skittered away from him, only to return with a resolute look. 'I wish to invite Lord Fenwick-Clyde to visit. Or rather, wish you to invite him.'

'What?' Hugo wondered if he had misheard. But, no, the look on his stepmother's face told him he had not. 'Isn't he Lady Fenwick-Clyde's stepson?'

Juliet nodded. She looked miserable, yet hopeful. Telling her 'no' would be like kicking a puppy, something Hugo would level another man for doing. Yet, if he told her it was acceptable, Annabell might leave. Devil take it, she might leave when he told her why he was going to London tomorrow. Not that any of that would keep him from doing what was right. Some things had to be done. Going to London to see Elizabeth and asking Fenwick-Clyde to visit for Juliet were two of them. Life was a series of risks, something he had learned very well during the Battle of Waterloo.

'This is your home, Juliet. If you wish me to invite the man, then I will.'

Relief flooded her expressive features, but she continued to wring her hands. 'I don't want to offend Annabell.'

'Neither do I, but this is your home. And, as you said before, if you leave then there is no chaperon. I imagine she can tolerate the chap for a couple of days.'

Juliet's pale face flamed. Hugo's eyes narrowed. 'It is for more than a few days.'

She nodded. 'I had hoped to invite him for several weeks.'

'I see.'

And he did. His stepmother was interested in Annabell's stepson. Could things get worse? He doubted it, but wouldn't bet on it.

'Now you understand,' she said, relief easing the wrinkle between her eyes. For the first time since she entered the room, her fingers stopped twisting.

Hugo found his fingers drumming on the top of his desk. He stopped them. 'When do you wish to invite him?'

'I would like the invitation to go tomorrow asking him for a week from that day. If you have time to do it that quickly?'

Her eyes held such a look of hope that Hugo was glad he had not refused her. Not that he would. This was her home as much or more than it was his.

'Is he in London?'

She nodded.

'I will deliver the message in person.'

She looked surprised. 'You are going to London?'

'Yes. I have some unfinished business.'

Her puzzled look intensified. 'I... That is, I don't mean to be intrusive, but I thought you and Annabell were doing very well together.' Her pale cheeks turned pink.

Hugo considered her. He and Annabell must not have kept their interest as circumspect as he had thought. Juliet would never pry like this if they had.

He considered his words carefully and kept his voice neutral. 'We enjoy each other's company, but we are not in one another's pocket.'

'Yes, yes, of course,' she murmured. 'I had rather thought it was more, but I must have been mistaken.'

Rather than lie to her, he said, 'Is there anything else you wish of me, Juliet?'

'No, nothing, and thank you, Hugo. I know this may be inconve-nient for you and Annabell.'

Hugo stood. 'That is not the issue, Juliet. But would you mind telling me where you met the man and how long you have known him?'

She stood as well, her head barely topping his shoulder. She was what the London beaus called a Pocket Venus. And she was a wealthy widow. Fenwick-Clyde had done well. Hugo stopped the cynical thought. Fenwick-Clyde was no fortune hunter by any stretch of the definition.

Juliet smiled and her face took on a contented glow. 'Last summer. After he returned from Waterloo. His wife had died in April and he had joined Wellington in an effort to forget. He is so sensitive.'

She looked besotted. Hugo swallowed a groan. 'You care for him, don't you?'

'Yes.'

Her hands fluttered, something he was not used to seeing in her. All the time he had known her he had never seen her lose her composure to this extent. He hoped things would work out.

'Does he return your regard?'

'Oh, yes,' she breathed, her voice full of wonder.

'Then I wish you the best of it.' He meant every word.

She gave him a beatific smile. 'Thank you, Hugo. You have always been so understanding and accommodating. I have been fortunate in my stepson.'

He smiled down at her. 'We are nearly of an age, Juliet. It is not my place to tell you what you can and cannot do.'

'Thank you anyway. You could have made this harder and you have not.'

'Only if I thought the connection would harm you, and then I would explain my concerns to you.'

'I know.'

She left the room, leaving Hugo to ponder the wisdom of what she had asked him to do. Her marriage to his father had been one of convenience. She had been barely seventeen and just out of the school room when she had married the late Sir Rafael Fitzsimmon. Their marriage had been happy, but far from ecstatic. Hugo was glad to see her finally find a man who made her glow. He just wished the man wasn't Annabell's stepson. Fortunately he had not heard any rumours that the son had his father's unsavoury proclivities. If he had, he would have refused to allow Juliet to extend the invitation. He hoped he was not making a mistake. Better to have the man under his roof for a period of time so he could watch him. He would also ask Annabell if she knew anything.

He sat back down and rang for Butterfield. This was one hell of a morning, and he still had the hardest part ahead of him. He had to tell Annabell about Elizabeth and his forthcoming trip.

Annabell groaned and forced her protesting muscles to lift her from the ground where she had been painstakingly clearing the dirt from what was definitely a mosaic floor in the Roman villa. She had left Hugo's bedchamber nearly lethargic from physical satiation, but had forced herself to dress and come to the site instead of going back to bed. She was determined not to let her liaison with Hugo interfere with her reason for being here. Her excavation had to come first.

She was a widow of independent means, and she fully intended to stay that way. Ten years of marriage to Fenwick-Clyde had taught her the downfalls of being legally attached to a man. The man owned his wife, and he could do *anything* to her that he chose.

She would not readily put herself in another man's power. Not even Hugo—should he ever ask. So far, neither one of them had mentioned wanting anything more than what they shared right now. She did not think he wanted commitment and marriage anymore than she did.

For a moment the sun seemed to dim, then everything was normal. Surely she was not upset because Hugo did not want more from their liaison. She had no reason to be so since she did not want more—or, at least, knew she should not want more.

'Annabell,' Susan Pennyworth's breathy, light voice intruded. 'What are you doing here by yourself?'

Annabell nearly groaned. She had not heard Susan arrive. She had been too focused on her thoughts of Hugo.

'I am excavating.'

Annabell kept her tone reasonable, even though she felt a spurt of irritation. It was barely nine in the morning. She had arranged for the men to arrive at ten to begin helping, and she wanted to get as much done as possible before they got here and she had to stop and direct them. Susan would remember that if she stopped to think about it. Ordinarily, she did not let Susan's inanity irritate her, but right now she wanted to be left alone.

Still, she kept her voice pleasant. She and Susan shared

a long history and, unless Mr Tatterly got his courage up, they would continue on together for a long time.

She tried again. 'I wanted to come here and get some work done before the men get here. Sometimes too many people make it hard to protect this precious mosaic. People tend to forget to watch where they step. After all…' she smiled as she warmed to her topic '…these are country folk. They are not used to valuing this type of discovery. They normally plough up a find like this and think nothing of it because to them the farm land is more valuable.'

Susan sniffed. 'Of course. Nothing like Mr Tatterly with his sensibilities. Why, just yesterday, he asked me how your work was going, and he was truly interested in what I had to tell him.'

Annabell smothered her laugh. Susan was several years older than she, but the other woman was as naïve as a school miss.

When she was sure she would not burst into laughter, Annabell said gently, 'I believe Mr Tatterly is interested in you, Susan.'

Susan flushed scarlet, her normally pale, nearly pasty complexion mottling. 'Oh, no, Annabell. You refine too much on his consideration. Mr Tatterly is university educated and very interested in anything having to do with science or history or the such.'

Annabell turned away to hide her smile, which she feared was closer to a smirk. 'As you wish, Susan.'

She was not going to argue with her companion. Susan would either see Mr Tatterly's interest or she wouldn't. Annabell knew from experience that there was nothing she could do to open her friend's eyes or change her friend's opinion.

'Do you have time to help, Susan?' she asked instead of continuing the previous conversation.

'Most certainly. I intend to stay here while you go back to the house. Sir Hugo has requested your presence.' Her voice lowered to a conspiratorial whisper. 'I believe he is going to tell us to leave. I heard the servants saying that Lady Fitzsimmon wants to invite other guests.'

Annabell stopped. More people would increase the risk of her and Hugo being discovered. Great as the damage would be if they were found out, she was not sure that even the increased danger to her reputation could keep her away from him now. He had penetrated her defences.

To cover her unease, she spoke more sharply than she had intended. 'Surely not, Susan. Rosemont is more than large enough for Lady Fitzsimmon to invite a dozen other people and still not require our rooms.'

She heard Susan sniff and realised too late that her tone had been curt. She had been reacting to her own fears about her relationship with Hugo and had hurt her friend. Susan talked too much and often did not make sense, but she was one of the most sensitive and easily hurt people Annabell had ever met. The slightest inflection of disdain or look of superiority and Susan was immediately cowed.

Annabell whirled around, instantly contrite. 'Susan…' She put her arms around the other. 'I did not mean to sound so short with you. I…I was thinking of something else that worried me and took that fear out on you. Please forgive me.'

Susan sniffed. 'No, no, Annabell, it is not your doing. I am too easily hurt. I must get a thicker skin, as you so often tell me. I know you did not mean anything by it. I can be irritating with my chattering. I know that.'

'No, you are who you are, Susan, and that is the way I like you.'

Susan smiled, her pale blue eyes lighting with affection. 'You are always so kind and ready to defend me.' She took a deep, steadying breath. 'But you must be on your way. Sir Hugo looked very upset. I shudder to think what must be wrong.'

Annabell nodded, her stomach clenching in worry. Hugo

never sent for her. It was an understanding they had reached. He knew how independent she was, and it did not look good to be seen together more than was necessary now they were lovers.

She sighed. This—relationship—was so complicated.

Annabell headed toward Rosemont, thankful for the modified pants she wore. They enabled her to move easily over the site without the worry of catching her skirts on a shard or upturned rock.

She reached the road and started walking, having decided against riding so that she could enjoy the crisp morning air without having it overwhelm her as it sometimes did when one travelled quickly on horseback. A brisk pace would put her at Rosemont in thirty minutes or so.

She heard a noise and saw a horse and rider coming toward her. She recognised Hugo's easy sway and comfort in the saddle. He must be very anxious to speak with her. She smiled and waved.

He stopped Molly several feet away and dismounted. The pale sunlight lit his chestnut hair, creating a sharp contrast with his grass-green eyes. He wore a casual jacket over a shirt that wasn't buttoned to the top. A handkerchief knotted around his strong neck gave him the aura of a sporting man. She knew he enjoyed sports, but realised with a start that she did not know which ones he participated in. It was unsettling to note that for all they had shared, she still knew so little about him.

She smiled as he closed the distance between them. 'Hello.'

'Thought I'd find you're here.'

Her smile widened. 'You know me too well.'

He strode to her. His thigh muscles rippled beneath the fine buckskin of his breeches. The hitch in his walk caused by his wound was only slightly more noticeable than usual. The poultice had healed the sprain better than she had thought possible. His Hessian boots sparkled from the champagne and blacking his valet used to polish them. He was, as always to her, magnificent.

'Admiring my manly attributes,' he said, his eyes sparking with an awareness she was very familiar with.

Her laugh was embarrassed because she had been so obvious in her perusal, but she retorted, 'Your boots are better polished than usual. Jamison must have had time on his hands.'

'That and the tavern wench.'

'Shame on you, Hugo.'

He shrugged. 'It is only the truth.'

'But I did not need to know that.'

'And why is that?'

'It is none of my business what your valet does.'

He stopped close enough that if she reached out she could touch him. Somehow, she resisted the urge to do so. But it was hard. She knew how his skin felt beneath her fingers; the sparks that flew between them when she touched him; the hunger that drove them to take risks they should not take.

'It can wait,' he murmured, closing the distance between them with one predatory movement.

She was in his arms and her fingers were undoing the knotted handkerchief before she quite realised what they were doing. Her hunger rose like a ravening beast as his mouth bent to hers. It was always thus, before his lips met hers and all conscious thought stopped.

He kissed her, the soft, moist sound of their joining exciting her. His hands slipped inside her pelisse and rubbed up and down her back, going lower with each stroke until they cupped her to him, nearly lifting her off her feet.

'It has been too long.' His voice was a hot breath against the side of her neck.

She arched into him. 'Only a couple of hours.'

'Too long.'

He rubbed his hips against hers to emphasise his meaning. She laughed softly and met his mouth once again with her own.

The kiss was long and wet and charged with need. She melted against him, his arms the only things holding her up. As though sensing her need for his support, he swung her into his arms and carried her to a patch of grass and dead leaves well away from the road. Bushes and trees screened them from any passers-by. He laid her gently down and followed her to the ground.

The scent of earth and growing things filled her nostrils. The sky behind his lowering head filled her eyes. She rose up to meet him.

With hands made deft from practice, he undid the buttons on her waistband and inched her loose-fitting pants down her hips until only her undergarments covered her. He unerringly found the place where her fine muslin opened. He skimmed a finger along her before slipping deep inside her.

He lifted his head, his eyes filled with wonder. 'You are ready.'

She nodded. 'For you.' Her fingers, not as skilled as his, fumbled with the buttons that held his breeches together. 'I fear I haven't your expertise,' she murmured against his lips.

'But you have something more important.'

Through the haze of desire that only he could create in her, she looked at him. 'More important than skill?'

He nipped at her mouth, tiny kisses that were as intoxicating as a deep penetration. 'Yes. You have a passion to match mine. That is a greater aphrodisiac than any skill.'

His fingers delved deeper, and she forgot what they were saying as her body reacted to his ministrations. Her hips matched his rhythm. Her heart beat erratically, and her breath came in sharp gulps.

His mouth suckled hers as his fingers brought her to climax. He swallowed the sharp cry of release she could not hold back.

She looked up at him and saw his eyes were now a deep green, his pupils nearly consuming the irises. 'Hugo...'

'Hush,' he said, pausing to put on his protection before slipping between her thighs. 'Now it is my turn.'

His breeches were open so that he spilled forth. She caught her breath, then caught him and guided him to her. He slid in and she gasped.

'Always,' she murmured. 'Always it is like this.'

His eyes barely focused, he smiled at her. 'Like nothing I have ever experienced before.'

Then he started moving and all else fled.

An eternity later, a second later, she lay beside him, both of them striving to get back their breath. She still tingled where minutes before he had caressed her, and she also felt a contentment she had never known before him.

He stroked the hair back from her face and gently helped her back into her harem pants. Only then did he pull her into the crook of his arm.

He kissed her on the forehead. 'Thank you, Bell, for the gift of yourself.'

She smiled at him. 'I receive more than I give, Hugo.'

He shook his head. 'Never.'

She put one finger against his lips. 'Let's not argue about who receives more.'

He laughed against her finger before catching it and kissing the tip. 'Let's not argue about anything.' He kissed her again, his lips lingering long enough for hunger to build once more in his eyes. 'Ever.'

Her stomach clenched with fresh desire. He had that power over her.

'Never,' she murmured, letting him keep her hand which he tucked against his chest.

They lay there while their hearts slowed. Drowsiness drifted over her, and Annabell knew she needed to get up or she would accomplish nothing this afternoon. She pulled her hand free and sat up, thinking to stand. He wrapped his arm around her waist.

'Bell, wait. I have something to tell you.'

He sounded so grave, nearly apprehensive, that she gave him a quizzical look. 'Susan said you wanted to see me.' She blushed. 'I thought we just finished doing what you wanted to see me about. Obviously I was mistaken.'

He continued to hold her hand. 'I couldn't help what we just did, Bell. I want you every waking moment.' He laughed wryly. 'And most of my sleeping moments as well.' His face sobered. 'But that is not why I sent Susan after you.'

She tried one last time to pull her hand free; when that failed, she tried to relax. But it was not easy. 'Talk to me while I work. I haven't all the time in the world to uncover this villa.'

He sat up beside her. 'Yes, you have. You have as long as you wish. I won't chase you off. I promise.'

Was his promise for time only, or did he mean something more? She stilled, the breath catching in her throat. She looked at him, searching for a meaning beyond the words. He gazed at her, but she could read nothing on his face.

Finally she spoke. 'I thought you wanted me gone from here as soon as possible.'

'How can you think that when I can't keep my hands off you every time I see you?' He shook his head. 'But it would be best for your reputation if you left. Still, selfish bastard that I am, I don't want you to go.'

He slid his palm up her ribs until his hand cupped one of her breasts. His thumb flicked the nipple that had hardened before he even touched it. She closed her eyes and sighed. It took so little for him to make her want him. So very little.

He pushed her gently back to the ground and she went willingly, so very, very willingly. Her body started to hum.

'Bell,' he said softly, tracing one of her black eyebrows, 'I need to go to London for a while.'

'London?'

He nodded.

She looked up at him, feeling the bed of leaves they lay on. The rich, earthy smell of decay filled her nostrils. Overhead the sun peeked from behind scudding clouds. It was a glorious day.

Yet, suddenly, a cloud seemed to move across the perfection of her world. She chided herself. He was likely going because of business. A small voice told her he was a man who had many mistresses. She was being unreasonable. They had made no promises.

She was not sure she could bear not to be with him at night. She told herself that loneliness was the source of the dread building in her. She had reached the point where she couldn't wait for night to fall and the house to quiet so she could sneak to Hugo's bed. And now he was leaving. But she could not stop him from doing as he wished, no matter how it might hurt for him to resume his old habits.

'For how long?' she finally asked, wondering if he was going back to gamble and womanise, and knowing it did her no good to think about it.

He rubbed her cheek with his thumb, sending a wealth of sensation coursing through her system. She wanted him to never stop touching her. But she knew he would. It was inevitable. Even now, he was preparing to leave her.

'A couple of days. No longer.'

Relief filled her, easing some of the pain and uncertainly of only seconds before. Surely he was not going to see someone else if he was only going to be gone so short a time? She knew if he came to visit her after a long absence, she would not let him leave in just a couple days. She would beg him to stay forever.

She would do what?

She stopped herself short. She was thinking like a woman

in love, not a woman who valued her freedom. She stiffened in his arms and drew slightly away.

'Don't pull away, Bell.'

His voice was deep and husky. His arm tightened around her, holding her so close she could feel the thud of his heart. She made herself relax. They had not promised fidelity to one another, or even love. He could do as he pleased. Still…

'Will you tell me why you are going?'

The words were out before she realised she was going to ask them. From the very beginning she had told herself this was a liaison only for her time here. When she was finished here, so were they. Now she was acting as though their affair meant more than that. She was crazy.

'Forget I asked that. It is not my place.'

'I came here to tell you, Bell.'

She turned on her side so she could see his reactions. 'You don't owe me anything, Hugo.'

'I know.' He met her gaze without wavering. 'But I want you to know. I want you to hear it from me and not some gossip-monger.'

Her stomach clenched in dread. 'You make it sound as though someone would enjoy telling me.'

'Some might…if they found out about us.'

In a voice smaller and tighter than she wanted, she said flatly, 'You are going to see another woman.'

He nodded. 'Elizabeth Mainwaring.'

Annabell went still in the circle of his arms where only minutes before she had felt safe from all harm. She had not counted on him being the one to hurt her. Not yet.

She had heard of Lady Elizabeth Mainwaring, the widow of Viscount Mainwaring. The woman was a fixture in the *ton,* although some wags said she was a fixture in the bed-rooms of the wealthy gentlemen of the *ton.*

She looked away from him. She did not think she could

bear to see what he thought when she asked, 'Is she your mistress?'

The words were hard to say, but she had to know. Lady Mainwaring was only linked to men whose beds she shared.

'Was.' He held Annabell tighter. 'Not since I returned here. Never again now that I've met you.'

She wanted to believe him, but… 'You cannot be sure until you see her again.'

'Annabell,' he ordered, 'look at me.'

The last thing she wanted to do now was look at him. He had the power to break her heart, something no one else had ever had. Power she had not realised he had until this very instant. It was a frightening realisation. Her hands turned cold.

He caught her chin in his fingers and forced her to look up. 'I meant every word I've ever said to you.'

She tried to look away, but he wouldn't let her. She settled for saying nothing. She was afraid of what she might say. She was still emotionally reeling from two blows: his departure and her realisation that he had the power to hurt her.

His fingers tightened and his voice lowered ominously. 'Don't you believe me?'

The anger in his eyes seared her. She had to say something, but she did not want to beg him not to go. Nor did she want to lose what little pride she still had where he was concerned.

She had to speak carefully. 'I don't know what to believe, Hugo.' And she didn't. 'I…' She licked her lips. 'My marriage taught me not to trust men. Except my brothers,' she added, unable to malign them even in such a small way.

His eyes narrowed into green flames. His voice filled with disgust. 'I am not Fenwick-Clyde. Nor have I ever been.'

She made herself look at him. His jaw was clenched. She could feel the tenseness in his arm that still held her close.

'I know. I just…' She took a deep breath. 'It's hard to get beyond the past.'

'You let me touch you.'

'Yes. I don't know why, but from the beginning I not only let you touch me, I longed for you to do so. But to trust…' She sighed. 'That is the hard part.'

She didn't add that his reputation made it even harder to believe he would not rekindle his affair. The last thing they needed now was recriminations over their pasts.

'I am not going to see Elizabeth to restart our affair, Bell. I am going to end it. You have to believe me.' His voice held such sincerity.

'I want to, Hugo. Truly I do.'

'Then do, Bell. Put your past behind you. Fenwick-Clyde had no honour. Not where women were concerned or men. He cheated at cards just as he cheated at everything else.'

She had heard rumours of her late husband's activities, but no one had ever told them to her face. She did not doubt Hugo's word. Then why did she doubt him about his own behaviour?

She looked into his eyes and saw sincerity and frustration. If they were going to continue their relationship, she would have to take the risk of trusting, and part of trusting was believing him.

She took a deep breath. 'Make love to me, Hugo. Now and tonight and tomorrow. Don't let me go until you leave.'

Tenderness softened the harsh angles of his jaw and muted the sharp glint in his eyes. He smiled down at her as his arm pillowed her against his chest, against the steady beat of his heart.

'Ah, never, Bell.'

Chapter Eleven

Hugo waited to be announced by Elizabeth Mainwaring's butler, periodically slapping his ebony cane against the side of his Hessians. As recently as two months ago, he would have entered her salon without thought. Now he did not. He intended his relationship with her to change.

'Sir Hugo Fitzsimmon,' her butler said in sonorous tones.

'Hugo,' Elizabeth purred, rising and coming to him, hands stretched out. 'You know better than to be so formal. It has been many months since last you were announced.' She slanted a seductive look at him. 'Before we became more than friends.'

Hugo made himself smile at her. It was not her fault he no longer wished to see her. She was everything a man could want in a woman. From the immaculately coiffed gold curls crowning her elegant head to the tips of her feet with their painted nails, she was perfect. Large periwinkle-blue eyes, tilted at the corners, thick lashes that were the pale brown of her true colour, to the full red lips that could drive a man crazy, she was Venus rising from the crumpled sheets of a well-used bed. Even in this cool room in the middle of the afternoon.

She did not have to stand on tiptoe to press her mouth to his. 'I knew you would come immediately.'

Her voice, husky as only a satiated woman's could be, caressed each word she murmured. It was a trick she had that titillated even though she was fully clothed and had not been pleasured recently. She used it well.

Just months ago, he would have been achingly hard and ready to take her here on the carpet. Now he felt nothing. The mind was a powerful thing, he mused.

He stepped away and released her fingers. 'What do you want, Elizabeth?'

She frowned at him. 'I wanted to see you, Hugo. It has been over two long months since you left me in Paris. I have missed you.'

'Have you?'

He moved to a chair and sat. He crossed one ankle over his other knee and looked at her. She was ravishing, and dressed to be ravished. It was the middle of the day, but she wore muslin as thin as netting. The rich red of her nipples showed large and engorged through the material of her bodice. The skirt clung to her full hips and dipped into the area between her legs. She was temptation personified.

After Annabell's artlessness, Elizabeth's calculated display left him not only cold, but mildly repulsed.

Hugo took a deep breath, glad to know he could be faithful to one woman. He had never been so before, and in spite of his assurances to Annabell there had been that tiny seed of doubt. He was, after all, a connoisseur of women and had always indulged himself regardless of the circumstances. Until now.

'Why do you really want to see me, Elizabeth?'

His voice was colder than he had intended, but there was no reason to let her think he felt something he did not. Honesty had always stood him in good stead. He didn't think it would fail him now.

She shrugged and moved to stand in front of him so the weak sunlight coming in the window limned her long legs.

'I want you to make love to me, Hugo. What else have I ever wanted from you?'

Tuberoses engulfed him.

'Money? Jewellery?'

'Sarcasm isn't one of them,' she said tartly, stepping back, her full mouth a pout. 'What has happened, Hugo? You were never like this before.'

He eyed her dispassionately. 'I had never before decided to end our involvement.'

She gasped, her eyes narrowing. 'You are seeing someone else.'

It was a flat statement that brooked no argument. It was spoken as though she knew without a doubt. It was his turn to narrow his eyes.

'And if I am?'

'She will not satisfy you for long.' She ran one long-fingered hand over her ample hip. 'You are insatiable. Most women are incapable of your stamina.'

He ignored her comment. The last thing he intended to do was drag Annabell's name into this. 'I am prepared to be more than generous with you, Elizabeth.' His voice dropped. 'More so than St. Cyrus will be.'

She blanched. 'Whatever do you mean? The Earl and I are acquaintances. I am known to most members of the *ton*.'

He let her comment go. There was no sense in being hurtful or disparaging or reiterating a fact she was prepared to deny. However, her willingness or need to lie to him did her no favour in his opinion. He should have ended this connection long ago. He had been lazy and not wanted to do without his comforts, and Elizabeth was very creative. Now he was paying the piper for that attitude.

'I have been to my solicitor and have drawn up papers leaving you sufficient funds to maintain your lifestyle without the need to present your favours where you do not wish.'

Without warning, she leaned forward and slapped him. Hard.

'How dare you, Hugo. I am not a whore, no matter what you seem to think.'

'No,' he said dispassionately, 'you are a well-born courtesan. If we lived during Charles II's time, you would be having one of his royal bastards. It is not an insult, Elizabeth, it is a statement of fact. A compliment, if you will.'

She stepped away, scowling. 'I do not need your money, Hugo. Mainwaring left me well provided for.'

'I know, but more never hurts. It will buy you the trinkets you enjoy.'

She turned and stalked to the fireplace. Turned and stalked back to him. 'I don't need your settlement, Hugo. I need you.'

Her voice was suddenly all business. His nerves started twitching, a signal he had learned to trust. The reaction had saved his life at Waterloo when he had felt an itching between his shoulder blades, and turned in time to see a French soldier he had taken for dead aiming a pistol at his back.

Carefully, he asked, 'What do you need me for, Elizabeth?'

She licked her lips until they glistened like ripe cherries. Normally he would have said she did so to be provocative, but there was no responding gleam in her eyes. A glance told him her nipples had lost their hardness. Sex was not on her mind.

'I am with child, Hugo.' Her voice dropped until he could barely hear it. 'Yours.'

He stared at her. If he had been standing, he would have sat down. 'You are carrying my child?'

'Yes.'

He frowned. 'I find that hard to believe, Elizabeth. I always used protection.'

She flipped her slim hand as though to toss away his

statement. 'A sheep's gut, Hugo? Don't be ridiculous. Those things are not to prevent conception, and if you thought they did, you deluded yourself.'

'You speak from much experience?' he said, acidly, unable to let her words go unchallenged.

The last thing he wanted was to be the father of her child—if she was with child. That was one part of his father's life that he had no desire to emulate. He did not believe he had any children by any of the women he had enjoyed.

He knew himself well enough to know that if such a thing happened, he would keep the child rather than giving it to some farm family to raise. He also knew his decision might be a mixed blessing for the child, as his father's had occasionally been for him.

Elizabeth's left foot began to tap, a habit he knew arose when she was agitated. He put aside his memories.

'You were not my first lover, Hugo. I was married.'

'And Mainwaring used sheaths?' He allowed the sarcasm he felt to drip from every word.

She flushed so quickly, he was not sure he had seen it. 'No.' She turned away and turned back as quickly, clearly anxious. 'No, but I was no innocent when you met me. I know those things do not work. They were never meant for the purpose you put them to.'

'True. But to the best of my knowledge, Elizabeth, I do not have any bastards, and I have never hesitated to do as I pleased.'

She glared at him. 'Perhaps one of your former lovers did not tell you?'

His stomach twisted at the thought before he thrust the possibility away. 'I cannot imagine a woman keeping that to herself. As you know, I make it plain from the beginning that I will provide for any child.'

'So you say.' Her full red lips curved down. 'But even

a woman's husband has been known to refuse to acknowledge a child borne by his wife.'

He had heard rumours that she had borne a babe during her marriage, and she had no children now. He had never asked her about it, respecting her privacy as he had expected her to respect his.

'That is rare, Elizabeth, and you know that.'

Now she did flush and the colour stayed on her high cheekbones. 'Yes. You are very eloquent, but I am adamant.' She raised her hand to keep him from responding. 'No more, Hugo. Suffice it that I know those flimsy things do not work. I carry your child.'

It sounded as though rumour was truth. He did not push her. Her past was not his concern. If she had truly carried a child during her marriage to Mainwaring and given the babe to some country family to raise as their own, then so be it. It was not unheard of in their circles. And it was still none of his business except in the way it affected her now.

Nor would fighting her change anything. He knew her well enough to recognise that she was determined to lead him to the altar, no matter what her true motive was. And he knew himself well enough to know he would not refuse when an innocent child was involved.

'I will not continue to argue with you, Elizabeth.'

'I do not want to bear a child without a father, Hugo.' Her posture turned defensive. 'You of all people should know how difficult that is. Even though your father claimed you and provided for you, you must have suffered some ridicule. In school if nowhere else.'

He had. And it had been difficult. Young boys could be cruel. He had thought himself beyond the hurt of the teasing he had received at school, matured. He was surprised to find the wounds could be so easily dredged up. He had been too sensitive.

Although he had been dearly loved, he had been a bastard. He knew several of his contemporaries were not their fathers' children, that their mothers had conceived with a lover, but the children had been born in marriage and everyone accepted them as the legal children with no shame attached. He would prefer any child of his be born in wedlock.

'Yes, Elizabeth, I do.' He did not try to hide the weariness weighing him down along with the knowledge of what he must do.

'What about St. Cyrus?' he pursued. It was one thing to let her deny the connection when there were no consequences, it was quite another to let her foist another man's babe on him.

She stiffened. 'I told you before, Hugo, you are the father.'

She sounded so certain that his heart lurched. He had been so careful, but he knew, as she had pointed out, that his method of protection was not foolproof. Most men of his station used them to protect themselves from disease when they bedded prostitutes. They did not care if the things kept them from impregnating the women. The suppliers did not care either.

'How can you be sure? We have not been together for nearly three months. Surely you would have contacted me sooner if I had caused your condition.'

Her anger of seconds before melted away. Now she was all softness and vulnerability. He mused cynically that she should have been an actress.

She knelt before him and rested her head on his knees. 'I wanted to be sure. I might…I might have lost the child.'

He did not touch her. Nor did he push her away. 'But you did not.'

'No, I did not.' She lifted her head to look at him.

He returned her look, wondering what he was going to do. His heart rebelled at what she wanted. His honour said he must do the right thing.

'Are you sure?' he asked, knowing she would tell him

once again that he was the father. But he wanted to hear her say it again and again, until, maybe, she might say he wasn't.

'Yes.'

He searched her eyes for a lie, wanting to see them shift away from his scrutiny. He wanted to see the corner of her mouth twitch from nervousness, from the fear of being caught in a lie. Neither happened.

He pushed her gently away and stood. 'I will send the announcement of our engagement to *The Times*.'

She stayed kneeling, but such a look of triumph lit her face that for an instant Hugo knew she had lied. He was not the father, he was simply her dupe. Then the look was gone and all he could discern was relief, as though she had thought he would refuse. He would have if he could have proved St. Cyrus was the one, but he could not. He would never know for sure unless the child was born several months early or late, proving it was conceived when they were not together. By then it would be too late for him, they would be married.

'I will call on you tomorrow afternoon.'

She finally stood. 'As you wish.'

He forced his shoulders to relax only to have his hands clench. He had to clarify things from the beginning. 'This is only a marriage of convenience, Elizabeth.'

'Surely you jest, Hugo.' She took a step toward him. 'Why should we deny ourselves the pleasure of each other's body?'

And why? he asked himself. She would be his wife and, after this fiasco, he would be lucky if Annabell even spoke to him, let alone let him touch her. Still, Elizabeth had won, but he was no longer interested in her as a woman. He would not do still another thing he did not wish to do.

'Because I am marrying you for the child's sake. Nothing more.' He eyed her coolly. 'And you may continue to see St. Cyrus after the child's birth.'

She reared back, her sensuous body poised like that of a hissing cat's. 'You are not making this any easier.'

'I did not intend to.'

He turned and got to the door before she spoke.

'Hugo, what is her name?'

He stopped an instant, no longer, and then was gone.

The next day he entered a jewellers, his hat tilted rakishly, ebony cane clicking on the flooring. Just below the surface veneer, anger simmered in him. The last place he wanted to be was here, choosing an engagement ring for Elizabeth. The only consolation was that he would not give her the Garibaldi sapphire. While it was not the traditional engagement ring given to the Fitzsimmon bride—Joseph would give the Fitzsimmon engagement ring to his bride— it was a ring left to Hugo by his Italian grandmother. It had been in her family for ten generations and went to a true love. He would not give that to Elizabeth.

A clerk appeared immediately. 'May I help you, sir?'

Hugo looked at the man, resisting the urge to snap. The situation wasn't this man's fault. 'I need an engagement ring.'

'Is there a particular type?'

Hugo paused. He had not considered what to get, only that he had to find something to replace his grandmother's ring.

He obviously looked undecided for the clerk said, 'Might I suggest this tray over here? They are already made so you can see immediately what they look like.'

Hugo followed the man and studied the rings displayed on a black velvet background. 'I want something more elegant than these. Nothing ostentatious.'

'I understand, sir. If you will give me a moment, I will go to the safe.'

Hugo cooled his heels reluctantly. The sooner this was

over, the sooner he could give it to Elizabeth and be on his way back to Rosemont and Annabell.

Annabell. What was he going to tell her?

'Ahem…' The clerk cleared his throat. 'I believe I have just the thing, sir.'

Hugo wished he had just the thing to turn this fiasco into a silk purse, but there was no way that he could see. Frustration made him brusque.

'I hope so.'

The man paled, but stood his ground, a tray in one hand. Hugo looked down and his eyes widened.

'It is a cabochon aquamarine, sir, circled by diamonds of the first quality.' He smiled proudly. 'We also have a necklace and drop earrings to match. They would make a stunning bridal gift, if I say so myself. The lucky woman could wear the engagement ring daily and the other pieces as she wanted.'

'They are very striking.' They would look perfect on Annabell with her silver-blonde hair and navy blue eyes. 'I will take them.'

The man bowed. 'I will have them wrapped.'

'And,' Hugo said just as the man stepped away, 'I still need an engagement ring.'

The man stopped, seemed to rearrange his thoughts and turned back. 'Let me see what else we have, sir.'

He left and Hugo wondered what he had done. Annabell did not wear jewellery. He doubted it was for lack of the baubles, since she was wealthy. Possibly she did not care for it. Still, he wanted to give her something, and most women enjoyed getting the things.

The clerk returned. This time, the tray held a large opal and diamond ring. It was lovely, but not striking. It would do.

'We only have the ring in this style, sir.' The clerk's tone was apologetic.

'I will take it.'

'Yes, sir.' The clerk bowed once more. 'I will have it packaged with the other set.'

'No, I want them separate.'

The man's eyes widened a fraction, but otherwise his face remained noncommittal. 'As you wish, sir.'

Not long after, Hugo left, as satisfied with his purchases as was possible. He didn't much care how Elizabeth felt about the ring, but he cared a great deal about what Annabell would think of her gift. Surely, a parure of jewellery like the aquamarines and diamonds would bring her enjoyment.

Trinkets had always been enough before, but no matter what he told himself, somehow he did not think they would suffice now. Before, his liaisons had been for pleasure and passion only. What he shared with Annabell was more, much more.

His stomach knotted. Dread such as he had never experienced before tensed his shoulders. He had not wanted to come to London, had not wanted to leave Annabell. More than anything he wanted to return to her, her warmth, her stubbornness and her passion. But things were different now.

She might leave him. And for the first time in his life, he understood what it was to know another person held the power to hurt him. It was not a pleasant sensation.

He signalled his coach. The sooner he gave Elizabeth the ring, the sooner his business here was done and he could return to Annabell. He had to convince her that they could stay together even if he did marry Elizabeth. An arrangement like that was not unheard of, just rare. It was the best he could offer now, but he had an awful feeling it wasn't going to be enough. She might have done it had he been single. But he had to try.

He should let Annabell go, but he was too selfish. It would hurt too much.

* * *

Annabell strode across the grass toward Rosemont, stopping to look at the daffodils beginning to turn brown. Soon the roses would begin their procession of colour and scent. Hugo's lawn would be full of blooming flowers. It would be lovely.

She entered the hall and handed her coat to the butler who appeared as though by magic. 'Thank you.'

He bowed, his demeanour everything that was precise. His gaze did not even stray to her unconventional attire.

She glanced down at her harem pants and boots. The hems of the pants were damp, but they weren't muddy. Neither were her wellingtons. She would get a book from the library to keep her company before going upstairs to change.

Hugo's absence had been harder on her than she had expected. The two nights had seemed unending; her bed cold, her body colder. And she did not know when he would return. How long did it take to give an old mistress her *congé?* She should have asked her brothers who certainly had plenty of experience in that area.

She pushed open the library door and entered, glanced at Hugo's favourite chair and froze. Someone was in it. She moved closer.

'Hugo?' She did not try to disguise her joy. 'Hugo, when did you return?'

He rose and turned to face her. A glass of brandy listed in his hand. His hair was disordered. His eyes were bright. His shirt was open at the collar. He was foxed.

She closed the distance between them and took the glass from his hand. 'What are you doing?'

'Drinking myself to the point of courage.' His words were only slightly slurred. 'That should be obvious.'

She would not have noticed if she had not known him so well. He held his liquor as well as Guy and Dominic and there were times when even she could not tell if her brothers were inebriated.

'Why do you need courage?'

Even as she said the words, her stomach tightened. He had no need of courage with her, unless he had something to say that would be unpleasant. Something like… She refused to finish that line of thought. Hugo would never do that after telling her he was going to break off his liaison with his former mistress.

He reached for the glass she still held, so she put it behind her back. Something was wrong. Badly.

He shrugged and sank back into the chair where he sprawled with one ankle over the opposite knee. 'Keep the drink. You might want to imbibe it, *bella mia.*'

He had never used that term of endearment. She frowned and set the glass down out of his reach. 'Why is that?'

He stared at the roaring fire as though trying to find answers to some world-shattering question. He looked utterly sad, as though he'd lost something he prized above all others.

She watched him without saying anything. Apprehension began to crawl up her spine. He had only been gone three days, but his behaviour made it seem as though the world had changed in that time. She sat gingerly in the chair beside him, wondering if she should run instead of stay. There was something about his whole demeanour that spoke of disaster.

Still he said nothing. She waited him out. One thing she had learned with her brothers and later her husband was that waiting was the best option when dealing with a man who had drunk too much. They would tell you what they wanted to tell you when they wanted to tell you. Most of the time, she hadn't wanted to hear their reason for drinking. Her heart told she didn't want to hear Hugo's either.

'Give me back the drink, Bell,' he said without looking at her.

'Not until you tell me what is wrong. Nothing should be

so bad that you could return home without coming for me and instead drink yourself nearly into a stupor.'

'You think so?' There was a flat tone in his voice that she sensed hinted at emotions too powerful to release.

'Yes, Hugo, I do. I thought we had reached an agreement with one another.' She paused, trying to think of how to say what she thought their relationship was. It was difficult. 'Not a legal commitment, but...but an emotional one.' When he continued to remain silent, she added awkwardly, 'For now at least.'

He angled his head to look at her. His gaze roved over her, making her hot, then cold, then hot again. He made her think of a condemned man looking at his last meal. Her imagination was running wild. She chided herself.

'What is wrong?'

He sighed and looked back at the fire. 'Would you be my mistress?' His voice was deep and raspy, nearly painful sounding.

Her chest contracted painfully. The word mistress was so demeaning. It made her remember how her brothers took mistresses, women they used, paid well and discarded. Although Guy no longer did so since marrying Felicia. But still, the word left a sour taste in Annabell's mouth.

Until he asked the question, she had not really thought about the reality of their relationship. She had already made love with him, numerous times. They weren't married and neither one of them had spoken of marriage. That made her his mistress already. She had thought it didn't matter to her. Now she wondered if she had been fooling herself.

'I thought I already was,' she finally said.

His laugh was harsh and bitter, seeming to rip from his chest. 'I suppose that literally you are right. But it never occurred to me to think of you that way.'

'Then why now?'

Her voice was low and careful, under control, or as much control as she was capable of. A sense of impending doom, unbearable hurt hovered on the edge of her consciousness. Something terrible had happened and it was going to change everything between them. She knew it.

He rose and came to stand in front of her. His beautifully formed mouth was a thin slash in a face white from strain. Before she realised his intent, he reached down, grabbed her upper arms and pulled her to her feet. His force was such that she stumbled against his chest where he held her.

His breath smelled slightly of rich, sweet brandy. His body smelled of cinnamon and musk. She had missed him so much. Even now, knowing he was somewhat inebriated and that he was about to tell her something that would hurt immeasurably, she wanted him. She wanted all of him: his mind, his body, his heart.

She was a fool.

'Ah, Bell,' he said, his voice an agonised groan, 'make love to me.'

She blinked, wondering where this was leading, then no longer caring when his lips touched hers. She sank into his embrace as they sank to the carpet. Nothing mattered but his mouth on hers, his hands undoing her garments, his body pressing her to the floor.

He cursed her harem pants and nearly ripped them as he pulled them down her legs. She was barely out of her garment when he opened his breeches. He sucked her tongue into his mouth and plunged his body into hers. It was a quick, sharp thrust that she rose to meet with all the passion in her soul.

'Bell, Bell,' he said over and over again.

His lips kissed hers, his tongue danced with hers. He shuddered. He swallowed her moans of pleasure and returned them to her with his own release.

She clutched him to her, her nails digging into his flesh, her back arching. Her body spasmed.

They collapsed with him still sheathed in her, her muscles still gripping him, her legs still cradling his hips. He looked down at her, his eyes deep green pools of pain.

'I have missed you so much. You will never know.'

She lifted her head to kiss him softly on the lips. 'I know, Hugo, for I feel the same.'

They stayed in each other's arms until their bodies cooled. Hugo finally rolled to the side and buttoned his breeches. She pulled her harem pants back on and secured them.

'Will you tell me now?' she asked quietly.

He gave her an inscrutable look. It was as though their passion had burned to ashes whatever had held him in its grips. Her chest clenched.

He stood and gave her a hand. She took it and he pulled her up. One arm cradled her to his heart while the other smoothed the tendrils of hair that had come loose from her braid during their lovemaking.

'You mean more to me than anything.'

She looked at him. He had not said he loved her. It was as though he could not say the word, but then neither could she. She understood his reticence. To love someone was to give yourself into that person's power. Neither of them wanted that. Or so she told herself.

He took a deep breath and let her go. She stumbled when his arm left her and he stepped away so he no longer supported her. She grabbed the back of the nearest chair, the one Hugo had been sitting in when she found him.

He shifted to the fireplace. Whatever he had to say, bothered him greatly.

He looked at her, looked away. 'I...I did not end it with Elizabeth, Bell.'

Her stomach lurched. 'You are going back to her.' Her words were flat from pain and disillusionment.

'I have to.' He reached for his nearly full glass of brandy that still sat on the nearby table and downed it in one gulp. 'She is carrying my child.'

Annabell reeled under the words. 'Surely not. You always use protection.'

His mouth twisted bitterly. 'She says so and I have no way of proving her wrong.' He closed his eyes as though in pain. 'Oh, Lord. I did not use protection just now.' He opened his eyes and looked at her, his countenance twisted as though he were being tortured. 'I am so sorry, Annabell. I did not mean to lose control like that. I have never done so before.'

He took a step toward her, his arm out to gather her to him. She moved backwards, her hand out to stop him. The bitterness of betrayal created a sour pit in her stomach. She felt as though she was in a nightmare, but knew she was awake.

The words spilled from her lips. Words meant to hurt him as he had hurt her. 'And if I get pregnant, Hugo, will you marry me as well?'

Chapter Twelve

Annabell curled into the sanctuary of the chintz-covered chair in her bedchamber. She had walked out on Hugo before he could answer her question. She had not wanted to know what he would say, knowing it would be too painful to bear. She felt as though someone had taken away her world. Tears tracked down her cheeks and she ignored them. Her chest was tight with pain.

Annabell gulped back an hysterical giggle. He was going to marry his former mistress. How ironic. How funny. How painful.

And she might be pregnant from their lovemaking in the library earlier. Her life could not be worse.

She dissolved into fresh tears.

A long time later, she stared into the dying fire. Surely she would not become pregnant from one time. Fenwick-Clyde had never done anything to protect her during their years of marriage and she had never conceived. She doubted she would now. It was some comfort.

But no matter what happened to her because of their lovemaking, she could not stay here. It would be too painful to see him daily and know he was going to marry someone else.

Not that she wanted to marry him, she told herself. She had made a vow after Fenwick-Clyde's death that she would never put herself in a man's control again. That meant never marrying. Yet…

He had asked her to stay, to be his mistress. His marriage was not a love match. Elizabeth Mainwaring carried his child. That was all. That was enough.

Annabell had thought her pain was too intense to worsen. She was mistaken. Her heart thudded, skipped a beat and her stomach twisted.

She could not ever remember feeling this devastated, not even on her wedding night. Fenwick-Clyde had demeaned her in ways she would not have imagined possible until they were done to her. But he had not broken her heart.

At the time she had decided she was in hell and death would be preferable. Now she knew better. Hell was losing the only man she had ever loved. No matter what Hugo said, she could not be his mistress. She could not do to another woman what had so often been done to her.

She would have to relocate to the inn that weeks ago had been full with sportsmen come to see the prizefights. Hopefully there would be room for her and Susan now. If she stayed here, she feared her resolve would weaken.

She struggled to her feet, feeling as though her body had aged fifty years in the past several hours. She would start packing. She usually packed her own things. The places she went often did not have servants. The activity would give her something to do. She didn't think she could sleep and she couldn't stand to keep thinking about what had happened.

Every piece of clothing had a memory of Hugo attached. Her brown harem pants. She folded them carefully and put them on the bottom of her portmanteau. She had worn them the first time she met Hugo. He had come upon her at the villa, and she had not known who he was. He had kissed her. She should have known from her reaction that he would mean more to her than she could ever have imagined. But she had not.

Her mauve silk evening gown. She had worn it the night she first went to Hugo. He had made love to her the entire night, erasing from her mind the horror of Fenwick-Clyde's groping hands and slobbering mouth. Hugo had shown her how wonderful the joining of a man and woman could be. She trembled with the force of the memory, her fingers stilled, the fine muslin crushed in her grasp.

Her head dropped and she shut her eyes, wondering why it was so difficult to shut out the memory of that night. But she could not forget his touch any more than she could forget to breathe.

Finally, exhausted from crying and from memories she could no longer endure, she collapsed on to the bed. Someday she would be over this. She had survived Fenwick-Clyde. She would survive Hugo Fitzsimmon.

Annabell woke the next morning to knocking. She felt groggy and disoriented, as though she had been the one consuming untold amounts of brandy. She didn't remember falling asleep. Finally, when the knocking became louder, she sat up abruptly then had to stay still until her dizziness abated. She fingerbrushed the hair from her face. She was still fully clothed, wrinkles and all. She grimaced.

She pushed off the bed and made for the door, her path only a tiny crooked. She was exhausted.

She did not open the door. 'Who is it?'

'Susan, Annabell. Let me in.'

Annabell groaned silently. Her companion's voice sounded more frazzled than usual, if that were possible. She must know about Hugo.

Annabell was tempted to tell Susan to go away, but knew it would only postpone the inevitable. 'Come in.'

She moved back to the bed and sat down. Her head ached and her mouth felt like it was stuffed with cotton. Briefly, she wondered how Hugo felt, but quickly pushed that traitorous thought away. She could no longer afford to care how Hugo felt.

'Annabell,' Susan gushed, slipping into the room and closing the door solidly, 'you'll never guess who just arrived. I nearly fainted. I could not believe my eyes. You know my sight is failing. I just know it is, but there he was. The last person I ever expected to see here. I mean, who would have thought he and Lady Fitzsimmon even knew each other, let alone well enough for Sir Hugo to invite him to stay.' She paused for a breath. 'Why, I never. You will never believe—'

Annabell put her hand to her throbbing forehead and closed her eyes. The absolute last thing she needed this morning was this chattering on about something that very likely didn't matter.

'Susan, please. I have a splitting headache. Just tell me and be done.'

A sigh gusted from the other woman's pinched mouth. 'Lord Fenwick-Clyde. He's here. Courting Lady Fitzsimmon, I swear, or I just fell off the turnip wagon, which I know isn't so. I'm all of thirty and five.'

Annabell groaned. 'Surely you're mistaken, Susan. Timothy doesn't know Lady Fitzsimmon. She is a widow of the utmost respectability. He is at least five years her junior, maybe more.' She shook her head, only to gasp at the pain caused by the motion. 'You must not have had your spectacles on.'

Susan sniffed. 'I most assuredly did have my spectacles on, Annabell. As for Timothy being too young, he is so starched and pompous one would think him a hundred. He is high in the instep and looks down his long nose at everyone. It was his father who was a lecherous old sot, not him.' She crossed herself. 'Forgive me for speaking ill of the dead, but truth is truth.'

This couldn't be happening. Annabell wondered if she

had died from the agony of losing Hugo and was now tor-
turing herself with even more difficulties. But she knew
better.

She stood, keeping one palm on the high bed for balance.
'When did Timothy get here?'

'Not more than thirty minutes ago. Lady Fitzsimmon is
with him. Sir Hugo isn't to be found.' She gave Annabell
a speculative look, her eyes bright like a bird's, but didn't
ask anything.

'Does Timothy know we're here?'

Susan shrugged. 'Not unless he saw me or you told him.'
She giggled. 'But I don't think he came here for us. He
was bowing over Lady Fitzsimmon's hand when I saw him.
The children were just going into the room, too.'

Annabell nearly smiled. She had never thought Timothy
was taken with children, but it seemed he could be persuaded. The situation was nearly comical, but her head still
ached and her entire body still felt as though she had abused
it.

'I had planned on our leaving today.'

'Oh, no. Never say so.' Susan's voice was high and tight.

Annabell nodded and instantly regretted it. 'I think it for
the best. Or had thought so until this. Surely Timothy is not
here to court Lady Fitzsimmon, but then why not?'

She needed more time to think things through. Her stepson was here. Before she knew it, Hugo's future wife would
be here. This was worse than any picture of Hades she
could ever have created.

'We were leaving?' Susan sounded as though she fought
back disappointment. 'I thought you and Sir Hugo had
come to an understanding.'

The woman looked frazzled. Her pale blonde hair, turning grey at the temples, was crimped around her narrow
face. Her big blue eyes were wide and startled, seeming
larger because of the spectacles she seldom wore. She
looked as though someone had taken away her most prized

possession. She reminded Annabell painfully of the way Hugo had looked last night.

Annabell sighed. 'Is there something you wish to tell me, Susan...a reason you don't wish to leave?'

Even though she asked the question, Annabell knew the answer. Mr Tatterly had been courting Susan since they first came here nearly three months before. Even Susan had finally realised what was happening and, it appeared, welcomed the attention. But Annabell wasn't going to tell her companion she already knew what was happening. It wasn't her place. Not yet.

Susan's pale skin turned beet red. Her gaze fluttered away and she put one hand to her throat. 'I...I am not sure, Annabell. That is, I think perhaps, but he has not said a word. I believe that just possibly.' She paused and blushed even more if that were possible. 'I don't mean to sound vain, you understand. Ordinarily I would never say, never think such a thing. But I believe—just possibly—that, ahem...'

Annabell took pity on her companion of many years and said gently, 'That Mr Tatterly is showing a marked interest in you?'

'Yes.' Susan pinched her lips together and collapsed on to the nearest chair, obviously overcome by the effort of being so concise. 'I think.'

Annabell went to her and took her cold hands into her own. 'My dear, he is besotted with you and makes no effort to hide his feelings.'

Susan looked up at her with eyes so full of longing that all Annabell could do was hope her friend would not be disillusioned and hurt. She knew how painful that was. She squeezed the other woman's fingers and let go.

'I wager that, given enough time to screw up his courage to the sticking point, to borrow one of my brother's less ladylike sayings, Mr Tatterly will announce his intentions.'

'Do you really think so?'

There was so much vulnerability in the question that Annabell's heart went out to her friend. 'Yes, my dear, I do.'

Even as she said the words, Annabell knew she could not move to the inn for she would have to take Susan with her. Mr Tatterly might call, and he might even still court Susan. But he was a timid man. He might just as easily think Susan did not care for his attentions if they moved. Mr Tatterly was nothing like his employer who would pursue the woman he loved to the ends of the earth. Would that Hugo had loved her. She chided herself for wanting, however briefly, something that was so impossible.

Annabell turned abruptly away, not wanting Susan to see the moisture threatening to spill from her eyes. Besides, how had she got from Susan's possible happiness back to her misery? Her self-centred selfishness.

Then there was Timothy. Surely he wasn't courting Hugo's stepmother. But maybe he was. She had never known him well. He had already been on his own when she married Fenwick-Clyde. Timothy had visited infrequently, and it had been obvious that there was no affection lost between him and her father.

Her voice was heavy. 'I think we will not move to the inn after all, Susan. Not today.' She took a deep, shuddering breath and made herself smile. Nothing would come of this self-pity and moping. 'Also, would you please have a servant bring up hot water so I can wash? I think it best if we let Timothy know we are here sooner rather than later.'

'Yes, yes, you are right, as usual.' Susan stood and scurried to the door, her former despondency gone as though it had never existed. She paused with her hand on the knob. 'Mr Tatterly has asked me to go into the village with him this afternoon. He has some errands to run for Sir Hugo and Lady Fitzsimmon. I did not think you would need me this morning. That is, I thought you would be at the villa, but that the village men would be there to help. If it is not convenient, then I will tell him no.'

Annabell blinked as she followed the rambling, contradictory words with an ease honed by experience. 'No, Susan. You go with Mr Tatterly. It will be much more fun than digging around in the dirt. And I haven't any new finds for you to draw.'

She gave Susan her best smile, knowing it didn't reach her eyes but also knowing Susan would not notice it. The other woman was caught in the throes of her first love.

Better to keep her pain to herself.

Dressed in a very proper white muslin morning dress with blue ribbon trim and a deep flounce around the hem, Annabell descended the stairs and headed for the salon. She even wore her widow's cap of white muslin trimmed with Brussels lace. Before last night, she would have gone to the library, hoping to see Hugo. Just the thought made her falter before she regained her composure. All she wanted to do now was avoid him, but she had to meet Timothy.

She slipped into the large, rectangular room and stopped to get her bearings. She had not been in here much. It was a cold room with two fireplaces that did little to ease the discomfort. The furniture was formal and grouped in precise little groupings. No, this had not the warm cosiness of the library, nor was Hugo here, she noted with a relief that seemed suspiciously like disappointment.

Juliet Fitzsimmon sat daintily on one of the bigger-than-life chintz-covered sofas with her hands folded demurely in her lap. As always, she was the height of fashion, from her Titian-red hair to the tips of her elegant little kid slippers.

Across from Juliet, in a stiff-backed wing chair, was Timothy Simon Fenwick-Clyde, the only son and heir of Annabell's deceased husband. She studied him dispassionately.

He was pale and slim, with hair the colour of weak sunlight cut into a Brutus. His eyes were a light grey, his lashes lighter than his hair and his brows a startling contrast of deep brown. His mouth was thin, but finely formed. His chin had a cleft. His hands were long and elegant. He was much like his father physically.

He was immaculately dressed in a navy morning coat and grey pantaloons. Had it been evening he would be in breeches. He had always followed fashion, unlike Hugo. She sighed and continued her study of her stepson. Timothy's boots were polished to a shine that reflected the nearby flames. He was never less than perfectly turned out. In this area he was totally at odds with Annabell's dead husband. Fenwick-Clyde had been more interested in his pursuits than his person.

'How do you do, Timothy?' Annabell strode towards the couple.

Timothy, Lord Fenwick-Clyde, started and jumped to his feet. 'Annabell.' His fair complexion reddened. 'I did not know you were acquainted with Lady Fitzsimmon.'

Annabell smiled and took the seat Juliet waved her to. 'I was not until recently. I am here to excavate a Roman villa.'

'Ah, I should have known.' The present Lord Fenwick-Clyde barely concealed his disapproval as he sat back down. 'You took up that hobby after my father died.'

Annabell nodded. 'It harms no one, gives me great pleasure and preserves our history for posterity. What more could one want in a hobby?' She was careful to keep her hackles over his attitude from showing in her voice.

As though sensing unease, Juliet waved one delicate white hand to indicate the tea table. 'Would you care for something, Annabell?'

Annabell, not wishing to fight with her stepson or cause her hostess discomfort, accepted. 'That would be wonderful, Juliet. I must confess that I have not broken my fast yet.'

'Then you most definitely shall have something to eat,' Juliet said in her light, clear soprano as she rang for a servant. 'Hugo would be appalled to know a guest of his was going hungry.'

The last was said teasingly, but Annabell didn't have the fortitude to smile. Just the mention of her former lover was enough to make her appetite flee.

'So,' Fenwick-Clyde said, 'Sir Hugo is in residence.' He cast a quick look at Annabell. 'I had thought he was still on the Continent, particularly since my stepmother is here.'

Juliet sat a little straighter. 'Annabell is my guest, Lord Fenwick-Clyde, and I imagine that I am ample chaperon for anyone and particularly for a widow.'

This time Annabell did smile. She had not thought Juliet Fitzsimmon had the wherewithal to speak her mind so forcefully. She was glad she had been wrong.

'My pardons,' Fenwick-Clyde said hastily. 'I did not mean to imply anything out of the ordinary.'

Annabell gazed at him. Susan had been right when she had described him as high in the instep. There were times he was insufferable. This had boded ill to be one of those times. Fortunately, Juliet had nipped him in the bud. She stole a glance at her hostess. Juliet might be good for Timothy. The real question would be whether or not he was good for Juliet.

To turn the focus from proprieties, Annabell asked, 'What brings you to Kent, Timothy? I don't recall any property in this area.'

Her stepson flushed deep scarlet before seeming to regain his composure, yet during it all he kept his attention on Juliet. 'I came to pay my respects to Lady Fitzsimmon. We met during the Season and have maintained a correspondence since then.'

Faint pink tinged Juliet's cheeks. 'Lord Fenwick-Clyde has been very generous with his time. I felt it only right that he be invited to visit. Hugo agreed.'

Annabell dropped her eyes to give the couple a moment of privacy and took a long drink of hot tea, laced with cream and sugar. It was hard not to smile at them. They were so obviously interested in each other and trying so very hard not to be obvious. Fortunately for them, nothing stood in their way. Timothy was too much of a prig to have had a mistress to get pregnant. He would be free to marry where he chose. And the age difference was not unheard of.

Not that she wanted to marry Hugo, she told herself sternly. She merely wished their relationship had not changed by his having to marry someone else. That was all. Nothing more.

She followed the tea with some toast just brought by a maid.

'How long will you be staying?' she asked her stepson.

Having never taken his attention from his hostess, he raised one sandy eyebrow. 'I don't know, Annabell.'

'As long as he likes,' Juliet said before he finished speaking. 'The children adore him.'

Somehow, Annabell could not imagine her starched stepson gambolling with Joseph and Rosalie. She could barely picture him unbending enough to kiss Juliet. And she could never think of him as passionate, although he had had a wife and had got her in the family way. She said nothing.

'Here you are,' Hugo's deep voice drawled. 'Butterfield told me Fenwick-Clyde had arrived. I see you have been entertaining him.' He strolled into the room. 'How do you do.' He held out his hand. 'I'm sorry I missed you when I delivered the invitation.'

Fenwick-Clyde rose and extended his hand. 'Sir Hugo.'

Annabell tried to surreptitiously study Hugo. He looked haggard, as though he had had a bad night. His hair was rumpled and his eyes were bloodshot. The lines around his beautiful mouth seemed deeper. His swarthy complexion looked sallow in the pale light coming from the many-paned floor-to-ceiling windows. She was not surprised to see him position himself close to the fire with just a barely perceptible hitch in his walk.

It hurt her to see that his thigh with the wound seemed

to pain him, making him hesitate in his walk, although she doubted anyone else had noticed. He was a naturally grace-ful man, but she knew him intimately now, and could see he did not move with his usual smoothness.

She forced her attention back to the other couple. They were much safer to her emotional well-being.

'Do you plan on staying long?' Hugo asked.

His tone implied that he didn't much care what Timothy intended to do, but Annabell knew better. She had learned that Hugo didn't ask unless he was interested in the answer. Otherwise he would keep his own counsel. She wondered if he worried that the old adage, 'like father like son', held true for Timothy. She would have to reassure him, for Ju-liet's sake, that to the best of her knowledge it did not. Timothy was the antithesis of his deceased father.

Again, Timothy hesitated as though he did not want to give the wrong response, and Juliet answered for him. 'Lord Fenwick-Clyde is free to stay as long as he wishes. Did you not tell me that, Hugo?'

Annabell shifted her attention to Juliet, amazed. That was twice in a matter of only minutes that the normally reserved and utterly polite Juliet had spoken with the intention of setting the record straight, so to speak. She began to see Hugo's stepmother in a new light.

'Of, course,' Hugo said. 'I did not mean to imply any-thing different, Juliet. I merely inquired so that I could pass the information along to Butterfield.'

He spoke so innocently and his face was so bland that Annabell nearly believed him. But she saw the hand that he rested on the marble mantelpiece tense. He was defi-nitely not comfortable with Timothy's visit. The small frown on Juliet's normally smooth brow told Annabell the other woman also realised Hugo was not perfectly sanguine. Timothy seemed unaware of any tension, but he did not know Hugo as the two women did.

'If it is not convenient, Sir Hugo, I can stay at the inn in the nearby village.'

'Not at all.' Hugo pushed away from the mantel. His gaze roved over the three of them, lingering briefly on Annabell. 'I hope to see you at dinner, Fenwick-Clyde. Right now, my estate manager is waiting.'

He made an inclusive bow and left. Annabell watched him, wishing she were going with him and knowing she never would. She turned back to the couple.

'Sir Hugo isn't the only one with things to do.' She smiled, a tight movement of her lips that did not reach her eyes. 'I must continue my work. The more time I spend at the dig, the sooner I will be finished, or...' she paused as she realised what she intended to do '...the sooner I will be able to turn it over to someone else to finish excavating.'

'Never say you are thinking of leaving?' Juliet said, genuine dismay in her light voice.

'I must some time, but not today and very likely not this week.' She rose. 'If you will excuse me?'

Both nodded, but it was obvious neither one cared. They were more involved in watching each other and discovering just how far they were to go.

Annabell walked from the room, envying them with all her heart.

Chapter Thirteen

Dinner that evening was uncomfortable in the extreme. Annabell nearly went so far as to excuse herself during the dessert course. Hugo watched her the entire time with a look of brooding awareness that made her stomach do cartwheels and her palms moisten. His attention was so marked that several times Annabell caught Timothy looking from Hugo to her and back again. She did her best to ignore everything, but could not stop her awareness of her host.

Finally Juliet rose and she and Susan followed suit. They escaped to the salon.

'Please excuse me, Juliet, Susan,' Annabell said before the other two had barely sat down. 'I don't feel well. Too much sun today, no doubt since I forgot my bonnet. I think I will retire early.'

Both women were glowing with pleasure at the knowledge that the men they were interested in returned their regard, but Juliet looked disappointed at Annabell's request. Still, always gracious, she said, 'Of course, Annabell. I will explain to the gentlemen.'

'Thank you.' Annabell smiled at Susan. 'I will see you in the morning.'

Susan nodded. 'Have you found something?'

'A pot, nothing fancy, but I think we should record it. I

don't think it is native to this part of the world. Possibly from Greece.'

'Oh, how exciting.' Susan clapped her hands. 'I shall be prompt.'

Annabell's smile softened. 'I know you will.'

But she did not want to linger. She did not know how long the men would spend with their port. She doubted it would be long since two of the three would be anxious to join the ladies. Before Susan could continue on or Juliet say anything else, Annabell left.

She fled, wondering if she was making a mistake by not moving to the inn. She reached her room and closed the door securely. Perhaps she would leave when Lady Mainwaring arrived. She did not think she could stand to watch Hugo with his future wife, no matter that Hugo did not love the woman. He was still marrying her. Lady Mainwaring still carried his child, begotten in passion.

The picture was too painful.

Annabell managed to undo the top buttons of her dinner gown so she could twist it around to the front and undo the rest. She slipped out of the thin muslin, shivering in the chill air, and left it wrinkled on the floor while she went for her robe. She looked back at the dress and decided to hang it in the wardrobe.

She had her head stuck in the recesses of the mahogany-and-sandalwood inlaid wardrobe when someone knocked. It was probably Susan come to talk about tomorrow.

'Come in,' she called, making room for the dress.

She heard the door open and shut, and expected to hear Susan. Instead cinnamon reached her. A *frisson* ran the length of her spine down to her toes. She pulled her head and torso out of the wardrobe.

'Hugo,' she murmured, turning around to see him standing too close for comfort. 'What are you doing here? Someone will see you.'

'No one saw me.'

He was magnificent. His too-long hair tumbled over his forehead and curled around the modest collar of his shirt. His black evening coat was unbuttoned and his black satin breeches were snug to his thighs and hips. His clothing left nothing to her all too active imagination. He was a man in all his glory.

She swallowed and looked at his face, only to see he was studying her as she had done him.

He gazed at her, taking in her dishabille. Self-consciously, she brushed the loose hair from her face. His attention lowered and she belatedly remembered she wore nothing but her chemise.

Hunger sharpened the angles of his face. 'I brought you something.'

She reached behind her and grabbed the first garment her fingers touched. It was a cape. She dragged it around her shoulders, embarrassed by her near nudity as she had not been before with him.

She spoke harshly. 'I don't want anything from you. Please go before someone finds you here. The last thing I need is to be linked with a man who's about to marry another woman.'

Even as she said the words, she realised their illogicality. The last thing she needed was to have *any* man in her bedchamber. The fact that it was Hugo only made it slightly worse.

His eyes narrowed. 'I want you to have these.'

He held out a square black velvet box. She knew it must be jewellery. The hard knot of pain in her chest slowly turned to steam.

'I am not your mistress, Hugo. I don't want jewellery from you, even if it is only a token of your appreciation for past favours. I know when men give gifts such as that to women. My brothers have done it enough. I don't want it from you.'

He opened the box to show the parure of aquamarines

and diamonds. The stones sparked with fire even from the distance separating her from them. It was a stunning set of necklace, drop earrings and bracelets.

'I bought them to complement your beauty.'

'You bought them to pay me off.' She took a deep, steadying breath and met him squarely. 'Get out.'

His face darkened and there was a dangerous gleam in his eyes. He set the velvet box down carefully. Too carefully.

She edged back.

He closed in on her.

She stepped back until the wardrobe stopped her. She put her hands up to ward him off. It was no use.

He pressed her to the hard wood, a hand on either side of her head. His face was too close.

'Don't send me away, Bell. I want you too badly to leave.' He took a deep breath. 'I won't leave, not while you look at me with desire as you just did.'

She closed her eyes to the ardour he radiated. 'You are mistaken. I don't desire you, Hugo. I am mad at you for your effrontery in offering me the same gift you would give a discarded mistress.'

'They are a gift, Bell. Nothing more. They belong on you.'

'I don't want them,' she repeated for what felt like the hundredth time. 'Take them and get out.'

'I have tried to be gentle with you, Bell, to woo you the way women want. Talking of emotions, finding out your likes and dislikes. Now I am going to seduce you with no regard for anything but your body and mine.'

She gasped, her eyes flying open. 'How dare you!'

He laughed, hard and sharp. 'I am desperate. I dare a great deal.'

His hand left the wardrobe and gripped her face. He held her for his kiss, his body pressed to hers. His lips met hers, hard and demanding, unlike any kiss he had ever given her.

His tongue forced her mouth open and plunged in. His fingers undid her braid and caught thick strands of hair, pulling her head back to expose her neck.

The pulse beat just where her collarbone showed. He moved his lips there and sucked. Shivers broke out on her skin.

Still holding her head back with one hand so her neck arched to give him access, he used the other hand to sweep off the cape she had so hastily donned. It fell from her shoulders to puddle in a brown heap on the floor. He pushed the chemise off one of her shoulders and down until her breast jutted exposed above her corset.

He lifted his head long enough to gaze at her exposed flesh, then he bent down and took her nipple into his mouth and sucked. She gasped and her back arched against her will so he had better access to her flesh.

Her hands, which had so recently pushed him, gripped the lapels of his coat and she hung on as though a storm raged through her body, pummelling her with its intensity. She could no longer resist him.

Sensing her surrender, he freed her hair and used the other hand to push the chemise off her other shoulder so that both her breasts glowed in the light from the fire. He raised his face and looked at her. She met his eyes, unable to turn away.

He took a deep shuddering breath. 'Tell me to leave now, and I will go.'

She gazed at him, seeing his need even as her own devoured any words of refusal she might manage to utter. 'I thought you intended to seduce me without regard for my wishes.'

His voice was deep and resonated with his arousal. 'I did, Bell. I did.' Pain twisted his mouth. 'But I cannot do that to you. You value your independence too much for me to take it from you simply to satisfy my appetites.'

She groaned, knowing his words had slipped between the

widening cracks of her emotional barrier. 'You have won,' she whispered.

'We both have.'

She closed her eyes, wanting what he was about to do to her, wanting him so badly she hurt with the need. When one of his arms went around her shoulders and the other behind her legs and he swung her up, she didn't protest. Let him take her where he willed, let him do to her what they both wanted.

He laid her on the bed and stepped back. 'Look at me, Bell.'

She didn't want to see him. She wanted only to feel him. Looking at him would be more than she could stand, for then she would have to admit to herself that she loved him. Had loved him from the first moment he kissed her. Her mouth twisted in bittersweet memory.

'Just kiss me and be one with it, Hugo,' she said, her voice hoarse with desire and denial and a loss that penetrated to her soul.

She heard him moving and the sound of cloth and knew he was undressing. The part of her that always revelled in his masculinity made her open her eyes. He stood naked.

The fire was behind him so the orange glow lined him, but she could still see him well enough. Dark hairs, crisp yet silky, covered his chest, circling his nipples. They formed a trail down the hard planes of his stomach past his stomach and lower. He was ready. She looked at his face and saw the tight line of his mouth and the blade edge of his jaw.

She lifted her arms to him.

He lowered himself to her so they lay side by side. His hands skimmed her bosom and stomach, his fingers touched her softly. She sighed as his mouth met hers. His kisses tantalised her, light then hard, shallow then deep. His fingers moved in unison. Her hips matched his ministrations.

She gripped his shoulders, shivering with need as he

moved. She felt his muscles tense and knew he was holding himself back.

She tore her mouth from his. 'Now, Hugo. Enter me now.'

He licked his lips. His pupils were so dilated that she could see her face in their black depths. She met his gaze without flinching even as her body pulsed from his attentions. He smiled, a look of power and barely suppressed passion.

And still he would not take her.

Her breathing increased. Her eyes closed and her back arched. She dug her nails into his muscles and rode the release he gave her.

When she could finally speak, she asked, her voice hoarse and weak, 'Will you take your pleasure now?'

He gave her an inscrutable look and, instead of moving between her legs, slid from the bed. Her eyes widened as she watched him go to his knees so that his face was level with the top of the mattress. The look he gave her was wicked and sensual. His lips parted and his tongue appeared.

He gripped her hips and positioned her for his deep kisses. She gasped with pleasure even as she tried to push him away.

'Stop, Bell. Let me give you this gift.'

She barely heard him over the rushing of blood in her ears. She had never experienced anything like this before. It was strange and embarrassing and—she gasped when he hit a sensitive spot—arousing her beyond her wildest imagination. He licked and sucked and used his mouth and tongue as he had his fingers and hand.

She writhed in exquisite torture. Just as she thought her body would explode, he withdrew only to return before she had completely calmed. He played her like a musician plays his instrument. He wrung from her every sensation her body was capable of giving.

Her soft moans and small gasps of pleasure filled the darkness in the room. She felt transported to a place where anything was possible. His mouth finally left her and she whimpered with frustrated need.

'Shh,' he murmured. 'I won't leave you like this. I promise, Bell.'

On one level she heard his reassurance, on a deeper level her body burned with desire not realised. Her nails clawed the sheet beneath her throbbing body.

'Look at me,' he ordered.

She opened her passion-heavy eyes to see him standing between her thighs, his masculinity firm and ready. He had already put on his protection. She reached for him and he caught her hands with one of his. With the other hand and his hips, he opened her wide. She finally realised what he meant to do.

He released her hand to grip her hips and hold her still. Then he thrust deep inside her. One strong, intense penetration and she exploded. She screamed with released tension as her body pulsated, and his hips pushed deeper and deeper. He seemed to touch something deep inside her that was both pleasure and pain. It was like nothing she had ever experienced.

Her mind numb, her body tingling, she hung on as he pounded into her. Suddenly, it was as though he had not already brought her twice to climax for she shattered again and again.

She gasped and sucked in deep gulps of air, her hips continuing to move with his. She was in a daze of satiation, yet still saturated with desire for this man who continued to move inside her as though he had just begun.

Suddenly, she felt him stiffen. He groaned, then spasmed.

Long minutes later, he still lay half on her, his feet on the bare floor, his chest covering hers. He kissed the side of her neck and smoothed the damp hair from her forehead. She turned to catch his lips with hers.

'I love you,' she whispered, not realizing she meant to say the words until they were out.

He looked sombrely at her. 'I know, Bell. I know.'

Annabell woke, wondering why she felt cold and bereft. Then remembered. Hugo had made love to her, such as he had never done before. In hindsight, it seemed he had taken her with desperation as much as passion.

She turned from side to side and swept her arms over the covers, hoping he was still with her and knowing he was not. He had been saying goodbye with his body.

Her mouth twisted. He had been showing her what she could never have. A lover who cared enough about his partner's pleasure that he would take himself to the limit in order to turn her inside out. But he was more than that to her.

He was the man she had fallen in love with despite her better judgement. In spite of everything she had ever told herself, her heart was his. She had not given it to him, he had taken it. And now he had returned it because he did not want it.

She curled into a tight ball as though she could shut out the pain. It was a futile action and she knew it, but there was nothing else she could do. He was gone and she loved him.

Hugo sat in the chair he had moved closer to the fire in his bedchamber and stared at the flames, seeing Annabell's face in each leaping glimmer. In another, he saw the curve of her breast. In another, the light in her eyes when he sheathed himself inside her body.

He would never touch her again. She wouldn't let him.

He emptied the last of the brandy into his glass. Instead of drinking the liquor, he threw it on the flames so they danced and reared to the top of the fireplace.

When she woke, she would find the aquamarines. He

should have taken them because she would despise him for leaving them, but they were for her. He had bought them for her, hoping she would remember him every time she looked at them. Hoping she would remember his touch every time she wore them. If she wore them.

He rose naked from the chair, his body exhausted but far from satiated. He could have made love to her all night. Even the thought of it aroused him. But he had not.

Tomorrow Elizabeth Mainwaring arrived.

The next morning, Annabell looked up from the piece of mosaic she was carefully uncovering. A post-chaise rumbled down the dirt road that skirted her dig on its way to Rosemont. She caught a glimpse of a crest. Lady Elizabeth Mainwaring was arriving.

Annabell slumped to the ground, careful even in her misery not to sit on something important. She pulled her knees up and hugged her arms around her calves, eyes staring at nothing. She had known this was coming. No one had made a secret of the fact that Hugo's future wife was arriving today. She should have moved to the inn, but that would have meant taking Susan from Mr Tatterly. A single woman, widow or not, did not stay in a public inn alone. And what if Mr Tatterly had stopped seeing Susan because of the relocation? She couldn't chance that just because she was not happy.

Nor could she leave the area completely and return to her brother's town house. That would mean leaving the dig before she was ready. She had decided long ago to devote herself to uncovering the past and exploring different lands and cultures. Not even the pain caused by her ended liaison with Hugo was going to change that. If anything, her heartache was going to make her vocation even more important.

But not this instant.

For a few moments and a few moments only, she was going to wallow in her misery. Elizabeth Mainwaring was going to get the only man Annabell had ever loved or ever would love. It didn't seem fair, but then she had learned long ago that life rarely was fair.

Her vision blurred. Eternity passed and was gone.

Annabell pulled herself together. Enough self-pity. She had work to do. The sooner she finished here, the sooner she could leave. The sooner she left, the sooner she would not have to see Hugo every day and know he would never be hers.

She jumped to her feet and swiped at her eyes.

A little more and she would have another mosaic unveiled. This one seemed to be the floor of what was probably the winter dining room. She thought it even had heating under the floor. Tomorrow she would need Susan to sketch it.

She bent back to her task, humming a country ditty. Anything to make herself feel less melancholy.

'Why don't you sing the song?'

She started, dropped the fine brush she had been using to remove dirt and craned her neck around. Hugo stood in the clearing. She hadn't heard him.

'I didn't hear you.'

He shrugged, his broad shoulders moving eloquently in the loosely-fitting brown jacket. 'You were entertaining yourself.'

'What brings you here?'

She turned back to her work. The last thing she intended to do was to let him upset her or, worse yet, to entice her. She didn't care that he was willing to carry on their liaison. She was not.

'Elizabeth just arrived.'

'And?' She was not about to tell him she had seen his future wife drive by.

'I wanted you to know so you would not be taken unawares.'

'That was nice of you.'

She was proud her voice was cool and nearly mocking. He would never know how much this hurt her. Never.

'You don't make anything easy, do you?'

She stopped swishing the brush, but did not look at him. 'Why should I? I didn't cause this situation.'

'Dammit, Annabell.'

She turned at that. He stepped toward her, and she put out her hand to stop him.

'Don't come near me, Hugo.'

His eyes smouldered. 'Why not? Don't you trust yourself with me?'

She stood so as not to feel overwhelmed by him. 'If you must know, then no. I don't trust myself with you. Or you with me. You are engaged to someone else, but you make no bones about the fact that you still want to bed me. I won't do it, Hugo. I won't. Not again.' Her voice cracked.

'Why not, Annabell? You enjoyed last night, I have the scratches to prove it,' he ended with a wry twist of his beautiful lips.

'I told you.'

Anger darkened his face. 'You told me you wouldn't do to another woman what was done to you. But that isn't your real reason, is it?'

She shrugged and pushed back a thick strand of hair that had come loose from the bun at her nape. 'Of course it is.'

'Very noble,' he said sardonically. 'Then if that is part of your reason, it isn't all.' He moved a step closer. 'It isn't as though you wanted to marry me yourself. Is it?'

'Not wanting to marry you myself and having you marry someone else are two totally different things.' But how could she explain something to him she didn't really understand herself. 'Had you remained single, we could have continued our liaison indefinitely.'

'We can continue it once I'm married.'

All she could do was look at him. Why didn't he understand? She had told him last night that she loved him and regretted having done so more than she could say. At least he hadn't thrown that at her. But neither had he told that he loved her in return.

'I thought last night was the end,' she finally said. 'I thought you came to me to say goodbye.' Her hands clenched. 'You left me those jewels.'

'I bought them especially for you, Bell. I would have bought them for you if Elizabeth had never existed. They are my gift to you.'

'I told you I didn't want them, but you left them. I told you I won't continue our liaison, yet you persist in hounding me.' Her voice rose in anguish. 'When will you listen to me and leave me alone?'

He stared at her, his shoulders tense, his mouth thin. 'I don't know, Bell. I can't seem to stop myself. No matter what has come between us, you are all I think about. All I want.'

She twisted around, her fist ground into her mouth to keep from sobbing. Her shoulders hunched. 'Please go, Hugo. Just go.'

Her misery must have reached him. She heard his footsteps and then Molly snorting, followed by the clop of hooves on the damp ground and then the dirt road. Annabell took a deep breath and willed herself to relax. Her shoulders slumped, her fist fell from her mouth and she turned.

He was gone. It was just as well. She had things to do. Thank goodness she had work.

Hugo rode away.

Why had he confronted her? Why was he provoking her? He was the one who had offered for another woman's hand. He was the one who had broken Annabell's trust even though neither one of them had ever promised the other exclusivity. He had never said *I love you*.

But she had. He had not answered her. It didn't matter what he thought. He was engaged to Elizabeth Mainwaring.

He must have yanked on the reins for Molly shied. He soothed her. 'Easy, girl. I didn't mean to do that.' She responded to his voice and calmed.

And why had he brought up marriage to Annabell? What good would it do either of them if he forced her to tell him she wanted to marry him? Nothing. In his rational moments he knew that. He had never intended to marry her in the first place, just as she had never wanted to marry him. So what was he doing now?

He didn't know…but he didn't want to go home to Elizabeth.

He whistled to Molly, their signal for a good run. The exercise would do them both good. He aimed her away from Rosemont.

Chapter Fourteen

Annabell studied herself in the full-length bevelled mirror. She was not a beauty. Never had been, and her silver-blonde hair was too out of the ordinary. Normally it didn't bother her. Hadn't bothered her until she had entered the hall and caught a glimpse of the sultry beauty Hugo was to marry. Even now, hours later, she could see Elizabeth Mainwaring in her mind's eye, and the scent of tuberose seemed to hang heavily in the air.

She made a face at herself. She had nearly worn the mauve gown, but the memories had been too fresh, too unsettling. Instead she had settled on this simple dinner dress of white gauze striped with blue. It was fancier than they had been wearing, but she sensed Lady Mainwaring would be dressed much more glamorously.

Unable and unwilling to do ringlets, she had braided her hair and wrapped it around the back of her head. She jabbed a small spray of diamonds into one side.

Against her earlier better judgement, she had even donned the aquamarines. They sparkled and shone in the light from the candelabra. Hugo had been right. They complemented her skin and hair colouring. They looked good on her.

But she hadn't wanted them. Had threatened to return

them. She even considered them an insult. Yet, in a moment of weakness she had put them on. She had wanted to wear something Hugo had given her when she met the woman who had taken him from her, who would likely be wearing his ring. Stupid and silly, but there it was.

She sighed and turned away.

She thought briefly of sending her excuses, then chided herself for a coward. She had never run from adversity or pain. Even when Fenwick-Clyde had been at his worst, she had faced him and lived through the ordeal. She might have cried later, but he never knew.

Nor would Hugo know.

Taking a deep breath, she lifted her chin and squared her shoulders. After she was through this, nothing would ever be hard again.

She made her way down the hall to the stairs and down to the salon where everyone gathered for a drink before dinner. A footman waited to announce her. She shook her head. The last thing she wanted was to draw attention to herself. Better to see what was going on before anyone knew she was here. More than anything, she wanted to see Hugo with his fiancée before he realised she was there. She just hoped he would not be hanging on Lady Mainwaring's every move or admiring her every gesture and ample curve.

Annabell sighed and passed one gloved hand briefly over her eyes, wishing she could shut out the world as easily as she could block her view.

She paused in the doorway to the salon. She had made sure she would be the last to arrive so she would have the least amount of time to mingle with the other guests before dinner was served. Seeing Elizabeth Mainwaring practically draped across Hugo's right arm made her heart ache and confirmed the intelligence of her decision. She had a long, miserable meal ahead of her.

Susan immediately bustled in her direction. 'Annabell, what took you so long? You are usually the first to arrive and tonight you are the last. I had begun to think I should send a servant to see if you were unwell.' She paused long enough to take a breath. 'You are very handsome tonight. The white and blue becomes you enormously. And the aquamarines. They are *magnificent.*' Her eyebrows rose, for she knew Annabell did not own such jewellery. When Annabell refused to answer her companion's silent question, Susan turned slightly. 'Don't you agree, Mr Tatterly?'

Tatterly, his square face looking frazzled, nodded. 'Very fine, Lady Fenwick-Clyde. You are absolutely correct, Miss Pennyworth.'

Annabell swallowed a groan. Leave it to Susan to mention the aquamarines. Silly as it now seemed, she had hoped no one would mention them. And Juliet and Timothy might not have. But Susan knew exactly what she owned right down to what she had brought with her. There was no help for it but to brazen it out.

'Thank you, Susan. Mr Tatterly.' She smiled at the footman who extended a tray of sherry. 'I was detained because I spent longer than normal today at the site.'

Juliet drifted over, a smile making her face radiant. 'Did you find something new?'

Annabell shook her head. 'Not really, but I am still uncovering my latest discovery. I want to be very careful not to damage anything.'

Timothy, who had followed Juliet, frowned. 'Do you think it is safe to stay so late? A woman alone?'

Annabell swallowed a sharp retort. That was just the thing she expected from him. He didn't mean any disrespect, he just considered women to be the weaker sex.

Patiently, she said, 'I am well able to care for myself, Timothy, but I thank you for your concern.'

'Oh, dear, yes,' Susan said. 'The places we have travelled. Why, we met on a packet ship coming home from Egypt. Annabell was the kindest possible, taking me under her wing when it became obvious I was having trouble with my lively charge who had decided she was enamoured of a gentleman. When he turned his attentions to Annabell, she made short shrift of him.'

'Really,' Hugo drawled, having wandered over with Elizabeth Mainwaring still draped across his arm like a serving towel. 'In what way, if I may be so bold as to inquire?'

Annabell pressed her lips together and forbore to give Susan a minatory look. The woman had no idea the trouble she caused when she tried to help.

'Oh, nothing out of the ordinary.' Annabell waved a hand as though to negate the story.

'Oh, no, it was more than that,' Susan interposed. 'Why, I saw Annabell push him over the railing and into the Nile. Nasty, dirty water it was too.' She laughed. 'When they fished him out, he was none too happy, but there was nothing he could do.'

'Indeed?' Hugo's eyes had an unholy gleam in them. 'Was he being impertinent?'

'No, really, Annabell,' Timothy Fenwick-Clyde said before she could reply. 'That is too bad of you. Surely there was another way to curb him. Wasn't there a British gentleman to protect you? Or was this one of your wild trips you took after m'father's demise?'

Annabell looked from one man to the other. Each wore a totally different expression, but she didn't appreciate either one. The urge to give them both a set down was strong.

'I may be *only* a woman, but that does not mean I am incapable of taking care of myself. That particular malady is more often than not a myth perpetuated by the male gender in order to keep the female subservient.'

The scent of tuberoses filled the air. 'A veritable Amazon,' Elizabeth Mainwaring drawled in her raspy, provocative voice.

The sensual sound reminded Annabell of a cat that was being scratched by a besotted owner. She wondered if it reminded Hugo of a woman who has been well bedded.

Her throat closed on the thought, and she had to consciously make herself relax. It would do her no good to dwell on Hugo and his sexual liaisons.

She looked at the woman. Elizabeth Mainwaring was provocation personified. She wore an evening gown in the latest London fashion, very high waisted and very low in the décolletage. The black satin, to differentiate it from the matte crepe of mourning, became her pale complexion and creamy bosom. The magnificent diamond necklace that seemed to drip like stars between her full breasts shone to perfection against her skin and gown. Her honey-blonde hair was curled around her perfectly oval face, accentuating her large blue eyes, before being braided around the back of her head. Her waist was small and her bosom and hips fully rounded. She was—stunning.

No wonder Hugo had made her his mistress and now his future wife. For the first time in her life, Annabell felt inadequate. Always before she had known she was tall and elegant with an adequate figure and with a mind that held its own in any company. Now, she appreciated painfully how a beautiful woman could mesmerise with nothing more than her body.

And there was the engagement ring, an opal surrounded by diamonds, not too big and not too small. The setting was modern, as though Hugo had recently purchased it. Annabell swallowed hard.

'Yes,' Hugo drawled. 'Lady Fenwick-Clyde is very like those mythical female warriors.'

His voice brought Annabell back to the conversation. She dragged her attention from the woman still curled around him. That sight only worsened her already sore heart.

She made her eyes meet Elizabeth Mainwaring's before moving on to Hugo's. 'A woman has many weapons in her arsenal to achieve what she wants. I choose to use my hard-won independence.'

Lady Mainwaring's blue eyes narrowed. 'And others do not?'

Annabell shrugged, regretting her hasty words. She didn't even know this woman, only by gossip and the picture she presented this evening. She had no right to judge her or to make veiled aspersions against her.

'Women are powerless in our society unless they are widows or dearly loved by the men in their lives. Any means to achieve happiness is worth using. I have chosen to use my independence since Fenwick-Clyde's demise to ensure that I am able to do as I wish.' She gave Timothy an apologetic look. 'I do hope you understand, Timothy.'

He nodded, but his complexion was pale. 'Perfectly.'

'Dinner is served,' the butler intoned, breaking the tension that had developed.

Hugo took his stepmother's arm and escorted her to the dining room while Timothy took Lady Mainwaring on one arm and Annabell on the other. Miss Pennyworth followed happily with Mr Tatterly.

Annabell heard Susan chattering on behind them. Thankfully someone had been unaware of the storm brewing so recently. Which was usual, since Susan had started it without any wish to cause trouble. It was simply her personality.

'How very difficult it must be for a gentleman of your sensibilities to have a stepmother of such independence,' Lady Elizabeth Mainwaring said in dulcet tones.

Annabell felt Timothy's muscles tense under her fingers. The other woman had hit the bull's-eye with one shot. That always had been the major source of friction between the two of them. They had finally reached a tacit agreement to smile politely, inquire about one another's health and then go their separate ways.

'Annabell more than earned her independence,' Timothy said. 'I am happy she values it.'

Annabell nearly stopped in her tracks. That was the nearest thing to an acceptance of her that she had ever heard her stepson say.

'Why, thank you, Timothy.'

He looked down at her, his eyes turbulent. 'You are welcome.'

He led each of them to their seats. Lady Mainwaring sat to Hugo's right in honour of her engagement to him. Lady Fitzsimmon sat at the opposite end of the table from Hugo as befitted the current Lady Fitzsimmon. Annabell sat on Hugo's left, a position she found disturbing, but could do nothing about. Her stepson sat beside her with Mr Tatterly across from him. Susan sat beside Mr Tatterly. They were an uneven number.

The first course began. Turtle soup and fish.

Annabell found she was not hungry, even for the turtle soup, a delicacy she normally relished. Across from her Lady Mainwaring ate sparingly, all the while keeping a light chatter going that included Hugo and Mr Tatterly. Both men looked interested, although Mr Tatterly made a point of trying to include Susan.

Annabell fiddled with her spoon and declined the salmon. Instead, she sipped steadily on her wine. She noticed everyone else also imbibed freely, particularly Hugo.

'Would you like some turbot?' he asked.

She looked directly at him for the first time since sitting down. He looked far from happy. Comfortable, yes, but then he was very experienced.

'No, thank you.'

'As you wish.'

His voice was bored and dismissive. It hurt. She took another sip of wine.

'Lady Fenwick-Clyde,' Lady Mainwaring addressed her. 'Do you find that London is quite flat with everyone on the Continent?'

'Not everyone is there and the Season is barely started.'

'True.'

Inanities, Annabell thought. A way for two women who want the same man to pass the time without being at each other's throat. And they still had several courses to go before dessert, after which she could plead a headache and escape to her room. *As she had done last night.* Only Hugo would not follow her tonight—or any other night.

The conversation buzzed around her. Her stepson, Timothy, concentrated almost exclusively on his hostess. A pretty flush made Juliet's skin glow. Her gown of a white muslin slip overlaid by a celestial-coloured netting further complemented her blue eyes and blush-red hair. She was pretty and gentle.

Annabell felt Hugo's attention on her. Heat crept from her stomach to her face. Fortunately the table was large enough that they were too far apart for him to touch her even by accident.

She finally turned to look at him, determined to act with more spine. 'Do you wish to say something to me, Sir Hugo?'

'You are wearing the aquamarines.'

Her flush deepened. 'Yes. They go perfectly with this gown.'

'They go perfectly with you.'

His brooding gaze rested on her like a heavy mantle of fur, warm and nearly suffocating. She glanced away from him and saw Lady Mainwaring look from him to her. She made herself smile at the other woman who merely looked at her for a long moment before turning her attention to Hugo.

'Hugo, my dear, please pass the salt,' she purred.

Annabell noticed every man at the table look at Lady Mainwaring as though unable to resist the call of her voice. The lady's smile was self-satisfied as Hugo acquiesced. She picked daintily at her food.

Unable to tolerate much more, Annabell was glad to see

the footman remove the dishes. The next course had to be better than this last one. It was not.

Annabell sat through dinner, feeling as though she were being tortured for wanting something she could not have. If she had never loved Hugo, she would not be suffering now.

The next course was removed. And so it went.

Juliet finally rose and Annabell followed suit with an alacrity that threatened to topple her chair. Without a backward glance, she followed her hostess from the room. They trooped back into the salon, a large rectangular room that never seemed warm.

Before the tea tray was brought in, Annabell rose. 'Please excuse me, Juliet. I have the headache and plead exhaustion.'

Juliet stood immediately, went to Annabell and took one of her hands. 'You poor thing. You have been working too hard trying to finish your excavation. Of course you are excused. I will send a maid up with tea and some laudanum to help you relax.'

Annabell smiled. She could easily understand what her stepson saw in this woman five years his senior.

'Thank you, but I don't need anything. I am merely tired. After a good night's sleep I will feel right as can be. I will probably miss breakfast too since I wish to spend every minute at the villa so I can finish this as quickly as possible and intrude no longer.'

Juliet shook her head. 'You are more than welcome here, Annabell, with or without the Roman villa.'

Annabell's smile deepened. 'You always make me feel warm and liked. Now, if you will excuse me.'

Susan, realising what was happening, scurried over. 'Oh, dear, oh, dear. I knew you were working too hard. Tomorrow you must rest instead of going out there. The men from the village will be able to carry on for a day without you. You know they will. I will go up with you and make sure that you get your tea and laudanum.' She turned to Juliet Fitzsimmon. 'What a perfect idea, Lady Fitzsimmon, to have laudanum sent up. Annabell does not have any with her. She does not like to take drugs of any sort, but she does look peaked. A good night's rest will be the best thing for her and laudanum will ensure that she gets it.'

Annabell nearly groaned. The last thing she needed was Susan's over-solicitousness. Her companion always meant well, but she could be exhausting.

'I will be perfectly fine, Susan, dearest. You stay here and enjoy yourself. The gentlemen will be arriving shortly.'

'Oh, no, I couldn't let you go up all by yourself.'

'Of course you can. I will be fine. A maid will bring the tea and laudanum, which I will take.' Susan raised both brows. 'I promise.'

'Well—'

'Oh, stop,' Lady Mainwaring's smoky voice interrupted. 'She has said she will do it. She is a grown woman with a penchant for exerting her independence. Let her be.'

Annabell's eyes widened slightly. She looked at the rival who had won the match and very likely didn't even know there had been a contest. Lady Mainwaring shrugged her delicately rounded white shoulders as though to say, what a fuss.

More flustered than ever, Susan said, 'Oh. Yes. I know that, Lady Mainwaring. I had just thought to help. Nothing more.'

Annabell, whose hand had been released by Lady Fitzsimmon, moved to touch Susan. 'It is all right. I know you only meant to help. You always think of others before yourself, dear Susan. But, as Lady Mainwaring said…' she cast a considering glance at the other woman '…I am fully capable of taking care of myself in this matter.'

'What matter is that?' Hugo's voice preceded him through the door.

'Nothing that need concern you,' Annabell replied

quickly. Then added, 'Sir Hugo. But thank you for your concern.' She turned to the other women. 'Goodnight.'

She felt Hugo's gaze on her as she left. Heat crawled up her back and made her head ache even more. She wished the excavation was done and she could leave. She would go join Guy and Felicia in London and Susan could remain here if that was acceptable to Juliet. That would give Susan more time with Mr Tatterly.

Annabell reached her room, closed her door and locked it, leaving the key in the hole so no one with another key could unlock it. She did not think Hugo would follow her with everyone here, but there were times when his passion was upon him that proprieties were the last thing on his mind.

She managed to undo her dress and let it fall to the floor and left it. She would wait till morning to hang it in the massive wardrobe. She would feel better then. She left the jewellery on.

Moving toward the mirror on the dressing table, she picked up a candelabra. She set the candles down and sank on to the chair. Her reflection, morose and exhausted, looked back at her from the mirror. Instead of unfastening the jewels as she had intended, she studied them. The flawless watery blue of the aquamarines were complemented and lent added sparkle by the circling diamonds. The white gold the gems were set in looked good on her pale skin. Hugo had picked well, so well that he might have had them specially made just for her.

Slowly, she unfastened the necklace, next the two bracelets and lastly the drop earrings. She picked up the box they'd come in from amongst the scattered bottles and vials. She carefully arranged them on the black velvet. She would not wear this gift again.

When the maid came with tea and laudanum, Annabell unlocked the door, and the maid saw that she was already dressed for bed. 'Thank you,' she told the young girl, who bobbed a curtsy. 'You may go.'

The girl bobbed another curtsy and scuttled back out the door. Annabell relocked it. That would keep Hugo out, but would it keep her in? In spite of everything, she longed to go to him, to touch him, to have him hold her. She was hopeless.

She drank the tea and left the laudanum. The opiate always left her feeling muddled in the mornings after she'd taken it. She would need her wits about her tomorrow.

Annabell rose earlier than was her habit, dressed and went downstairs. She doubted that her daily provisions were ready yet or that breakfast had been set out so she would go to the kitchen and get a bit of toast and some tea. She moved quietly on the carpeted hall and was just about to round a corner when she heard voices. She stopped.

'Miss Pennyworth,' Mr Tatterly's solid voice said, 'you are up early.'

'Yes, Mr Tatterly. I have chores to finish before I can join Annabell at the villa.'

Susan's voice was even more breathless than normal. Annabell smiled.

'Perhaps if I helped you, you would have some time to take a stroll through the gardens with me? They are very nice this time of morning.' There was a hesitation to Mr Tatterly's voice, as though he were not sure of his ground.

'Why, thank you,' Susan said.

Annabell could imagine the smile on her companion's face. Things were progressing nicely between the couple. She would find another way downstairs to give the two some privacy, but the next words stopped her.

'I have something I wish to ask you in private.'

Tatterly sounded as though his cravat was too tight and he had to force the words past the constriction. Annabell sympathised with his nervousness. She anticipated that he wished to ask Susan to marry him, and that would make any man nervous, let alone one as shy as Mr Tatterly.

'Oh, my.' Susan, on the other hand, sounded thrilled. 'Of course I will walk with you. Shall we go now?'

'What about your chores, Miss Pennyworth? I don't wish to interfere with them.'

'You shan't, Mr Tatterly.'

Annabell walked back to her chamber door to give the couple time to get down the stairs. She would soon lose her companion, but while she was sad she was also glad. Susan would be happy with Mr Tatterly.

After several moments, she retraced her steps to find them gone. She descended to the ground floor. The delay had been long enough that her food hamper stood in its regular position by the front door. She fetched it and started out only to see Lady Mainwaring on the front steps dressed for riding.

Annabell paused for an instant before nodding. 'Good morning, Lady Mainwaring.'

'The same to you, Lady Fenwick-Clyde. I hope you are feeling better today.'

Her sultry voice seemed to cling like honey to every word. No wonder Hugo had taken her as his mistress. And that was without taking into account her considerable beauty. Her rich gold hair was swept up and under a navy blue velvet hat with a single ostrich plume that curved so the end tickled her flawless cheek-bone. Her lips were full and red as the evening sun. Her figure was outlined to perfection in a tight-fitting habit. A waterfall of fine lace spilled from her jabot to draw attention to her voluptuous bosom.

Annabell felt completely inadequate in her practical harem pants, man's plain white shirt and loose-fitting jacket. She felt absolutely clumsy in her wellingtons. Well, there it was and nothing she could do about it. She and Lady Mainwaring were the complete antithesis of one another.

With only a tiny pang of jealousy, Annabell replied, 'I am much better today, thank you. A good night's sleep is the best cure for ailments.'

'Generally.' Lady Mainwaring laughed and a wicked gleam entered her eyes. 'Are you off to your Roman villa?'

'Yes.' Annabell wondered what the woman was up to. She couldn't be interested in something so unfashionable as an excavation.

'Hugo has told me a little about what you are doing. Very commendable.' She flicked the riding crop against her lower leg. 'But what I find utterly fascinating is your independence. I don't know another woman who would do as you are.'

Annabell studied the other woman's face, looking for derision or malice. There did not appear to be either.

'I do as I please and have done so since Fenwick-Clyde's death. If that is independent, then so be it.'

'Do you follow your own desires in everything?'

Now there was a hint of something more than interest in the lady's voice and expression. Annabell wondered if she was prying into her personal life. It was none of her business if that was the case.

'I do as I see fit, Lady Mainwaring. Nothing more and nothing less.' She picked up the wicker basket she had set down when the two of them had started talking. 'Now, if you will excuse me, I have work to do.'

'Of course,' Lady Mainwaring murmured. 'And I have a ride to enjoy. I look forward to seeing you at dinner.'

Annabell smiled but said nothing. She did not look forward to seeing anyone at dinner tonight. Perhaps she would plead another headache and have a tray sent up to her room. That would be easier.

Every time she saw Hugo's former mistress and soon-to-be wife, she felt a pang of jealousy and pain that was far from pleasant. She had never considered herself a petty person, but she did not enjoy seeing Lady Mainwaring's extraordinary beauty or hearing her sultry voice. She had to let that go. She could change nothing.

And for now, she had work to do.

Chapter Fifteen

Annabell slipped on to the veranda while everyone else was in the salon talking or playing cards. She had been unable to continue seeing Lady Mainwaring draped over Hugo's arm and hanging on every word he said. Weak and petty, but she was rapidly learning that where he was concerned she was not as strong as she had always thought.

The scent of roses reached her. The moonlight showed a gravel path through the gardens. A walk might calm her down, help her regain her equilibrium.

She moved down the steps, smiling at the lion rampant that guarded the entrance to the rose walk. To her fanciful imagination, he was a large tabby cat rearing on hind legs to catch a butterfly. She smiled and realised with a start that it had been a long time since she had seen anything whimsical in life. If nothing else, falling in love with Hugo had given her a deeper appreciation for everything around her.

She stopped and cupped a large red rose to her face. She inhaled the intoxicating scent.

'They are most beautiful in the moonlight,' Hugo's voice said from behind her. 'But their smell is strongest in the full afternoon sun.'

She started and moved away. 'I did not know you were behind me.'

She did nothing to keep the accusatory tone from her words. She did not want him here. It was too painful.

He stretched his lips, showing white teeth. It was a predatory action. She took a step back and caught herself. She was not going to turn tail and run from him.

'Why are you here, Hugo?'

He gazed at her, his eyes brooding. 'Because of you, why else?'

'Then leave. I don't want you here.'

He closed the distance between them. 'Don't lie to me, Bell. Lie to yourself if you must, but not me.'

Her heart thumped painfully. 'I am not lying.' But she was.

He grabbed her upper arms and pulled her to his chest. 'You want me here as badly as I want to be here.'

She stiffened and flattened her palms on his chest and pushed. She didn't move an inch, he held her so tightly. 'Have you been drinking?'

He laughed harshly. 'A little. But that is not what runs hot in my blood.'

The moonlight turned his swarthy complexion sallow and accentuated the hollows of his cheeks. It made his eyes dark pools of passion and pain, his sensual mouth a slash of promised delights.

She drew a shaky breath. 'Let me go, Hugo. This is not right.'

'Right?' His voice was hard. 'What is right? My engagement to Elizabeth?'

'No, but necessary,' she said, her voice weaker than she liked. 'You must pay the piper for your actions.'

'Or another man's,' he said bitterly.

'You can't change the situation,' she managed to say, through lips gone numb with pain. 'You agreed to this marriage.'

He groaned, his fingers tightening until she knew she

would have bruises the next day. 'I have to, Bell. I couldn't let her deliver a child out of wedlock.'

'Why not?' Even as she asked, she knew why. And she would have thought less of him if he had.

He set her away. 'Because. Because as much as my father protected me, there were still the sly glances and quickly hushed words. My father loved me dearly, but I knew with a small boy's insecurity that my father had not married my mother. I might be in much different circumstances if he had married and had another child sooner than he did. As it was, I was his only child for many years.' He turned his back to her so she could barely hear him. 'I would not do that to another child.'

'Even though you do not love the mother?' The words were a cry from her heart.

He rounded on her. 'Even though I do not love Elizabeth. Can you understand?'

She nodded. The hurt he had inflicted did not keep her from understanding what he did and why he did it. But it didn't make it easier to watch him and Elizabeth Mainwaring together either.

'Yes,' she sighed. 'I can understand.' He took a step toward her. She put her hand up. 'Please, Hugo, no more. While I can understand, it still hurts. Please, leave me alone.'

She thought he would refuse, but then he bowed his head. 'You are right. My pursuing you only makes it harder.'

'Yes,' she murmured.

Without another word, he left, taking her happiness with him. Something was going to have to change. She couldn't take much more of this. With feet that felt leaden, she made her way back to the veranda, her pleasure in the rose garden gone like it had never been. She climbed the shallow steps and saw a shadow moving, sensed another person.

'Lady Fenwick-Clyde?' Elizabeth Mainwaring's rich, honeyed voice penetrated the darkness of the veranda.

Annabell faced the other woman. 'Yes, Lady Mainwaring?'

For an instant only, she pondered the inanity of them calling each other by their titles, given to them by men now no longer living. Still, the formalities provided distance that she, for one, sorely needed. This was the woman who had taken Hugo from her. Plain and simple, nothing more, nothing less. She took a deep breath and wished it did not feel as though her throat was closed.

'I would like to speak with you. If you have a minute.'

Annabell considered her answer. The last person she wanted to talk with was the woman in front of her. Yet, she could not blame Lady Mainwaring without also laying blame on the woman's partner—Hugo. He had been an active participant in their liaison. While society might wink and turn away from Hugo's involvement, she would not— could not.

'What do you wish to say?' Annabell finally said, suddenly tired beyond imagining.

Lady Mainwaring stopped when she was close enough for her lowered voice to reach Annabell. The full moon sparked off her pale blonde hair and made her skin appear like the finest Limoges porcelain. Her eyes sparkled like sapphires. She was a very beautiful woman.

No wonder Hugo had taken her for his mistress. He was a connoisseur of female beauty even though he had erred when he chose her for his latest dalliance. He had said she was beautiful to him. That had been enough for her.

Pain, tight and breathtaking, took her. She had thought herself past this. She had thought her independence would be enough. Had she been wrong?

'This is not easy.' Hugo's future wife kept her voice low.

Elizabeth Mainwaring's sensual alto penetrated Annabell's agony. She forced herself to let go of what had been. The woman before her was Hugo's past and his future, not her.

Her voice rough, Annabell said, 'Nothing ever is, is it?'

She sighed from exhaustion, wishing this was over and she was in her own room, locked behind a concealing door where she could release her grief and pain instead of holding them in. She did not want this talk, but she would not turn away from it. She was made of stronger stuff, or so she had always believed.

'No, but then life isn't easy,' Lady Mainwaring said. 'I want to tell you the truth.'

Annabell laughed a short, sharp bark that did nothing to conceal her hurt. It was the best she could do.

'What if I don't want to know the truth, Lady Mainwaring?'

Elizabeth Mainwaring looked at her from the corner of her eye. 'Then leave. I won't follow you, and I won't try again.'

Annabell turned away. That would be the simple solution. She could walk away tonight and tomorrow she could leave Rosemont. Susan and her Mr Tatterly were very likely settled, therefore Susan could stay here or not as she chose without jeopardising her relationship with her fiancé. She could go to Guy's London town house. But running away would accomplish nothing, especially on her excavation. Still, she thought she would go anyway. She was tired beyond imagining. She could always return later, hopefully when Hugo and his new bride would not be in residence.

She angled a glance at the other woman. Elegant and beautiful as she was, Elizabeth Mainwaring did not look happy. Bitterness flooded Annabell. The woman had Hugo, but she was not ecstatic. What irony.

Perhaps it would be better to hear her out. If nothing else, one of them might walk away from this encounter feeling better.

'What do you want to say?' She didn't try to keep the resignation from her voice. 'Let us air the dirty linen and be done with it.' She looked at the expanse of grounds, silvered by the full moon, and refused to feel regret. She made a sudden decision. 'I shall be leaving first thing in the morning.'

'You don't need to.'

She shrugged. 'There is no reason to stay. The initial excavation is done. Jeffrey Studivant will be arriving tomorrow afternoon. He was originally going to assist me. Now he can finish it all. He is eminently qualified.'

'Ah. So you aren't running away. I had wondered.'

Annabell felt the heat of anger burn through her chest, easing some of the previous pain of loss. 'No, Lady Mainwaring, I am not.' Then honesty made her add, 'Only a little. I would have left for a while no matter what. My brother and his wife have just had a baby. I would like to spend time with them.'

Only a small white lie. She did want to see Guy and Felicia again and little Adam. The fact that she would not have gone for some time if Lady Mainwaring had not arrived was only a small matter.

The other woman lifted her elegant and rounded white shoulders in a very Gallic gesture. 'I would have left had I been in your place. I have never believed a stoic face worth the effort. Better to leave behind whatever is hurting you.'

The admission took Annabell by surprise. She turned to look at her nemesis. 'I would imagine you have scant experience of being hurt and consequently having to be a stoic.'

'You would have been wrong.' Her voice was ironic.

'How little we know each other,' Annabell murmured.

'True. But we are both women and as such, we both live with our emotions close to the surface.'

Annabell looked sharply at Lady Mainwaring. 'You are marrying Sir Hugo, yet you sound sad.'

'Perhaps I am.' She turned to face Annabell. 'Perhaps I wish things had turned out differently, but they have not. That is why I sought you out.'

A pang of discomfort lodged in Annabell's gut. 'Don't feel you must tell me anything, Lady Mainwaring. Sir Hugo and I were not engaged, not did we exchange vows of any kind.'

'No?'

Annabell shook her head slowly. 'No.'

'Then am I mistaken in thinking you care for him?'

Annabell's fingers froze in the act of pulling her shawl close. She had to pick her words carefully. Lady Mainwaring might speak as though she intended to bare her soul, but so far she hadn't. And Annabell didn't think she could make herself more vulnerable to this woman than her love for Hugo already made her.

She spoke slowly. 'In the time I have been here, I have played cards with him, gone on picnics, sat across from him at the dinner table. He even taught me how to waltz. I would be lying to say that after all that he means nothing to me.'

'A friend, nothing more?'

Annabell took her time folding the ends of her scarf across her breast, wondering why she was suddenly so cold. The night was nearly balmy. But she knew why. She felt caught in a situation with no easy solution. It made her defensive.

'Why are you doing this?'

Lady Mainwaring turned away and leaned over the stucco railing so that she seemed poised to fly into the night air. 'Guilt?'

'Guilt?' Annabell was certain she had misheard.

Arms still on the railing, Elizabeth Mainwaring looked at her. 'No matter how you skirt around your feelings, Lady Fenwick-Clyde—which I call you because I sense you don't like or trust me—I believe you care deeply for Hugo. I also believe he cares for you. That is something where Hugo is concerned.'

She turned back to gaze over the rose bed that spread

from the house nearly to the artificial pond. The scent of its blooms wafted on the breeze.

'I have known him for many years. He knew my husband,' she added. 'After I became a widow, I waited the acceptable year and then approached him.' Her perfectly formed mouth twisted. 'As you can probably imagine, he accepted my offer.'

Annabell sucked in air, but said nothing. She must have made a sound, though, for Lady Mainwaring looked back at her.

'Does that shock you?'

'Should it?' But it did. As independent as she professed herself to be, she did not think she could pursue a gentleman.

'Not if you knew me.' She turned back to her contemplation of the moonlit garden. 'Anyway, he took me up on my offer. That was nearly a year ago. I even went to the Continent when he did. Although, in all honesty, it was not so much for Hugo as for the excitement. Everyone was there.'

'So you and Hugo have been lovers for nearly a year?'

'Yes. But he dropped me when he met you, even though he had made arrangements to return to London when I did and to carry on as we had been doing.'

Another sharp intake of breath. Hugo had been telling her the truth when he said Lady Mainwaring was no longer his mistress. For what good it did now.

'And his action would not have bothered me.' She stopped speaking for so long, Annabell began to wonder if she had finished. 'You see, I cared for someone else.' Elizabeth Mainwaring gave a bitter, disillusioned laugh. 'I was a fool, but I loved him. I cuckolded Hugo with him.'

Annabell seethed with indignation. How dare she treat Hugo like that, betray him with another? She had thought only the married did such things.

Lady Mainwaring shrugged. 'At the time nothing mattered to me but this other man. And, if Hugo knew, he did not let on. However, looking back, his visits did lessen. Yet, he was always careful in what he said, and it was easy for me to be so with him. He is a wonderful lover, but I do not love him so I was never caught in the throes of impatience. When Hugo paused for his protection, it was more than acceptable. I did not want to bear his bastard any more than Hugo wished me to.'

She turned around and leaned backward on the parapet, closing her eyes. Her voice lowered. 'I had already borne someone's bastard, delivered it and given it up to a tenant farmer. A little girl.' Her voice caught. 'My husband did not take lightly to being cuckolded. Charles told me to give up the child or run away with my lover, who would not have me for he was married himself, or find myself turned out with no support.' She opened her eyes, but Annabell sensed she did not see anything but the past. 'I gave up the child.'

Annabell gasped. She could not help herself. But she instantly regretted it. 'What you did is not so unusual in our circles.'

'No,' Lady Mainwaring agreed. 'But, nonetheless, it was not easy to do. I was in a fit of melancholy for at least a year afterward. I vowed that I would never get myself into that position again, and if I did, then I would keep the child.' She gave Annabell an apologetic look. 'That is why I am so very sorry to do this to you, but I will not give up my baby again. Nor will I raise the child as a bastard. Hugo had an easy life of it, but his father was a powerful man at court and in society. No one dared ostracise Sir Rafael or his illegitimate son. I am not so fortunately placed. And society will accept much from a man that it will not condone in a woman.' Bitterness dripped from her last words.

Annabell could do nothing but stare at the woman. Pity mingled with rage in her breast. Pity for the situation Lady Mainwaring was in and the pain she had experienced when giving up her previous child, and rage that the woman had decided to force Hugo into marriage.

'Is Hugo the father of your child?'

Lady Mainwaring's striking blue eyes glowed softly as though tears filled them. 'I don't really know.'

Annabell kept a tight rein on her voice, willing herself to show none of the disgust she felt. 'Yet you are forcing him into marrying you.'

'To provide a name for my child. Yes.'

'What of your other lover, the one who might just as easily be the father? Why don't you make him marry you?'

For the first time since her arrival, Elizabeth Mainwaring faltered. Her elegant fingers clutched tightly to the plaster railing, and her magnificent bosom rose and fell as though she fought for air.

And Annabell knew why. 'You love him.'

'Yes.'

'And he does not love you in return.'

Elizabeth Mainwaring shook her head. Her voice was soft and hurting and lost. 'No, he does not.'

'I am so sorry.'

And she was. After falling in love with Hugo and then losing him to this woman, she understood the agony of not having the person you love. Just a short time ago she would not have understood, but now Lady Mainwaring's pain was an emotion she knew only too well.

Suddenly she understood. 'That is why you won't tell him about the child.'

Elizabeth Mainwaring's breath caught. Annabell sensed the other woman's tension.

'Yes. He…' she turned away so Annabell could not see her face '…he told me from the first that he would not marry. He has been hurt before.'

Annabell did not try to keep the sarcasm from her voice. 'Haven't we all?'

'Yes.' Elizabeth Mainwaring's was just audible. 'And

even should he change his mind and marry for the child…I do not think I could marry him, loving him as I do, and have him not care anything for me.' Her beautiful mouth twisted. 'I have not your strength.'

Annabell found herself hating and despising this woman. Elizabeth Mainwaring had made her own situation, and she was ruining another person's life because of her own self-ishness and weakness. Yet, she truly understood, now that she had loved and lost Hugo, what it was like to be emo-tionally devastated.

'Will you tell Hugo?' Lady Mainwaring's voice cracked.

Annabell blinked back tears of anger. Would she tell Hugo? Would she make Elizabeth Mainwaring's child a bastard? Even for her own and Hugo's happiness? Perhaps if Hugo had ever told her he loved her, but he had not. In all likelihood, he would eventually be as happy with Eliz-abeth Mainwaring as he would have been with her. And she would get over this. Pain was not constant, it faded with time. She knew that from her parents' death. The first days and weeks, even months, she had felt as though a heavy weight lay suffocatingly on her chest. Then slowly, it had eased. Now when she remembered them it was with joy and love for what they had meant to her. Eventually that would happen with her feelings for Hugo. It had to.

'No, I won't tell him. It is not my place.'

Rather than stay and hear any more, Annabell turned away. She would walk in the rose garden and delight in the silvered beauty of the blooms and heady scent of their rip-ening. Tomorrow she would leave.

She descended the steps to the gravel path and began to wander aimlessly. She told herself that in time none of this would matter anymore. In time.

Chapter Sixteen

Dawn barely crept over the late spring sky when Annabell stepped into the travelling chaise that had brought her to Rosemont a few months before. She told herself that in time her chest would no longer feel as though someone had pried it open and ripped out her heart. But not yet.

'Annabell.' Susan's voice penetrated Annabell's misery.

'Yes, dear?' Annabell leaned forward in her seat to look out the window. 'I thought I told you not to bother getting up. We will meet up in London soon enough.'

Worry puckered Susan's pale brows. 'Yes, you did, but I could not help but feel concern. As I told you last night, your departure is so sudden. Are you sure you are not sickening and need me by your side?'

Annabell made herself smile, but she knew it was a poor thing. 'Quite. Guy and Felicia have asked me to visit in London. They have gone there for the Season so Guy can take his seat in Parliament. Besides which, Mr Studivant will be here tomorrow. You will be completely occupied helping catch him up to where we are. And I know he will want you to stay as long as possible to continue your illustrations.'

'Yes, I understand all that,' Susan said peevishly, 'but I still can't help but worry at this suddenness. It is not at all like you. You never leave something unfinished. At least, I have never known you to do so, and I have known you for these many years.'

'Five, dear. Perhaps six. I was much less reliable in my younger days.'

'Faugh! You are being purposely obtuse.'

'Yes, I am,' Annabell said gently. 'I don't wish to discuss my reasons with you, Susan. Please respect that.'

Susan's mouth formed an astonished *O* seconds before her eyes filled. 'I'm so sorry, Annabell. I didn't mean… don't wish to pry. I just…' She took a shuddering breath. 'I was just worried. You have been different since Sir Hugo's arrival, but it seemed a happy difference. Now you seem distracted and sad.'

Once more Annabell forced a smile that didn't reach her eyes or ease her heart. 'I need to go, Susan. Take care and join me in London as soon as you can. We must plan your wedding. And I shall miss you.'

Susan blushed a rosy pink and started speaking, but Annabell rapped on the carriage roof and the coach lurched forward. She waved to her friend.

Fortunately it was a beautiful day and the trip to London promised to be quick and uneventful. She needed something in her life to go simply.

She pulled the curtain over the window, thought better of it, and hooked the heavy green velvet back. The morning sun would improve her disposition. Consequently, when the carriage drove past the Roman villa, she could not help but see it and the workers she had hired from the village who were rapidly erecting the more permanent awning where the temporary tent had been. She would come back later, perhaps next year, and stay at the village inn.

Hugo would be married by then…and a father. The unhappiness that thought caused was like a rock in her stomach. She hiccupped as she tried to stifle the tears that seemed to insist on falling. She had cried more than enough last night, yet here she was doing so again. She was a watering pot.

She finally gave in to her misery.

Later, she pulled the handkerchief from her reticule and blew her nose with force. Somehow she felt that if she did everything with determination, she would manage to keep going forward with her life. After all, she had not wanted to marry Sir Hugo. After Fenwick-Clyde, the last thing she wanted was to put herself at another man's mercy.

So what if Hugo was nothing like her husband? Fenwick-Clyde had seemed a reasonable older man when she first met him. She had not wanted to marry him, but neither had she feared and loathed him. Instead, she had been young and impressionable and had still thought she would find a grand passion.

What a fool she had been. Was.

She sank back onto the velvet squabs and closed her eyes. Even more recently she had found herself longing for a love that would complete her life.

She had watched Guy and Felicia's stormy courtship with all its pain and passion and found herself wanting to care for someone like they cared for each other. They had defied the conventions of polite society and now neither was accepted by the sticklers of the *ton,* but they were ecstatically happy. They had each other and their baby.

She shifted, trying to get more comfortable. Sleep had eluded her last night and exhaustion rode her like a demon. Still, her thoughts would not quit so she could rest.

She was being as silly as Susan so often was. She was happy. Finding someone would only complicate her life. Particularly someone like Hugo. He was a rake, with every charm and flaw that epitaph epitomised.

But there is no man more faithful than a reformed rake, a tiny voice said in the back of her mind. That voice had been more and more persistent as her liaison with Hugo had progressed. She had nearly believed it.

Then Elizabeth Mainwaring had arrived.

Annabell turned again, frowning at her inability to get comfortable. She finally gave up, sat up and stared out the window. The lush Kent countryside passed by her window, bringing the fresh scent of growing green things. She loved this time of year. Spring always seemed to promise new futures. It was the time the Romans had believed Persephone returned from the Underworld, bringing rebirth with her. She believed they were right.

She was unable to distract herself for long from Hugo. Her thoughts returned to him will she or nil she. He had lodged in her heart and remained there no matter what she told herself.

Her hands clenched the seat cushion, her nails sinking in. If only it didn't hurt so much.

And what if the child Elizabeth Mainwaring carried wasn't Hugo's? What if she had left him to the woman when she might have fought to keep him? What if?

Her decision was made. If Elizabeth Mainwaring truly didn't know who the father of her child was, then it was Lady Mainwaring's place to tell Hugo. If she chose not to, it was not Annabell's right to tell him what had been told to her in confidence. This situation was between them. Hugo had slept with the woman of his own free will. Unfortunately for her, she was suffering more from the consequences of that passion than Hugo.

And Elizabeth Mainwaring was hurting as well. Annabell had to concede that. The woman was in love with one man and marrying another. It had to be hard. But that was the way of their world, and, deep down, Annabell admired Elizabeth Mainwaring for doing what was necessary to keep this child and to raise it as legitimate. That took a lot of courage.

But the consequences still hurt. She could rationalise all

she wanted. She could tell herself she did not want to marry Hugo, would not have even had he asked. But the fact remained that she loved him and had lost him.

The fact remained that her heart still felt as though it had been ripped from her chest.

Hugo turned from the window, letting the heavy gold-velvet curtains fall back into place. The travelling carriage was long gone, and with it, Annabell.

Annabell of the silver hair and inquisitive mind. Annabell with a passion to match his own. He had lost her before he had even truly had her. And all because of his own actions. He had lived the life he wanted, and had revelled in the pleasures of the flesh. He still did. Only now, he wanted to share those delights with Annabell. And she was gone.

Fury and frustration coursed through him.

He moved to the mantel and swept his hand across the top, sending candelabra and fresh flowers crashing to the floor. The resulting sound of destruction brought no satisfaction.

'Jamison,' he bellowed. 'I'm going riding.'

The valet appeared so quickly it was likely he had been standing on the other side of the dressing-room door. He eyed Sir Hugo with a jaundiced air.

'No use taking your anger out on them gee-gees, Captain. Only cost money to replace them and a maid to clean up the mess.'

Hugo turned on his retainer. 'And what do you suggest I do, Jamison? Drink myself into a stupor?'

The man shrugged. 'Could do worse.'

Hugo's hands fisted, the urge to hit something nearly impossible to resist. Somehow he managed to unclench his hands before he did something he would regret. 'Go away, Jamison.'

'You wanted me to get out your riding clothes.'

Hugo scowled. 'Go away. I will do something else.'

'Ain't like you intended to marry Lady Fenwick-Clyde,' Jamison said as though he hadn't heard the order to leave. 'You was merely amusing yourself. Seen you do it more times 'n I can remember. Do it meself.'

'You are being impertinent.' Hugo's voice was cold enough to frost a frying pan.

Jamison ignored the reprimand. 'You even carried on with Lady Mainwaring off and on for nearly a year. Some would say you gotta pay the piper.'

Hugo's teeth clenched. 'Get out before I forget what we have gone through and throw you out.'

'Some would also say you swallowed Lady Mainwaring's story without so much as a peep. Wonder why?'

'Now.' Hugo's voice was dangerously low.

When in London he practised with Gentleman Jackson weekly and was accounted a good pugilist. The urge to land his valet a facer returned with a vengeance.

'I'm goin', Captain. But I think yer should consider what y'er doin'. Don't seem like you've given it much thought.'

On those words, he quickly moved to the door leading to the hallway instead of the dressing room. He tossed one parting shot. 'Know I went too far, but you needed to hear it and for sure Lady Mainwaring wasn't going to say it. Nor Lady Fenwick-Clyde. I owe you too much to stand quietly by while you ruin yer life.'

Hugo stared at the closed door for a long time before sprawling into a large chair. He ran his fingers through his hair to get it off his forehead and—unbidden—remembered Annabell doing the same thing. She had done so after their first bout of lovemaking. He turned his head to look at the bed. There.

His loins tightened painfully as the memories flooded back. She had been eager and insatiable. She had made him feel like a young buck with his first woman. She had made him feel special. It had been a long time since someone had made him feel special.

Perhaps Jamison was not far off the mark.

* * *

Annabell arrived in London after dark. The mist had rolled in from the Thames and made the going slow. The carriage lanterns cast an orange glow that reflected back. As they progressed further into the city, heading for exclusive Mayfair, the houses began to have gas lighting in front of the doors. Soon the night took on an eerie golden hue. Yes, she was in London during the Season.

The coach pulled to a stop in front of Guy's imposing Georgian town house. Instead of waiting for the servant to open the door and lower the steps, Annabell took a bunch of skirt in one hand, held on to the door strap with the other and jumped into the street. Luckily for her it hadn't rained or she would have soaked her half boots.

The front door opened and Oswald stood haloed by the light from the hall lamps. 'Miss Annabell,' he said in his most proper English butler voice. 'We were not expecting you.'

Annabell mounted the steps. 'I decided at the last minute. Surely Guy is still here. I see the knocker is on the door.'

Oswald stepped back to allow her in. 'His lordship and Lady Chillings have gone to Brighton for the week. His Highness, the Prince of Wales, specifically invited them.'

Annabell stepped further into the hall and instantly felt at home. She had spent more time here during her marriage to Fenwick-Clyde than at her husband's London residence. 'And the Prince of Wales is not to be gainsaid. Is Dominic here?'

'Yes.' His tone was censorious in the extreme.

'Up to no good, I take it.' Annabell undid the ribbons on her travel bonnet and tossed the confection on to a nearby table. 'I would expect nothing else.'

At that moment, a loud whine came from the door leading to the servants' work area and the steps to the kitchen. Annabell raised one brow in query.

'Mr Dominic's latest waif. A mongrel of less than impeccable blood lines.'

'That is certainly like my brother.'

Annabell laughed for the first time in what felt like ages, although she knew it had not been long since Lady Mainwaring had arrived at Rosemont. It felt good to find pleasure in something as minor as her younger brother's propensity to rescue the underdog—literally.

'Are you referring to Fitz?' Dominic's pleasing tenor demanded.

Annabell turned to see her brother descending the stairs, dressed in formal black satin breeches and coat. He had her height and slimness and high-bridged nose and dark blue eyes, but that is where the similarities ended. His hair was black as pitch and his complexion was swarthy as a tinker's thanks to the inordinate amount of time he spent out of doors pursuing his sporting interests.

'Where are you going rigged out like that?'

He snorted. 'Nowhere interesting, trust me, Bell. Almack's.'

'Almack's? Don't you detest that place?'

He gave a long, exaggerated sigh. 'Immensely. But that is where Miss Lucy wishes to go, so that is where I will escort her.'

'Miss Lucy? As in Lucy Duckworth?'

'The same.'

She frowned. 'I thought Guy warned you away from the chit. She is barely out of the schoolroom and much too innocent for the likes of you.'

He returned her look with a scowl of his own. 'I keep my own counsel, sister, just as you do.'

'Really?' She stood taller and squared her shoulders. 'And what do you mean by that remark?'

Instead of answering directly, he asked sweetly, 'Have you had the pleasure of meeting Fitz? My newest acquisition.'

Dawning realisation made her eye him with ill-disguised ire. '*Fitz*, as in…'

'Exactly,' he drawled. 'Fitzsimmon.'

'How dare you name a dog after Sir Hugo!'

'I dare very well, thank you. After all—' he settled his chapeau at a rakish angle on his ebony curls. '—they are much alike. Roustabouts with a taste for the ladies and less than impeccable antecedents—as Oswald so quickly informed you.'

'The pot calling the kettle black, don't you think, Dominic?' She could barely contain her irritation. 'Yet how like you.'

He made her an elegant, mocking leg, showing a calf any woman would be pleased to admire and any man would long to have. 'If you insist on digging at me about Lucy Duckworth, then I will continue to remind you that Sir Hugo Fitzsimmon is a rake of the first order and someone you should stay well away from.'

She snorted very much in the same way he had. 'I will do as I please. At least I am a grown woman and a widow. Lucy Duckworth is still a child.'

'A delightful one,' he said with a sly grin that quickly turned to disgust. 'Unfortunately, she comes well chaperoned.'

'Ah, Miss Duckworth.'

'Yes,' he said, his tone implying dislike. 'Miss Sourpuss. I swear she criticises everything. Nothing I do pleases the woman.'

'You would please her if you quit pursuing her young sister. Had you thought of that?'

'Ah, but that would not please me.'

'How typical.' She shook her head in resignation. 'But mark my words, Dominic, what you are doing will come to no good.'

He moved past her, turning to look over his shoulder.

'You think so? Then one can only hope it will be interesting.' He sailed out the door to his waiting phaeton.

She watched him with a worried frown. He was such a rakehell and ne'er-do-well, but she loved him. For all his ramshackle ways, he had a heart of gold. Even if he did name his latest charity case after Hugo.

Oswald coughed. 'Excuse me, Miss Annabell, but your luggage is ready to go up to your room. The same as usual?'

'Yes, thank you, Oswald.' In her altercation with Dominic she had completely forgotten that the loyal family servant witnessed it all. She threw caution to the wind and asked, 'Is Dominic getting himself in too deeply?'

Oswald's eyes clouded. 'I believe he might be, miss. It is as though he is driven to chase Miss Lucy, even though Miss Duckworth has been here several times to demand that he stop.' He shook his head in resignation.

'I can see him doing something like that.'

And she could. Something was amiss here, but goodness knew Dominic would never tell her what it was. In the meantime, she had her own concerns to deal with. But she would keep a watch on Dominic.

'So,' Annabell said, sweeping her gaze around the theatre of the Surrey Institution, aware nearly everyone in her audience was male, 'in conclusion, the discovery of a Roman villa in Kent so soon after the discovery of one in Sussex provides further proof that our shores were as fertile and welcoming to the Romans as they are for us today.'

There was a light smattering of applause to which she nodded acceptance before stepping down. Tomorrow she would speak to the Society of Antiquaries. For them, she would be more specific in what she found.

'Excuse me, Lady Fenwick-Clyde.' A gentleman stepped from the group just leaving the bottom row of seats. 'If I may be so bold, would you mind answering some questions?'

A little taken aback, but flattered nonetheless, Annabell stopped. He was a very presentable person. He wore a nicely fitted navy coat over a starched white shirt with points that just barely touched his jaw. His cravat was simple but well done, a point she recognised because of Guy's finesse with the things. And his pantaloons were grey and well-made. Very presentable.

She smiled at him. 'I hope I can answer your questions, sir. I did not stay to complete the excavations, Mr...'

He smiled back at her, showing strong teeth. He had a pleasant face with open blue eyes and a wide, if thin, mouth. His hair was sandy blond.

'I am Mr Daniel Hawks, and I am sure you can answer anything I ask. I know you have been involved in more excavations than this one.'

Her curiosity piqued, she asked before considering, 'How do you know that? I do not think we have met before.'

His face warmed, but he maintained a relaxed yet interested attitude. 'I have heard you speak before at the Society for Antiquities. You seem every bit as informed as your male colleagues.'

She blushed with pleasure. 'Why, thank you.'

He made her an abbreviated bow. 'Fully deserved. But I am wondering if this particular villa had mosaics of the seasons. I understand that another one not too distant does, or did. I believe originally there were depictions of all four seasons but that now only one remains.'

She nodded as she listened. 'Ah, yes. You are speaking of Bignor. I don't believe it has been fully uncovered yet.'

'Correct. I have listened to Mr Samuel Lysons read his second account of the excavation to the Society. I was wondering if you are finding similarities.'

'Some. As must be expected, the coloured mosaics are made from the same materials. And there are a number of rooms that have, or had, heated floors. Of course, we have found what appears to be bathing rooms. Nothing unusual.'

He nodded as he scribbled down her words.

'May I ask, sir, are you an antiquarian?'

He gave her his friendly smile. 'I am an amateur.'

'Aren't most of us?' she said. 'I hope I have helped you, Mr Hawks. I must be going now.'

'I am sorry if I have kept you from an appointment.'

'No, nothing of the kind. But my carriage should have arrived and the tiger hates to have the horses standing for long. They are my brother's and he is very particular.' She smiled to soften her words.

'Yes, yes, perfectly reasonable. Thank you so much.'

He made her a perfect leg, as though he were asking her to dance instead of bidding her goodbye. And if he was more graceful than Hugo, it was of no matter. She nodded and left.

She stepped outside and beckoned Tom, Guy's tiger, who was her tiger for the afternoon. He led the horses up and held them in place while she clambered into the phaeton. Luckily for her, this was not Guy's high-perch phaeton so she did not feel perilously high from the ground.

She glanced back at the elegant portico of the Surrey Institution to see Mr Hawks standing between the Ionic columns. She managed a small wave before Tom released the horses and clambered on to his spot in the back of the carriage. They were in Blackfriars Road and had some way to go to get back to Guy's house. Fortunately it was summer and the sun would be up for some time.

She flicked the reins and off they went.

She was a fair hand with the ribbons and could let her mind wander as she drove. Mr Hawks's attention had been very gratifying, and she wondered for what must be the hundredth time if she should write a paper about this excavation. Up to now, she had decided against it because women did not do that sort of thing. But then, women did not travel to Egypt alone such as she had done. Nor did they choose to live there as Lady Hester Stanhope was doing.

Perhaps she would write that paper after all. It would give her something to concentrate on besides Hugo. She smiled spontaneously for no other reason than she felt a glimmer of happiness. It was the first time in weeks.

With hard work, she might even forget Hugo. Hah!

Chapter Seventeen

'La,' Lucy Duckworth simpered. 'You are so naughty, Mr Chillings.' Suiting action to words, she swatted Dominic on the sleeve with her fan.

He grinned and appeared completely infatuated. If there was a gleam of ennui in his dark eyes, only those who knew him best would see it.

'Only with you, Miss Lucy.'

Annabell thought their inane flirting would make her nauseous, but she still managed to smile and nod and wonder what she was doing at Almack's with them. She had only been in London a week and Dominic had managed to drag her with him in lieu of Miss Duckworth as chaperon for Miss Lucy Duckworth.

Miss Lucy laughed a light trill that sounded straight out of the schoolroom. Annabell turned her attention elsewhere. She had not been to Almack's since her own coming out many years ago. It hadn't changed. The rooms were unadorned, the food was mediocre at best and the company convinced it was the finest in the land.

Annabell sighed. So much for an enjoyable evening. But she could keep an eye on her brother.

'Bell,' Dominic said, 'Miss Lucy and I are going to have the next dance.'

'Don't monopolise her.' She flashed a smile at the young woman. 'It isn't done.'

'Yes, Lady Fenwick-Clyde.'

Miss Lucy Duckworth flushed with excitement. One would think she had never been here before, which Annabell knew was not so. Dominic had brought her last week. Of course, this was probably the first time the chit had been here without her older sister.

The music began and Annabell watched the couple join the group forming for a quadrille. She noted that a number of ladies followed their progress with envious looks. Her brother, rakehell that he was, was still considered a very desirable catch. He had an air about him of danger and passion that was nearly irresistible.

She turned from watching them to see Mr Hawks before her. 'Oh!'

'Pardon me,' he said, bowing. 'I did not mean to startle you.'

She smiled at him, noting he was once again impeccably dressed. 'No, do not apologise. I was thinking of something else and did not hear you approach.'

'Do you mind?' He indicated the chair beside her.

There was no polite way to tell him no, and she was not sure she wanted to. It would be nice to have company other than Dominic and his silly Miss Lucy. She wondered how the very serious and proper Miss Emily Duckworth managed. But that was none of her concern—she hoped. So long as Dominic behaved and did not go beyond the bounds of propriety, Miss Lucy would continue to be Miss Duckworth's problem.

'Ahem…' Mr Hawks cleared his throat.

'Oh, dear, I am sorry, Mr Hawks. Please be seated.'

'Thank you.' He took the chair and angled himself to look at her. 'Do you come here often?'

She laughed. 'No. I haven't been here for years, but my brother talked me into coming tonight.'

He looked at the closest set of dancers. 'Mr Dominic Chillings?'

'Yes, do you know him?'

She was not sure that knowing Dominic was a good recommendation. He often moved with a very fast and loose crowd. But then so had, did, Hugo, and that had not kept her from falling in love with him. The unbidden memory instantly dampened her spirits.

'Is something the matter?' Mr Hawks's voice held concern.

Annabell realised her emotions were showing on her face. Where was the stoic countenance she had worked so hard to perfect when married to Fenwick-Clyde? She would have to resurrect it.

'No, nothing is wrong.' She forced her voice to lightness and pressed him, knowing the surest way to make someone leave behind one topic of conversation was to insist they answer a question. 'You did not answer my question. Do you know Dominic?'

'No. Merely hearsay.'

'Really?' She lifted her chin, prepared to give him a setdown if needed.

She did not like his tone of voice. It implied that Dominic was unsavoury. She might often think that, but he was her brother. For a perfect stranger to think it was unacceptable.

Mr Hawks reddened and had the grace to look uncomfortable. 'Pardon me, Lady Fenwick-Clyde. I did not mean anything derogatory.'

'I am glad to hear that, Mr Hawks.'

He gave her a rueful smile. 'I seem to be at sixes and sevens with you this evening. Nothing I say or do is correct, which is my own fault. Perhaps I should leave, then come back and try again.'

That made her laugh. 'Don't be ridiculous.' Taking pity on his obvious discomfort, she asked, 'Do you come here often?'

'More than I should, no doubt.'

'Why is that?'

He gazed around the room and Annabell looked where he did. The glittering throng dipped and swayed, simpered and flirted to the rhythm of the music. Some of the finest jewels in the world glittered under the light from massive chandeliers, and some of the greatest minds in the country mingled with some of the most empty.

'I am supposed to be here in London to make contact with Mr Samuel Lysons. I wish to work with him, but so far I have done nothing but listen to him.' He finished with a grin. 'But that is nothing to concern you. May I have this next dance?'

Annabell blinked in surprise. 'Are you saying you wish to be more than an amateur antiquarian?'

He reddened. 'I have ambitions in that direction.'

'How interesting.'

She smiled at him. He returned her smile, his with a hint of interest she did not return. She decided it would be wise to change the subject. A country dance would not be amiss. It would put some distance between them and end this conversation.

'I would be delighted to dance—as long as it isn't a waltz. I am not good at that.'

His face lit with pleasure. 'I am sure you can do anything you set your mind to. However, if the music is any indication, I believe the next dance will be another quadrille. They are popular.'

It was not the dance she had hoped for, but it was better than sitting here and talking. She took one quick look around to locate Dominic and Miss Lucy. They were at the refreshment table talking to several other people. For the moment, she might leave them to their own devices.

Mr Hawks stood and gave her his hand. When her fingers met his, no shock of awareness made her tingle. Nothing. She had reacted to Hugo from the first, even when she didn't know who he was and he kissed her. For a moment she stared at nothing as the memory of Hugo's lips on hers made her ache for what she would never have.

'Lady Fenwick-Clyde?' Mr Hawks's concerned voice finally penetrated her reverie of joy and pain.

She turned her lips up into the semblance of a smile. 'I am so sorry, Mr Hawks. I keep thinking of other things. I believe I am tired.'

His blue eyes filled with sympathy. 'Would you like me to escort you to your carriage instead?'

Her smile turned genuine. 'You are so nice. Too nice for me not to keep my word.' She moved slightly ahead of him. 'We will dance.'

He followed with alacrity.

They took their places, he bowed and she curtsied. The music began. They moved through the steps, touching, then parting, then touching again.

She enjoyed the music and the movement, but there was nothing special when his fingers touched hers or his eyes met hers. Nothing at all. It was as though she was physically numb.

The music ended, he bowed, she curtsied and they returned to her seat to find Dominic and Miss Lucy already there. She still felt nothing for the attractive, nice man who stood at her side. She glanced at him and turned away with regret.

'Dominic,' she said to her brother, who was in the act of signing Miss Lucy's dance card. 'Miss Lucy has already danced with you twice.'

He stopped. 'And what if she has? That is just one of Society's bugaboos.'

She raised one brow.

'Very well.' He gave the young woman a rakish, lopsided grin. 'You will have to make do with this gentleman here.' He indicated Mr Hawks.

Taken by surprise, Mr Hawks did a credible job of concealing any sense of ill use he might have felt. Instead he bowed. 'If Lady Fenwick-Clyde will introduce us, I would be honoured to dance with the lady.'

Annabell's mouth thinned at Dominic's rudeness, but she made the introductions. Lucy Duckworth would be considerably safer with Mr Hawks than with Dominic. After the couple had joined the group forming on the floor, she rounded on her ne'er-do-well brother.

'Dominic, what game are you playing? That was appalling.'

His eyes narrowed. 'I am doing as I please, just as you have since Fenwick-Clyde stuck his spoon in the wall. You, of all people, should understand what that means.'

And she did. A tiny bit of her irritation with him evaporated, but still… 'That is all fine and good and I do understand, but that is no reason to ruin the chit. Unless…' An appalling thought occurred to her. 'You don't wish to marry her, do you?'

Totally affronted, he took a step back. 'Absolutely not.'

'Then stop making her the latest *on dit* with your pursuit. You are sometimes a loose screw, but this is outrageous even for you.'

He stiffened and his hands paused in the act of straightening his cravat. 'If you will excuse me, sister, I see an acquaintance.'

He stalked away without hearing her response. Just as well, she decided. He would not have liked her reply. He was behaving strangely, even for him.

'Lady Fenwick-Clyde,' a deep, honey smooth baritone said from just behind her.

Annabell's skin goose-pimpled and her stomach clenched. The room seemed suddenly hot and close, as though there wasn't enough air. One hand went instinctively to her throat.

She turned to see Hugo.

'Hugo.' She couldn't keep the note of joy from her voice.

When his sombre face lightened into a smile, she was glad she had not been able to.

'I called at your house earlier and they said you were here with your younger brother and Miss Lucy Duckworth.'

He had called at Guy's? In spite of knowing he should not have done so, she found herself happy he had. She was a mass of contradictions, had always been where he was concerned.

'That was very bold of you. An engaged man does not call on another woman, at least not a respectable woman, and I believe I am still considered one.'

The smile fled his face, leaving it harsh and hard angled. 'There is no reason for you not to be. I gave the excuse that I was looking for Dominic.' When her eyes widened a fraction, he added drily, 'We have been known to see each other at some of our haunts.'

'Of course, I had momentarily forgotten how much the two of you have in common. Although,' she added, irritation making her words bite, 'I don't believe I ever heard of you pursuing a chit barely out of the schoolroom.'

He lifted his quizzing glass to one clear green eye and surveyed the room until he found Dominic. 'Not since my salad days at least. Is it Miss Lucy Duckworth?'

Annabell sucked in her breath and bit her lower lip. 'Is it common gossip?'

'Didn't I just hear you tell him it was?'

She scowled at him. 'Were you eavesdropping?'

'You were not whispering. Besides, it is common knowledge. I have only been in town a day and have already heard the comments.'

She would swear there was a look of pity in his eyes. 'Don't pity me for my fool brother.'

'I don't. But I do understand your concern. It is not the thing to dally with someone of Miss Lucy's years—unless he intends marriage.'

Annabell sighed. 'You likely heard him say that was not the case.'

'I did. But if he continues as rumour says he has gone on, then he might find himself forced to it by a duel with the girl's father or brother. They are a ramshackle pair, but even they value their good name.'

Annabell's shoulders drooped. 'Very true.'

'But come,' he said, his voice dropping to a provocative challenge, 'forget Dominic. There is a waltz beginning, and I believe you could use another lesson.'

She eyed him askance. 'I don't think that is wise.'

He shrugged, but there was a hunger in his eyes and in the curve of his erotic mouth that told her he meant to have this dance. 'When have we ever been wise about each other?'

'So true,' she murmured.

'Then why start now, Bell? I want to hold you. It has been too long.'

There was an intensity of longing in his words that caught and held her. She realised with a mingling of fear and happiness and anticipation that she could not deny them both this small pleasure.

'All right.'

She moved to the dance floor, sensing he followed her without having to look. Her blood sang with his nearness. This dance was so little compared to what they had had, to what they had lost. But it was all they would get. She would take and revel in the closeness of his body to hers. She would take what he offered for the next too-short minutes and never regret it.

The music began.

Annabell looked up at Hugo and smiled. He met her gaze steadily with no easing of his sombre demeanour, but the hunger in his eyes burned brightly. He put his arm around her waist and swung her into the waltz.

Unlike their first dance, her feet followed him flawlessly.

It was as though what had passed between them since that time had somehow joined them so her body knew his without hesitation. She became one with him.

'I have missed you.'

His voice was low and seductive, the words full of promises. She responded to him in spite of her better judgement. But this line of unreason would benefit neither of them.

'Don't,' she whispered, her throat tight with regret. 'Don't do this to me, Hugo.'

'Why not?' Anger tinged his voice, lurking on the edges, ready to come forth. 'You know you feel the same way.'

He spun her around and around until she was too breathless to respond immediately to his demand. At the same time, his arm tightened so that she was closer than acceptable. Her breasts brushed his chest and fire, scalding and molten, flowed through her. It was all she could do not to press herself to him.

And the memories. They erupted from the dark corner where she had tried so desperately to bury them. Her face burned. Her body ignited.

'Hugo,' she gasped, her voice deep and raspy, 'take me back.'

A smile that was neither nice nor comforting transformed his face into a mask of desire with an edge of danger. 'No.'

He pulled her closer so that with the next turn, his hips brushed hers. Her eyes dilated and her mouth formed a soft *O* of arousal and need.

'You are remembering, aren't you?' he said. 'Remembering the other times I held you like this.'

She nodded, nearly unable to speak. But she had to. This had to stop. 'Hugo, this is not the place.'

'Then where is?' he demanded. 'Will you come to me?'

She stared at him aghast. 'I can't. You know that.'

'Then this is all I have.'

He twirled her again and again. Cinnamon and cloves

filled her senses. The music filled her ears. And Hugo kept her close.

Dimly she knew other couples danced around them, but they were a blur of colour and then they were gone. Nobody mattered but the man holding her. She revelled in this moment in time. It was one more treasure to add to her memories, one more example of what he could do to her.

Annabell finally noticed they were no longer moving. His arm remained around her, and their bodies stayed too close for propriety. Her chest rose and fell in rapid gulps as she tried to regain her sangfroid.

'Hugo,' she finally managed, 'you are holding me too close.'

He released her and offered his arm. She wanted to refuse, fearing that touching him again would only make it that much harder to let him go in a few minutes. Or worse, that she would sway towards him, thus telling anyone who bothered to watch that she loved him. Still, appearances dictated that she put her fingertips on his forearm. She did so and he led her back to her seat where Mr Hawks waited.

She was surprised to see the other man. For some reason she had thought he would leave when he saw her with Hugo.

Mr Hawks gave her a reproachful look. 'You waltz very well, Lady Fenwick-Clyde.'

She remembered what she had told him less than thirty minutes before and had the grace to blush. 'Sometimes I surprise myself, Mr Hawks.'

'Of course,' he said courteously. He bowed and made his departure.

'Who is that?' Hugo's voice was low and ominous, nothing like the tone he normally used with her.

Annabell gave him a considering look. 'What is wrong?'

His mouth thinned. 'An upstart makes a comment to you that implies he has a right to an answer no man should have a right to, and you ask me what is wrong? Don't be naïve.'

Her eyes widened as realisation hit her. 'You are jealous.'

He drew himself up ramrod straight as though she had insulted him. 'Think what you please, but answer my question.'

His high-handed assumption that she would kowtow to him was too much. 'I think not, *Sir* Hugo.' She sniffed. 'It is not as though you have a right to know whom I see or speak with. You are—after all is said and done—engaged to another woman.'

His face darkened and his hands clenched and unclenched. 'How convenient for you.'

She fumed. 'And where is your lovely fiancée?'

His jaw clenched. 'She is over by the window.'

For a fleeting moment pain such as she had hoped never to experience again seared through her chest. 'Oh.' It was all she could do to get the single word past the tightness of her throat. She dared not cry here, in front of him.

She pulled in a deep breath, heard it wheeze through the contraction of pain, and looked where he indicated. Sardonic amusement bit between the strands of hurt she felt.

Lady Elizabeth Mainwaring was gazing raptly up into the golden-skinned face of a man who had the bearing and gifts of a Greek Adonis. His hair was as gold as the sun, and even from this distance Annabell could see the intense flash of his blue eyes. His shoulders were broad in the formal black coat with tails and his legs were long and well muscled in the black breeches and white stockings. Whatever was going on?

'Who is the gentleman with her?' She turned back to watch Hugo.

'That is St. Cyrus,' her former lover said drily. 'He shared Elizabeth's favours with me for some time.'

Annabell gasped, not certain she had heard correctly. Lady Mainwaring had said he might have known, but for some reason, Annabell had preferred to think he had not.

'What? What did you say?'

His mouth curled. 'You heard me. Elizabeth was bedding him while she was also sleeping with me.'

'And you didn't care?'

After the jealousy he had just demonstrated over her, she found it hard to believe he would countenance a woman of his choosing seeing another man, no matter what Lady Mainwaring had said. He had definitely made it plain he would not willingly allow her to do so.

He shrugged. 'I didn't really care. My liaison with Elizabeth was for one thing and one thing only. I never wanted or expected anything else. If she chose to see someone else as well, as long as it didn't interfere with my pleasure, then she was free to do so.'

'Like a marriage of convenience without the marriage.' It was a bald statement, but his words had been so matter of fact, nearly callous, that her description seemed perfect.

'Exactly.'

'Then it doesn't bother you that they're together now?'

He pinned her with his gaze. 'No, it does not. I'm with you, and even if I weren't, it still wouldn't bother me.'

A shiver ran up Annabell's spine. He was so cold, nothing like the man she had fallen in love with. 'I see.'

'Do you?'

He still would not let her look away; the intensity in his eyes and the aching sharpness of his features held her. 'I don't know, Hugo. I would hope your marriage would turn out to be more than an arrangement to give a child a name.'

His laugh was a harsh sound. 'The child may not even be mine.'

She stilled. Surely Lady Mainwaring had not told him what she had spoken about on the veranda? The woman was not stupid. She tore her gaze away from Hugo to look at the couple. Yet, Lady Mainwaring was obviously hanging on every word St. Cyrus said. He must be the man she loved who did not love her. For a brief moment, she pitied the beautiful Lady Mainwaring.

'Look at me, Bell,' Hugo ordered.

When she did not, he reached for her, but caught himself in time. She finally turned back to him. 'Do you really believe you might not be the father?'

He shrugged. 'It is possible. As you know, I take precautions. Not every man does.'

She flushed. 'Hush, Hugo. There are people around us.'

He glanced around, a haughty look on his face that dared someone to approach them. No one did. 'They are too far away to hear what we are saying, and if you do not give us away with your blushes they will never know.'

She continued to look at him, not sure if his blunt speaking was irritating her or if she was just in a bad mood because of the entire situation she found herself in. She decided it was a combination of everything.

'Very well, Hugo. I will try and control my body better.' She did not try to keep the trace of sarcasm from her tone.

He sighed. 'I am sorry, Bell. I do not like this situation any better than you do. I wish there was some way I could find out if St. Cyrus is really the father but, short of Elizabeth telling me that, I can't. I even—' he looked from her to the couple '—brought her with me tonight, hoping he would be here and she would go to him—as she has.'

Annabell laid a cautioning hand on his arm before she realised it. He looked down at where she touched him and she jerked away.

'This is not the place, Hugo, no matter if no one is near. What you are talking about is too private, too important.'

He sighed in exasperation. 'You are right. What do you suggest?'

She bit her lip. There was no easy answer. No right answer. She wanted to see him, and she wanted to talk this through. More than anything she wished Elizabeth Mainwaring carried St. Cyrus's child and could be brought to admit it—provided the woman even knew. But to see Hugo in private—that was risking much.

'I…' she took a deep breath and let it out in a rush as she spoke '…I don't think we should see each other again. What you are talking about is between you and Lady Mainwaring. I have nothing to do with it. If, by some chance, she calls off your engagement, then…then I no longer know.'

She could see that her answer angered him. His eyes narrowed and his mouth thinned.

'Annabell,' Dominic said imperiously, 'it is time to take Miss Lucy home.' His face hardened as he glanced at Sir Hugo.

She nodded, casting one last look at Hugo. His face was stony, but he said nothing. She followed Dominic and Miss Lucy from the rooms.

Hugo watched her go and wondered that it could bother him so much to see her and not possess her. He had never felt this way. And now, he had lost her and all because of past indiscretions.

He watched his fiancée with the man he knew she preferred and wondered if Elizabeth had approached St. Cyrus and been denied. From the look on her face and the way her body swayed toward him, she wanted him.

He turned his attention to St. Cyrus. The man was a dandy, but had also been a soldier and done well from all reports. He was considered a man of honour. Then why would he not take on the burden of marriage to Elizabeth? Because she did not think he was the father. That was all he could think of.

He no longer wanted to stay. It was hot and too many dowagers with their wagging tongues watched him. He made his decision.

He sauntered toward Elizabeth and her companion, nodding to acquaintances but keeping his expression closed. The last thing he wanted was to be approached and forced into conversation. That was not his purpose for being here.

He reached the two and drawled, 'Elizabeth, St. Cyrus, I

believe it is time to leave. Anyone who is anyone already has.'

Elizabeth's violet eyes sparked and she opened her mouth in what Hugo knew would be a protest. St. Cyrus laid his hand lightly on her arm for a moment, no longer, and she composed herself. Interesting.

'I believe you are correct, Sir Hugo,' the other man said. 'I was just telling Lady Mainwaring that I must be leaving. I have another engagement.'

Elizabeth's cupid-bow mouth thinned, but that was the only sign that she was not happy. Hugo found himself admiring her ability to keep her feelings to herself. It was a skill he had always prided himself on possessing. Now it seemed he was slipping. He did not like that.

He extended his arm. 'If you will, Elizabeth? My carriage should be brought 'round shortly.' He nodded to St. Cyrus. 'I hope to see you around.'

St. Cyrus bowed to Elizabeth and nodded to Hugo. 'I am sure of it. We do frequent the same clubs.'

Hugo studied the other man for a long minute, wondering if there was more to his words. When St. Cyrus remained sanguine, he decided the man meant exactly what he said. Apparently he had shared Elizabeth's bed simply for the pleasure with no emotional ties. Just as he had. Hugo almost found it in himself to feel sorry for her. And he might have, if she had not picked him to be her sacrificial goat.

He nodded curtly to St. Cyrus, put a palm to the small of Elizabeth's back and escorted her outside to his closed carriage. He helped her into the carriage but, instead of joining her, closed the door and rapped on the side of the vehicle, telling the coachman to take her home. Here in London, Elizabeth stayed in her own town house.

She stuck her head out of the window the instant she realised what he was about. 'What are you doing?'

He looked at her beautiful face, so perfect in every detail even though she was pouting. 'I am doing as I please, Elizabeth. We may be engaged, but that does not require me to squire you everywhere.'

It was obvious from the pinched look around her mouth that his words did not make her happy. Instead of replying, she dropped the curtain back into place and closed the window with a snick of the latch.

Hugo watched the coach until it turned the corner and was lost to sight. There was nothing for him at home and he was not sleepy. Nor did he intend to share Elizabeth's bed, even though she had indicated that he would be welcome. Of course, her invitation had come before she had met St. Cyrus again.

He would go on to Brooks's. Of all the clubs he belonged to, it was his favourite. And the walk to St. Timothy's Street would do him good. He was still tense from the encounter with Bell.

He set off, swinging his ebony cane with an occasional swat at nothing simply because he needed to do something or he would explode. She was the only woman who had ever made him care if he never saw her again. And he'd be damned if he wouldn't. Even if he did end up married to Elizabeth, he would see Bell. It would be better if he could find something to link St. Cyrus to Elizabeth's current state, but he had a feeling that information would have to come from the man.

Watching Elizabeth with St. Cyrus had told him much about their relationship. St. Cyrus was the dominant one. He would be the one to determine if there was more to their liaison than shared passion.

Rain started and Hugo picked up his pace.

A night ending with gambling and drinking. It could be worse. He could be in his bed alone.

Tomorrow he would call on Bell whether she liked it or not. He would also arrange to meet up with St. Cyrus.

Chapter Eighteen

Annabell sat stiffly in the carriage and wished she had never agreed to accompany Dominic and the simpering Miss Lucy to Almack's. And from the look on her brother's face, he was going to set into her as soon as they left Miss Lucy on her doorstep. Well, he had another thing coming if he thought anything he said would make a difference. Dominic was everything he accused Hugo of being, and he was younger.

In the meantime, she had to sit and watch the two. The chit blushed and giggled. Dominic barely skirted the edge of propriety. No wonder Emily Duckworth was beside herself. Annabell wasn't sure if she wanted this spectacle to end so she would not have to agonise over what was going on or if she dreaded the end of this little trip because then she would have to listen to Dominic's tirade.

Either way, they arrived at Miss Lucy's London residence and Dominic helped the chit from the carriage and walked her to the front door. Annabell winced when he raised the girl's gloved hand to his lips and instead of kissing the back of her hand, turned it over and kissed her wrist. Very Continental and calculated to further ensnare a girl as susceptible as Miss Lucy appeared to be.

As soon as the chit was in the door and he turned around,

the smile left Dominic's face. Annabell was tempted to signal the coachman to drive away. It wouldn't hurt Dominic to walk home. But she hesitated and the chance was lost.

He climbed in, then sprawled across the seat opposite her, his relaxed pose at direct odds with the look on his face. She knew him well enough to know he was ready to explode with fury.

'What did you think you were doing, dancing with that man?'

She kept her countenance bland. 'Do you mean Sir Hugo? Or Mr Hawks?'

Through clenched teeth he said, 'You know exactly whom I mean, Bell. Don't try my patience.'

'Don't try yours?' She leaned forward. 'What about you trying mine? What I do is none of your business, Dominic. I don't care that you are my brother. I am a widow and older than you. And…' she paused ominously '…my reputation is considerably better than yours.'

He wagged one finger at her. 'Don't drag my reputation into this, Bell. It has nothing to do with your association with Sir Hugo Fitzsimmon. The man will ruin you—you won't be accepted anywhere in polite society.'

She sniffed. 'I don't see that it has harmed Felicia not to be accepted by the sticklers. Nor would it bother me. I never go about in society as it is. I only went tonight to give poor Emily Duckworth a reprieve from seeing you seduce her young, silly sister.'

'Don't bring Miss Sourpuss into this either,' he retorted.

'I can't imagine why you call Emily Duckworth such an uncomplimentary name. She has done nothing to you.'

He scowled. 'Don't change the subject. This discussion is about you and Sir Hugo. If you don't value your reputation, then at least show some pride. The man is engaged to be married. Rumour says Elizabeth Mainwaring is carrying his child. If that is so, and I don't doubt it since the two have been lovers for at least a year that I know of, then the last thing you should be doing is throwing yourself at him.'

Her scathing reply died before she could even think what it was going to be. She turned away from her brother's all-too-discerning gaze. The last thing she wanted was to cry in front of Dominic. She had become a watering pot and what for? A man she could never have and wasn't even sure she would marry if she could have him. Not that he had asked. But… Damnation, she was a mess.

'Bell?' Dominic's voice had softened. 'What is the matter?'

She took a deep steadying breath. 'Nothing, Dominic. I am merely tired…from being out later than usual and from arguing with you.' She pushed back a strand of hair that had come loose from the elaborate braid circling the back of her head. 'Please, no more talk. You are perfectly right about Sir Hugo and I know that. All right.'

He sat up. 'You agree?' His voice held incredulity.

She sighed wearily. 'Yes, I agree. Can we let it go?'

'Then you won't see him again, and you definitely won't dance with him again?'

She would have smiled at his persistence if she hadn't been so tired of it all. 'I very likely won't see him again, and I'm positive I won't be in another situation where the opportunity to dance with him will arise.'

He opened his mouth to say something, but she held her hand up to stop him. 'No, Dominic, some promises are better not made.'

He shook his head. 'You always were stubborn to a fault, Bell.'

She raised one slashing black brow. 'And you aren't?'

He laughed. 'I believe it is a family trait. If I remember correctly, both our parents were burdened with it.'

'At least we come by it honestly, as the saying goes.'

Fortunately the carriage pulled to a stop in front of Guy's town house before Dominic could start berating her again.

She slid to the door, opened it and clambered out before he or a servant could help her. The last thing she intended to do was give him the opportunity to take her arm and keep her captive while he continued his rant.

The next morning, Annabell entered the sunlight-flooded breakfast room with less than her customary appetite. Oswald stood near the sideboard, waiting to hear whether she wanted tea or hot chocolate, but instead of his normal welcome, he looked uncomfortable.

'Good morning, Oswald.' She smiled at him and took the chair held by the footman. 'I won't be needing ser— What is this? An old copy of *The Times?*'

Oswald cleared his throat. 'Mr Dominic left it for you.'

Unease settled into Annabell's shoulders. She picked the paper up and realised it was only a page showing the engagement announcements. One of them was circled. *Sir Hugo Fitzsimmon announces his engagement to Lady Elizabeth Mainwaring.*

Ten simple words.

Annabell closed her eyes and felt the tension move to her stomach. She took a deep breath. This was not the time or the place. Please, don't let her cry.

She placed her hands flat on the table and pushed herself to a standing position. She felt like an old woman, aged before her time.

'I believe I will have tea in my rooms, Oswald. Nothing to eat.'

To give him credit, the old family retainer merely said, 'Yes, Miss Annabell.'

She couldn't even look at him for fear she would see pity on his face and that it would be her undoing. She walked from the room, back straight.

She managed to reach her rooms.

Why seeing the announcement had bothered her so much, she couldn't say. It was nothing but words. And she had known about the engagement. Had known about it for far longer than the announcement had been public. But there was a finality to the written word that the spoken word did not share. Perhaps that was it.

Either way, it did not matter. Seeing the announcement in black and white negated any hope she had sustained the night before. Hugo might find out that Elizabeth Mainwaring's child was not his, but it was too late. He had already placed the announcement in *The Times*. Only a scoundrel would cry off after that, and whatever else Hugo was—and he was many less than savoury things—he was not a scoundrel or a loose screw. He would not break the engagement.

Lady Mainwaring would have to do that.

The following afternoon, Hugo knocked at Viscount Chillings's town house. The door was opened by a very proper butler who looked him up and down.

'Yes, my lord?'

Hugo handed over his card. 'Please let Lady Fenwick-Clyde know Sir Hugo Fitzsimmon is here to see her.'

The butler's eyes widened a fraction, but his voice remained completely noncommittal. 'Please come in, my lord.'

Hugo entered the hall and handed his beaver hat to the waiting servant. 'Come this way, please, my lord.'

He followed the butler to the drawing room where he was left. There was a portrait over the mantel of Annabell and her brothers. There was a marked resemblance between her and Viscount Chillings. He vaguely remembered hearing they were twins. The younger man also had a likeness of them, but where their hair was silvery blond, his was black as night. And there was a mischief in his eyes that was missing in the others.

'Damn if it isn't you,' a male voice said.

Hugo turned to see the younger man standing in the doorway. His black brows were drawn together.

'Dominic Chillings.' Hugo kept his voice pleasant even though he sensed the man's anger. 'Pleased to see you again.'

'Well, I am not pleased to see you. Nor do I intend to let you see my sister. She is better off without you.' Dominic paced into the room, his very posture a challenge. 'Go back to your fiancée.'

Hugo stood his ground. 'I am here to see your sister, not you. And I believe she is old enough—and independent enough—to do as she damn well pleases.'

'Well, she won't wish to see you or even hear from you when she learns what's been written in the betting book at Brooks's.'

Surprised, Hugo asked, 'What do you mean?'

Dominic scowled. 'Don't play the innocent with me, Fitzsimmon. It doesn't sit well on a man of your ilk.'

Hugo took a deep breath and reined in his rising temper. 'I have only been in town two days. I stopped briefly at Brooks's last night, but did not stay late. I didn't look in the betting book and no one mentioned it to me.'

Dominic sneered. 'Then the bet must have been placed some time between when you left and this afternoon when I was there for lunch. Not much time.'

'And just what bet are you referring to?'

Dominic's voice lowered ominously. 'The one that reads: *What knight is engaged to one woman who carries his child while in love with another? A monkey he jilts the one to have the other.*'

'You jest.'

'Not about my sister.' Dominic's voice was as cold as Hugo's.

There was a cold pit in Hugo's stomach. That was exactly what some cur who imagined himself to be a wit would write. And it was close to the truth. Too close.

'Bloody cur,' Hugo growled.

'My sentiments exactly,' Dominic said. 'And it is all because of you.'

'Perhaps no one knows who the blackguard is referring to.' Even as he said the words, Hugo knew it couldn't be true. The bet was too precise.

'Not after the way you behaved at Almack's last night.'

Hugo had never before regretted any of his actions. Not even having Elizabeth Mainwaring for a lover. But he regretted this. And the realisation surprised him.

'So,' Dominic continued, 'I want you to leave this house, and I don't ever want to see you near my sister again or I will be forced to call you out. Do I speak plainly enough, Fitzsimmon?'

'Perfectly.'

Hugo bit the word off, wondering who infuriated him more, the worthless cad who had placed the bet or the young man who stood defiantly before him. Both had made it impossible for him to continue pursuing Annabell, something he knew he should stop. If only he could. Nor could he duel with this young hothead. Annabell would never forgive him if he hurt her brother. But he could find out who had written in the betting book.

'Whatever is going on here?' Annabell demanded from the drawing-room door.

Hugo spun around. He had not heard her come in and, from the look on his face, neither had Dominic.

'Nothing,' both men said at once.

Annabell came nearer, a suspicious look on her face. 'Then why do both of you look like little boys caught with your fingers in the biscuit tin?'

Hugo looked at Dominic, who was looking at him. For once they both had a common goal, to keep the sordid truth from Annabell.

'I was telling Fitzsimmon to be off,' Dominic said. 'Told him you didn't wish to see a man who was engaged to another woman.'

Much as the words irritated him, Hugo had to admire Dominic's quick thinking. She would believe that and it was the truth.

'And I was telling him that I wanted to hear you dismiss me yourself.'

She looked from Dominic to him. 'He is right. I don't wish to see you.'

Her words hurt more than he would have expected. He had thought the musket ball in his thigh had been painful, but it had been nothing compared to this. This went deeper than physical agony. But he knew she was right. He needed to leave her alone. If he continued this, someone would notice and her name would eventually be dragged through the worst the *ton* had to offer.

He kept his gaze on her as he bowed. 'I won't bother you again, Lady Fenwick-Clyde.'

Her eyes widened slightly as though she had not expected him to agree so readily. His mouth twisted. She did not know about the bet. Were it not for that, he would not have accepted her dismissal so quickly. He would not have accepted it at all.

He took his leave before she could pry deeper. Better to never see her again than to drag her through the gutter. A nearly impossible decision to make, but a necessary one for her sake.

Hugo made his way to Brooks's. It was early, but the betting book was always there. Perhaps there was a clue that would tell him who would do such a despicable thing. And there would undoubtedly be members there just to get away from home.

He signalled his tiger and jumped into the seat of his high-perch phaeton. With an accomplished flick of the wrist, he set his pair in motion. At St Timothy's, he pulled to the curb and waited for the tiger to go to the horses' heads before getting out.

'I probably won't be in very long, John. Don't go far.'

'Yes, sir.' He took the reins and started walking the team up the road. He would continue to do so until Hugo returned.

Hugo entered the cool, dark club and handed his beaver and cane to a waiting footman. 'Brandy.'

'Yes, sir.'

The man left and Hugo went into the central room where the bulk of the gambling was done. The long crimson curtains were closed. The chandelier provided enough light for gambling and reading the papers.

He found the betting book and opened it to the last page. The bet was even uglier in writing than it had been coming from Dominic Chillings's mouth. He set the book down and his fists clenched till the knuckles turned white. He looked around, wondering if any of the people here were responsible. A few men watched him surreptitiously. No one came over.

The servant found him sitting in one of the corners, his feet stretched out in a pose of seeming nonchalance. He was far from it.

'Thank you,' Hugo said, pouring a generous measure.

Someone was going to lose a great deal of money. Much as he didn't want to marry Elizabeth Mainwaring, he was going to. As for Annabell, he hadn't asked her to him marry even before this fiasco, and she would have told him no if he had.

He downed the brandy and poured more.

'Mind if I join you?'

Hugo looked up, starting at the interloper's immaculately polished Hessians, past a perfectly fitted jacket that even Beau Brummell could not have found fault with, to the intensely brilliant blue eyes of St. Cyrus. He did mind, but shrugged.

St. Cyrus took that as permission. 'Mind if I share?'

Hugo took another drink and eyed the other man. 'Yes.'

St. Cyrus's chin jerked a little, but he waved to a servant. 'Bring me a bottle of whatever this is.'

'Brandy,' Hugo said.

'Brandy.'

Hugo waited St. Cyrus out. They were not friends, nor had they served together during Waterloo. In short, with the exception of Elizabeth Mainwaring, they had nothing in common.

The second bottle of brandy arrived and St. Cyrus poured a glass and drank the contents in one gulp, his Adam's apple bobbing behind the intricate folds of his cravat. He set the empty glass down and turned to face Hugo.

'Your engagement to Lady Mainwaring was sudden.'

Hugo took another drink, wondering where this was going. 'It depends on how you look at it.'

St. Cyrus took a sip of his brandy. 'Perhaps. She had barely returned from Paris when it was announced.'

'True.' Hugo angled to look at the other man. 'However, it is none of your business.'

St. Cyrus set his glass down sharply. 'Are you sure?'

'The lady assures me that it is so.'

'And you believe her?'

Hugo looked away, checking to ensure no one was close by. Their discussion was private and, if overheard, damaging to Elizabeth's good name, or what she had of one. Still, in spite of the situation, he did not want her hurt. He turned back.

'Shouldn't I?'

St. Cyrus's perfect features reddened. Hugo eyed the man sardonically, wondering how indiscreet he would be.

St. Cyrus cleared his throat. 'I think the lady might have acted in haste.'

Hugo's heart lurched. Surely he had not heard what he thought he had heard. Elizabeth had led him to believe she had already spoken with St. Cyrus.

'Really?'

It was hard to keep his mounting interest out of his voice, but if St. Cyrus was about to admit to something, he did not want to scare him off by seeming too eager. He took another drink.

St. Cyrus had stopped drinking. 'It is very possible.'

Hugo chose his next words with care. 'Then what do you intend to do about it?'

'I have arranged to speak with her this evening. At the theatre.'

Hugo started. 'I am taking her there.'

St. Cyrus had the grace to look uncomfortable. 'I know, but…'

She had sent St. Cyrus a note. Hugo's mouth twisted. 'I see. That is not a very private place.'

'No, it is not.' St. Cyrus's hands clenched on his thighs. 'That is why I wanted to speak with you. It is a stroke of luck to find you here.'

'It is the stroke of a very malicious pen,' Hugo muttered.

'I beg your pardon?'

Hugo eyed him with dislike. 'The betting book. Perhaps you even wrote it.'

St. Cyrus drew himself up straight. 'I am not in the habit of writing in the blasted thing.'

Hugo snorted. 'From what you have hinted at these past minutes, you would certainly stand to gain if the bet came true.'

St. Cyrus's eyes turned frosty. 'I will see what you are talking about.'

Hugo shrugged. 'As you wish.'

He watched the other man make his way to the infamous book, and wondered what was going on. From the implications of the conversation, St. Cyrus was not happy that Elizabeth was engaged to someone besides himself. Interesting.

St. Cyrus read the last page, and Hugo saw his elegant body stiffen. The other man swept his cold gaze around the room. No one looked at him. So, Hugo decided, St. Cyrus was not the target of the bet, nor was he the perpetrator—unless he was a superb actor.

St. Cyrus stalked back to the seat beside Hugo. 'When I find out who wrote that, I will see to it that he does not write anything else.'

'My sentiments exactly.' Hugo was mildly surprised to see that he and St. Cyrus could agree on something besides bedding Elizabeth Mainwaring.

'But for different reasons, I would wager.'

Hugo watched the other man through narrowed eyes. 'For the nonce, my reasons are my own.'

'Understood.' St. Cyrus stood. 'I will be calling at your box tonight.'

Hugo nodded. He had a season box at Covent Garden. Juliet used it more than he, but he got it every year.

He watched St. Cyrus leave, wondering what would come of this. And what would he do if St. Cyrus did ask Elizabeth to marry him? Would he ask Bell to wed him? He didn't know.

That evening, Hugo sat in his box and looked casually around the theatre. As usual, all the *ton* had come to Covent Garden Theatre. The boxes were full and the pit was crowded. The women were in evening gowns and masses of jewellery. The men had their quizzing glasses raised. At least, a quizzing glass was one affectation he did not aspire to.

He heard Elizabeth flick open her fan. 'La, Hugo, it is hot in here. Would you get me something to drink?'

He turned to her. As usual, she was stunning. She wore a black evening dress with white trim of some sort. The neck scooped low to show her milky breasts. And there was a brightness in her eyes and a flush on her fair complexion. His mouth twisted sardonically. She was excited about St. Cyrus's visit. Far be it from him to interfere.

'Of course, Elizabeth.' Hugo rose to leave.

She nodded graciously. 'Take your time.'

Even as she spoke to him, her eyes scanned the nearby boxes with an eagerness that was almost painful to watch. He was not accustomed to seeing her expose her emotions openly. For the first time since this fiasco began, he felt sorry for Elizabeth. She might have created this intolerable situation, but she was no more happy than he.

Hugo bowed and left, swinging his ebony cane jauntily. With luck and another man's jealousy, tonight might see him a free man.

With that thought, Hugo searched to see if Annabell was here. There was no reason to believe she would be since she was not at all interested in society and where it congregated. Still, he would like to see her, and if she was here he would go so far as to visit her. Nothing ventured, nothing gained.

He found her. She was across the theatre in a box with a group that included Dominic Chillings, Miss Emily Duckworth, who looked as though she had just eaten a lemon, and her sister, Miss Lucy. He would wager the tension in that box could be cut with a knife.

Without pausing to consider his actions, Hugo made his way to the box and knocked. Dominic Chillings came to the door and stepped out.

'You are not wanted, Fitzsimmon.'

'By you or your sister?' Hugo asked coolly.

'Both.'

Hugo looked the younger man in the eye. There was a belligerent set to Dominic Chillings's jaw that spoke of determination. If he forced the issue, Annabell's brother would be glad to help him cause a scene. That was the last thing any of them needed. Nor was it fair to Annabell. She had already told him to leave her in peace. It was not her fault he was unable to do so.

Hugo took a deep breath and made himself do the right

thing. 'I will leave for now.' He didn't bow, but pivoted on his heel and sauntered away, working to keep the simmering irritation he felt from showing. It was bad enough that anyone watching had seen him turned away. Now the gossip-mongers would have a feast, but at least it was no worse. There would be no challenge to titillate everyone.

He paused and looked at his own box, which was in the first circle. St. Cyrus was there. He and Elizabeth had their heads together. She even had her hand on his forearm. They were so obviously a couple that Hugo decided to leave. St. Cyrus would see Elizabeth home—his or hers. It didn't matter. All he wanted was a note telling him the engagement was off because she was to marry St. Cyrus.

Nothing else mattered.

Chapter Nineteen

Hugo found it impossible to sleep after the theatre. He paced his room and dozed, with more pacing than dozing. Morning couldn't come soon enough. Having never really slept, when morning finally arrived Hugo found himself even more impatient, if that were possible.

Now he had to wait until afternoon when Elizabeth would be up. He knew from the past that she was not an early riser. And then he would have to be patient and see if she would send for him.

And what if she didn't?

He wouldn't think about that. She would or she wouldn't. If she did, then he would be free to go to Annabell. If she didn't, he would marry a woman he didn't love because of a child he might or might not have fathered. Simple, no matter how the second action would hurt.

Half past noon, Butterfield knocked on the library door. 'Excuse me, sir, but there is a message for you.'

'Thank you.'

Hugo jumped up from the leather wing chair he had been lounging in, trying to read and being unsuccessful. As at Rosemont, the library here was also his favourite room. He liked books and maps. Always had.

He picked up the sheet of paper, which was sealed with red wax. The scent of tuberose engulfed him. Relief eased the tension in his shoulders.

Opening the note, he read: *Dearest Hugo, please call on me immediately. I have something of great importance to tell you. EM.*

He tore the sheet into pieces and threw them on the grate. When the fire was lit this evening, the paper would be ashes. He trusted his servants, but this was a private matter.

'Butterfield, have my carriage brought 'round.'

'Yes, sir.' There was only a hint of curiosity in the old retainer's eyes.

'Don't worry, old man, you will know soon enough.'

Hugo could no longer go to Butterfield with his trials and tribulations, but he still cared for the man. And he knew Butterfield had been troubled by his engagement, although the butler had never said a word.

'Yes, sir.'

Hugo smiled. 'Where is Jamison? I need a coat at the very least.'

'I believe he is upstairs, but he could also be out.'

'True,' Hugo said, more amused than irritated at the possibility. 'He does like London and all the possibilities it provides.'

He went up the stairs two at a time. He should have put a coat on first thing upon dressing, but it was hotter than normal today and he liked his comfort before he cared for fashion.

He entered his chamber. 'Jamison.'

When the valet didn't appear, Hugo went to the dressing room and found a bottle-green coat. He shrugged into it, thankful he did not believe in tailoring to the point that he needed help to dress. He didn't always cut a dash, but then his lack of polish had never hurt him either.

He went down the stairs as quickly as he had gone up

them. His phaeton waited. He jumped up, took the reins and signalled the tiger to get into position.

He found himself more anxious by the minute. What if he was mistaken and Elizabeth had not summoned him to release him from their engagement? What would he do then? He would deal with that if and when it happened. There was no point in borrowing trouble.

He consciously relaxed his shoulders and made himself pay attention to his driving. The streets were busy as usual at this time of year, and he did not want to cause an accident or be in one of another person's making.

He reached Elizabeth's town house and gave the reins to his tiger. 'Walk them. I might be a while.'

Not waiting for a reply, Hugo ran up the front steps and rapped. Elizabeth's butler was prompt.

'Good afternoon, Sir Hugo,' the butler said. 'Her ladyship is expecting you.'

'Hello, Edwards.'

He followed the butler in and was shown to the drawing room. It was done in the Egyptian motif of several seasons before. He had always thought the drama of it was the perfect foil for Elizabeth, who could be quite dramatic if she felt it suited her.

'Sir Hugo Fitzsimmon,' the butler announced.

Hugo walked in and immediately saw Elizabeth by the window. She sat stiffly in one of the very uncomfortable settees. She was obviously as unsettled as he was. But there was a glow about her face that told him she was either excited or happy—probably both.

'Elizabeth,' he said, coming to a halt in front of her. 'Is something the matter?'

He sounded inane, but he was afraid to say anything that might worsen the situation. He was suddenly very aware that he wanted her to break their engagement more than he had ever wanted anything in his life—with the exception of Annabell. Nothing had prepared him for what Annabell had come to mean to him.

Even now, the realisation stunned him and he missed Elizabeth's first words.

'—so, you see, I think it for the best.' There was such hope in her eyes that Hugo's hopes soared.

'Pardon me, Elizabeth, but I was not paying proper attention. Would you please repeat what you just said?'

He had never been this gauche, and he would have been ashamed if he were not so nervous. But he wanted this so badly.

She gave him a cold look. 'Do you need to sit, Hugo?'

'No.'

She licked her full, red lips. 'Well, I just told you St. Cyrus has asked me to marry him.'

Hugo sat. It was either that or shout for joy. He was a free man. But he did his best to keep his spirits under control. It would not be right to parade his relief in front of her.

'And what did you say?' he asked, careful to keep his voice pleasantly curious only.

She tilted her head to one side. 'Hugo, aren't you happy? I thought you surely would be.'

'That depends on what you told him, Elizabeth. If you remember, you told me I am the father of your child.'

He couldn't keep a slight tinge of irony from his words. Happy as he was to know his freedom was in sight, he still harboured a little bitterness about the situation her demands had created. Annabell had been hurt. She might refuse to take him back, and he couldn't blame her.

'You are not making this easy, Hugo.'

'Should everything be easy for you, Elizabeth?'

She had the grace to blush. 'I suppose not.' She took a deep breath and determination settled over her like a mantle. 'I told St. Cyrus yes.'

'Is he the father of your child?'

Why he was pursuing this, Hugo didn't know, but he was piqued that she had nearly ruined his life and Annabell's and now she acted as though nothing had happened.

She shrugged. 'He might be as easily as you. Probably more so for the reason you and I have previously discussed.' Her blush deepened.

'Ah, protection,' Hugo said softly.

'Hugo!'

He eyed her. 'Does he know the situation?'

She nodded. 'He is willing to raise the child as his.' Her face took on a blissful look. 'He loves me. I didn't believe so when we parted on the Continent.' Now she looked the tiniest bit sorry. 'That is why I sent for you.'

Hugo just looked at her. His joy at being released was like a balloon that threatened to explode if he wasn't careful. But at the same time, his irritation with her was not easily put aside and it made his voice crueller than it should have been.

'I was your ace in the hole.'

'To put it crudely, yes.'

'Then you will send a retraction to *The Times*.' He made it a statement.

'Yes. You are free to marry your Annabell, Hugo.'

He stood and looked down at her, ignoring her last words. What he intended to do was none of her business. 'I wish you the best.'

'Goodbye,' she said softly to his back.

Hugo did not look back.

Annabell sat by the front window, watching the pedestrians: men in beaver hats and spotless coats, women in walking dresses. Occasionally a maid scurried on her mistress's errand. Sometimes a nanny with several children in tow passed.

The last reminded her of Joseph and Rosalie. She wondered how they were doing, and Juliet. She smiled, but it was melancholy. She would very likely see them again. Unless she missed her guess, her stepson intended to wed Lady Fitzsimmon.

She sighed and rose. It was time to dress for the lecture at the Society of Antiquaries. Mr Jeffrey Studivant was presenting his paper on *her* Roman villa, a follow up on the first paper she had presented several weeks ago.

She moved slowly, determined not to think about what had been in yesterday's *Times*. Dominic had shown her.

She stopped and her heart thudded painfully. Lady Mainwaring had announced that her engagement to Sir Hugo Fitzsimmon was broken. Hugo was free. But he had not come to tell her even though the separation had to have happened several days before.

Had all his words, all his pursuit been nothing? She feared so.

She blinked, realised she had stopped moving, and forced herself to continue to the door. She needed to dress. She needed to go out so she would not sit here and descend into melancholy.

And to think she had wondered if she could have brought herself to marry Hugo, should he ever ask. She was a fool, a self-delusional fool. She loved him. It seemed she had loved him her entire life.

But he had not come for her.

The drawing-room door opened and Oswald stood there with a very pleased look on his face. 'Sir Hugo Fitzsimmon.'

Surely he jested. But, no, Hugo was right behind the butler. Her former lover strode into the room, and she wondered how she could have ever thought she would not have him if he offered. But he hadn't, so her fall from independence was immaterial.

She dredged up all her pride. 'Good afternoon, Sir Hugo.' She smiled, knowing it was thin and unwelcoming. 'I fear you have come at a bad time. I am just on my way out.'

He did not return her smile. 'What I have to say won't take long, Bell.'

She started at his use of her family name. 'Lady Fenwick-Clyde.'

He took a step nearer. 'Bell. My Lady Spitfire.'

She blanched and tried to walk around him, but he shifted so that she could not pass. Nor was there anyone to call for help. Coward that he was, Oswald had already left and closed the door behind him. He had known something was afoot. Where was Dominic when she needed him? Gone out with Lucy Duckworth.

She threw caution to the winds. 'Why are you here, Hugo? The announcement was yesterday.'

Nor could she keep the hurt and disappointment from her voice. That shamed her. She had fought for her independence and now she would gladly give it up. No, she would beg to give it up to Hugo. She shook her head and made herself stand tall and proud.

He closed the distance between them.

She edged away, not wanting him to touch her. Whenever he touched her she lost all resolve, no matter what her reason for resisting him might be. She had learned that lesson well during her stay at Rosemont and, later, here in London, that night at Almack's.

He moved with her. 'I couldn't come sooner, Bell.'

She frowned. 'Couldn't or wouldn't?'

The look he gave her was tender and loving. She wondered if her brain had gone soft as her body was threatening to do. Surely he was not looking at her the way she thought he was. If he were, he would have rushed to her as soon as he knew he was free—days ago.

'Wouldn't, Bell.'

She stared mutely at him, unable to speak. The last thing she wanted to do was cry in front of him. What had happened to all her independence, her determination to make a life without a man's hand on her? Gone. Lost the first time he kissed her, only she hadn't realised it then.

She lifted her chin. She could still be independent. She was strong. 'Please leave.'

She was proud her pain didn't show in the clipped words. She would get through this, just as she had gotten through his engagement to Elizabeth Mainwaring.

'Not until I ask you to marry me.'

'What?' Surely she hadn't heard him correctly.

'Marry me, Bell.'

His words were soft, almost hesitant. If she didn't know him better, she would think he was unsure of himself. Yet, there was that determined gleam in his green eyes.

She gaped at him, then anger came to her rescue and stiffened her resolve. 'Your jest is in poor taste, Sir Hugo.'

He shook his head, the too-long hair framing his sharp cheekbones. For a second he looked wild. 'No jest, Bell.' His magnificent lips curved. 'I have never jested with you. And I have never lied to you.'

She looked long and hard at him, searching for the truth of his words. She didn't think she could stand to be hurt by him again. She had only survived the last time because of her determination and strength. If he failed her again…

She sucked in air, wondering what would happen if the dizziness overtaking her won. She would fall to the floor and awaken later, remembering this only as a dream. She had longed so much for him to come to her like this.

'If you truly mean what you say, why did it take you so long?'

Now a little bit of her agony was in her voice. She flushed at the realisation that she was so vulnerable to this man, and she had let him know.

'Because I wanted you to have this when I proposed.'

He held out a velvet box. She shuddered.

'Another piece of jewellery?' Bitterness tinged her words. She drew back.

'Yes.' He closed the distance between them and fell to one knee, wincing.

Concern swelled up in her. 'Don't, Hugo. Your injury doesn't do well when you kneel. Please stand.'

He looked up at her and opened the box. Inside was a ring. A star sapphire, large as a pigeon's egg, surrounded by diamonds, winked up at her. It was large enough to span one knuckle.

'The Garibaldi engagement ring, my grandmother's gift to me. I want you to have it.'

She gasped, her left hand going to her throat where her pulse beat rapidly. The first words from her mouth were unintentional, but came from the depths of her hurt soul.

'That isn't the ring you gave Lady Mainwaring.'

'No,' he said, taking the ring from its satin bed. 'I would have never given it to her. She is not the bride of my heart. The ring is always given to a true love. That is why I'm giving it to you.'

The tears she had tried so hard to hold back welled up and over. They spilled silently down her cheeks. She couldn't stop them.

'Hugo.'

He caught her unresisting left hand and slipped the ring on to her finger. It fit perfectly.

'I love you, Bell,' he said simply, but there was such a wealth of emotion in the words that she could not doubt him.

She sank to her knees beside him.

He smiled tenderly at her. 'The sapphire came from India back in the late sixteen hundreds. It was given to one of my Garibaldi ancestors by a Maharaja as a token of esteem. Legend says that as long as the gem goes to a true love, that union will be blessed with happiness and many children. My ancestor had it made into an engagement ring.' He cupped her cheek with his hand, his thumb rubbing her bottom lip. 'I could have never given it to anyone but you, Bell.'

She kissed him gently at first, then more passionately. 'Hugo, I love you so much.'

He pulled away just enough to say, 'I know.'

Their wedding was a small affair, held in the small chapel at Rosemont. They had invited immediate family only, and Susan Pennyworth and Tatterly.

The minister beamed at the couple before him. 'You may place the ring on her finger.'

Hugo looked at Annabell as he slid the sapphire-studded wedding band on to her finger. 'I love you.'

The minister closed the Bible. 'I pronounce you man and wife.'

Annabell smiled at her husband. 'I love you forever.'

'Hear, hear,' Dominic Chillings's voice rose above the hearty clapping. 'Kiss her like you mean it, Fitzsimmon. No pecking. You put her through enough to get here.'

Hugo felt Annabell stiffen. He lifted his head enough to look at his brother-in-law. 'You are a reprobate, Dominic, but occasionally you do have a good idea.'

The other guests cheered.

Hugo turned back to his bride and smiled. 'Shall we show them how it's done?'

She blushed, but there was a glint in her eyes. 'By all means.'

He placed his mouth on hers and forgot the initial challenge as he fell into the passion and love they shared. Her lips opened and he plunged inside, wishing he could do more than kiss her. His body ached to do more.

When they came up for air, she was flushed and he was aroused. He buried his face in her hair and whispered, 'Thank goodness we are home and can go upstairs. I am about to embarrass myself.'

Her laugh was throaty and full of promise. 'We don't want that, love.'

He nipped her ear. 'No, we don't.'

He turned her to face their guests. Guy, Viscount Chillings, had given Annabell away. He stood to one side with Felicia and their very healthy baby son, Adam. Dominic was now heckling Susan Pennyworth, the future Mrs. Tatterly. Tatterly stood nearby, watching the byplay with a besotted look on his face. Juliet and the children beamed at him. Timothy, Lord Fenwick-Clyde, stood close. They had not announced their engagement, but Hugo sensed they would do so soon. He hoped they would find the same joy together that he had found with Annabell.

Hugo guided his bride through the well-wishers. Annabell glowed with happiness.

She turned to him, 'I am so glad we had our wedding here.' She looked around the chapel, decked out in the last of the summer roses. 'Rosemont has been like a home to me since I first came here.'

'Since you found that Roman villa here, you mean,' he teased.

'That too.' She smiled up at him.

'Here, here, you two,' Dominic said, closing the distance. 'Don't forget you have guests and we still have breakfast. Then you can show us around.'

Hugo shook his head. 'Not this time. We are too old to stand by society's practices.'

Dominic raised both brows. 'Really? Then what do you intend to do, leave us to our own devices? Hardly gracious.'

Hugo laughed. 'Too bad.'

'For that is exactly what we intend to do,' Annabell finished for her husband.

She wanted him as badly as he did her. They had remained chaste since their engagement, knowing the self-denial would make their wedding night all that more memorable.

Everyone had heard her words, but she did not care. There was clapping and a few indiscreet remarks followed.

'Not done, old fellow,' Dominic continued to press. 'The same to you, Annabell. You should be blushing from the top of your gown to the roots of your hair.'

She laughed. 'But I am, little brother.'

'Wait until you are wed,' Hugo said to Dominic. 'I venture to guess you will be even more impatient than we are.'

Dominic turned brick red as though Hugo had caught him in the act of something forbidden. Hugo gave him a speculative look, but said nothing. His brother-in-law would do whatever it was he intended to do. He knew the man well enough to know there would be no sense in prying.

Besides, he had other interests. He turned to Jamison, who had been his groomsman. 'Lady Fitzsimmon and I are retiring. See that no one disturbs us.'

'Yes, sir,' the valet replied, a twinkle in his eyes. 'I'll stand guard outside the door.'

'You don't need to go that far,' Annabell protested before seeing the mischievousness in Jamison's smile.

'Yes, my lady,' Jamison said, barely able to suppress his guffaw.

Hugo shook his head and propelled Annabell through the door and up the stairs before anything else was said. When they reached the door to his chambers, he stopped her.

'I intend to carry you over the threshold.'

She laughed. 'Absolutely not, Hugo. The last thing I want on our wedding day is to injure your leg.'

He dipped his head to kiss her. 'If I hurt that, it won't stop what I have in mind for this afternoon, evening and all day tomorrow.'

Her blush returned and her grin was wicked. 'No, but that would make it painful for you, my dear, since I intend to see that you live up to that boast.'

He opened the door, then swung her into his arms and carried her into the room and to the bed. He dumped her in the pile of silk and satin cushions where she lay very still, gazing up at him.

'I love you,' she said quietly, all of her previous humour gone. 'I love you so much it hurts.'

'And I you,' he said, meaning every word more than he had ever meant anything else in his life. 'Now and always.'

She sighed and reached for him.

He went to her.

When they lay naked in the sheets, he caught her bottom lip with his thumb and rubbed. 'I want to remember this for the rest of our lives.'

She twinned her arms around his neck. He meant so much to her. 'We will, love. We will.'

He gazed at her with more love in his heart than he had ever imagined himself capable of. Then he kissed her, deeply and passionately. She opened to him.

Annabell revelled in the desire he always ignited in her. With him she felt that anything was possible. She stroked the unruly hair from his face and dug her fingers into the silken strands to hold him to her.

He drank in her bounty, his hands cupping her breasts. His fingers stroked her swollen flesh until her nipples hardened and she gasped. He ached for her, ached so it hurt.

She rubbed one hand down the back of his neck to his shoulders, marvelling in the muscles that rippled beneath his skin. Her fingers raked gently down the ridges bracketing his spine. He was so strong and so beautiful in his masculinity.

He broke away from her lips and gave her his rakish smile. 'You are mine.'

When her slumberous eyes opened and her moist mouth smiled, he thought he would lose control. His manhood strained against the slight swell of her stomach. But he wasn't ready to enter her yet.

Annabell saw the passion in his eyes and felt her stomach

twist as sensation started radiating through her. She was more than ready for him. She moved her hips suggestively.

'Not yet,' he murmured, kissing her chin lightly in passing.

He nuzzled the sensitive skin on the side of her neck and down to the hollow at the base of her throat. His hands shifted downward, skimming over her ribs and abdomen. He felt her nails dig into his hips and knew he was exciting her. He chuckled low in his throat.

Then his mouth was at her breast and he sucked powerfully so her back arched and a small whimper came from deep in her chest. He continued to pull and nip while his fingers moved inexorably lower. When he entered her, she was moist.

Pleasure filled him. He wanted her to remember their first time together since being wed. He wanted that so badly that he could postpone his own release until he had completely satiated her.

Annabell felt his fingers inside her and thought she would explode. She gasped and tingles started at the small of her back and rushed outwards. She gripped him tightly, urging him deeper. Her mind grew fuzzy and the only thing that mattered was what he was doing to her.

She was on the brink when he withdrew. She gasped, 'Hugo.'

'Easy, my love. I won't leave you like this. I promise.' He kissed her mouth lightly, then deeper. 'I want you to remember this time for the rest of your life.'

Tears welled up and she did nothing to stop them. 'You make me so happy.'

'Don't cry, my love,' he murmured, licking one salty drop from her cheek. 'This is only the beginning.'

She nodded and pulled his lips back to hers. 'Always.'

He sank into her embrace, his body over hers. When her legs opened, and his hips settled, he was lost. 'I am sorry,

Bell,' he gasped. 'I had wanted this to last longer, but I can't hold out.'

She hooked her ankles around his hips. 'Pleasure me now, Hugo. I cannot take any more.'

He kissed her long and hard as her hips rose up to meet his. He wanted her so badly he hurt.

For one last moment of sanity, he held himself back. 'I am not protected.'

She smiled at him, her lips swollen and moist. 'I want your baby, Hugo.'

He thrust forwards until he thought he would die from the tight heat of her. Her gasp of pleasure joined his as she rose to meet him. Their hot, wet skin met and slipped together in a passion that mounted with each penetration.

Her moans filled his mouth, her nails dug into his shoulders, urging him to greater heights. He withdrew, thrust forward again and again. Their bodies moved together as though they had been made for one another.

She sucked his tongue deep, and he felt her contractions start. She pulsed around him, pulling him inside so deep he thought he had died and gone to heaven. Then he joined her. The ache in his loins became such exquisite delight he was not sure where he ended and she began.

Only much later, still sheathed inside her, did he come back to himself. Propped on his elbows, he gazed down at her. 'I thought you were going to take me so deep inside yourself we would become one,' he murmured, his breathing rapid.

She smiled. 'I wanted to consume you,' she said, her voice deep and raspy. 'I wanted to have what you were doing to me never end.'

He shifted and realised he was ready again. 'It won't end just yet, love.' He moved so that she gasped and the small of his back tightened in pleasure.

She moaned and matched the motion of her hips to his.

* * *

Later still, exhausted but happy, he rolled to her side and pulled her into his arms. 'I love you, Lady Spitfire.'

She smiled at him. 'Lady Fitzsimmon.'

He watched her. 'What happened to your independence?'

'Nothing. I finally realise I can be independent and married. It took me a long time to understand that.'

He smoothed a strand of silvered hair from her forehead. 'I didn't help with my own situation.'

She caught his hand and turned her head to kiss his palm. 'You are a man of honour. You did the right thing.' Her smile broke through. 'And we were fortunate enough that St. Cyrus was also a man of honour.'

More cynical than she, he added, 'And in love with Elizabeth.'

'That too.' She put a finger to his lips. 'But enough of that. Make love to me again.'

He gave her a mock look of shock. 'Again?'

She pressed her lips to him. 'How else am I to get pregnant with your child before we leave this room?'

Joy and love filled him so that tears sprang to his eyes. 'You are my life, Annabell. I love you more than I ever thought possible. If we have a child, then I will be doubly blessed.'

Smiling, he pulled her on top and entered her safe haven.

She bent to kiss him, this man who meant more to her than life. 'Just love me, Hugo. Just love me.'

* * * * *

Regency

High-Society Affairs

Rakes and rogues in the ballrooms – and the bedrooms – of Regency England!

Volume 8 – 2nd October 2009
Sparhawk's Angel by Miranda Jarrett
The Proper Wife by Julia Justiss

Volume 9 – 6th November 2009
The Disgraced Marchioness by Anne O'Brien
The Reluctant Escort by Mary Nichols

Volume 10 – 4th December 2009
The Outrageous Débutante by Anne O'Brien
A Damnable Rogue by Anne Herries

Volume 11 – 1st January 2010
The Enigmatic Rake by Anne O'Brien
The Lord and the Mystery Lady by Georgina Devon

Volume 12 – 5th February 2010
The Wagering Widow by Diane Gaston
An Unconventional Widow by Georgina Devon

Volume 13 – 5th March 2010
A Reputable Rake by Diane Gaston
The Heart's Wager by Gayle Wilson

Volume 14 – 2nd April 2010
The Venetian's Mistress by Ann Elizabeth Cree
The Gambler's Heart by Gayle Wilson

NOW 14 VOLUMES IN ALL TO COLLECT!